COLD SNAP

"Bestseller Cameron's exciting fourth novel featuring quick-thinking Deputy U.S. Marshal Arliss Cutter (after 2021's *Bone Rattle*) takes Cutter once again from his home state of Florida to Alaska . . . Cameron piles on the complications in the thrilling finale, played out in a remote wilderness setting, with an icy storm on the horizon and a hungry 800-pound grizzly looking for his next meal. Well-developed characters complement the nonstop action. Cameron viscerally conveys Alaska's austere beauty as well as its unexpected dangers."

—*Publishers Weekly*

"*Cold Snap* by Marc Cameron is another riveting novel featuring his main character, Deputy US Marshal Arliss Cutter. The author worked in law enforcement as a US Marshal, so he keeps the plot realistic. Cameron puts the reader in the middle of the Alaskan wilderness. They feel the wind at their face, and the bitter cold from the downpour of snow. Animals also become a factor with wolves and an 800-pound grizzly bear trying to get their next meal. There is no means of communication, few supplies, and prisoners who want nothing more than to kill Cutter. He must use all his skills to protect himself and others found in the wilderness. The plot and characters are enthralling."

—*Military Press*

COLD
SNAP

MARC
CAMERON

PINNACLE BOOKS
KENSINGTON PUBLISHING CORP.
www.kensingtonbooks.com

PINNACLE BOOKS are published by

Kensington Publishing Corp.
119 West 40th Street
New York, NY 10018

All Kensington titles, imprints, and distributed lines are available at special quantity discounts for bulk purchases for sales promotion, premiums, fund-raising, educational, or institutional use.

Special book excerpts or customized printings can also be created to fit specific needs. For details, write or phone the office of the Kensington Sales Manager: Attn.: Sales Department. Kensington Publishing Corp., 119 West 40th Street, New York, NY 10018. Phone: 1-800-221-2647.

Pinnacle and the Pinnacle logo Reg. U.S. Pat. & TM Off.
First Kensington Hardcover Edition: May 2022

First Paperback Printing: April 2023
ISBN: 978-0-7860-4764-2

ISBN: 978-0-7860-4766-6 (ebook)

10 9 8 7 6 5 4 3 2 1

Printed in the United States of America

For Irene
best mother-in-law in the whole world

*"The winter! The brightness that blinds you,
The white land locked tight as a drum,
The cold fear that follows and finds you,
The silence that bludgeons you dumb."*

—Robert W. Service, "The Spell of the Yukon"

PROLOGUE

1986
Port Charlotte, Florida

Nine-year-old Arliss Cutter paused from whittling and shielded his eyes with the hand holding his knife. A trickle of sweat creased his cheek. His grandfather was worth watching anytime, but Arliss especially liked observing the old man on his patrol boat that was tied alongside the wooden dock, even if it did mean he was leaving. The boy's ratty tennis shoes were stained green from tending to the freshly mowed Saint Augustine lawn that stretched behind the dock and up a slight incline to a modest frame house. Beside him, a well-used Zebco rod and reel was propped between an Igloo ice chest and battered metal tackle box.

Far across the channel, or "gut," known as Little Alligator Creek, past the tangled thatch of silver buttonwood and gumbo limbo trees, and beyond row after row of stucco tract houses, a steamy evening sun settled over the Gulf, turning the elder Cutter and his slate-gray uniform of a Florida Marine Patrol officer into a hazy silhouette. A gold badge over his heart caught the light each time he turned. The Colt Python revolver jutted slightly away from a narrow hip, his black leather holster perfectly canted for a quick draw.

To Arliss Cutter, his grandfather was godlike, or nearly so. He did cuss once in a while.

Arliss dusted a pile of wood shavings off his lap. Cutoff jeans revealed tanned but scarred knees. The grimy bill-fishing T-shirt that had been handed down from his brother clung to bony shoulders on its last threads. The boy's face remained passive, almost frowning as he squinted into the sun, but inside he glowed with the sure knowledge that his grandfather was the best lawman in Florida, and probably on the whole planet. Called Grumpy by friend and foe alike, Officer Cutter was not a tall man, but he had wide shoulders and strong hands that looked like they might never let go if they got ahold of you. Arliss's older brother, Ethan, looked more like their late father, but Arliss took after Grumpy with straw-colored hair, a prominent brow, and the propensity toward a resting mean mug no matter his mood.

On the boat, Grumpy stowed his pump shotgun in a slot beside the console as he talked. When he looked up, his gray-eyed gaze lingered on the Barlow pocket-knife in his grandson's hand.

"Whatcha makin'?"

Arliss brushed a shock of sun-bleached hair out of his face with the back of his carving hand and studied the hunk of cottonwood in the other, rubbing a bandaged thumb over the grain.

"Some kinda fish, I expect."

"I'll take you fishing tomorrow," Grumpy said, stuffing a canvas warbag full of gear into one of the boat's lockers. "I should have given your brother the Barlow and you the whittler. You'd have used it more."

"I like the Barlow just fine." Arliss went back to work on the cottonwood with the tip of the fat blade. "I keep it plenty sharp, just like you showed me."

"Very well," Grumpy said. "But be careful. I'd just as soon you had both your thumbs attached when I get back."

"Yessir."

"Where *is* your brother?"

Arliss looked up. Grumpy didn't like it when he tried to do two things at once—like carve and pay attention. "Next door, doing homework with Pammy-ann."

His grandfather's eyes narrowed to icy slits. "*You* don't have any homework?"

"No, sir."

Grumpy's boots clomped on the dock as he hopped over the gunnel of his patrol boat. He hunkered down on the balls of his feet beside Arliss so they were eye to eye, and tipped back his uniform ball cap. The Colt Python revolver jutted out prominently, adding to the old man's mystique.

"How old are you now? About fifteen?"

Arliss had heard this before. "You know I'm nine."

"Well, sir," Grumpy said. "I reckon nine is old enough for you to fill in your brother on where I'm headed."

"You have to work this evenin' instead of going fishing." The boy knew that much.

"Yep," Grumpy said. "Sometimes you gotta go

straight at a thing. It can't be put off, not even for an afternoon with your grandsons."

"Like bustin' punks?"

Grumpy half smiled, then looked the boy up and down for a minute, like he might impart some secret wisdom. He must have thought better of it, because he said, "I have to run over to Hog Island."

"What's over at Hog Island?"

"Two outlaws robbed some folks who were out there just minding their own business," Grumpy said. "Sent one of the victims to the hospital. Fishermen radioed in a sighting, so it falls to me to hunt down and capture those bad men before they hurt somebody else."

Arliss gave a slow nod. "And make 'em pay for what they done."

"What they *did*," Grumpy corrected, hitching up his gun belt. "But no, I merely bring 'em in. The judge decides the rest."

"Man-rule twenty," Arliss said.

"That's the one," Grumpy said.

"Let no guilty man go free."

Grumpy stood, the slightest of smiles crossing his weathered face as he tousled his grandson's hair.

"Exactly."

Arliss took a deep breath and studied his grandfather's craggy face. It didn't look particularly kind, even when he smiled, but Arliss always felt better when the old man was around. Calmer. Steadier.

Safe.

"Bad men gotta pay," the boy said, a catch in his throat.

"That is a fact." Grumpy mussed his grandson's hair again before turning to cast off the lines. He stepped aboard his boat.

Arliss resumed shaving off thin pieces of cottonwood with the Barlow. Behind him, a screen door slammed. Heavy footsteps tromped quickly up the dock. He turned to find Ethan sprinting toward them, fishing rod in one hand, tackle box in the other. He was taller, darker, and cared more about his image than his little brother did. Even at eleven, Ethan insisted on spending his own money for barber-shop haircuts, where Arliss let Grumpy cut his.

"My homework's all done," Ethan said, slowing to a suspiciously tentative walk when he got closer. "Arliss, why aren't you in the boat?" He slumped when he saw Grumpy in his gray uniform, and let the tip of his fishing rod thwack the dock. The disappointment was clear in his voice. "We're not going, are we?"

"There's a package of drum in the freezer," Grumpy said. "Arliss, you cook. Ethan, you pull dish duty."

"Yessir!" the boys said in unison.

"Good job finishing your homework, Ethan," Grumpy said. "Arliss'll fill you in."

The old man pushed the throttle forward and waved over his shoulder as he turned the boat away from the dock and into the gut.

Their mother gone, their father dead, the boys stood side by side as their grandfather and legal guardian headed south on Little Alligator Creek toward Gasparilla Sound. Arliss's nine-year-old eyes were sharp, allowing him to focus on the Colt Python revolver until

Grumpy and his boat were little more than a fuzzy speck on the glass-calm water.

"I'm not doing the dishes by myself after you spill flour and cornmeal everywhere cookin' the fish," Ethan muttered. "Where's he going this time?"

"Punks robbed some people over on Hog Island. Somebody's gotta pay."

"I know, little brother," Ethan said. "I just wish it didn't always have to be us."

CHAPTER 1

Present day
Dutch Harbor, Alaska

*T*he bow of the little skiff slammed into another frigid wave, sending Supervisory Deputy US Marshal Arliss Cutter's badge flying out the collar of his immersion suit. The silver circle-star hung suspended in the air as Cutter caught a chatter of icy sea spray full in the face. He gasped and tucked the badge and neck chain back down the front of his suit, snugging the zipper all the way to his chin for the duration of the ride.

Cutter rubbed seawater off his face with the back of a neoprene glove, getting a better look at the Russian ship a quarter mile ahead. Salt stung Cutter's eyes, making him hyperaware of the scratches on his cornea he'd gotten from flying rock debris in Juneau less than two weeks before. The wounds weren't quite healed, but Cutter squinted through the sting and, as with much else in his life, kept it to himself.

There were four of them in the little skiff, all wearing bright orange Mustang exposure suits with wide reflective SOLAS patches on each shoulder. The insulated coveralls were supposed to give them an extra few minutes before they succumbed to hypothermia if anyone fell overboard in the thirty-nine-degree water, but the main purpose was to protect him from the wind and waves. Cutter suspected the most realistic benefit would be as a brightly colored visual aid to the Coast Guard in body recovery.

The dark hulk of the Russian freighter pitching in the sea ahead stood out in stark contrast to the snow-covered mountains that loomed over the semi-protected anchorage.

Another green-water wave swelled before the boat. Cutter had been in worse seas, and he'd spent countless hours in small boats, but never at the same time. He braced himself, feeling the Colt Python under his Mustang suit wedge against the aluminum gunnel.

They wallowed up the brow of the swell—not huge as swells went, maybe a six-footer, but big enough to toss the skiff around. The prop on the 150-horse Honda outboard growled in protest, cavitating as the little boat crested the swell, and picked up speed racing down the backside. They smashed the bottom of the trough hard enough to loosen fillings, bringing a sheepish grin from the youthful driver clinging to the wheel at the center console.

His name was Spence, a tall, oafish kid with an easy smile and sophomoric attitude that probably got his ass kicked a lot in high school. He was so far out of his depth as to be laughable, had boating over bone-chilling water to board a hostile ship been a laughing matter.

Cutter had seized dozens of vessels as a deputy in Florida—a huge Bayliner belonging to a podiatrist convicted of Medicare fraud, cigarette boats used by narco terrorists, an entire shrimping fleet, and even a cruise ship the owners of which had gotten crossways with the EPA for dumping 15,000 gallons of raw sewage overboard within three miles of shore.

Working on the water could go from mundane to dangerous in a quick minute—unhappy skippers, glowering crew, and rats . . . there always seemed to be rats.

Someone who did not know Arliss Cutter might blame his stony expression on the prospect of boarding the massive Russian ship looming on a lumpy sea ahead. Perhaps he was angry to find himself getting pelted with rain and spin-drift in an open aluminum boat in the Bering Sea when he could have been floating in the sunshine in his home state of Florida. Or maybe the turbulent 800-mile flight from Anchorage to Dutch Harbor had left him feeling bilious.

In truth, Cutter was smiling inside. Rain or shine, danger or calm, on all but the rarest occasions Arliss Cutter's face brimmed with all the glee of an Easter Island statue.

Spence continued to bounce the little boat across Broad Bay toward *Magdalena Murmansk*, the 107-meter Russian ship moored to the emergency buoy west of Unalaska. Cutter's partner, Deputy Lola Teariki, sat amidships, hunkered down with her back to the bench, using her bent legs as shock absorbers. Jimmy McElroy, a rawboned local hard hat diver and ships' pilot, sat near the bow, across from Cutter.

One moment Cutter and the other passengers on the insignificant little craft found themselves at the bottom of a valley staring at walls of dark water all around them, then the next saw them thrust upward on the peak of a quavering swell. Each time they rose, the dark blue hulk of the *Magdalena Murmansk* hove into view, pitching and bobbing as if trying to escape its mooring.

The idea of pulling alongside the freighter at least twenty times longer than the skiff didn't appear to bother young Spence for the moment. He was trying to impress Lola with his vast knowledge of the sea—and in that endeavor, he was sinking. Fast.

At least once a day another law enforcement officer, or even a recently arrested fugitive, tried to flirt with Deputy Lola Tuakana Teariki, Cutter's partner on the US Marshals Alaska Fugitive Task Force.

Spence had started innocently enough, complimenting her hair as she boarded the skiff, but then turning the conversation quickly to his healthy blond beard—which he thought made him look more like an old-time sailor, and how he was thinking of taking up pipe smoking to bolster that image on his Instagram account. He lost a few more points when he rushed to help her put on an auto-inflating life vest. The ride from the docks to the ship was estimated to take twenty minutes, and the kid had spent the first ten telling enough sea stories for a man three times his age. Cutter and McElroy had ignored him for the most part, chalking his behavior up to the hormonal flush of youth. Lola Teariki sat hunkered in her spot amidships, shielded from the wind, but fully exposed to Spence's bluster. Of Cook Island Maori descent, she'd tucked thick black hair beneath a waterproof nor'easter rain hat. High cheekbones and mahogany eyes peeked above the collar of her Mustang suit.

Everyone on the skiff emerged from their private thoughts as they neared the Russian ship, and Spence's words floated to the surface again.

". . . gotta love the smell of the sea," Cutter heard him say. The kid had to yell above the whining outboard and chatter of water against the metal hull. Already sure of himself, the shouting made him sound extra committed to each and every word he spoke.

Lola shook her head, heaving a heavy sigh that was visible even in the thick overalls.

"That's not the sea," she said.

Spence canted his head, giddy for any sign he'd gotten her to speak with him, but unaware of the dangers that lay in that endeavor.

"What's not the sea?"

Lola smiled broadly, a lioness savoring her meal before she tucked into it.

"That odor you're smelling—"

The kid cut her off. "It's great, isn't it? I think I was born for the sea, the smell of it just—"

It was Lola's turn to interrupt. "That's the smell of land," she shouted. "Where it meets the sea. If you'd ever been out to sea, I mean truly out in blue water, you know that the ocean smells clean if you can smell it at all. You're breathing in the odor of rotting kelp, boat fuel, and unlucky fish who've gotten themselves caught at low tide." She shrugged. "But you can think of it as the smell of the sea if you want to. Whatever floats your boat."

"I-I guess that's . . . I mean—"

Cutter came to the rescue. The kid was harmless,

just too self-absorbed to realize Lola came from a sea-faring culture and might know a thing or two about Mother Ocean.

"They're expecting a diver to clear the prop." Cutter pointed a gloved hand at the Russian freighter, now less than a hundred meters away. "They don't know how many of us are coming aboard, but it's best they think we're all here to support Mr. McElroy until we're on the bridge."

"Copy that," Lola said, going over her part of the plan. Teeth clenched, she arched her back against the seat, stretching her arms skyward with a shudder born of sitting too long on the floor of the boat. "I'll shoot a text to the Coasties as soon as we make it up the ladder and our boots hit the deck."

The US Coast Guard cutter *Douglas Munro* patrolled a few miles away. Named for the only Coast Guardsman to ever be awarded the Medal of Honor, the 378-foot Hamilton Class high-endurance cutter was a frequent visitor to the Bering Sea. Armed with numerous heavy deck guns and a MH-65 Dolphin helicopter, the *Douglas Munro* would provide the seafaring muscle to back up the deputies' swagger once they were aboard the ship.

At least that was the theory.

Magdalena Murmansk had visited Dutch Harbor the year before, sailing as the *Pravda*. The outlines of the foot-high letters were still visible under several coats of flaking blue paint on either side of the ship's prow. As *Pravda*, the ship that eventually became the *Magdalena* engaged in a series of violations of maritime and US law, accepting a dozen vehicles that were believed to have been stolen from a smaller cargo vessel sailing out of the Port of Anchorage. *Pravda* had been captained then by a Russian named Koslov—the same man who'd called in her most recent mechanical troubles that required her to moor to the emergency buoy in Broad Bay.

She'd run across a submerged cable two days prior, fouling her prop badly enough to require a hard hat diver to go down and cut it out. The observant skipper of F/V *Violet Dawn*, a pacific cod trawler, happened to be a recently retired Alaska State Trooper familiar with the vehicle smuggling case. The harbor master slow-walked his response for assistance to the Magdelina long enough that the former trooper could get word to the US Marshals in Anchorage, who held the maritime court order to seize the vessel. With all her ops deputy marshals tied up in court, injured, or detailed to special assignments in other parts of the country, Chief Deputy Jill Phillips had assigned Cutter and Teariki from the fugitive task force to fly out and nab the *Magdalena*. Cutter went where he was pointed, and Lola Teariki was always up for something new, so long as she got in her daily workout. Fortunately, the Grand Aleutian Hotel had a serviceable gym—which she'd visited twice in the twelve hours since they'd arrived.

Spence slowed when they were still twenty yards from the *Magdalena*, allowing the skiff to settle and wallow on the waves, momentum and the currents shoving her forward. The pilot's or "shell" door through which they would have to enter the cargo ship was fifteen feet up the side of the pitching vessel. A swell thrust the ship upward at the same time the skiff surfed into a trough, putting the pilot's door almost thirty feet above them. A moment later, when the swells and troughs switched places, the angles reversed as well, making it look as if they could jump straight across the water and into the opening. A simple misstep, faulty lines, or a rogue swell might drop any one of them between the two vessels—grinding them to paste.

There was a reason Marshals Service policy forbade deputies to board ships on the open ocean. Theoretically, the mooring buoy would be safer—but the sea didn't appear to realize that.

Cutter looked up at the pitching ship and then back to a grinning Lola Teariki. She wanted assignments that were new and interesting—and she was about to get her wish.

CHAPTER 2

*T*here was something undeniably sinister about the Russian ship—somber faces of the two crewmen peering down from the pilot's door, lines of rust weeping from beneath flaking hull paint, and something else that Cutter couldn't put his finger on. A flutter in his gut.

Despite his sophomoric flirting with Lola, Spence turned out to be a steady boat driver and brought the little launch expertly alongside the mooring buoy. McElroy tied off the bow, and both the ship and skiff began to rise and drop in time with the swells. The danger of getting crushed if any of them fell between the two vessels was lessened slightly, but was far from nonexistent.

A rope ladder with iffy-looking sun-bleached wooden rungs banged against the hull, held away only slightly from the sloping metal by a weathered piece of lumber that rested on large stopper knots in the ropes at the base of the door. Regulations stated a ship's pilot—the local person who guided the way in to each port—had to be able to board via a ladder that was no more than nine meters from the water's surface. The skipper of the *Magdalena Murmansk* apparently fretted over that regulation as much as he did about transporting stolen cars. It was impossible to be sure from his angle in the skiff, but Cutter estimated the climb was well above thirty feet if the swells weren't timed just right.

Cutter caught the ladder at the bottom of its dive, riding it upward as a swell lifted the larger ship. Rain and sea spray slicked the rungs, and he tested each treacherous step as he climbed, alternating hands and feet to retain his balance on the swaying ropes. His two sidearms—his grandfather's Colt Python revolver and the regulation Glock that kept him in Marshals Service policy, were hidden beneath the thick orange Mustang suit—which meant they were also difficult to access. The sailors who helped him aboard, both young men bundled in wool hats and foul-weather slickers, welcomed him with disinterested grunts, assuming he was part of the team come to untangle the propeller. Their Turkic features brightened when Lola Teariki peeked over the rail and grabbed their offered hands. The *Magdalena Murmansk* probably had few female visitors. The taller of the two removed his wool watch cap and wrung it in both fists, attempting small talk in halting, broken English.

With the sailors' attention on Lola, McElroy hauled himself aboard, using the upright posts at the top of the rope ladder.

"Your captain?" McElroy said, interrupting, if not breaking, the spell Teariki had over the men.

"Da," the tall sailor said, stretching the hat back over his buzzed head. He had a small and crudely drawn tattoo of a dolphin under his left eye. He glanced aft, toward the raised whitewashed wheelhouse that loomed two stories above the main deck, then back at McElroy as if he wasn't too keen about going to see his boss.

Captain Dimitri Koslov stood with his knuckly hands clasped behind his back, large beak of a nose to the window peering down at the newcomers. His angular face dripped with the disdain of a pirate toward the lesser folk who allowed themselves to be constrained by the petty laws of man. Koslov kept the thermostat in the wheelhouse cranked up high, allowing him to wear his preferred T-shirt and cargo shorts no matter what kind of gales blew out on deck. It was good for his crew to see the scars—the bite of a tiger shark that had taken much of his left calf muscle, the obscenely white flesh left behind on forearms from molten metal during a deck fire when he'd been a much younger man. Lines from a broken vodka bottle webbed the bald flesh over his right temple and down the side of his ruddy check, visible even when he wore a hat. All were constant and helpful reminders to the crew that their captain was a man accustomed to great pain. At six feet two with hardly an ounce of fat, Dimitri Koslov seemed a knotty rope of bone and joint and sinew. His men often described him as "a bag of hammers," and he liked that very much.

Vasiliev, a blond man with an equally angular face who served as first officer, informed him the American underwater welder wanted an audience before he got to work on the cable.

Still facing the window, Koslov gave an almost imperceptible nod.

Koslov needed the Americans to cut the fouled propeller free of cable, but he wanted them off his ship as soon as possible. There was far too much at stake to have strangers nosing around.

The captain tilted his head sideways, as if to gain a better vantage point. "Is that . . . ? Did he bring a woman with him?"

"It would seem so, Captain," Vasiliev said.

Nikolai Nikolaevich, the knock-kneed Ukrainian boy standing watch by the helm, glanced up. In his late teens, he had a pale, round face and blue eyes that seemed always on the verge of tears. The other crewmen would look at any woman on the ship as possible companionship. The boy would certainly think of her as a mother, someone who might rescue him from his rough crewmates.

Koslov did not approve of women on his ship, but he had to admit that this was a handsome one. She'd unzipped her heavy orange survival suit shortly after coming on board and was on the mobile phone with someone. He'd sailed enough of the world's seas to recognize a Polynesian beauty when he saw one.

Every man on the bridge, including young Nikolai, moved to the window and pressed his nose against the glass for a better look.

"It is good these waters are so cold," Koslov said. "Otherwise I am afraid some of the men would jump ship."

"My thoughts exactly," the first officer said. "Who do you suppose she is talking to, Captain?"

Koslov licked his lips, then stepped away from the window, shaking his head. Beautiful woman or not, strangers on this boat would be a problem. "Their launch driver perhaps," he said. "It does not matter. Get them working at once. I want to be free of this place an hour ago!"

Footsteps clanged on the metal ladder outside as the boarding party made their way up to the bridge. The door creaked open and one of the crewmen, an Azerbaijani named Yaadan, who was fond of giving himself crude tattoos, ushered the three visitors inside and then excused himself.

Koslov recognized the hard hat welder from the McElroy Diving website—but a large blond man stepped forward as if he were the one in charge. The captain bristled immediately, sensing danger. He glanced back and forth, figuring the odds. The girl would be no problem—but Nikolai would be no help. That left the engineer, the first officer, a radio man, and Koslov to deal with McElroy and the frowning blond man.

"Are you the captain?" the big man said, staring at Koslov with blue eyes as cold as the sea outside.

The Russian gave a curt nod, fists clenching at the same time his stomach sank. This man was law enforcement, or military, maybe both. The lines were often blurred at sea. Either way, he was going to be a problem.

Koslov wanted them off his ship—fast.

* * *

Cutter had unzipped the Mustang suit to the waist by the time he reached the bridge, giving him access to his credentials, the paperwork, and his sidearm if it came to that.

The inside of the wheelhouse was sweltering and smelled like pine disinfectant, absent of all but the faintest hint of grease and human body odor.

Cutter locked eyes with the mass of scars wearing a T-shirt and shorts.

"You are the ship's master . . . ?"

"Captain Koslov," the skipper said, eyes flitting between Cutter and the door. He spoke heavily accented English, phlegmy, like a TV spy villain. "I am guessing you are not here to fix propeller?"

Cutter shook his head. "Afraid not, sir." He used his left hand to hold up the black leather case displaying the silver circle-star—keeping his right hand free. "Pursuant to a court order and maritime warrant of arrest in rem, I am seizing the vessel formerly known as *Pravda* and now known as the *Magdalena Murmansk.* A hearing date will be set at the United States Courthouse in Anchorage. I'll leave you a copy of the paperwork. There's a telephone number that the attorneys representing the shipping company may call with any questions."

Captain Koslov nodded again, slower this time, then barked something to a sad-looking boy who seemed to be trying to melt into the corner of the wheelhouse. Whatever he said caused the boy's mouth to fall open in dismay. He shook his head. The captain repeated himself, sterner this time. The boy raised both hands, continuing to resist. Cutter didn't speak Russian, but he understood the word *nyet* when he heard it.

Koslov took a menacing step toward the youth, as if he might strike him. Cutter moved to intercept, but another man whom Cutter took to be the first officer, raised both hands.

"I will go, Captain," the man said in English. "Please forgive young Nikolai Nikolaevich. He is frightened."

Lola Teariki gave the first officer a wary side-eye. When she was tense or tired, she spoke with the shortened vowels and nonexistent Rs of her father's Kiwi accent. "What's he scared of?"

"You are taking ship," the first officer said. "She is our . . . livelihood. Intercom is down, so Captain asked him to go inform engineering."

The boy stared at the floor, shoulders quaking.

"We'll let the crew know in a minute," Cutter said.

Koslov picked a bit of lint off his T-shirt and flicked it toward Cutter. "There are only three of you," he said. "How do you propose to take my ship with such small party?"

"You are in United States waters, and I seized this vessel pursuant to a lawful court order."

Koslov pursed his lips in thought and then smiled. "You think to board my vessel like some Somali pirate in Tom Hanks movie. And yet, you have only three pirates." Koslov thumbed his chest and wagged his head. "I have crew of nineteen men. Maybe they not comply with order of American pirate court. What you say to that, Mr. '*I am captain now*'?"

"I say I have a lot more than three," Cutter said, nodding toward the bow.

The radio man said something in rapid-fire Russian. It was Lola's turn to sneer. "I'm guessing he just told you that a very large US Coast Guard cutter is bearing down on us as we speak."

Captain Koslov gazed out the window, seeming to look well past the approaching *Douglas Munro*—a thousand-yard stare. At length he pounded a fist into his palm.

"Very well," he said. "The ship is yours. What will become of crew? You have . . . what do you call . . . 'arrest in rem' warrants for us as well?"

Cutter shook his head. "Immigration officials will be out shortly to get you all processed and returned home."

"I see," the captain said. He barked something in Russian again.

The first officer turned to leave, but Lola sidestepped, blocking his path.

"What's your hurry?" she asked. "The ship's not going anywhere."

"I follow Captain's orders," the first officer said through a saccharine smile. "I will go tell crew now to listen to you."

Lola shot a glance at Cutter.

The boy piped up. "He lie!"

The veins on Koslov's neck bulged. His face flushed bright red. *"Ublyudok!"*

Young Nikolai plowed ahead. "Captain order me throw in sea, drown before you find—"

Koslov snatched a two-foot piece of steel pipe from the chart table and rushed the hapless boy.

Cutter planted a boot hard on the side of the man's knee. Koslov screamed, listing sideways, the joint bending a direction knees were not designed to bend. Far from out, the captain spun swinging the pipe at Cutter. It whooshed past, inches from his nose.

Cutter was vaguely aware of the first officer moving to assist his boss and heard the loud smack as Lola gave him a slap across the ear to change his mind. Breaking someone's eardrum didn't exactly fall within the Marshals use of force policy, but they were on their own until the Coast Guard arrived. This wasn't the time to tiptoe gently into an arrest, especially after the captain orders someone thrown overboard.

Cutter waded in on the Russian's backswing, closing the gap and getting inside the steel pipe before he could swing it again. Cutter caught Koslov under the chin with the heel of his hand, pushing up, then rolling over and straight down toward the deck—as if spiking a basketball.

Koslov dropped the length of pipe, flailing in vain to catch himself as he fell backward, snapping one wrist in the process and likely spraining the other.

Cutter kicked the pipe away and looked back and forth between Koslov and the boy. He spoke slowly, unsure of how much English Nikolai understood.

"Throw who overboard?"

"My job," the boy said, tears in his eyes. "My job . . . take care of them. They so beautiful. He say to me throw over before you find."

"Beautiful?" Lola took a half step forward. "What are you talking about? Throw who over? Are there prisoners on this ship?"

Koslov spoke through clenched teeth, clutching his shattered wrist, grimacing in pain as he glared at Nikolai. *"Zatkni past!"*

The boy ignored him, looking from Cutter to Teariki, pleading.

"*Frantsuzskiy* . . . I not know how you say . . ."

Lola brightened. "France? French?"

Nikolai nodded. "Yes! French *shchenok*."

Lola shook her head, butchering the pronunciation. "Shenak?"

The first officer slumped. "Puppies," he whispered. "French bulldog puppies."

Cutter cocked his head. "Puppies?"

Nikolai nodded. "Much valuable."

The first officer, seeing where this was going, rubbed a hand over his face and turned to Cutter. "Captain buys puppies from breeder in Russia. One hundred dollars for each. He sells in Seattle for fifteen hundred dollars. Big profit. Small risk. Not like drugs."

"How many puppies are we talking about?" Cutter asked.

The first officer rubbed his face again, speaking through his fingers. "Three hundred."

Nikolai gave an emphatic nod. "Yes. But many puppy is very sick . . ."

Lola twitched, looking like she might jump out of her skin at any moment. Cutter released her with a nod.

She gave Nikolai a tap on the shoulder. "You come with me. Let's go check on those sick puppies."

"Hang on," Cutter said. "Do we need to worry about the crew?"

The first officer shook his head. "They hate captain," he said. "Will be happy."

Koslov grabbed a wood handrail on the chart table and attempted to pull himself up. Bloodshot eyes bored holes into Cutter. "You . . . you have no right to do this on my ship—"

"Oh no." Cutter tapped the stack of documents on the chart table with the handcuffs he'd gotten from his belt. "This is *my* ship."

"What is to happen to me?"

"That depends," Cutter said, head down, eyes narrowed, "on the condition of the pups down in your hold."

Cutter had briefed Customs and Border Protection officials in Unalaska before the seizure, and it took them less than an hour to get personnel on-site. Spence had to move the skiff off the mooring buoy in order to give them space to board. The *Douglas Munro* hove to off the bow of the *Magdalena Murmansk*, the deck guns on the 378-foot US Coast Guard vessel a big-stick reminder to the Russian crew that they should comply with the marshals' orders.

Cutter and Teariki charged the captain with assault on a federal officer. Immigration officials saw to the crew, including young Nikolai, to whom Cutter gave his cell phone number.

Customs officials begrudgingly took custody of the three hundred squirming and hungry French bulldog puppies that were now evidence against Captain Koslov in a soon to be filed smuggling charge.

Lola's phone buzzed as they waited on *Magdalena*'s deck while the skiffs were jockeyed around for their transport back to Dutch Harbor/Unalaska.

They were in the middle of a prisoner move, sur-

rounded by men who wouldn't mind terribly if they
fell in the sea, but Cutter nodded at her to take it, in
case it was something to do with the vessel seizure.

She cupped her hand over the phone to block the
wind, listened intently, then ended the call. Her lips
were set in a tight line when she turned to face Cutter.

"Everything okay?" he asked. Lola was not one to
overreact to a phone call—or much of anything.

She shook her head. "That was a friend of mine
from the Troopers. Another body washed up out near
Beluga Point. APD is on scene working it now."

Koslov turned up his nose and muttered, "Decadent,
murderous Americans . . ."

Cutter ignored him. "A body?"

"Yeah." Lola groaned. "Well . . . a piece of one anyway."

CHAPTER 3

Anchorage, Alaska

"*D*on't even say the words *serial killer*," Officer Sandra Jackson said over her shoulder, sliding down the loose shale on the sea side of the Alaska Railroad right of way. "It riles up the brass."

It was just past eight in the morning, in the hours where midnight shift and day shift overlapped—offering light that mid-shifters like Officer Joe Bill Brackett were not accustomed to after a long, dark winter. Low clouds clung to the mountains directly across the Seward Highway. Turnagain Arm had some hellacious tides with over thirty feet of fluctuation when the moon was full. When the tide went out, it left the shallow arm of Cook Inlet looking like a desert moonscape. If conditions were just right, the incoming tide rushed in all at once, in a long, continuous wall of silty water called a *bore tide*.

Tourists and locals alike lined the pullouts along the

Seward Highway to watch the phenomenon. Once the jagged pad ice was gone, surfers would don dry suits and ride the wave in. The latest bore tide had come in the middle of the night, not huge, just a four-footer. That was six hours ago—and the tide was out now, leaving barren sand, scattered chunks of muddy ice—

And a body.

Spitting rain plastered locks of dirty-blond hair to Jackson's forehead. She wore little makeup, but what she did have around her eyes was smudged from standing so long in the weather, and maybe, Brackett thought, vomiting into the bushes before he got there. She was in her early twenties, about Brackett's age, but with a couple of years seniority in the department.

"Why can't we call it what it is?" Brackett asked, hopping from a large chunk of granite riprap along the railroad bed to the grassy slope that led to the beach. "It's just us. Bradley can't hear."

Jackson stopped short and turned, tut-tutting him with her index finger. "Don't even say the words—to anyone. Just forming them in your mouth will put you in the habit. Next thing you know, you'll be blabbing about serial killers to some reporter from Alaska Public Radio."

Brackett gave a noncommittal shrug. The killings had to be connected. How could they not be? Severed limbs, torsos washing up around Anchorage.

"Doesn't not admitting we have a serial killer out there just make the public trust us less?"

"The ways of the chief's office are not our ways," Jackson said. "They know shit we lowly folks aren't privy to. Or, at least you should keep telling yourself that or you'll go insane."

Jackson slid down the last few feet of slope to the base of two massive basalt rocks. One was the size of a house, the other qualified as a small hill with a couple of scrubby storm-blown trees on top. Brackett had always thought they looked like sleeping dinosaurs when he was growing up.

Rock gave way to sand, forming a small, hidden beach before turning into silty mud that looked solid but could suck a boot off of a foot or, worse, trap an unsuspecting tourist up to their thighs until the tide rolled in and drowned them. It was a favorite story of Alaska parents to scare their children into staying away from the mudflats.

Like all things treacherous the mudflats drew people in, now there was the added lure of a mutilated body. Cars were already lining up in the Beluga Point overlook lot with gawkers piling out to see what was going on. As one of the newest members of the department, Brackett knew he'd eventually be relegated to traffic control, so he wanted a quick look at the scene. Just over two weeks earlier, a similar torso had washed ashore on Point Woronzof. It was his very first call after being cut loose from his training officer to work on his own. Then he'd responded with Jackson to Bootleggers Cove, where a passerby discovered a female foot with multicolored toenails. He knew it was stupid, but these killings felt personal to him.

It would be raining APD officers soon—brass, homicide detectives, crime scene. But for now, there were only three of them. A patrol officer named Bradley had arrived at Beluga Point first and now stood guard at the edge of the mud by the body. Jackson was designated uniformed investigator, so she got all the interesting calls. Fortunately for Brackett, he'd been working off Huffman and was already far enough south he could hightail it down to Beluga Point before anyone could tell him not to.

Officer Bradley had been around so long he'd given Brackett's mom a ticket when she was in college at UAA. He'd seen enough dead bodies to last several lifetimes and was happy to yield the scene and go attend to traffic control when the two "piss-and-vinegars" got there.

The body—or what was left of it, was mired five yards away from solid ground, making closer approach impossible until crime scene got there with plywood with which they'd build a flat path that would distribute their weight over hungry mud.

"Just like the one at Point Woronzof," Brackett whispered, unable to tear his eyes off the battered corpse.

"Preach on, brother," Jackson said. "But listen. If you ever do end up talking to the media—"

"The last thing I'm going to do is talk to journalists about an active case." Brackett scoffed. He rubbed a hand over his dark hair, curly, damp from the rain. "That's so far above my paygrade—"

"You'd be surprised," Jackson said. "Reporters have a way of hunting the young ones and separating you from the herd. But whoever you talk to, you might want to steer clear of phrases like 'a bunch.' Be specific. We've recovered five body parts: an upper arm last spring off the beach below Kincaid Park, the foot at Bootleggers Cove a couple of weeks ago, the torso you found off Point Woronzof last week, Rainbow Toes at Bootleggers Cove, and now this torso."

"Yeah, well," Brackett mused. "Five seems like a

bunch, but I hear you. People could read anything they want into it."

"Now you're catching on," Jackson said. "Just trying to keep you from stepping on your own pee-pee when homicide rolls onto the scene. Anchorage may be a big city, but we've got a small-town psyche. Folks in New York or LA expect there to be killers lurking in the greenery. Gazelles are accustomed to being hunted by lions. They're wary, but go on with their lives with one eye peeled." She whistled, low, under her breath. "But let a herd of domestic cattle catch the scent of a lion on the breeze and they're apt to run off a cliff in a blind-slobberin' panic. I hate to say it, but with all the newbies who move in from the lower forty-eight every year, we got our fair share of cattle right here in Anchorage."

Brackett suppressed a smile despite the situation. He always enjoyed listening to Sandra Jackson. Her parents had run a trapline with a small dog team north of Fairbanks near the tiny berg of Livengood—pronounced to rhyme with "alive and good." Her descriptions and observation of life—and death—were heavily influenced by growing up in a remote sixteen-by-twenty log cabin in the shadow forests along the mighty Yukon River. Brackett's dad was raised just a little south of there, near Fox, and he was the same way.

She used the telephoto lens of her camera to study the body in the mud for a few seconds before passing the camera to Brackett.

He zoomed in as close as he could with the lens. "Missing head, hands, and feet. Been in the water for a while . . ."

"See the marks around her shoulders?"

Brackett nodded without lowering the camera. The body was nude, hardly recognizable as a body really, more like a mound of mud, or home plate after a heavy rain. Long gashes, rips in the flesh deep enough to expose white bone, hatched both shoulders.

"Sharp pad ice?" he guessed.

"I don't think so," Jackson said. "I think it was whales."

Now Brackett lowered the camera, giving his brain a break from the gruesome image. "You think a whale killed her?"

"Not at all," Jackson said. "She was murdered like the others. It's spring. Schools of hooligan will be coming in to spawn soon. The beluga whales are already hanging around waiting for them. The body's been in the water for a few days, judging from decomp and how much the sea lice have eaten. I think the belugas probably tossed her around, chewed on her a bit, but decided she wasn't worth the trouble."

"Alaska crime scenes . . ." Brackett whispered.

"You ever see those movies where the serial killer hangs around the crime scene to admire his handiwork?"

"That's pretty much all serial killer movies."

Jackson chuckled. "I know, right." She shot a glance over her shoulder at the crowd gathering in the Beluga Point parking lot. "All this commotion, cop cars and whatnot . . . He could be up there watching us right now."

The rain picked up, turning into a mixture of snow and rain—*snain*.

Brackett shivered and looked through the camera

again. "I heard some swing-shift guys calling these the Phantom Swede Murders after some bootlegger who used to sell booze here during Prohibition. I guess Bootleggers Cove is named after him."

"First off," Jackson said. "Don't trust anyone on swing shift. They're too worried about their pretty haircuts to get any real policework done. And second, I'm not so sure about that theory."

"About the Phantom Swede?"

"About Bootleggers Cove having much to do with our killer."

"Okay," Brackett said. "You've been UI on three of these crime scenes. If anyone deserves to have a theory, it's you."

He cringed inside, thinking that came across more flirtatious than he'd wanted it to.

Jackson heaved a great sigh, shuddering under the stress of a long night shift and the weight of finding a butchered female torso on this cold and rainy morning.

"Honestly," she said. "I got nothing. This one looks like it's going to be a bust. No clothes, no identifiers unless her DNA is in the system. I'm banking on there being someone who will know a girl who paints her toes like that last foot that washed up. We may not be able to call this asshole a serial killer, but if we solve one murder, we solve them all. Am I a sick person because I wish we could find a head floating around out there? At least that way we could get some dental records."

"I hear you," Brackett said. He'd thought exactly the same thing.

Jackson groaned, taking her camera back. "Did you know Alaska swallows up something like two thousand people every year? An overwhelming number of them are Native women."

Brackett didn't need to say it, but that was one of the little Alaskan factoids people talked about all the time in the lower forty-eight. That, and the fact that the state consistently topped the FBI's Uniform Crime Report for sexual assault and other violence against women.

Jackson went on, building up a head of steam. "Of course, that number of missing people includes lost hikers, hunters, boats that sink, planes that go down—people who gee when they should have hawed, as my musher dad used to say, and end up getting eaten, or freeze to death, or consume poison berries, or fall through the ice, get buried in an avalanche, or just sit down in the wilderness and die of despair. It's tough enough living here without some maniac hacking you into pieces and tossing you out like another Eklutna Annie."

"You think this is another Butcher Baker type thing?" Brackett mused. The thought was on everyone's mind, law enforcement and civilian alike. Between 1971 and 1983, Anchorage baker Robert Hansen had kidnapped, raped, and murdered at least seventeen women. Many of his victims he'd flown to his remote cabin so he could hunt them like animals. The first remains anyone found turned up north of Anchorage off Eklutna Road. The unidentified female had been stabbed to death. Authorities dubbed her Eklutna Annie.

"That's a strong possibility," Jackson said. "Most of Hansen's victims were women without much of a connection to society. A significant number of those who go missing here—cities and the bush—are women. At least two dozen females in the Anchorage municipality have been reported missing and are still unaccounted for. Similar cases in the Mat-Su Valley and Kenai Peninsula. And that's only what we know of. Those numbers don't take into account the women who go unreported. Most of these missing women are prostitutes or migrants, sometimes both, with few people to even notice they're gone. I can't begin to tell you how many young women I've detained during my relatively short career whose parents were astonished as hell to find out they'd made it all the way to Alaska. Girls like that might get reported missing in Omaha or Albany, but some nutjob could grab them off the street here in Anchor-town and we wouldn't even know to look for them. It wouldn't be a stretch to think we could have double the reported number of missing women."

"Thank God we only have five bodies," Brackett said.

"Only five that have washed up so far," Jackson said. "What does that tell you? The location, I mean."

Brackett turned the idea over in his head for a moment. It seemed like a simple question, but he didn't want to look stupid in front of Jackson.

"Four along the Coastal Trail," he said. "We're, like, twenty miles down the Seward Highway from where the other bodies washed up, so this one's an outlier."

"That's where the beluga whales come in," Jackson said. "She could have easily been killed in the same place and then brought here."

"By whales?"

"Like you said, Joe. Alaska crime scenes . . ."

"Right," Brackett said. "Cook Inlet has some of the biggest tidal fluctuations in the world, like thirty feet or something. The bodies could have been dumped across the inlet on the Point MacKenzie side, especially with all the ice out there this winter grinding them around and shoving them back and forth." He brightened as the theory firmed up in his mind. "Maybe something about the ocean current brings the pieces to the coastal trail." He shot a glance at Jackson. "Unless the whales grab it. I'll bet the Coast Guard could put together some kind of predictive model and backtrack to figure out where the killer is dumping the bodies."

"Maybe so," Jackson said. "But think on this, youngling. Last I heard there are at least thirty known brown bears and countless blackies inside Anchorage city limits. There's already enough light this time of year to get them up out of their dens. Hell, my garbage can has claw marks all over it. Both the Ship Creek and Portage wolf packs frequent parts of the beach. That doesn't count the foxes, coyotes, pine martens, wolverines, and eagles that could be snatching bits and pieces. For all we know, there are woman parts washing up all around the inlet. Maybe there are feet and hands and elbows strewn from the mouth of the Susitna River all the way around and down to the Homer Spit. They're either getting eaten by animals, or maybe we keep finding body parts along the coastal trail because this is where the people are to find them."

"So you think there are more victims out there?" Brackett asked.

"Don't you?"

"I guess I do," Brackett said.

Jackson stabbed the air with her index finger, driving home her point. "Somewhere out there, maybe up in the parking lot watching us right now, is a twisted son of a bitch who has murdered a shitload of women. At least one of those women was playful enough to have multicolored toes—and that animal chopped her into pieces with an axe."

CHAPTER 4

*R*ita Taylor's last client left at two thirty in the morning. He'd been a sad sack, crying and moaning about how he never did this sort of thing, like he should get a first-timer's discount or something. She'd stopped listening the instant he started talking about all his problems at home. Criers weren't the worst kind of client, but they were near the bottom rung of the ladder for sure. Listening to their whiny shit was exhausting, and she was tired enough already. Barely five feet tall and all of ninety-five pounds, Rita didn't have much energy in reserve.

She stood at the motel room door when Crybaby left, holding a flimsy cotton robe closed tight against her throat to ward off the sudden gush of cold wind. She was tired of that too—cold rain, shitty slush, and if it ever stopped raining long enough for things to dry out, clouds of moldy dust left behind from receding winter.

"Anchorage ain't a snow globe this time of year," her last boyfriend had observed, philosopher pimp that he was. "It's a dirty mop bucket."

The motel room smelled of curry and carpet cleaner. A squat, two-story affair of wood and shingles, all the doors faced Merrill Field—the busiest municipal airport in the world—and Fifth Avenue, the only road leaving Anchorage to the north. The parking lot out front had been paved at one time, but frequent scrapes of the snow plow and very little maintenance from the owners left it a muddy lake with a few islands of piled gravel and filthy snow.

Rita closed the door and lit a cigarette. The room had a NO SMOKING sign on the door, but nobody cared. This wasn't that kind of hotel. She thought about grabbing a shower, but Grace would be there any minute, and her place didn't have a fungus ring around the bathtub.

Alone at last, Rita's cigarette hung from her lips as she slipped on a pair of sweats. She pulled on a loose gray hoodie that zipped up the front, wanting to look as far from sexy as humanly possible. She washed down her nightly dose of nitrofuran with the last swig of an Alaskan Amber. The doctor had prescribed the antibiotic to keep her UTIs at bay. One after "each time you have sex," he'd said. She'd asked how many doses a day would be safe. He'd settled on two. That was a joke.

Grace's court hearing was at ten. Rita looked at her watch, doing the math. If Grace got there soon, she'd be able to crash for a few hours, make it to the clinic in time to get her methadone, and still be at the courthouse to show her friend support. She swallowed the last of the beer and peeked out the window, making sure Crybaby had actually driven away. She did a double take when she saw Grace's little blue Subaru parked at the end of the row.

Empty.

"Where you at, girl?" Rita whispered to the dusty miniblinds. Maybe she'd gone to the lobby for a coffee while she waited for Rita's last customer to leave.

Five minutes later, there was still no sign of her. Rita tried to call her cell—three times—but it just went to voice mail. Maybe she'd leaned back her seat and gone to sleep. Yeah, that had to be it. Rita grabbed her jacket and went to check, seeing the front seat was upright before she even made it out the door. The hood was cool to the touch. Grace had arrived a while ago, while Rita had been inside with Crybaby.

Rita looked up and down Fifth Avenue, which was practically deserted this time of night—then back at the hotel. Had her friend met a client, gotten a room? Rita shook her head. That was impossible. There was no way Grace would have started turning tricks again, not with the hearing to get her kid back. No, something had to be wrong.

Always on the verge of paranoia, Rita called out to the darkness, soft and mewling at first, then a full-throated yell. No answer.

Mitch, the fat guy at the front desk, knew Grace but said he hadn't seen her.

"Corsica stopped in with some *slow*," he said. "I'll sell you some if you want."

Slow, *brown*, *down*—it was what Mitch called heroin.

Rita thought about it, then shook her head. "I'm good," she said. "But I need to figure out where Grace went."

Mitch's eyes fluttered. He'd already done some of his *slow*. "Corsica didn't mention her," he said. "Just some tall dude hanging around in front of your door. She thought he was one of your . . . dates."

Rita's throat convulsed, like she'd swallowed a sharp stone. "A tall man?"

Mitch's head lolled on his fat neck. "That's what she said . . . or maybe it was thin man . . . or tin man . . ."

"A tall man," Rita said again. "That's what she called him?"

The desk clerk's eyes fluttered and he loosed a long, squeaky fart. "Sorry, I'm not . . . I mean, the memories are just sort of there, but I can't get to them. . . . You know what I mean?"

Rita was out the door before he'd finished his sentence, running like a child scrambling up from her parents' basement with some imaginary monster behind her. She ducked inside her room and stood with her back to the door, panting, clutching her hair in both fists. Every working girl in the city knew about the bodies washing up along the Coastal Trail.

The Tall Man . . .

No! Rita couldn't go there in her mind.

She paced for five more minutes, checking the window every few seconds.

The grimy parking lot remained empty and dark.

Phone in hand, Rita took a deep breath, steeling herself, and then punched in 911. There was no way in hell some cop was going to believe a prostitute reporting another prostitute as a missing person.

Despair washed over her as the 911 operator picked up.

If the Tall Man was involved, then Grace was dead already.

CHAPTER 5

*G*race Ayuluk woke slowly, her mouth full of dirt. Cold, slick, musty with decay. Dizzy and fighting nausea, she licked her lips. Wincing, tasting blood.

Cheek pressed flat to the muck, she chanced wiggling her jaw. Her tongue found a broken tooth, one of her molars, sheared off at the gumline. Glass-like edges made hamburger out of her cheek, but any pain was eclipsed by the molten blue pulse throbbing in the center of her head. Her skull was surely cracked. Someone had hit her, hard.

She stifled a cough, pushed decaying leaves away from her mouth with the tip of her tongue.

Oh, Grace . . . What have you gotten yourself into?

The thought of her real name hit her like a bucket of cold water. She had been Tawny Hill for ages, nine years—since she'd run away from Nunam Iqua, her village at the mouth of the Yukon River. The name of the tiny town meant "Land's End" in her native Yupik.

To a fifteen-year-old girl, it had seemed like the end of everything. She would have given anything to have been there now instead of waking up facedown in a shallow grave.

Her Christian name, Grace, sounded like one of her aunties, like someone running a church rummage sale. Maybe if she prayed as Grace Ayuluk instead of Tawny Hill—

There was movement above in the darkness, the shuffle of a boot on wet leaves, a snapping twig.

She groaned reflexively, regretting the sound the moment it happened. The weight of her situation pressed her deeper into the dirt. All the girls in her line of work knew about the killings, the body parts—the Tall Man.

She tried to tell herself that some drunk had dragged her into the trees behind the hotel, too looped to carry out his plan to get a freebie.

But she knew deep down that this was the guy all the girls were talking about. He had her. He. Had. Her.

She sobbed again.

A twig snapped in the blackness, amplified by her fear. Wet leaves rustled, like a bear nosing around in the duff—or the boots of a man who didn't care if he was heard or not.

Assholes like this guy got off on fear—and Grace was drowning in it. Her body shook so badly it rattled the decaying leaves. She could almost hear him smiling.

Her hands were tied behind her back, tight. She could still feel them, tingling, burning, which made her think she'd not been tied for more than a few hours. A bastard oil exec had once left her tied up all night with the cord from the miniblinds when she'd tried to lift his Rolex. Her hands had gone completely numb that time. They still gave her trouble on really cold nights. Like now.

She held her breath, straining to hear some clue as to where she was. No traffic sounds. Just wind in the trees and the patter of rain on the dead leaves and the back of her jacket. Above her, the man began to hum softly. Her heart sank when the humming grew louder and she realized there was no one there to hear him.

She opened her eyes a crack. Clouds covered a full moon, but there was enough ambient light to make out the tangle of low berry bushes directly in front of her face. Snotty leaves piled against wet plants, black and slick with rot from a long winter beneath the snow. She had to turn her head to keep from suffocating.

Grace was still dressed, if you could call it that. Her skimpy skirt and a tight leather coat were meant for heating up guys, not keeping her warm. Snippets of memory came shooting back, pounding in time with the throbbing orb of light in her skull. She was clean, if you didn't count methadone, with a gig as an Internet model in a room at the by-the-hour motel across from Merrill Field. She planned to use the money to show the judge she should get her son back. The thought of that little boy stabbed her like a dagger through the heart. She'd finished filming a little early and made it to Rita's just after two a.m.

Everything ran together after that.

She tried to wriggle into a seated position. An immediate wave of nausea caused her to gag.

If he noticed, the man ignored her, and kept humming his creepy little tune.

Then she remembered hearing the song before, when she'd turned to lock her car.

Her last ounce of hope spilled out of her like water from a broken jar. Nobody gave a shit that she'd quit using, how impossible that really was. She'd been a junkie whore when they took her little boy and in the court's eyes, she'd always be a junkie whore. When she didn't show up for her meeting this morning, child welfare would just assume she was passed out next to a guy somewhere with a needle between her toes.

Nobody would miss her. Hell, they'd be happy she didn't show up for the hearing. One less bad mother for everyone to worry about. All clean and tidy with the junkie whore mom out of the picture. She sobbed again. Better for the boy . . .

A single-engine plane buzzed overhead. Hope fled as quickly as it arrived. Bush planes were as common as cars in Alaska, but it was too dark to see a lone woman in a black leather jacket and matching skirt, even if the pilot happened to glance down.

The breeze rattled bare branches overhead, swallowing up the drone of the bush plane. The man in the shadows stopped his humming. Footfalls kicked through wet leaves above the little grave as he came closer.

"I know you're awake, Gracie," the voice said. It came on a whisper, grating her nerves even worse than the humming. He must have gotten her name from her driver's license. She cowered against the putrid mud, clenching her eyes shut. He moved closer. "How about we give the Sleeping Beauty act a rest."

She nodded, ruffling the forest duff with her breath.

"Okay then," the man said, a verbal shrug. "I'm sorry to say, the friend we had picked out for you decided not to play by the rules. I'm sure I don't have to tell you that that is a problem for us."

This guy was acting like she was a part of some big plan—hog-tied and pitched in a shallow grave. As terrified as she was, Grace's tolerance for bullshit had always been low.

"What are you talking about, asshole?"

He was going to kill her anyway.

He laughed. High-pitched, stilted, like a crazed bird, or someone only pretending to laugh.

"I'm saying we now have to go to the trouble of finding you a different friend." A strong hand wrapped around her ankle where it was tied to her hands, and dragged her backward. She tried to kick, but it was useless and only cut into her wrists. Unable to shield her face, she bounced along the ground as he dragged, her chin plowing a furrow of leaves and mud.

She tried to scream, slicing the inside of her mouth with the broken tooth, tasting blood again.

The man suddenly let go, allowing her to roll on her side. She tried to crawfish away. Useless. He switched his headlamp on, full in her face, causing her to freeze. The light swayed back and forth as he shook his head and gave an exhausted sigh.

"They always think they can run." The hand reached out again from behind the blinding halo of light. He chuckled. "But you know what? That shit never gets old."

Grace shuddered at his tone. "Just . . . just tell me what you want me to do, mister. I'm really good at a lot of things."

A fog of vapor from the man's breath swirled from the blinding curtain of light. He was thinking about her offer. That was good. Maybe he would cut her loose. Guys did weird things when their motors got going.

At length, he laughed again. "Nah, I don't think so. As much as I'd enjoy that, he'd kill me. Anyway, we have to hurry. I got somewhere I need to be." His grip tightened around her ankle. He turned mechanically, giving her a silhouette of his towering height as he dragged her through the muck. Not skinny, but not fat, either. A dark shadow. It was him. The specter all the girls were all talking about.

The Tall Man.

On her side now, sliding on her hip and shoulder, she began to pick up pieces of her surroundings.

He turned his head back and forth as he slogged, checking his path. The ghost-gray bark of a stump reflected in the light to his right. Too thick for a birch tree, it was probably a cottonwood, about as big around as Grace's waist and sawn off flat two feet above the ground. A long-bladed knife stuck tip-first into the wood. Not a machete, this was meant for stabbing—for close work. It was still plenty large enough to chop if the need arose.

Dark lines of red streaked the sides of the stump. Blood. Lots of it. Grace recoiled at the gruesome sight, throwing herself from side to side. Thrashing. She screamed until she thought her voice would shatter.

This was where he did it. She was going to die here, cold and alone amid rotting leaves and sloppy mud, hacked to death by a maniac.

But the man kept dragging, past the killing place toward a white birch set aglow by his headlamp.

He dropped her foot, like he was setting down a bag of groceries, to unlock his door.

She tried to skuttle away on hip and shoulder, hyperventilating, cursing, out of her mind with terror and pain.

A chain rattled. Cut branches and camouflage netting fell away to reveal a metal door secured by a stout padlock.

He took a key out of the pocket of his overalls—dark blue, like a mechanic, or someone who didn't want to get blood on his clothes, might wear.

Grace continued to caterpillar away, which only made the man chuckle when he turned, blinding her with the headlamp again.

She screamed. "You . . . you don't . . . have . . . have . . . to do this!"

"Aahhh," the Tall Man said, grabbing her foot again and twisting the ankle against her own body weight to make her comply. The latch handle gave a loud clunk, and the heavy door squealed as he pulled it open. "You're right. *I* don't have to . . . But you do."

CHAPTER 6

Two days later

*R*ose Fulton knew someone or something was in the trees as soon as she got out of her car at Beer Can Lake.

She should have turned around then and driven somewhere more populated, but reasoned if she didn't run in Alaska because there might be something dangerous in the woods, she'd never run. It was probably a moose. Or maybe a bear. About time for them to be waking up this time of year. Kobuk, her two-year-old German shepherd, bounded ahead, making her decision for her as he tore down the trail beside the lake.

She sucked up her fears—and ran after him into the early-morning fog.

The 11-27 call came over the radio as Officer Joe Bill Brackett patrolled Spenard Road. He was working his way slowly around the end of Lake Hood, looking at floatplanes and pondering about whether or not to get his pilot's license. As busy as it was, night shift had a significant amount of time for pondering life goals.

The dispatcher was terse as per usual: *"Female jogger reports assault by possible homeless white male on the jogging trail adjacent to Beer Can Lake. Attacker fled into the woods. Unknown direction of travel."*

The facts, ma'am, just the facts.

Little Campbell Lake had been called Beer Can for as long as Joe Bill could remember, due to the propensity of Anchorage kids to use its secluded banks for parties. Brackett broke up at least one kegger a week.

The initial information from dispatch provided enough detail that responding officers could get the job done safely, but not so much as to clog up radio traffic.

EMS was also in route.

Curt Jacobs, the 24 Alpha unit, attached himself to the call. Kincaid Park and Little Campbell Lake were in area 24—adjacent to Brackett's patrol assignment. He whipped into the Marriott parking lot and hit the brakes, taking a moment to read the 911 operator's notes on the mobile data terminal in his car. Suspicious activity calls were common on midnight shift, and it was easy to become numb to the harsh realities of them, especially for older, more jaded officers. Only weeks out of field training and on his own, Brackett's pulse still raced at almost every call. He scanned the hotel parking lot out of habit while cuing up his MDT, making sure no threats were walking toward his cruiser.

The notes read, he threw the car into gear and made

a U-turn, lifting his radio mic from the console as he rejoined morning traffic to speed south toward Jewel Lake Road.

"21-A-2," he said. "Attach me to the 11-27 at Beer Can, responding from Spenard."

He got his sergeant on the phone about the time he drifted around the corner onto Raspberry Road, passing the Tastee Freez, heading west, wigwag lights strobing, siren wailing.

"You think this might be more than a simple assault, Sarge?" He spoke into the earbud so he could keep his eyes on the road. "An attempted kidnapping, maybe?"

Sergeant Hopper liked Brackett, which made things easier. "You seeing this as our Bootlegger Cove killer?"

Hopper was a Texan, not one to beat around the bush, but even he wouldn't say the words *serial killer*.

"He's out there somewhere, sir," Brackett said. "I mean, Bootleggers isn't all that far. Point Woronzof is even closer to Kinkaid Park—and Beer Can."

"I don't disagree with you," Hopper said, and went to work doing what sergeants did, moving pieces around on the chess board without going overbudget.

Moments later, Tom Alcorn, K9 Blitz's handler, broke squelch on the radio, dispensing with the Ten-Codes for plain talk. "Copy the possible assault at Beer Can Lake. Show me and Blitz en route from Jewel Lake Training Center."

Sergeant Hopper directed units to meet Airport Police at the Kulis Business Park Gate and set up a northern perimeter by the time Brackett turned right off Raspberry toward Beer Can Lake. Kincaid Park spanned both sides of the road; units from mids and day shift would form a southern perimeter along Raspberry. No way the bad guy could have made it that far.

A cavalry of sirens screamed behind Brackett. Kinkaid Park was a 1,500-acre greenbelt at the end of a point on the western edge of Anchorage, making Raspberry the only main road in. He hoped the brass was calling in someone with a boat in case this guy had a skiff stashed on Cook Inlet. The Troopers based a chopper at the airport, but it would take time to get it in the air—and exponentially longer to get the FBI or US Marshals planes up. No, this was going to be a boots-on-the-ground search for the moment—and Joe Bill Brackett wanted to make sure his were some of the first boots on scene.

The bastard had slipped up.

Now they had him.

CHAPTER 7

*A*rliss Cutter was up, showered, and tying his boots when the phone call came in from the chief deputy. He hated tying boots. It reminded him of the military, but the snow and ice of Alaska terrain had caused him to trade his beloved post-Army Tony Lamas in favor of Zamberlan hikers for the added traction.

As usual, Cutter's subconscious had nudged him awake a few minutes before his six o'clock alarm. The return flight from Dutch Harbor had arrived after midnight. By the time they jockeyed around vehicles at the airport and got an extremely disgruntled Captain Koslov tucked in at Anchorage Jail, Cutter didn't get home until almost three in the morning.

His body could have used more sleep, but his mind wouldn't allow it. Getting up and moving was far preferable to staying in bed and ruminating on his past.

Chief Jill Phillips gave him a BLUF, bottom-line-up-front, rundown of the events that were unfolding at that moment with the assault in Kincaid Park. Cutter could hear her baby crying in the background while Phillips puttered around nonchalantly talking about bloody assaults and serial killers, phone on speaker while she soothed the fussy child. She was an expert, using these same skills to lead a squad room of fussy deputy marshals.

"Captain Osborne with APD is a friend of mine," Phillips said in her sleepy, exhausted-mom Kentucky accent. "I've mentioned your abilities as a man-tracker to him several times. They got a perimeter up right away and have a K9 unit arriving anytime. They could well grab the guy and this'll be over before you get there."

Boots tied snuggly and double-knotted, Cutter stood. He kept his voice low so as not to wake anyone else in the house.

"No ego here, Chief," he said. "I hope they do get him. Trackers don't usually lay hands on the person we're after anyway. We find a direction of travel and pass it on to forward teams." He glanced at his watch. "I can be there in twenty minutes."

"Go ahead and call Lola," Phillips said.

"She's probably at the gym."

"Call her in anyway," Phillips said, putting a stop to further discussion.

"Roger that," Cutter said, ending the call so he could get on his way. He'd call Teariki from the road.

In addition to the normal "war bag" of essentials he carried with him to lead the Alaska Fugitive Task force each day—radio, extra magazines for his Glock and speed loaders for his Colt Python, a flashlight, gloves, etc.—he kept a rural go bag for times when tracking was the primary mission. First responders rarely thought about calling in trackers, what with so much technology at their fingertips. And in the rare event they did decide to get a tracker involved, initial responders had to be trained not to muck up the scene before one arrived. Cutter understood completely. It went against a law enforcement officer's mind-set to stand by when there was a trail to follow. The few times since transferring to Alaska that Cutter had assisted other agencies had been search and rescue calls. A lost sheep hunter up the Peters Creek drainage above Eagle River. A college freshman who'd gotten separated from his group on Pioneer Peak. Cutter knew from experience that tracking missions in Alaska might mean an overnight bivouac, so he packed for it just in case.

A streamlined chest rig made by Haley Strategic held a spare fire steel, extra flashlight, Leatherman Wave, measuring tape, a disposable bivy bag, light silicon tarp, 550 cord, a wound kit (including a SWAT-T tourniquet), orange flagging tape, a bottle of water, a couple of energy bars, and among a few other odds and ends, a notepad and pencil.

He grabbed both the war and tracking bags and headed for the door.

His twin nephews argued over something in the next room, getting ready for school. The shower turned off—probably his sister-in-law Mim. His sixteen-year-old niece Constance had early classes, so she'd be about ready to head out the door too. He'd come in so late the kids didn't know he was home—a good thing in Constance's case. They used to be good buds, but shortly after Arliss had come to Alaska to help out after his brother's death, she'd turned cold, distant.

She and Mim walked out of their respective rooms at the same moment, when Cutter was making his way toward the door.

Dressed in her puffy pink terry cloth robe, honey-colored hair still wet from her shower, Mim brightened when she saw him.

Constance did not.

Lola Tuakana Teariki was standing with a knot of APD brass when Cutter arrived at Beer Can Lake. The parking lot was a circus of APD officers moving between the lake and their respective Tahoes, Impalas, and Ford Explorers. More unmarked than marked—mostly detectives and bosses. The chief's friend, Captain Osborne, stood talking with Lola and some of his men around an open laptop computer on the hood of a white unmarked Expedition. He held a radio in one hand and shielded the laptop from the spitting rain with a file folder he held in the other. He was a big man with thinning hair that was pasted to his head with drizzle and fog.

Lola's condo was on the north side of the airport, little more than five miles away. It made sense that she'd beat him here. A black North Face rain jacket matched her dark hair, piled high in a tight bun. Cutter's identical issue jacket along with their khaki slacks gave the deputy marshals a semi-uniform appearance. Both wore silver-star badges suspended on chains around their necks.

Lola gave a nod to the APD brass when she saw Cutter drive up, and walked over to meet him.

Cutter gave her a "hello" toss of his head. "You made good time."

She shrugged, scrunching her nose and raising her brow to show the whites of her eyes. If Cutter hadn't known her so well, it would have been slightly terrifying. "I've been up for hours," she said. "My mum always told us kids a guilty conscience makes the best alarm clock."

Cutter almost smiled at that. "Explains why I'm always up so early . . ."

"Anyway," she said through a long yawn. "Looks like they found the victim's German shepherd."

Cutter threw on the chest rig while he listened, shrugging his rain jacket over top.

"The poor dog is cut up some," Lola continued, grim. "But they say he should mend okay."

Cutter locked his SUV. "The bad guy?"

"Still at large," Lola said. "Blitz had no trouble sniffing out the wounded doggo, but it sounds like there's a lot of blood. It's taking a bit to sort out the track. The captain was just on the radio with the guys on scene when you—"

A shout erupted from the group of officers at the makeshift command post. Osborne's fist pumped the air.

"Got the son of a bitch!" The captain gave Cutter a thumbs-up. "Sorry to get you out here for nothing."

"No problem at all," Cutter said, shaking the captain's hand when he reached the group and then greeting the other officer in turn. "I'm interested, though. Was the bad guy in a camp?"

"Hiding behind a pile of deadfall," Osborne said. "Officers on scene recognize him as Henry Farris, a homeless guy with a history of violence. Hurting women would be right up his alley. I shouldn't be happy about it, but Blitz got a good bite to go along with the ones the other shepherd gave him."

"He injured that girl pretty bad," a female sergeant named Mirada said. "No telling what he had in store for her if he'd gotten her into the woods. I hope Blitz dragged him out of the brush by his balls."

Cutter took a slow breath, thinking. "Since we're already here, would you mind if we go take a look at where they got him?"

Osborne spoke into his handheld radio. "Brackett, a couple of marshals coming your way." He nodded at Cutter, pointing into the fog with a knife hand. "Just down the trail alongside the water. Take the footbridge over the marsh at the end of the lake and then hang a right into the birch trees. You'll likely hear them. They know you're coming. They're treating Farris's injuries before they walk him out, so they'll be there a few more minutes."

Cutter thanked the captain and then moved out quickly, hoping to reach the scene while there were still officers there. Lola fell in behind him.

"What is it, boss?" She snugged her jacket around her neck against the morning chill. "What can we do if they already got the guy?"

"Just curious," Cutter said. "If Henry Farris is the person responsible for all these recent killings, APD might need help with an evidence track. Chief sent us here to help, so we might as well help."

Cutter pointed out the area where Farris had made

his initial attack as they passed the scuffed dirt and overturned leaves. There was blood too, probably from Farris when the victim's dog got him. He had to be hurting now, with bites from the German shepherd and a Belgian Malinois. As Osborne predicted, the sounds of K9 Blitz's whines begging for another piece of the bad guy carried through the fog by the time they reached the footbridge.

There were five uniformed officers on scene, the handler and four others. Cutter had watched APD K9 tracks before. Customarily, four officers worked a diamond formation, providing overwatch and security so the handler could focus on the dog. Now, two officers stooped beside a mud-covered Henry Farris, bandaging the worst of his wounds. The jogger's shepherd had nailed him on the point of his chin before he'd discouraged it with a knife to the shoulder. Blitz was a much more practiced biter. Still, Farris had apparently tried to fight, smacking the K9 in the head with a piece of birch after he'd dropped his knife. The dog, in turn, had latched on to Farris's groin. The bite had missed the femoral artery, but blood soaked the front of his grimy jeans.

A youthful officer with dark hair and the slightly giddy expression of someone new to the job approached Cutter and extended his hand. He introduced himself as Joe Bill Brackett.

"You're the marshals," he said, stating the obvious.

The other officers looked up and nodded. Blitz studied Cutter and Lola with expressive amber eyes, like they might be the main course after the amuse-bouche provided by whatever he'd bitten off of Farris.

"What is it you're looking for?" Brackett asked. Too new to be tarnished by any parochial jealousy, he seemed genuinely interested, almost puppy-like.

Cutter was already poking around the area, which had seen enough activity in the past few minutes to look as if it had been plowed.

"Your crime scene folks will be here shortly to work an evidence track," Lola said, sounding confident. Not like Cutter had just explained it to her five minutes before. "Cutter is a tracker. Captain Osborne asked him to get started with that, see if he can't find where Farris came from."

"Mind if I come along?" Brackett asked. He shot a glance at the officers around Farris. "That is, if you guys don't need me here."

A female officer with her med kit spread out on the wet ground glanced up at Brackett and smiled. "Go ahead, fed." She chuckled. "We all had you pegged for going over to the dark side after the academy anyway."

Lola started to joke, but Cutter shook his head. They were, after all, trying to find where a possible serial killer was butchering women. Instead, she gave the kid a pat on the shoulder. "Come on. We could use the extra set of eyes."

Cutter worked backward from the deadfall where Blitz had located Farris, pointing out a spot a few yards through the trees where he'd squatted and watched, apparently moving south before thinking better of it and going back to the deadfall, where he was eventually captured.

Cutter gestured to the divots in the duff formed by Farris's elbows as he'd lain flat, peeking from behind a small clump of highbush cranberry—called "cramp bark" by indigenous people because of its medicinal properties.

"He watched his backtrail from here for a bit," Cutter said, pointing through the trees to the north. "Hard to be sure with so much moose activity, but I'd guess he came from here first. I imagine he was going back when he heard the K9 closing in and thought better of it."

Lola squatted low, getting a view of the trail from a different angle like Cutter had taught her. "Like he didn't want to lead them back to his lair?"

"Exactly that," Cutter said. The ground was covered with decaying leaves and spring muck, offering plenty of evidence of disturbance, but few clear tracks. Still, he could tell from the scuffs when Farris was running. The stride and straddle changed considerably after he'd gotten his first bite from the shepherd, allowing Cutter to judge with a fair degree of certainty which line of sign was made on his journey in before the assault and which was made after he'd started favoring his left leg. The birch trees were still bare of anything but tiny spring buds, but periodic stands of black spruce, alder, and highbush cranberry cast the forest into perpetual shadow, even without a full crown of leaves, making for many excellent hiding spots.

It took Cutter a few minutes of looking, and some help from Lola, but he eventually found Farris's back trail. His camp wasn't far, merely hidden in a shaded hollow of a low draw, surrounded on three sides by prickly devil's club. He'd come and gone through the spreading trunks of an alder, his hands having rubbed the bark smooth and red as he used the stout branches to pull himself up the incline and out of his hide.

Cutter took the lead, with Lola behind him, picking their way through the trees.

"My dad calls this pucker brush," Brackett said. "Because of how your sphincter reacts to it when you're in bear country."

Lola chuckled. "Pucker brush . . ."

Cutter stopped short, still in the tangle of alder branches, but at the edge of a large, room-like clearing.

Lola crowded in beside him and gasped, "Holy shit . . ."

Brackett pressed the radio mic clipped to his lapel.

"Sarge," he said, his voice a hushed whisper. "You're gonna want to see this."

CHAPTER 8

"What are we looking at?" Lola pointed to a mound of dirt the size of a small cabin behind a tattered dome tent.

Cutter cocked his head, peering through the trees at an earthen lump covered with overgrowth. It was about fifteen feet high at its peak, with steep, sloping sides, a rivetted metal front, and heavy steel door.

"I'm guessing it's an old ammo bunker."

"The padlock looks new," Lola said. "You know, a bunker would make for a nifty lair."

"Then why the tent?" Cutter mused.

"I'd call that evidence," Lola said, nodding at a stump to the right of the tent.

"Looks like blood," Brackett said. "A shitload of blood."

"Yep," Cutter said, grim. He took out his phone and snapped photos from several angles, but he didn't move from his spot.

"And one big-ass blade buried in the wood," Lola said, starting forward. "My cousins would call that a boar-sticking knife."

Cutter touched her arm, stopping her. "Our work here is done," he said. "We tracked him to his camp. Now we'll wait until crime scene arrives."

"But, boss . . ." She gave a disappointed shake of her head.

"We wait here," Cutter repeated. He locked eyes with Lola to make sure she understood, and then looked up, surveying the scene.

The morning breeze had pushed away the fog, leaving the clearing cold and gunmetal gray. Rain dripped from new alder buds and last year's brown seedpods that hung from the branches like tiny pinecones.

"Either of you ever play Kim's game?" Cutter asked.

Lola glared at him though narrow slits, like it was a trick.

Officer Brackett shook his head, still focused on the blood-soaked stump at the edge of Henry Farris's camp.

Lola wiped the rain off her forehead with the back of her hand, sullen, wanting badly to go and investigate. "I guess I've heard you mention it. Remind me."

"Kim, the spy kid in the Kipling novel, trained his mind by memorizing a tray of items that were put in front of him for a short time. I'm sure you've played a similar game at parties. Military snipers have a version of it, memorizing terrain features and whatnot. I use a grid to help me remember."

"You want us to *memorize* what we see?" Brackett mused.

"No disrespect toward APD," Cutter said, "but it's

human nature for all of us to let ourselves get pulled into things. It's especially common when urban investigators work a rural case. All these browns and greens tend to run together like one of those Bev Doolittle paintings. Important details get missed because the human eye glosses over them. I say we use this time to our advantage. We can identify places that should be searched when your team gets here. Make a plan. We . . . you . . . can nudge them toward things we've noticed as they're going in."

Brackett scoffed. "I'm barely out of field training. Nobody's going to listen to me at a crime scene."

"Sure they will," Lola said. "They'll take your suggestions and then they'll take the credit . . ."

"Okay . . ." Brackett said, unconvinced.

"Let's start like this," Cutter said. "Where did Farris sleep?"

Lola shrugged. "The tent . . . or maybe the bunker."

"My guess is the tent," Cutter said, "judging from the well-trod ground out front. Let's use that as a focal point in the camp and work outward. Find me the most prominent path leading from the tent."

Brackett shot him a side-eye. "Find it from here?"

Cutter nodded as he scanned. "Yep. Any trail to the bunker?"

Brackett shrugged. "Not a very big one."

"The leaves are darker there," Lola said. "Going behind and slightly to the north of the tent toward that clump of bushes."

"Right," Cutter said. "My guess is that he dug himself a cathole . . . a dedicated latrine. I'm not seeing any fire ring, but look at all those yellow bottles in front of the tent door."

"Heet," Lola said, squinting to read the labels. More than a decade his junior, her eyes had the edge of youth over Cutter.

Brackett gave a slow nod. "A gasoline additive. Basically methanol. So, Farris is cooking on an alcohol stove instead of a fire . . ."

"A what?" Lola asked.

"Fairly easy to make a camp stove out of a beer or soda can," Cutter said. "Gas stations often keep cases of fuel additive outside the main door, making them relatively easy to swipe."

"Explains why Farris was able to keep his camp hidden," Brackett mused. "No campfire smoke."

Lola scanned the camp, putting it all together. "He makes an alcohol stove out of *aluminium* cans?"

Brackett looked sideways at how she added an extra syllable, making the word ah-loo-minium.

She went on. "So he doesn't have a camp fire to give him away, but with all that blood, there had to be screaming. Hard to hide that."

"If the victims were alive when he cut them up," Brackett said. "Or maybe he used the bunker as a kill house."

"True enough." Lola groaned. "I've seen some stuffed things in my life, but that bloody stump spooks the shit out of—"

Voices in the trees behind them cut her off.

"We're over this way," Brackett said, guiding in his bosses.

Captain Osborne hauled himself through the tangle of alder branches with a grunt a few seconds later, followed by two more uniforms and two in plain clothes whom Cutter didn't recognize. The nearest introduced himself as Detective Nakamura from homicide."

"Cool." Lola beamed, shaking his hand. "My mum's mother was a Nakamura from a little village at the base of Mount Fuji."

The detective looked at her, deadpan. "My mom's mother is from Seattle."

Lola shot Cutter a grimace. "All righty then. Anyway, we're here to help . . ."

Osborne radioed back to the parking lot for a pair of bolt cutters and then, to his credit, kept everyone on the edges of the clearing until crime scene techs arrived half an hour later.

"You were right," Cutter whispered to Officer Brackett as the group gathered around the door of the bunker, hands on or near their sidearms in anticipation of what they might find. "A few tracks and some disturbed duff on the forest floor, but I see no established trail leading here."

Detective Nakamura made quick work of the lock with the bolt cutters. He had to beat on the hasp. It didn't appear to have been moved in years, maybe even decades. It took two of them and the edge of the bolt cutters to pry open the door, which squealed in protest on rusty hinges when they finally got it moving.

"Empty," Nakamura said under his breath, sleepily, as if he was noting the weather. If he was disappointed, he didn't register it.

Cutter understood. Sometimes, the best investigators were the dogged types armed with a keen mind but completely lacking in bubbly personalities—or personality of any sort. Lola was turning into a terrific enforcement deputy—a manhunter—but so far, at least, she lacked the patience to put together the sophisticated case needed to prosecute a murder suspect. Cutter didn't blame her. Patience wasn't exactly his strength, either.

Investigate. Arrest. Take to jail. Begin again. He'd leave the thick case files and lengthy reports to his friends at the FBI.

The bunker looked to be a bust, but crime scene techs sprayed the dusty interior with luminol and scanned with a blacklight anyway, on the off chance that they might find blood or semen. For their trouble, they found dust and a pulsing orb of daddy longlegs the size of a soccer ball.

Cutter and Lola helped walk a grid, moving step by step, calling out anytime they found possible evidence—a scrap of paper, a bit of hair. APD personnel logged it all in.

The stump looked to be covered in blood, as did the heavy butcher knife embedded in the wood. Captain Osborne squatted next to it and adjusted his glasses, careful not to touch anything. "What do you make of this?" he said to whomever happened to be nearby.

Cutter stepped in next to him and gave the stump a slow once over. It was wide for a birch, but it *was* a birch, so barely a foot across at its widest point. Not really ideal for a butcher block, but few trees around here would be.

Still, people made use of what they had.

Cutter could make out bits of something white embedded in the battered wood.

"Bone fragments?" he said.

Nakamura became animated at the mention of bones

and strode across the clearing. Not quickly, but quicker—
a sloth on a mission. "We'll need to take the entire
stump," he said.

"Makes sense," the captain said, and called to have
someone bring in picks and shovels and a chainsaw
while they were at it.

Brackett's hunch about the Heet was proved correct
when evidence techs found two puck-shaped stoves
made from aluminum cans and a cook pot fashioned
from a twenty-four-ounce Heineken.

Nakamura retrieved what looked like five scalps of
matted gray-white hair from inside the tent and held
them aloft in his gloved hand.

"I've got blood on these," he said, his emotions
ticking up a tiny notch. "Whatever the hell they are."

Brackett leaned in for a closer look. "Snowshoe
hare pelts. Hare and lynx run on a seven-year cycle,
give or take. Lots of hare mean lots of food for preda-
tors. Lots of lynx means the hare population drops,
which makes for less food, so the lynx population fiz-
zles. With few lynx to hunt them, the hare population
grows . . . Rinse and repeat every seven years. We're
at the top of the hare cycle now, so they're everywhere.
Farris was probably eating them."

"Nice biology lesson," Nakamura said. "I just realized, you're that newbie who keeps bugging us to help
out with this case."

Brackett gave a sheepish nod.

The detective held the furs out in front of him. "You
wanna be involved. You can go ahead and bag these."

Apart from the furs, the tent held little but a filthy
sleeping bag and a makeshift mattress of tarps and
foam couch cushions.

One of the crime scene techs came out of the trees carrying an evidence baggie in his blue nitrile glove. "We found something by the guy's shitter."

"What is it?" Osborne called, still guarding his find beside the stump.

"A wallet," the tech said. "ID says it belongs to a Lacy Geddes."

A female patrol officer's head jerked up at the news. "Geddes is a hooker who used to work down by the bus station. She dropped out of sight about a month ago."

"All right," Captain Osborne said. "That's a place to start. It's a good bet that one of our torsos or other body parts turns out to be Ms. Geddes. Let's take this slow. The highway department has ground-penetrating radar. We should start looking for anything that might be a grave."

Detective Nakamura kicked the ground and said, "I doubt we'll find many of the bodies here, Captain. The dirt is still frozen probably a foot down, maybe more. Too hard to dig without good equipment—which Henry Farris doesn't appear to have."

"True enough," Osborne said. "We'll get this stump back to the crime lab and order up some toolmark comparisons between the knife and the recovered limbs." He looked hard at Nakamura. "Can we tie Farris to this spot?"

"The marshal backtracked him here," Nakamura said. "He can testify to that. Right?"

Cutter gave a nod. "Absolutely."

"Plus any DNA we find," Nakamura said. "Oils on his sleeping bag, stool samples from his latrine . . ."

"Good," Osborne said, punching his open hand with

a fist as he thought. "Blood, bone fragments in the stump, toolmarks from the knife . . . and a missing woman's wallet. Yeah, I'd call that a damn good start."

"Farris is our guy, Captain," Nakamura said, turning away to talk on his phone.

Lola leaned against a tall birch tree at the edge of the clearing, frowning. She looked at Brackett, who'd remained with her and Cutter instead of his peers. Cutter suspected it had something to do with the way the two youngsters had been exchanging glances. They were close to the same age, and Cutter had to admit, Lola Teariki did have a certain gravitational pull.

"You thinking what I'm thinking?" Lola asked.

"Depends," Brackett said. "If you're thinking that this doesn't add up."

"I know, right?" She kept her voice low so the APD officers and techs couldn't hear her. "I mean, this guy's cooking rabbit soup in an old beer can. Do you think he's sophisticated enough to lure a half-dozen women into these woods, murder them, and not get caught?"

"Could be he's a roamer," Cutter offered. He didn't believe it, but it helped to play devil's advocate. "Maybe he didn't kill them all at this location."

"I don't buy it," Lola said. "Henry Farris has as much in common with a serial killer as chalk and cheese. I mean, he's stupid enough to try and grab a girl in his own backyard. Guys like that get caught pretty quickly. He's violent, probably schizo. Maybe he did kill someone on that stump, but he doesn't strike me as smart enough to get away with a string of unsolved murders."

Brackett watched the other members of his department at work, and then gave a slow shake of his head.

"I know they have to try, but I don't see them finding any bodies here. The killer hacked up his victims and threw them into the Inlet. He didn't bury them."

Lola raised her brow, wagging her head at the young officer. "Then the question is, what are we going to do about it?"

Cutter gathered himself up to move, nudging her with his elbow. "*He* can do what he wants. You and I are going back to the office."

"Boss!" Lola said. "I don't mean to whine, but I bet you don't believe for one second that Farris is our serial killer."

"You would be correct," Cutter said, deadpan.

Her mouth fell open. "Then we have to do something. Maybe we list the reservations we have in our supplemental reports."

"You'll want to think that through." Cutter gave an emphatic shake of his head. "Our reports state facts, not opinions. If it turns out we're wrong and Farris is the killer, defense attorneys will use our initial misgivings to cast doubt to the jury during trial."

"I guess that's why you make the big money," Lola said, peeved, so her Kiwi accent reared up again. "But what if we're right? That means a maniac is still out there. We can't just call it a day."

"I'll give Captain Osborne a shout later," Cutter said. "Let him know what we're thinking. He seems like a straight shooter. Don't forget, though, these APD guys know what they're doing. Once they get the lab results back on the blood and toolmarks, they'll come to the same conclusions."

"I know," Lola said, scuffing her boot toe against the forest floor. "I just really want to catch this guy."

Then, when she thought Cutter wasn't looking, she tucked a business card in Officer Brackett's hand and mouthed, "Call me."

Cutter saw it all. He stifled a chuckle but said nothing. He was young once. More than that, he couldn't blame Lola for what she was feeling about this investigation. Everything about him wanted to jump into APD's business with both feet and track down this killer before anyone else got hurt.

CHAPTER 9

A ssistant US Attorney John Stapely sauntered around the Court Security screening desk in front of the Marshals' Office at the same time Cutter got off the parking garage elevator almost a hundred feet away in the open atrium. Stapely's assistant, Kaydra, followed him like a cleaner fish—or maybe a lamprey (Cutter couldn't decide which)—trailed a reef shark. Cutter saw the AUSA first and pulled up short before he came out of the elevator alcove to cross the wide hallway toward the Fugitive Task Force offices. Close behind, Lola, who was on her phone, ran into Cutter, knocking him into the open so they caught the AUSA's eye.

"Sorry, boss," Lola said, shoving the phone in her pocket.

Stapely was a lean man with smallish, deep-set eyes and the habit of wearing running shoes with his ill-fitting business suits. His voice reminded Cutter of a table saw when the blade first started to spin—but that had more to do with the things he had to say than the manner in which he said them. He was civil division chief for the US Attorney's office in Alaska. His assistant, Kaydra, had drawn up the paperwork for the *Magdalena Murmansk*.

Cutter groaned when the attorney raised his cardboard coffee cup to hail him down. A court security officer standing at the second-floor railing above saw what was happening and shot Cutter a sympathetic look.

"Hey there! Deputy!" Stapely's buzzing shout echoed across the open atrium, his accent a pinched transatlantic, like he was clenching a cigarette holder in his teeth. "I need to talk to you."

Cutter stood fast, making the attorney come to him. Lola took up a position to Cutter's immediate right. Kaydra hung back a half step behind her boss, probably so he couldn't see her eye rolls.

"I have to ask," Stapely said as he got closer. "Were you trying to screw up this vessel seizure?"

Cutter raised a brow but didn't answer.

Stapely plowed ahead. "You have got to be aware of the hard and fast rule, agreed to by the Marshals Service, that we do not seize things that have to be fed. Last I checked, dogs have to be fed. Seriously, I can't fathom how you could possibly think encumbering the United States Government with the care of three hundred French poodles would be a good idea."

"Bulldogs," Cutter corrected. "What you can or can't fathom doesn't concern me, John."

"Well, concern yourself with this then. Your little stunt in Dutch Harbor is causing my Customs agents a shit-ton of extra work."

Lola bowed up. "What did you expect us—"

Cutter raised a hand to shush her, then peered down at Stapely, who was half a foot shorter. "You done?"

"Hardly," the lawyer said, grinning, playing a trump card. "Captain Koslov has filed a formal complaint with the US Attorney's office—"

"I'll bet he has," Cutter said. "I gave him a pretty good smack."

"See!" Stapely scoffed, throwing a disgusted look over his shoulder at his assistant. "That's what I expected. You don't give a shit if you—"

"Oh, I give a shit," Cutter said, voice low and even. "I do. That's why I didn't put up with his behavior."

"You can't go around slapping a Russian national on his own ship."

"First," Cutter said, "I was under the impression it was *our* ship once I hung paper on it. Second, Koslov's nationality has nothing to do with what happened."

"Oh, but it does."

Cutter gave a slow, contemplative nod as if considering whether or not to give Stapely a smack of his own. "So, you'd let a Russian national rob the bank down the hall?"

Stapely scoffed, incredulous. "No."

"How about letting him kick a woman?"

"Of course not."

"Even if she was on his ship in US waters?"

"I see where you're going with this and it's not the same thing."

"Yeah," Cutter said. "It is. Koslov attacked a kid who was cooperating with us. For that matter, he swung a steel pipe at me. You seem to be awfully worried about *your* Customs agents. How about you show a little love to *your* deputy marshals? I mean, we're all on the same team. Right?"

Stapely's nostrils flared, but he said nothing.

Cutter waved off any notion of further conversation. "Doesn't matter," he said, stifling the urge to smack this smarmy guy in the ear. "Better if anything else is taken up with Chief Phillips."

"Oh, it will be," Stapely said.

"See you around then," Lola piped as the AUSA stalked off, runners squeaking on the polished brick floor, Kaydra scampering meekly after him.

Cleaner fish, Cutter decided.

"I'll check in with the chief," Cutter said. "You can touch bases with the TFOs and see if we have any pressing punks to bust." A TFO was a task force officer from an agency outside the Marshals Service.

"All the same to you, boss," Lola said. "I'd like to tag along. Chief's an animal lover. I want to see what she's gonna do about all the puppies."

"US Customs has the pups," Cutter said. "We only have custody of the ship."

Lola gave him a wink. "We're talking about Jill Phillips. She uses her mighty cosmic power for good." Lola's phone started playing a song from Disney's *Moana* in her pocket. She fished it out and her eyes widened when she saw the number. "It's Joe Bill," she muttered, nodding to herself, apparently pleased.

"Who?" Cutter said, still walking toward the Marshals' Office.

"Officer Brackett." Lola stopped. "I should . . . I'll catch up with you."

*   *   *

"I thought you'd be asleep by now," Lola said after Cutter walked away. She strolled toward the expansive indoor planters that occupied the atrium of the federal building, full of ferns, rubber tree plants, and spiky mother-in-law tongue year-around, no matter how much snow fell outside. Phone to her ear, she took a seat on the low brick wall that surrounded the freshly watered plants. The comfortable ozone smell reminded her of the lush jungles of her father's home island. "Didn't you just work all night?"

"I can't turn my brain off." Brackett's voice was husky, exhausted. "Too much on my mind."

"I know what you mean," Lola said. "This thing has had me wrapped around the axle for a while now. I don't like having my hands tied."

"Me neither," Brackett said. "So . . . I was think-ing . . ."

His voice trailed off, and for a moment, she thought she'd dropped the call.

"You still there?"

"Yeah," Brackett said. "I'm not very good at this . . ."

"Good at what?" Lola asked, teasing.

"I mean . . ."

"If I'm being honest," Lola said, "I thought you were going to ask me out at the crime scene. That would have been way weirder than this."

"Okay," Brackett said. "Less weird is good, I guess. Anyway, no way I was going to ask you out with that grim-looking dude you work with standing beside you."

"Cutter?" Lola chuckled. "He's a pussy cat . . . Well, not really, but he's not . . . Okay, he's grim, but his heart's in the right place."

"You guys aren't . . . I mean . . . you don't have anything going?"

"He's my boss," Lola scoffed. "I mean, he's a good-looking man with all sorts of . . ." She paused, shook her head, and then laughed. "Nah, he's more like a protective uncle. Besides, he has his own thing going."

She left out the fact that Cutter was sweet on his widowed sister-in-law.

"So," Brackett said. "You want to have dinner or something this evening. We could talk about the murders."

"Well, don't you just know the way straight to a girl's heart."

"We don't have to—"

"I'm in," Lola said quickly. "We are what we are, Joe . . . Should I call you Joe or Joe Bill?"

"Either," Brackett said.

"I like Joe Bill," Lola said. "Anyway, people like you and I will end up talking about the killings for sure. No reason to pretend otherwise."

Lola heard him whisper "Outstanding!" under his breath. He said "Okay" into the phone. "What time do you get off work?"

"Depends on what's going on," Lola said. "Today is a catch-up and paperwork. I have an appointment in the afternoon, but I should be done by five. If it's job related, I can cut out a little earlier."

"I usually wake up around four or five and don't have to be at fallout until ten thirty. We can grab dinner and compare notes."

"Sounds fun . . . seriously."

"I have copies of a lot of the case files."

"Really?" Lola said, genuinely surprised. "They let a rookie carry around case files?"

"Well," Brackett said. "I have photos of the case files on my phone. Nothing official. They don't even know."

"Yeah, Joe Bill Brackett," Lola said. "You and I are gonna get along famously. We'll probably get ourselves suspended, but we'll get along."

Brackett yawned. "Good deal. Text me your address and I can pick you up."

"Righto."

"I usually stop at that little Sodas and Smore's in Eagle River for a Truelove when I get up. Want me to bring you one?"

"A Truelove?"

"Dr. Pepper and coconut cream," Brackett said, mimicking a Caribbean accent. "My favorite. Like the islands, mon."

"You do know I'm from the South Pacific?" Lola said. "Not Jamaica."

"I know that," Brackett said. "I'm too tired to get the accent right."

CHAPTER 10

Constance Cutter's sixteen-year-old friend, Audrey Lipton, stood on tiptoe and scanned the crowd of students in the South High School common area with crazy eyes and pinched lips. Constance, who sat by herself drinking a Diet Mountain Dew and eating a Subway wrap, saw her and waved. Audrey pointed at her, the wild eyes warning of dire consequences if Constance didn't stay put. Evelyn Brant was with her, bottle blond in counterpoint to Audrey's dark features. As always, the two were joined at the hip. Not quite as spun up as Audrey, Evelyn glanced back and forth as they wove their way through the crowd of students, like she expected someone to jump out and grab them at any moment.

Her back to the wall, a loose black and white flannel billowed down around Constance's faded jeans. Rips in both knees exposed pink knees. She'd drawn little death's head skulls on her black Converse sneakers with a ballpoint pen. The other girls were dressed in the latest fashion, designer jeans and cashmere sweaters, the works.

"What's up?" Constance said when they got closer.

"You're not going to believe it," Evelyn said, a gushing whisper.

Instead of speaking, Audrey slid down the wall beside Constance and held out her iPhone, letting it provide the explanation.

"This is crazy," Evelyn said, hugging herself as she took up a spot flanking Constance. She leaned in so she could see the screen too.

"What am I looking at?" Constance asked. "A guy . . . two guys at your—"

She gasped as the man in the lead reared back and kicked Audrey Lipton's front door. It didn't break at first, but he kept kicking until it did.

"What the . . ."

"I know, right?" Audrey said, nodding at the screen. "My mom is going to lose her shit if she sees this."

The video was from a security camera located under the eave above the Lipton's front porch. Constance watched as the two men—one big, probably Samoan or Tongan, one slightly smaller and white—looked over their shoulders, apparently to see if anyone heard their commotion, and then barreled into the Lipton home.

"The big Samoan dude is Koko," Audrey said. "The other one's Bodie. My supplier's . . . I don't know . . . henchmen. Not my favorite people in the world if you want to know the truth of it."

Constance checked the scrolling time stamp in the corner of the screen and shot an astonished look at Audrey.

"This is less than five minutes ago!"

"No shit, Sherlock."

"Is your mom home?" Constance said. "Is she okay?"

"She's in Portland," Audrey said. "Thank God."

Constance gave a breathless nod. "You've got to call the police! They could catch them in the act."

"Keep your voice down," Audrey whispered. "We can't call the cops. With my luck, these dipshit home invaders will completely miss my stash of tab acid and the cops would find it."

Constance glanced up. "Any cameras inside the house?"

Audrey moaned. "I sure as hell hope not. Can't imagine my mother having eyes on me all the time . . . Anyhow, she's too busy with her own train wrecks to spy on my shit."

"So, they're still in there?" Constance asked. "Inside your house?"

Audrey tapped an icon on her phone and split the screen so she had a view of the front and back doors. The back door was still secure. "Looks like it."

"What about an alarm?"

"My mother felt like this camera thing was cheaper."

"I hate to say it," Constance said. "But do you think . . ."

Audrey finished her thought. "That that bitch Imelda is behind this? That's exactly what I think."

The girls had taken Imelda Espita under their wing. The Guatemalan girl was probably illegal and worked for Audrey's weed dealer. Audrey had invited her in during their last slumber party, feeding her pizza and even giving her a pedicure. Giddy at the prospect of something so girlish, the poor thing had playfully asked Audrey to use a different color of polish on each of her toes. The entire arrangement had set Constance's nerves on edge, but Imelda had seemed like a normal girl—as normal as a teenage undocumented immigrant drug mule could be when she was doing who knew what else for the man she lived with.

Audrey growled. "That ungrateful little bitch saw my stuff and told her pimp about it!"

Evelyn squirmed. "Wait . . . Imelda has a pimp?"

"My dealer, her pimp," Audrey said. "Same, same. The point is, I befriended her and she betrayed me. It explains why she hasn't answered my calls."

Evelyn reached for the screen. "They're coming out."

"Look at that!" Audrey said. "Those bastards are stealing my pillowcases."

"And your PlayStation," Evelyn said.

"And my mom's emerald ring, no doubt," Audrey said. "I'm supposed to inherit that ring!"

The men hustled out of view with the full pillowcases. Koko, the big Polynesian dude, had a book in his hand. Audrey gasped when she saw it.

"That son of a bitch has my journal."

Both other girls turned to look directly at Audrey.

Constance spoke first. "You keep a journal? Do you mention us?"

"Maybe," Audrey said. "Well . . . yes."

"Where we live?" Evelyn whispered.

"I can't remember. Okay?"

Constance studied the video, watching Koko flip through the pages as Bodie looked over his shoulder.

Maybe her Uncle Arliss was rubbing off on her, but these two were looking for information, not just burglarizing a house. Instead of tossing the diary, Koko stuffed it in one of the pillowcases to take with him.

Audrey touched the screen again, pulling up another camera to show an older blue-gray BMW sedan leave the driveway.

Audrey stood. "I'm going over there."

Evelyn groaned.

Constance looked up in horror. "Go over where?"

"To Imelda's."

"You said you haven't heard from Imelda," Constance said.

"I haven't," Audrey said as if it were all so simple. "Not for days. That's why I'm going over there. I'll tell her she has to give my shit back or I'm going to call the cops."

"You wouldn't," Evelyn gasped.

"Of course I wouldn't," Audrey said. "But Imelda doesn't know that."

"Wait," Constance said. "You know where she lives?"

"Sure, I know," Audrey said, lowering her voice even more. "My dealer has a house off Blueberry not far from Dimond High. I told you before. This is the twenty-first century. Everyone knows where everyone else lives."

"Have you thought that Imelda might be not answering your calls for a reason," Constance said. "Maybe something's wrong."

"Something's wrong, all right," Audrey said. "She's ripping me off, and she knows it. That's why she's avoiding me."

"What about those guys that robbed your house?" Constance said. "I mean, they're burglars. If you're right and Imelda is involved, they're drug dealers too. They could have guns." She shook her head. "I don't think you should go over there alone."

"Oh, sister," Audrey said, looking back and forth at the two other girls. "Who said anything about me going alone?"

CHAPTER 11

*A*rliss Cutter's eight-year-old nephew, Michael, stood in the middle of the kitchen holding a sagging circle of pizza dough almost half his size. Flour dusted dark hair and the tip of his nose.

"Wait, wait, wait," he said. "I can get this."

Cutter stood back and let him try, and fail, and try again to spin the now-oblong and rapidly thinning circle of dough above his head. It had already hit the floor twice, so there was no chance it was going to become an actual pizza. Matthew, the younger of the twins by twelve minutes, stood a few feet from his brother, giggling, but doing better since he was attempting to spin a damp dish towel instead of dough. His blond hair—matching his uncle Arliss—also bore a liberal dusting of flour from recent attempts with the real thing.

"Three hundred," Mim said from her spot at the kitchen table. "That's a lot of puppies."

She'd changed out of her scrubs as soon as she got

home from her shift at the hospital and now wore plaid
pajama pants, thick wool socks, and a loose University
of Florida sweatshirt. The oven clicked and ticked, on
its way to 475—as high as it would go. Burning spruce
crackled and snapped in the fireplace in the adjacent living room. Cutter, too, had changed from punk-busting
clothes into a sweatshirt—his army gray.

There were icicles outside the kitchen window again,
under that broken spot in the gutters that he needed to
fix. Winter was refusing to surrender peacefully this
year—leaving everyone in need of comfort food like
homemade pizza.

Cutter gave the twins a rare grin as he cut thick
coins of fresh mozzarella from a ball he'd picked up at
Carr's grocery on the way home from work.

"Keep trying," he said. "Grumpy let me and your
dad goof up a lot of dough before we finally got it
right. I'm telling you, though, the cup towels are easier."

He put down the knife and began to spin his own
damp towel above his head, using the tips of his fingers. He turned to Mim as he demonstrated. "You're
right. That is a lot of dogs. US Customs is trying to figure out how to take care of them all."

Mim scrunched her smallish nose and brushed a
lock of honey-colored hair out of her eyes, seemingly
mesmerized by his pizza-towel-spinning abilities. He
had to admit, her approval mattered even more to him
than impressing the twins. She looked sad lately. Not
her usual missing her husband sad, but something else
Cutter couldn't quite put his finger on. He knew her
well enough not to press her.

"I can't believe that Russian captain was going to dump them all in the ocean," Mim said.

The twins growled at the idea of someone drowning hundreds of puppies. It was a hard lesson, but Mim had thought talking about it was a good way to make her boys aware that there was evil in the world.

The buzzer on the oven went off. Cutter bumped Matthew out of the way with his hip as he opened the door and retrieved the cast iron skillet he'd been heating.

"Watch your noggins!" he said, carrying the heavy pan to a cork trivet he'd set aside earlier. The boys stopped their attempts at spinning and gathered round to watch as Cutter placed a clean circle of pizza dough that he'd prepped into the greased pan while it was still piping hot.

"It's already cooking," he said, carefully adjusting the edges before spooning on sauce, cheese, pepperoni, and black olives.

Matthew shot him an accusing look as he slid the pan back into the oven. "But I wanted sausage," he said.

"Sausage goes on the next one," Cutter said. "Your mom worked all day. Remember Grumpy's rule—"

"Ladies first," both boys said, though neither was happy about it.

"Mom," Matthew said. "If there's three hundred puppies out there, maybe Uncle Arliss could get us one. I like those little bulldogs."

"Not that easy, champ." Cutter began rolling out another circle of dough with a thick wooden dowel. "Anyway," he said, spinning it a couple of times over his head. "A lot of folks in Customs and the US Attorney's office are pretty mad at me."

Mim blanched at that. "What did they expect you to do when you found them?"

"That's exactly what Lola asked," Cutter said. "People don't need a *good* reason to be mad. Just *a* reason."

As if on cue, Constance blew in from the garage, slamming the door behind her. She hid behind her earbuds, ignoring everyone, and started straight for her room without speaking.

"Hey!" Mim said, not quite a yell—but awfully close. "Hello there!"

Constance took out one earbud and turned her head sideways so a sullen flap of dark hair fell over one eye. "Hello." She wagged her head. "Was there anything else?"

"Pizza's almost ready," Mim said, sighing, obviously suppressing the urge to say something she would regret. "I thought you were studying with Audrey and Evelyn. I'd planned to come get you."

Constance shrugged. "I'm not hungry. We're finished. Audrey brought me home." She dared her mother to say more but avoided Arliss's gaze altogether. "Was there something else?"

"Did you guys study at Audrey's house?"

Something dark flashed on Constance's face.

"No . . ." she stammered, but caught herself with a headshake. "We stayed at school. Audrey's mom is out of town."

Mim caught the look too, and studied her daughter just long enough to make her uncomfortable. She would have made a good interrogator.

"I worry about Audrey," she said. "Her mom travels a lot."

There was the flash again, this time it was panic. Mim saw it too, probably counted on it.

Constance gasped. "How do you even know that?"

"Audrey's mom and I talk," Mim said. "You do spend a lot of time together. We care about our daughters."

"Mom—"

Mim wagged her head, mocking. "Constance . . ."

"Oh my *gosh*. You don't have to check up on me and my friends' mothers."

Mim gave a slow nod. "Wash up for dinner."

"I told you, I'm not hungry."

"Wash up anyway," Mim said.

"My stomach is killing me, Mom. Okay?"

The darkness crossed Constance's eyes again. Cutter had seen it before, many times, just before somebody lied to him.

Mim gave her a little nod. "Okay."

Whatever she was hiding, it wasn't small—at least not from her point of view. He'd never known his niece to blow things out of proportion. If anything, she downplayed disaster. If she was worried enough to stand there and lie, it was something important.

He didn't say anything. It wasn't his place, but it didn't stop him from worrying.

Constance shut the door to her room—quietly, so her mother wouldn't have a fit—and then wedged her backpack against the base. Her mom wouldn't allow locks, but the bag would at least slow down the brats if they tried to barge in on her. She collapsed on her bed, fighting back tears from the overwhelming stress. Staring up at the ceiling, she punched in Audrey's cell number. She had to work hard not to hyperventilate.

This was all just crazy—like something out of a bad movie where all the stupid teenagers eventually got murdered.

It felt like years before Audrey picked up, sounding groggy when she did. She'd probably hit her stash of weed as soon as she got to Evelyn's. No way she was going back to her house, no matter how brave she was. Not after what they'd seen.

Evelyn giggled in the background.

Audrey coughed. "What's goin' on, sister?"

"I'm freaking out," Constance said, her voice cracking. "My mom is all up in my business. I'm afraid she saw how scared I was on my face."

"Just keep your mouth shut," Audrey said. "This'll all be fine."

"Did you know my mom's been talking to your mom?"

Evelyn mumbled something, then laughed again.

"So?" Audrey's voice was thick with effects of the weed. "My mom's cool. Wait . . . Are you implying my mom would rat on us for doing a little weed?"

"No," Constance said. "I'm not saying that. I just mean we have to get our stories straight. And anyway, that's not the main thing. What are we going to do about those guys?"

"Koko and Bodie?"

"Yes, Koko and Bodie," Constance said. Sometimes talking to Audrey was like talking to one of the twins. "Your mom will be home in two days. Imelda's boss knows you're the buyer, and he apparently knows Imelda spent time with us in that house."

"Of course he knows," Audrey said. "Because she told him. That's why Koko and Bodie showed up to rip me off."

"I was thinking about that after you dropped me off. You heard them talking. It didn't sound like the boss is very happy with Imelda."

"You think they thought she was at my house?"

"It sounds like they're looking for her," Constance said. "I'll bet you they go back too."

"Why do you think I'm staying at Evelyn's?"

"But this problem isn't going away," Constance said. "What if they still haven't found Imelda in two days? What if they go back and question your mom when she gets home? Maybe we . . . I don't know . . ."

"Maybe we what?" Audrey said.

"Maybe we should tell someone," Constance blurted before she changed her mind.

Audrey gasped. "You are seriously blitzing my buzz here. I am warning you, missy. Do not breathe a word of this to Uncle Marshal! A shit-ton of variations in the space-time continuum can occur over the next two days. There is zero reason to panic just yet." Her voice cleared, deadly sober now. "Are we clear?"

"Yeah," Constance said. "We're clear."

"Good," Audrey said. Constance heard her whisper, "Can you believe this shit?" Evelyn probably had her ear to the phone. Then louder, "Get some rest. We'll make a plan tomorrow. One that doesn't entail all of us getting locked up in McLaughlin Youth Center. Are we tracking?"

"Yes," Constance said. "But be careful, okay. Remember what you said about the Internet. Those guys might know where Evelyn lives too."

"Geesh!" Audrey said. "Go to sleep. You're killin' me."

Constance let the phone fall to her chest and lay there staring at the stupid bumpy 1970s popcorn ceiling that her dad had talked about fixing all the time . . . before he died. He'd always told her to go with her gut. Those guys were pissed at Imelda. Pissed enough to hurt her.

She pulled a pillow tight over her face and screamed until she was out of breath. Then, she shook it off and sat up, swinging her legs off the bed. She steeled herself to go out and face her mother and uncle—or whatever he was to her.

Imelda Espita was in danger—and so was anyone else who tried to help her.

CHAPTER 12

Deadhorse, Alaska

*B*oth the Aurora Hotel and Deadhorse Camp were full, unless you wanted to sleep on the floor. The New Arctic, which was pretty swank for the oil patch, had a few vacancies, but the Prudhoe Bay Hotel had Nolan Lamp, and Nolan Lamp had a poker game. Edward Nix parked his Kenworth and got a room there for one night.

The hotel looked like a train of mobile homes and ATCO trailers strung together on gravel and ice. He'd had to wade through exhausted roustabouts and roughnecks who walked the halls with holey socks, but he knew many of them from taking their money at cards. Two hundred sixty bucks a night got a warm if dusty room with two beds and, if you were lucky, your own bathroom. If not, shared facilities were down the hall.

He wore the stupid paper booties housekeeping at every hotel forced guests to wear inside. There were a limited number of places to stay in town, so guests paid their exorbitant rates, ate what they served, and wore their stupid booties.

Stiff and sore from the 850-mile trip from Anchorage, Nix had contemplated a shower, but it was late and he didn't want to miss the action. He stowed his duffel and made his way straight to Lamp's room for the game. The room, which was identical to his, had changed little since the hotel had been built during the pipeline boom. Wood paneling and scratchy industrial carpet added a dark air of broodiness, like a long-forgotten Polaroid from an aunt's shoebox. Baseboard heaters ticked and clanged along the wall, working to keep ahead of the single-digit temperatures on the other side of the paneling. Besides the two beds, there was a framed picture of some caribou and a night stand with a December 1974 issue of *National Geographic* on top. Wedged in the cramped space at the foot of the beds, four men sat in metal folding chairs around a rickety card table.

Nix swirled the ice cubes in the hard, plastic tumbler someone had swiped from the cafeteria, and then drained the last of his drink. A green lizard, they called it. The ban on alcohol was strictly enforced on the North Slope—a good way to get your ass booted off the job. Heaven forbid you brought weed or pills. But a medicinal evening toddy of Sprite and NyQuil went more or less unnoticed. The concoction tasted like shit, and too many of them could kill you because of the acetaminophen, but Edward Nix didn't worry much about the little things. After all, this was the end of the road, a place to relax. He didn't have to be so "on" here.

Besides, he'd never expected to see forty. Every day from here on out was a gift.

Nix looked the part of a stereotypical ice-road trucker. A mop of mussed black hair was plastered to a high forehead from two days straight wearing a John Deere ballcap. Intense brown eyes gave him the appearance of someone who might be slightly funny—or extremely dangerous. His hands were large, chapped from working outside in the cold. Greasy breakfasts and gas station burritos were starting to give him a bit of a gut. Otherwise, he was reasonably fit with strong arms and a naturally bullish neck. Fleece-lined Carhartt trousers, buffalo plaid shirt, and Filson wool vest fleshed out the trucker look. He'd made a pretty good go of it for being just forty-two years old. His own trucking company. A big house on the hillside overlooking Cook Inlet. A twenty-six-foot Sea Sport.

The farm across Cook Inlet.

Nix had contracts with most of the oil and gas equipment supply companies operating on the North Slope. There was rarely a day of the week that at least one of his trucks wasn't somewhere on the Haul Road coming or going to Prudhoe Bay. Nix was the boss and didn't have to drive a single route, but the road provided interesting opportunities that were harder to come by in other places.

Life in Prudhoe Bay was like he imagined it would be on another planet, a place where you could drink green lizards and play poker. A break from the madness. He had time to step away from the rest of his life, to catch his breath—and forget about everything except the game.

He plunked his glass down on the card table with a

boisterous sigh and wiped his mouth with the back of his sleeve while he studied the cards in his rough, oil-stained fingers. It was a good—no, a great—hand. A full house, kings over nines. He grinned, like he always did—great hand or dud, raised, and then looked to his left. It was still winter up here—eight degrees outside, cold enough to gel the fuel in his diesel if he wasn't careful. That was bad enough, but the ache that was stabbing at an old rib injury told him the barometer was dropping for real. A storm. There always seemed to be a damned storm up here. No matter the time of year.

A vacuum cleaner droned back and forth in the hallway. Shifts of roustabouts came and went twenty-four/seven, so housekeeping worked at all hours too. The roaring went quiet, followed by hushed voices just outside the room.

Everyone at the table had something to hide. Noises, newcomers, anything out of the ordinary made them all uneasy. Some just had better poker faces.

Nolan Lamp, who sat directly across the table, sat up a little straighter, eyes darting from his cards to the flimsy wooden door. For a moment, he looked as if he might try and bolt out the window. In point of fact, Lamp always gave the impression he was about to flee the scene of some crime.

A weasel in both appearance and demeanor, he was not quite five and a half feet tall. He wore thick glasses over eyes that were tiny, shifting dots sunken into a gaunt face. With no meat to speak of on his bones to keep him warm, he was rarely found without a thick shawl-collar cardigan. He always wore heavy boots that looked ridiculously cartoon-like on his small feet.

Nix thought he probably wore them as anchors against the very real possibility that he would topple over in the Arctic gales that whipped across the North Slope.

Operating as "The House," Lamp skimmed a little off the top of each game for his trouble—which was fine, because he was a horrible poker player and, more important, smart enough to lose when Nix was at the table.

Still, when the house took money, a friendly game of poker turned into illegal gambling. Another reason to worry about unseen voices in the hallway.

The vacuum started up again and everyone relaxed a notch.

Nix took a slug of his green lizard, grimaced at the taste of it, but welcomed the warm rush to his belly.

The rawboned roughneck to Nix's left had as much of a past as anyone at the table, but he pretended to ignore the noise in the hall and Lamp's skittishness. Chance Spivey wore an oval silver buckle with a gold bucking horse on the face of it. He liked to remind people he was from Houston, and that he'd ridden rough stock and worked offshore well before he ever came to The Slope. Nix tended to respect the battered knuckles and cauliflower ears more than the swagger. Spivey had also spent time in prison.

The cowboy scratched his bent nose, the way he did every time he had a good hand, and raised.

Nix kept his smile passive. He rubbed his ribs with an elbow. Yep. This storm was going to be a bad one. Bitter wind, blowing sideways in a day or two. He'd get some rest and get his truck back on the road before dawn—which still came late this far north.

The vacuum outside the door fell silent again. More

voices. They were female, so Nix dismissed any notion of danger.

Lamp raised as well, though Nix could tell he had a bust hand by the way he kept sucking on his top teeth. The creepy little shit toyed with the few poker chips he had left and glanced at the kid who sat to Nix's right, waiting for him to decide what to do.

The fourth player at the table couldn't have been more than twenty-five, on the pudgy side with an innocent, baby face that seemed to scream to the older men to take his money. He was single, Nix knew that much, and working back-to-back-to-back two-week shifts, which kept him on the Slope for six straight weeks— making a shitload of overtime. All that dough was burning a hole in his pocket. Ripe for the fleecing, he was. So far, he didn't seem to care.

His name was Reuben.

"Where you from again?" Nix asked. He was getting bored, so he might as well screw with the kid while he tried to concentrate.

"Tulsa," Reuben said absent-mindedly, focused on his cards.

Nix looked at Spivey, who answered without being asked—as Nix knew he would.

"I'm from a little town outside Houston, Texas," Spivey said.

Nix swirled his glass again, chuckling under his breath. "This girl at the gas station in Coldfoot said to me yesterday, 'Happiness is an Oklahoman leaving Alaska with a Texan under each arm.'" He saluted the other men with the dregs of his green lizard. "Lookin' at you two, I can see her point."

Spivey wagged his head and raised his middle finger. Reuben gave a goofy grin over the top of his cards.

Nix heard a muffled thud in the hallway. The knob rattled, causing Lamp to spring to his feet, spilling his chips.

Then a knock.

"North Slope Police Department!" The voice was husky, direct, and to Nix's relief, female. The North Slope Borough was a municipality that covered the towns and villages in roughly the top third of Alaska from Barrow to Point Hope to Anaktuvuk Pass. There were only so many officers to go around, which meant they usually operated on their own. Nix had never seen more than two at any given time in Deadhorse.

"Nolan Lamp!" the voice said through the door. "I've got a warrant for your arrest. Open the door."

Nolan looked back and forth at the other men.

Nix growled, low under his breath. There was paper on him too, for violating probation on a domestic violence charge. It was years old, but things like that didn't go away.

He considered going out the window. No one even knew he was here. If he could get back to his room, he'd—

The doorknob shook again.

"Nolan!" the voice said. "Open up."

Lamp was looking at the window too. Nix decided the puny dude was on his own. Lamp probably didn't even know his real name. With any luck as soon as the bitch cop got her man, she'd lose interest in whoever flew out the window.

Nix shoved his way past the other men, making it to the window at the same moment the door popped open.

"You can stop right there," the lady cop snapped, hand on her pistol, which was still holstered.

That was a stupid, stupid move, Nix thought.

He turned back toward the window, but she stopped him with a sort of *tut-tut* sound. It reminded him of his grandmother sending a chill down his legs and causing him to freeze.

Nix recognized the officer as Janice Hough. Her husband did books for the local Haliburton office so she was a frequent flyer at the Deadhorse police posting. They pronounced the name like "huff."

Her cheeks pinked from a recent walk from her cruiser to the hotel, Officer Hough wore a dark blue North Slope Borough uniform. A fake fur hat with the earflaps pulled down against the cold kept most of her curls confined. She filled out the uniform nicely, Nix thought, though he'd much rather have seen her without the bulky Kevlar vest. Housekeeping even made the cops wear the puffy cloth covers and she had a pair stretched over her boots.

She saw how Nix was eyeing her and darkened, her hand drifted to the butt of a yellow Taser on her belt opposite the Glock.

"You!" she barked at Nix, her direct tone leaving no room for misinterpretation or argument. "Take a seat on the bed. Hands where I can see them. The rest of you sit back down while I sort you out."

Lamp and the kid plopped into their chairs around the card table, but Spivey kept his feet. The room was small, barely fifteen feet across, but even the short distance between Spivey and Nix forced the cop to divide her attention.

"I'll stand," Spivey whispered.

Nix put his back to the window but stayed where he was.

"Is that so?" the cop said, glancing from the cowboy to Nix, without becoming fixated onto either one. Nix had to admit, she was pretty good.

"It is a fact," Spivey said. His hands were up, but he edged ever so slightly away from the table, giving himself room to maneuver.

"It'd be so much better if you sat," Hough said. "We'll sort this out with Lamp, and the rest of you can be on your way."

Nix raised his hands. "That sounds good to me," he said, though he knew it would never go down that way. This bitch was eyeing him like she was the one in charge. Cops never let you walk. They always ran everybody's ID. This one looked the type to rub their noses in all her power and authority.

"Then sit down," she said, nodding at the bed beside Nix. Her fingers continued to tap the Taser on her belt.

"Looks to me like you're all by your lonesome," Spivey said. He gave a disdainful chuckle and then shrugged. "Four grown men against one girl."

"Seriously?" Officer Hough said. If she was frightened, she didn't show it. "All four of you?"

The kid piped up, voice quavering. "Not me!" he stammered. "I'm not a part of this. I'm just playing cards. I got no beef with you, ma'am."

Spivey clicked his teeth and glared at the kid, then turned his attention back to the officer. He shrugged. "Doesn't change anything. Three men against one girl."

The cop exhaled slowly, her face set in a funny half frown. This bitch was far too smug to Nix's way of thinking.

"You boys are scaring me," she said, sounding any-thing but. "And that's so very bad for you."

Spivey nodded. "You should be scared. How about we just shut the door and have us a good old time. Hell, I'll bet you could make a man out of this kid without even trying—"

"See," Hough said. "That right there is what scares me."

"Yep," Spivey said. "All alone—"

"Exactly," Hough whispered. "I am alone—and in fear for my life."

Lamp's head looked like it might rattle off his bony shoulders. "I . . . I don't think—"

"Shut your mouth," Spivey said. He glanced at Nix, who said nothing but nodded to show he planned to back the cowboy's play.

A smile spread over Spivey's battered face as he looked at Hough's Taser. "You can't shock us both," he smirked. "And nobody's given you cause—"

Nix heard the electric crackle of the Taser before he saw Hough move. She'd fired with her left hand, point shooting. The metal darts, barbed on the end like fish-hooks, caught Spivey in the solar plexus and left thigh, locking up his muscles. Rigid, he fell backward, slam-ming his head into the baseboard heater. He twitched on the floor, teeth clenched, body arched between his heels and the back of his head.

Hough kept the Taser pointed at him, while drawing her Glock with her right hand and training it on Nix. "On the ground!" she barked. "Or I might get confused about which trigger I'm pulling."

Five seconds gone, Hough immediately sent Chance Spivey on another Taser ride.

Nix seethed, staring at the maw of the Glock, which was pointed directly at his face.

Spivey's body went slack—and Hough hit him a third time.

"Hey," Nix said. "You didn't have to do that."

"Sure, I did," the officer said. "I told you. You big strong men are scaring the shit outta me. I'm all by myself here. Now . . . do us both a favor and plant your face in the carpet."

CHAPTER 13

*C*utter hung up his desk phone with a little more force than he should have and swiveled his chair back to his computer. He would have preferred a root canal to all the paperwork that went with being a supervisory deputy. The morning had started better. Lola picked him up early so they could sit on a house and watch for a fugitive sex offender they'd been hunting for over a week.

Just after eight—noon in DC—Cutter got a hair-on-fire call from an HQ weenie in the Investigative Operations demanding reports that he'd failed to turn in. Nancy Alvarez, the task force officer on loan from APD, had come to take his place on the surveillance, and he'd driven Lola's G-car back to the federal building to whip out the reports.

Now, less than an hour later, Lola called to break the news that she and Nancy had just followed their sex offender into his mother's house, where they found him hiding under the bed in the basement. The idiot had tried to scuffle—and Lola smacked him with a Bible from beside the bed and broke his nose. She'd called to give Cutter a blow-by-blow description, playfully taunting him that there had been violence and he'd missed out.

She'd been doing "God's work," she said, while poor Cutter was chained to his desk, dotting i's and crossing t's for the Marshals Service's Investigative Operations Division.

IOD—sometimes simply called "Enforcement" by old-timers like Cutter—was the USMS Headquarters component that oversaw multiagency task forces. The wheels of justice . . . at least the Justice Department, appeared to be greased by reports and goal-setting proposals. No one had said anything about Task Force Office fuel budgets when Cutter applied for the supervisory deputy gig. He tested, interviewed—and then the Service-wide promotion list came out by email letting him know he'd gotten the job. He filled out the paperwork for a government move for the meager amount of personal goods—and then hitched a ride north on the Justice Prisoner and Alien Transportation System airlift. The "Con Air" plane happened to be heading north and it saved the taxpayers money.

He'd hit the ground running. One day he was a POD—a plain old deputy—and the next day he was a supervisor. There was always talk of a supervisors' school, but so far, he'd learned what he needed to do from networking with other SDUSMs, or waiting for someone from HQ to squawk because they didn't have some report he didn't know he was supposed to submit.

Still, nobody from HQ seemed to want to come to Alaska and do his job. As long as he was reasonably close to being on time, they left him alone with little more than periodic frantic emails.

The latest one today was about fuel receipts, thankfully interrupted when the electronic blip of the Hirsh ScramblePad outside the task force door sounded, alerting him to a visitor.

His office was directly across the small squad room from the secure door, and he leaned forward to see the chief walk in. She was dressed for the gym in blue Grundéns leggings with images of swimming salmon and a loose gray Marshals Service sweatshirt. Her cheeks were flushed, highlighting the splash of freckles across her nose. Since she would have changed from her work clothes in the gym, Cutter assumed that she'd been in the middle of a workout when she decided to come see him.

He stood and met her in the middle of the squad room beside the oval conference table that was cluttered with powder-blue warrant folders and Wanted posters. It spared her the sight of the messy desk in his office, which he was hardly ever in anyway.

"Ma'am," Cutter said, genuinely happy to see her. "What brings you to our side of the tracks?"

"Looking for Lola," she said. "I have an assignment if you can spare her the rest of the day."

"We'll make it work," Cutter said. "She's on her way in from the jail—"

The Hirsh scramble security pad blipped in the hall again. A moment later, the door opened and Lola Teariki burst in, mid-conversation with Nancy Alvarez about some potential boyfriend—probably that Joe Brackett kid. She froze when she saw Chief Phillips, grimacing at Cutter.

"Geeze, Louise, boss," she said. "You could have warned me that the big boss was here to see you."

Phillips laughed and shook her head. "I'm here to see you," she said.

"Hey, Jill," Nancy Alvarez said, before ducking into the office she shared with a TFO from the Alaska State Troopers.

"What's up?" Lola's eyebrows bounced on her high forehead in anticipation. "Something exciting, I hope."

"If you call a prisoner trip exciting," Phillips said.

"An extradition?" Lola said. "Europe? Australia maybe? I heard the Aussies just nabbed that Ponzi scheme guy. Are you sending me to—"

Phillips shot a glance at Cutter, then back to Lola. "The North Slope Borough PD has three prisoners in Prudhoe Bay that need to be picked up. Two are on federal charges, one on state, but I told AST we'd bring all three since we're going up anyway. Heavy weather brewing out that way, so I need you to leave today. A quick up and back. I already called Bill Young. He's on his way in now from Chugiak."

"Today?" Lola said, looking at her own feet, thinking. "Okay. I just need to make a call."

"You shouldn't be too late," Phillips said. "I doubt there will even be any overtime. The Alaska Airlines charter heading north leaves in a little over two hours. I have you two seats reserved."

"No worries," Lola said. "I've never been to Prudhoe. It'll be interesting. I just need to postpone an appointment."

"You have a medical?" Cutter said, reading between the lines.

Lola gave a sheepish grin. "I have an appointment at 3:00 to sneak out and get a mammogram."

Phillips gave her a side-eye.

"I know what you're thinking," Lola said. "She's awfully young for the old boobly squish."

"It's none of our business," Phillips said. "But are you okay?"

"Oh, I'm right-as," Lola said. "My mum and two of my aunties have a history, that's all. I've been getting the girls checked since I was twenty. Seriously, no worries. I'll just reschedule."

"Not a chance," Cutter said. "You keep your appointment. I'll take the prisoner trip."

"No kidding?"

"Of course." Cutter didn't have to say it. Both women knew his fourth wife had died of breast cancer.

"Seriously, boss," Lola said. "I appreciate this."

"No problem," Cutter said, almost grinning. "You can make it up to me by doing the Task Force Officer fuel reports while I'm gone."

"Okay then," Phillips said. "Arliss, I'll leave it to you to get with Bill Young and hash out the logistics. Have you ever worked with him before?"

Cutter shook his head. "We've crossed paths working court."

"You're gonna love Bill," Lola said. "He's a bit of a talker, but a really fun guy."

Always struggling for enough personnel, the Marshals Service relied on a shadow workforce of contract guards, called in when needed to keep up with court

and prisoner transport duties. Active or retired law enforcement officers. Some were armed, some were not,
but they were always paired with an actual deputy
marshal. Bill Young was a former Alaska Department
of Corrections officer, reasonably fit for a sixty-year-
old, and from what Cutter had heard, a hell of a shot
with his Smith & Wesson 686 revolver. Cutter had
only met the man in passing, going to or from court,
but the fact that Young carried a wheel gun lifted him a
notch higher in Cutter's estimation.

"I'm off to finish up my time on the stair climber
then," Phillips said, turning toward the door.

"What about the puppies?" Lola asked. "Any word
from Customs? I mean, they can't just put them back
on a boat to Russia. They'll be murdered."

Jill Phillips flushed red. A notorious animal lover,
she'd been known to adopt old laying hens as pets
when they were past their prime. "It's really out of our
hands," she said. "But I did mention the puppies during my interview with Channel 11—and provided
them copies of the photographs you took, Lola."

Lola gushed. "I know, right? They look like little
bats with those big ears. Aren't they the cutest—"

Phillips sighed. "They are, and several national out-
lets have picked up the story. Three hundred French
bulldog puppies make for a bigger and sexier news
cycle than any ship seizure. Headquarters is pissed,
and my counterpart at Customs and Border Protection
wants to send *me* to Russia, but it's all over the Internet
and cable news now. Whatever happens to the little
critters, the world is going to know about it."

Phillips headed for the gym, leaving Cutter and Lola
in the Task Force Office.

"I'd hate to have her mad at me," Lola said. "Anyway, thank you again for taking this trip. Probably not a good thing to remind you of, but it's still winter that far north." She held up the weather app on her phone. "Minus three in Prudhoe Bay as we speak—and there's a storm stalled out over the Bering that could start moving east any day now. I'd be a shitty partner if I didn't say it was okay to change your mind."

"Nope," Cutter said. "You're not getting out of doing my fuel receipts that easy."

CHAPTER 14

*B*ill Young met Cutter at the federal building, duffel in hand and a huge parka over one arm. Cutter had all the gear he needed at work, so the two took a caged minivan straight to the airport, staging it for when they returned with the prisoners.

Young had a full head of snow-white hair and the pink flush of a man who enjoyed more than a few whiskeys each evening before bed—to soothe the pains of age and a misspent youth, to hear him tell it. Young proved to be just as Lola described him, chatting away about this and that as they drove, dropping names of people he and Cutter might know in common, generally checking the pulse of who he was going to be working with. It turned out that some of Young's extended family worked for the police department in Ft. Meyers, Florida, and they actually did know some of the same people.

The law enforcement family could make the world a very small place.

This prisoner trip to Deadhorse was supposed to be a quick up and back, but Cutter had learned even before transferring to Alaska that he needed to be prepared to RON—remain overnight—for any assignment more than a few miles from home. Here in the far north, that could mean being completely self-sufficient—a sleeping bag, water, food, and wound kit—or just a toothbrush and change of underwear. Deadhorse was connected to the road system, such as it was this time of year—some eight hundred miles north of Anchorage. A cursory web search showed there were hotel rooms and a handful of places to eat. Law enforcement backup would be sparse or nonexistent if North Slope Borough officers were busy on other calls. He planned to be on his own operationally—and in truth, preferred it that way.

Cutter dressed as he normally did for rural work: layers of smart wool, Fjällräven pants, wool shirt, fleece jacket. He made it a habit to carry a thin wool watch cap and wool glove liners in his jacket pocket. His rural kit included, among other things, Hestra insulated leather gloves and a pair of beaver over-mittens. He draped a thick Wiggy's parka through the handles of his duffel bag. His dear friend, Birdie Pingayak, from the Yupik village of Stone Cross, had sewn him the mittens as a Christmas gift, as well as a wolverine fur ruff for his parka hood. The Wiggy's was exceptionally warm, and he wanted to keep it within reach, but it was far too hot to wear on the plane. He'd swapped his Zamberlan hikers for a pair of insulated

high-top Danner Canadians. Prisoner moves often involved a lot of standing around and waiting on the cold
tarmac. As an afterthought, he tossed in a pair of NEOS
overboots that would add another twenty degrees of in-
sulation to the Danners if he had to tromp around town
for very long in subzero temps.

The task force kept a half-dozen cases of MREs in
the storage closet. He grabbed two, one for his guard
and another for himself, both Meatball Marinara—
mostly because of the First Strike protein bar in that
particular meal pouch.

A long gun would have been too cumbersome, so he
made do with his grandfather's Colt Python and the
baby Glock 27.

Bill Young had lived in Alaska for half his life and
knew his way around the outdoors. Cutter quizzed him
about his kit, as he would any partner, and nodded in
satisfaction at his response. As the contract guard,
Young took care of the prisoner files and the olive drab
military tool bag containing the restraints—handcuffs,
belly chains, and leg irons—often called three-piece
suits by deputies.

"You think we'll need to black-box any of these
guys?" Young asked as Cutter took the ramp off Min-
nesota onto International Airport Road.

A black box—more often than not actually dark
blue—was a hard plastic clamshell with a metal collar
that was secured over the handcuff's keyholes with a
heavy padlock. Their use was generally left to the dis-
cretion of the deputy. "Black-boxing" made it virtually
impossible for a prisoner to shim or otherwise pick the
cuffs, or even swivel his wrists. They came in handy
for escape risks, but Cutter steered clear of them unless

there was a compelling reason. Grumpy could be one of the toughest men on the planet when it came to dealing with outlaws, but he wasn't a bully. Ever. And Cutter didn't intend to be one, either.

"Bring them," he said, "We'll see about it when we get there."

Young flipped through the three packets, each a "holey joe" federal memo envelope with a black and white photo and descriptors of the prisoner affixed to the face with clear tape.

"Nolan Lamp, white male, forty-one years of age. Warehouse operator for North Hill Oil and Gas. Rap sheet shows racketeering, larceny, illegal gambling . . ." Young nodded to himself. "He's a little dude. This shows him five-five, a buck forty. State and federal warrants, both for larceny.

"Edward Nix, white male, six foot, two-forty. Owner of Nix Trucking. He's got no federal paper, just a state warrant for probation violation stemming from an original conviction of domestic violence."

"Yeah," Cutter said. "We're going up anyway, so we're helping the Troopers out by hauling him back."

Young tapped the face of the last file. "Chance Spivey is our winner," he said. "Six-four, two-sixty. Two felony assault convictions and a misconduct involving a weapon charge. I remember him. He did a three-year stint in Goose Creek Correctional for shooting up a bar in Seward. Theory is that he was trying to kill his ex-girlfriend but was too drunk to realize he was aiming at her reflection in the mirror behind the bar. A couple of off-duty soldiers from JBER tackled him. He broke one of their jaws, but the other soldier was an MMA fighter and beat him half to death."

"Always somebody bigger." Cutter gave a knowing nod. "Sounds like he deserved a little laying on of hands."

"Spivey is a piece of work if I ever saw one," Young said. "I was a CO at Goose Creek for a bit before I retired. Seems like he was always in a fight or in the infirmary from being in a fight. Frankly, it surprises the hell out of me that he made it out of prison alive. I'm glad Lola sat this one out. This guy had something against female corrections officers. Oh, he hated us all, but he reserved his most intense form of hatred for women. Went out of his way to intimidate them."

"Well," Cutter said. "He would have met his match with Lola."

Cutter dropped Young off at Departures with their gear, parked the van, and met him back at ticketing.

Bags stacked at his feet, Young held up both hands as Cutter approached.

"Don't kill the messenger," he said. "But we've hit our first snafu of the trip."

Cutter sighed. "One of many, no doubt," he said. "What is it?"

"The North Slope Alaska Airlines charter flight is on mechanical delay. Pressurization or some such. The point is, sounds like there's a chance the flight will be canceled until tomorrow."

"Can't be helped," Cutter said. "We can't go, we can't go."

"Not like I'm trying to milk out extra hours," Young said. "But the gate agent told me there is a Ravn flight leaving in two hours. It's a Bombardier turboprop commuter, so it'll take half again as long, but there are seats."

"Okay," Cutter said. "Let's do that."

"There are seats going up," Young said. "It's full coming back. And anyway, it's going to Fairbanks after Prudhoe."

"So we overnight and catch a flight back tomorrow," Cutter said, thinking he might get the opportunity to see where Ethan had been working when he died.

"No Alaska flights tomorrow," Young said. "We'll have to figure out another way back. I've been up there a half dozen times on prisoner transports. There are always a couple of bush pilots flying Cessna Caravans and Piper Navajos in and out of Deadhorse. One of them could get us as far south as Fairbanks and then we could commercial it back. Honestly, that wouldn't even be the most convoluted prisoner trip I've ever heard of in Alaska."

Cutter fished his cell out of his pocket. He reached an empty hand toward Young. "Let me see that file with the North Slope officer's contact info. We'll see if this might still be doable."

Young passed him the file. "It's plenty doable, if you don't mind riding squished into a little Navajo, knee to knee with Chance Spivey."

Cutter punched in the number with his thumb and glanced at Young while he let it ring. "Spivey . . . That's the cowboy son of a bitch who likes to bully women?"

"That's the one."

Cutter gave a smug nod. "I sort of hope I do get smushed in next to him."

"This is Jan," a voice on the other end of the line

said. It was awfully perky for this late in the afternoon. She reminded Cutter of Lola minus the Kiwi accent.

"Officer Hough?"

"That's me," she said. "What can I do for you?"

"Arliss Cutter, US Marshals Serv—"

"Wait," Hough broke in. "Did you say Cutter?"

"Yes, supervisory deputy with the Marshals."

"Arliss Cutter . . ." Hough said, as if she couldn't quite believe it. "I . . . I've been expecting your call."

"Okay," Cutter said. The chief had probably phoned ahead and let North Slope PD know to look for him instead of Teariki. Or maybe Lola had. He ticked off their list of logistical problems and asked Officer Hough if she could help find a flight as far as Fairbanks.

"Yeah, sure," she said without hesitation. "We're used to that up here. It's not a problem at all. I know a guy who can take you. He's got a light load going south tomorrow anyway. I'm sure he'll be glad to get paying passengers."

She took the details of the Ravn Air flight and agreed to meet them at the airport.

Cutter was about to end the call when she cut him off.

"So, you're just coming to pick up the prisoners?"

"Correct," Cutter said, the hair suddenly standing on the back of his neck.

"I thought you were calling about something else," Hough said. Garbled voices sounded in the background as a radio broke squelch. "I am so sorry. I've got to run to this call. A polar bear if you can believe it."

"Hang on," Cutter said, instinctively turning away from Bill Young and the pile of baggage. "What did you think I was calling about?"

"You're Ethan Cutter's brother," she said. "Right?"

Cutter felt the blood drain from his face. "I am."

"Okay," Hough said, tense, as if waiting for the other shoe to drop. "Like I said. I've been expecting you."

CHAPTER 15

*F*lat on her back in the tub, Mim held the open letter in both hands, high above her face, keeping it out of the water. It hardly mattered. The paper was stained with tears, and she'd folded and unfolded it so many times to read it over the past two days that it was about to fall apart anyway. Her attorney, Coop Daniels, was working down in Juneau, but he'd called to let her know the letter was coming. She should have been ready, but seeing the actual words in print made it difficult to breathe.

Her hair blossomed in the water around her oval face. She liked it hot, and steam rose from the surface as it swirled from the rhythmic rise and fall of her chest. Water in her ears at once muffled and channeled the creaks and hums of the house. She could hear the boiler running. The singing hiss of water in the pipes that fed the dishwasher at the other end of the house . . . Ethan's house.

A sudden squeak down the hall made her hold her breath. She raised her head above the surface, turning to clear her ears.

The inner door to the arctic entry opened, then shut.

She'd thought about oiling the hinges, but Arliss had wisely pointed out that loud hinges and squeaky floorboards were a good first line of defense when you had teenagers in the family.

Her skin chattered against the porcelain tub as she scooted into a sitting position. Remnants of a Lush jasmine bath bomb the twins had given her for Christmas lapped at her skin. She held her breath, listening, squeezing the letter in her fist like a weapon.

Footsteps, the refrigerator door . . . and then the buzz of music through earbuds—turned up far too loud.

Constance.

"I'm having a bath!" Mim yelled.

"Knock yourself out," Constance said.

A bedroom door slammed.

Mim volunteered for every hour of overtime she could get, and this rare day off meant that she and her daughter might actually have a few minutes of overlapping time at home without the twins underfoot.

She refolded the letter carefully and returned it to the envelope before setting it on the magazine rack beside the tub. She pressed herself up with both hands and then threw on a thick terry cloth robe, twisting a towel over her wet hair like a turban. The image peering back at her in the foggy mirror looked an awful lot like her own mother. Dammit.

Mim stashed the letter in the nightstand beside her bed and then, gathering her courage, went to check her daughter's mood.

She stood in front of Constance's door for several seconds, planning the approach to her young hedgehog of a daughter—cute enough, but prickly. Eggshells didn't begin to describe the fragility of conversations with this little demon-child. Mim could not remember a time when she'd been so moody as a teenager. Mim's mother had a temper—and quite a past to hear her grandmother tell it. Maybe the rattlesnake gene skipped a generation.

"You were a teenage girl," Mim muttered to herself. "At least you can speak the language."

She knocked softly. Then louder when she got no answer, but not so loud as to appear confrontational.

"What?"

Mim could almost hear the disgusted eye roll. She translated it as "come in" anyway and opened the door.

Constance was sitting on her bed, back to the wall, legs straight out in front of her, eating a yogurt and reading something on the laptop on the mattress beside her. As usual, her hair hung in a sullen mop like a privacy screen over her face. She'd kicked off her sneakers and her big toe stuck out of a hole in her left ankle sock.

"What?" she asked again, barely looking up.

Mim leaned her shoulder against the door frame. She'd considered telling Constance about the letter but decided to wait. She fought the urge to fold her arms. That might send the wrong message. Instead, she gave a smiling nod to her daughter's naked toe. "We can afford to buy you new socks."

"Don't worry about it."

"We don't get to talk lately," Mim said. "There's always so much going on."

"We talk," Constance said. "You assign me chores or give me crap about my friends. That's talking."

Mim stood quietly, feeling the water drip from her wet hair and run down her neck.

"I have homework," Constance said. "Was there something else?"

Mim sighed, staring at her daughter, desperately trying to remember when she was younger. Nicer.

"I'm not here to argue," she said.

Constance scoffed. "That's a relief."

"Have I done something to offend you?"

Constance shook her head. "I already told you how I feel. You just don't listen."

"You've told me?" Mim wanted to scream. "What? What did you tell me? That you're afraid I'm forgetting your father?"

"Mom . . ." Constance pounded the mattress with a fist. "Look at yourself. I—" She buried her face in her hands and began to sob. Mim rushed to her little girl's side, tried to put an arm over her shoulder, but she jerked away.

"Please let me in," Mim whispered. "We used to be close . . ."

Constance's head snapped up, her face wet with tears. She sniffed. Rubbed her nose. "I know. Okay?"

Mim kept her voice low and steady. She was the adult here. "What is it that you know, sweetheart?"

"Everyone can see how much I look like him," she said, sniffing. "How you look *at* him. How he looks at you . . . I just . . . I don't understand how you could have done it."

Mim's face flushed. "What are you talking about?"

"I'm talking about you and Uncle Arliss," Constance said. "Tell me the truth."

"Wait," Mim said, struggling to breathe. Her stomach lurched like she might throw up. "You said he looks like you . . . You think Arliss is your father?"

"Tell me I'm wrong!" Constance said, so smugly that Mim had to grit her teeth to keep from screaming.

Instead, she shot to her feet—as if she'd been slapped. "Oh, you foolish, foolish child. Is that seriously what's been going through your brain all this time? That sixteen years ago I snuck off and opened my legs for my husband's brother? What is the matter with you? To think so little of me? Of Arliss?"

"But you—"

"Be quiet!" Mim snapped. "You have no idea! I . . ." She paced, then spun on her heels, glaring, head shaking. "Don't you see? I chose your father over Arliss all those years ago." A sob clicked in her throat. White-hot fury seethed low in her belly. She could not remember ever being this angry. "You awful, selfish child. You're too caught up in your own petty problems to grasp the magnitude of what you're saying. I know now and I knew then that my decision broke Arliss's heart. It crushed him, but I chose your dad anyway. No one forced me." She stood in silence, chest heaving, getting angrier with each breath. "Don't you dare imply that I . . . that we . . . I chose your father, and I would choose him again if he were here, but he is not. Do you realize how hard it must be for your uncle to know that, to know how I feel, and still drop everything to come and help after your father died?"

"I . . . I don't—"

"No," Mim snapped, disgusted. "You don't, because you're too caught up in your own woes, worrying about how this is all affecting you. You never take time to notice that this whole situation is killing your little brothers . . . what it's doing to me. The only thing that is keeping this family going has been your uncle Arliss. Do you hear me?"

"Are you sleeping with him now?"

"No!" Mim roared, sending her daughter recoiling on the bed. She wheeled and stormed out of the room without another word, before Constance caught the rest of the answer in her eyes. Because the truth was, the only reason she'd not slept with Arliss since he'd moved to Alaska was that he'd never asked.

CHAPTER 16

*N*orth Slope Borough PD officer Janice Hough was waiting inside the Deadhorse airport terminal nursing a tall Yeti mug of something hot when Cutter and Bill Young lugged their bags through the doors and out of the bitter wind. Cutter decided not to read too much into the earlier phone call. She'd either known Ethan or known of him. That didn't mean anything.

She was smiling now, sipping from her mug, getting warm, and apparently happy to help out. Her free hand clutched a fake fur hat, which, judging from the flattened nest of blond curls, she'd just removed from her head. She wore heavy "pac" boots that came halfway up her shins, and insulated Carhartt coveralls unzipped and rolled down to her uniform gun belt so the empty arms trailed beside her legs. It looked odd but was necessary to keep from overheating. The walk from the little Ravn Air turboprop—Young called it a flying cigar tube—had been numbingly cold. The biting wind and blowing snow made the trudge feel much longer than the fifty yards it actually was. Cutter wasn't yet sure how cold it was, but the tiny hairs inside his nose froze together, which usually started happening somewhere around ten degrees. The chills seeping through the legs of his pants told him it was considerably colder than that.

"Marshals?" Hough said, toasting the air with her steel mug to let them know she was their ride. She smiled at Young, then surveyed Cutter up and down, giving him a slow once-over. "You must be Arliss Cutter."

"I am," he said. "We appreciate you picking us up."

"Remarkable," she said, giving him another up-and-down scan. She took a sip from her mug again, continuing to study him, as if expecting him to say more.

Young let the bag of prisoner chains fall to the floor with a jingle, and slipped off his glove to shake the officer's hand.

"What the hell happened to spring, right?" Hough said, grinning, a tinge of nerves wobbling her voice. She waved the hat toward the frosted window overlooking the wind-scoured taxiway.

"I wondered about that myself," Cutter said, stomping his feet to get the blood flowing. "Seriously, thanks for meeting us. We'd have likely gotten lost and frozen to death between here and the jail."

"Well," Hough said, still tentative, but relaxing by degree. "Six below is a balmy spring day here. They don't call it Deadhorse for nothin'. Come on. I have you one room at the borough building and one at the hotel. We keep a couple of rooms for itinerant teachers, nurses, and cops. Even had a traveling shrink here last week, checking on our mental health." She gave the men a toothy grin and toasted again with her drink. "You know, making sure we're crazy enough to work up here and all. Anyway, only one to spare at the moment." She leaned in close to Cutter. "The borough room is better."

"Copy," Cutter said. "Bill can have that one."

She looked at Cutter with a wan smile, a smile that hid unspoken words. "You really are Ethan's brother . . ."

Young must have sensed the tension in the air. "What time are we losing light this time of year, Officer Hough?"

"Call me Jan," she said. "That's the good news. Days are getting longer even if it's colder than . . ." her voice trailed off, obviously deciding she didn't know these men well enough for the rest of her metaphor. "Anyway, it won't get dark until after nine. Let's drop your bags and I'll give you a tour before dinner."

Bill Young decided he'd seen enough blowing snow for one day by the time they reached the borough building. He opted to go to his room for a short nap before he met them for chow later that evening. In truth, he was aware of his surroundings enough to realize Cutter wanted to talk to Officer Hough about Ethan in private.

"Any chance you could take me to where my brother died," Cutter said once he and Jan Hough were alone in the relative warmth of her patrol Tahoe. He'd bundled up with virtually every stitch of clothing he'd brought with him, including the beaver over-mittens, which he carried on a leather harness over the shoulders of his parka.

"Wish I could," Hough said. "But Ethan was killed at a pad near the mouth of the Kuparuk River. That's over twenty miles away on the other side of Pump Station One. I'm still on duty, so I need to stay closer to town."

"Understood," Cutter said.

She brightened. "I can still show you around. Take you to other places he worked."

She talked as she drove, pointing out oil and gas company buildings, the boxy hotels, and the tiny clapboard and metal store. In many ways, it had the industrial, utilitarian look of a Soviet-era town in Russia.

"Ethan's engineering firm is there," she said, nodding to a light blue ATCO construction trailer.

Cutter studied the place as they drove past, watching the ice fog blow and swirl, shrouding the idling trucks out front. He couldn't shake the feeling that his brother had died on some Venusian outpost.

The radio on the dash squawked, and the dispatcher reported another polar bear sighting on the east side of town, past the espresso shop.

"Are bears a big problem?" Cutter asked.

"Depends on what you call big," Hough said. "The bears are big, and they will definitely hunt and eat you if given the opportunity, but it's not like we're living *30 Days of Night* with marauding carnivores. They're beautiful animals, luminous really—but with so many human eyes on them, they sometime seem a little bewildered at the way things are going."

Cutter nodded, still looking out the passenger window. He had zero experience with polar bears, so he had no opinion to offer.

Hough made a quick left down a foggy alley alongside a two-story warehouse. She drove slowly, scanning as she wove her way through lines of parked pickups and box vans. To Cutter, it looked like they were driving inside a cloud.

She gestured toward the rear of the building as they drove past. "See those bars?"

"Looks like a cage," Cutter said.

"That's exactly what it is. Like a shark cage, but for bears, that extends off the back exit. Polar bears are ambush killers. They like to wait on the ice for a hapless seal to poke its little head out. They've learned over the years that the door from that building is like a hole in the ice. Good treats come out of it. The metal cage allows workers to take a step or two out, away from the building a few feet so they get a wider field of view before committing to walk to their vehicle."

"The bears actually lie in wait?" Cutter asked.

"They would," Hough said, "if we'd let them hang around. I don't mean to make it sound worse than it is. It's not like they're waiting behind every truck, but they do consider humans to be a food source."

Cutter wanted to hear more about Ethan but decided not to press. For now.

Hough pulled herself forward in her seat with the steering wheel, craning her head back and forth to study the surroundings as she spoke, a natural teacher. "An Iñupiat elder from Nuiqsut—a village between here and Utqiagvik—once told me that his great-grandfather used to catch the big polar bears by getting them to try to catch him. According to my friend, they'd take long strips of springy baleen from a bow-head whale—the stuff they used to use in ladies' corset stays back in the day—and sharpen them to a point at both ends, shaving them down thin like a leaf spring so they could be rolled up in tight coils. Then they'd take this coil of razor-sharp whale baleen maybe a foot long and freeze it in a ball of seal meat the size of a fist."

Hough rolled to a crunching halt in the gravel parking lot and turned to look Cutter in the eye. "When the hunter crossed the track of a polar bear, he'd start dropping these boobytrapped meatballs every couple hundred feet. The ice was cold enough to keep the balls frozen, but when a bear picked up the trail and started after the man, he found treat after treat on the ground. Of course, it didn't take long for the body heat inside the bear's gut to melt the meat and let the little baleen spikes snap open, one by freaking one. Bears move fast when they pick up a trail, so chances were good it would have eaten a dozen meatballs before they started to thaw and do their work. Get the picture? Twelve or more spikes, basically spring-loaded punji sticks, cutting the bear's guts to shreds. . . ."

Cutter grimaced. "Tough way to die."

Hough looked like she was about to say something and then thought better of it.

She suddenly hit the gas, speeding through the gray-white fog.

"Got you now, *Nanook*."

Cutter leaned forward, recognizing the Iñupiaq word for "polar bear." He saw nothing but the gray outline of buildings and a whirling curtain of fog.

And then the bear was just there, as if it had materialized out of a snowdrift. A magnificent hulking thing, it seemed to Cutter to be as large as the SUV, certainly larger than any bear he'd seen up close. Massive shoulders rolled and flexed under fat and fur. Haunches that looked like the back end of a Volkswagen Beetle drove the animal forward at a steady, waddling walk down the street. The big bear looked over its shoulder once, noted Officer Hough's SUV, and then ignored her, moving at a sure but unbothered pace. Cutter guessed the creature easily weighed over eight hundred pounds and would have towered over him if it decided to stand on hind legs. For now, it remained on all fours, sauntering down the road like it hadn't a care in the world.

They were close enough to see the wind ruffling through the great bear's thick yellow-white fur.

Hough glanced sideways, taking her eyes off the animal long enough to look at Cutter's belt. "What are you packing? As far as a sidearm, I mean?"

"Colt Python," he said. ".357."

Hough gave a barely perceptible nod. Impressed. "Better than most, these days," she said. "But still puny when it comes to this guy. It would only piss him off unless you hit him just right." She toggled a switch on the dash beside her steering wheel, freeing the Remington 870 pump shotgun from its rack with an electronic click. "Hold on to this for a sec if you don't mind," she said. "Then pass it to me when I get a little closer."

Cutter looked at the bear, then at her. Surprised at the way this was turning out. "You're planning to kill it?"

"Oh, hell no," Hough said. "This is a big male. See how he's walking? He's tippy-top of the food chain—

the great one. My Iñupiat elder friend believes these
guys decide when the hunter is worthy enough to hunt
them. They're also responsible for punishing folks
who break important taboos. You look at this one and
you can believe it. He ain't scared of anything. We just
have to give him something to make him decide to
leave town. I'll smack him in the butt with a couple of
rubber bullets. These are magnums, so they'll hurt like
hell, but they won't do any lasting damage. You hit the
air horn for me when I shoot." She grinned. "I need to
get out of the truck to get on target. These guys can
move quick, though. The third and fourth rounds in
this shotgun are Brenneke slugs, but be ready to back
me up with your pea shooter if this guy runs the wrong
way."

The less-lethal projectiles Jan Hough used on the
polar bear were about the size of her thumbs and made
of dense rubber for maximum stinging effect. The first
round smacked the bear high in the hip, a glancing
blow. It caused him to hump up, run a few feet, and
then stop cold before turning to look over his shoulder
at what sort of puny, insolent creature had tried to hurt
him.

Cutter opened his door wider, thinking he might
have to get out if the bear turned and Hough didn't get
back in the truck. He'd already unzipped his parka and
had one foot on the ground, giving him access to the
Colt.

Hough's second round hit the bear square in the
ham, cracking like a whip. The startled animal tucked

its rear end as if to downshift, and loped away, apparently heading for another zip code. A moment later, it vanished into a curtain of blowing snow.

Hough took the time to top off the shotgun with two more shells before she got back in the Tahoe. The next threat might prove to be a little more dangerous than a polar bear, so these rounds were double-aught buckshot. Cutter watched her make certain the gun was patrol ready—chamber empty, bolt released, magazine full, safety off. All she had to do was rack the action to feed in a fresh round and then pull the trigger—if it came to that.

"Thanks for your help," Hough said, stowing the shotgun and settling herself behind the steering wheel. She unzipped the insulated coveralls to her waist, warmed by the bear encounter.

"You did the heavy lifting," Cutter said. "I just stood by in case."

"Yeah, well," Hough said. "The 'in case' can kill you out here, so thank you. I appreciate it." She smiled, hands on the wheel. "Your coloring is different from Ethan, but it's easy to see you two are brothers. Same self-deprecating manner. Though, I've gotta say, he did smile a bit more than you do."

Cutter shrugged, feigning a frown. "A lamppost smiles more than I do. Sounds like you knew Ethan pretty well."

"I did," Hough said. "Same goes for a lot of people in Deadhorse. Stay here long enough and you're sure to hear some wise quote from his grandfather."

"Grumpy." Cutter nodded, almost smiling. Then he took a chance. "May I make an observation?"

Her knuckles turned white as her grip tightened on the steering wheel. "Of course."

"Maybe I'm reading something into this," Cutter said. "But it seems to me you're holding something back from me about Ethan."

Hough took a deep breath and then let it out slowly. "To be honest, when I heard you'd switched places with the deputy who was originally supposed to come up . . . I was sure you were here for a different reason."

"And what reason is that?"

"To solve Ethan's murder," she said, almost a whisper.

Cutter thought he'd misheard. "What?"

"Ethan's murder," Hough said again.

Little in the world shocked Cutter anymore, but he suddenly found himself on shaky ground, as if the world as he knew it was yawning open to swallow him up.

"Murder . . ." he said, mulling over the word, what it meant—what the idea of it would do to Mim if she found out.

"There's not much to do up here," Hough said. "Which makes the place ripe for a rumor mill. Still, there were things that made me wonder."

"Things?" Cutter said. "Rumors? What are you talking about?"

Hough glanced at her watch. She put the Tahoe in gear and began to drive again, eyes focused on the road—as if to avoid Cutter. "Some of the rumors were pretty ugly."

"Just tell me," Cutter said, fighting the urge to raise his voice.

"About his engineering firm, for one," Hough said.

"What about them?" Cutter asked. "Ethan's wife has been dealing with them in court. They say his design was flawed and so he was responsible for his own death. They're treating my sister-in-law like trash, holding up his life insurance."

"Assholes," Hough said. "On top of everything else—"

Cutter half turned in his seat. "On top of what?"

Hough rubbed a hand across her face, exhausted. "I know Prudhoe is almost a thousand miles away from Anchor-town, but holy crap. I can't believe none of the tabloid crap trickled south. Though, I guess it's a blessing that Ethan's widow was spared the sordid stories. Like I said, some of them are pretty ugly. Look, I'm an idiot for bringing it up. I . . . I just assumed you already knew."

"Well, I didn't," Cutter said.

"Everything is unsubstantiated, mind you. I'm afraid hearing them will be like eating one of those booby-trapped meatballs. They could end up gutting you from the inside out."

"I'll deal with that," Cutter said, his tone leaving no room for argument.

"Okay . . ." Officer Hough threw her head backward against the seat and groaned. "Some people have claimed that Ethan was involved in illegal gambling. So, there's that. People swear they have seen him at a couple of games organized by Nolan Lamp—one of the guys you're here to transport back to Anchorage. That little shit has been putting together poker games for years, though. Just playing at one or two doesn't mean a thing. Playing cards and even betting on them isn't a big deal. The house making money off the game is illegal. And like I said, rumors. I'm not even sure Ethan really went to any of the games."

"It doesn't sound like him," Cutter said. His mind was moving a million miles an hour, and he had to concentrate to keep his knee from bouncing. He steeled himself for what came next. "You said 'for one thing.' What else?"

"Well," Hough said. "This is completely unsubstantiated—and believe me, I've done a shitload of digging—but more than a few people believe Ethan's engineering firm is being so vindictive because he was going to blow the whistle about something."

"Blow the whistle about what?"

"I wish I knew," Hough said. "I took as deep a dive as I could without getting a warrant, and I found zilch."

Cutter kept his eyes trained on Hough. "Is that it?" He could tell from the look on her face that she was holding something back.

"You seriously don't know?"

"Jan!"

"Okay, okay. There were rumors he was having affairs," she said.

"What do you mean?" The word not registering when used in connection to his brother.

"Affairs," Hough said. "Sexual liaisons."

Cutter gave a slow nod, digesting this new information. "With who?" he asked, knowing the answer before he spoke the words.

"Well," Jan Hough said. "Among others . . . me."

CHAPTER 17

*T*ires chattered on frozen ground as Jan Hough made a quick right into the lot of Cutter's hotel. Instead of parking, she pulled up to the front door and rolled to a slow stop. She put the Tahoe in park, but left the engine running. Her hands gripped the steering wheel, rocking her body back and forth, thinking. She looked straight out the windshield, far into the distance.

She gave a little shrug, barely noticeable in the heavy coveralls. "It's not true, you know. I mean, Ethan was my friend. Yeah, I felt stronger about him than my husband would have liked." She chuckled softly, nervously. "The guys have this saying on the Slope that there's a woman behind every tree." She waved her hand across the barren landscape. "It makes the handful of women who do work here mighty popular if everyone wasn't so exhausted from working all these hours. But . . ."

"But people being people," Cutter said.

"Exactly," Hough said. "Sure, affairs happen. But not Ethan. Oh no."

Still coming to grips with these new revelations, Cutter waited for her to say more.

Instead, she checked her watch, then gave a nod toward the hotel, seemingly eager for a break in the conversation. "Listen, I'm sorry, but I really do have to run to the office for a few minutes. There aren't many places to eat in Deadhorse, but all of them serve four shifts a day, all you can eat. People burn a ton of calories working in the cold. This place is good as any. One of our borough public works guys is bringing Bill Young over to meet you here for dinner."

Cutter didn't move.

"Seriously," Hough said. "We'll talk some more. I promise. But I have a meeting that I can't miss. I don't think it'll take more than a half hour. Forty-five minutes tops. I'll come straight back afterward. We can talk all night if you want. Hell, stay an extra day if you can work it out with your boss. The prisoners can cool their heels in our holding cell."

"What about that storm?" Cutter reminded her.

"There's always a storm in the Arctic," she said. "We're used to it. But I guess if you stay too long you could be stranded for a few days."

Cutter heaved a deep groan. There was nothing he could do about this, so he might as well let things play out on Hough's terms. If he pressed too aggressively, she might clam up. He opened his door to go, but she reached across the seat and touched his arm, looking him dead in the eye when he turned back, a plea for understanding.

"Ethan Cutter would never have cheated on his wife," she whispered. "Even if he'd had the opportunity. I'm one hundred percent sure about that."

Tori Whitlock paused inside the swinging metal doors that separated the kitchen from the big dining hall. She took a deep breath, gathering her wits. It should not have been this difficult to walk thirty feet and top off the coffee urn. But he was out there, waiting for her, holding a stupid silk rose he must have brought with him all the way from Fairbanks. Tori tried to convince herself he was harmless, but something in her gut said otherwise.

Working the dining hall in this sea of lonely testosterone was bad enough, even though ninety-nine percent of the guys were great . . . Okay, maybe closer to ninety-five percent. There were a few real assholes who didn't quite understand the idea of personal space. Gene Richards was the worst. She grimaced at the idea of even talking to him, let alone accepting a dusty cloth flower.

Eww. Just Ewww.

He never said anything rude, or even off-color. She would have found that easier to deal with. No, Richards was always polite—maybe too polite, like he was putting on a show, an act. It creeped her right out. He was hot looking enough, with shaggy black hair and a perpetual three-day scruff. Too tall, though, and too broad. Tori was only five-two and liked her guys around five-nine or ten. Gene was at least six three and probably weighed in around two-sixty. He was probably juicing. She'd dated a guy on steroids once and wasn't about to go through that again.

He reminded her of a darker version of that I-Will-Break-You Russian dude in the *Rocky* movies her dad liked to watch.

The zipper tab on his jacket was festooned with lift tickets from ski resorts around the world, signaling to everyone he met that he not only hit the slopes, but was a world traveler as well. Okay, most men bragged. It was evolutionary, strutting their stuff to show they'd be a good mate.

Worst of all, this dude was old enough to be her dad.

She was twenty-two, saving money to start nursing school at UAA in the fall. Richards was what? At least forty. Tori's dad was only forty-three. *Ewww*. Just a couple of weeks earlier, Richards had Instagram stalked her, found a throwback photo of her as a cheerleader at Bartlett High, which wasn't that long ago, and commented with a string of hearts and googly eyes. Any man who used that many emojis instead of plain words turned her off anyway, but a forty-year-old man who used them about a photo of her when she was a sixteen-year-old . . .

Beyond ewww.

She peeked through the little oval window in the swinging door, formulating her plan. Richards wouldn't take rejection well. Something crazy flashed deep in his eyes every time she dropped a hint that she wasn't interested. She couldn't shake the feeling that telling him flat out would turn a suitor into a stalker. She even confided in her manager, Mr. Hollifield, what she was planning to do. He was a big guy, soft and timid, but still imposing if he worked at it. Okay, maybe not big enough to intimidate Gene Richards, but he would at least be a witness. Mr. Hollifield had begged her to wait until she wasn't in the cafeteria for any kind of brush-off. Anywhere else. She said she would try, but now Richards was out there lying in wait, ready to ambush.

This had to stop, once and for all.

Tonight.

Metal coffee pitcher in hand, towel over one shoulder of her dark blue uniform, Tori Whitlock closed her eyes, took another deep breath, and bumped the swinging door open with her hip.

Cutter stomped the snow off his boots on the metal ramp outside the front doors. Nerves made him tromp harder than he needed to, and the steel grating vibrated and sang as he tried in vain to work off some frustration after Janice Hough's revelations.

An affair? Not a chance. No. Way. In. Hell. Ethan was a one-woman man.

Arliss, on the other hand, had been married four times, enough that his friends called him a serial monogamist.

The smell of baked bread and fry oil hit him in the face as he opened the outer door. A wall of heat and even more intense food smells met him when he opened the second, interior set of doors that formed a dead air space against the bitter outside cold.

Cutter shucked off his hat, did a quick scan of the lobby—habitual, each time he entered any room. He nodded to the Filipina woman leaning over the front desk on both elbows, watching a video on her phone. This was the end of the road, and there were few drop-in guests at this time of year. Signage on the walls pointed the way toward the cafeteria, but it wasn't necessary. Cutter only had to follow the buzz of voices and clatter of silverware and plastic trays toward the smell of food.

The cold had made him hungrier than he thought he was. He grabbed a tray and napkin-roll of flatware so he could eat now and make use of all the time he had later to quiz Jan Hough about Ethan. Grumpy always said people don't know what they know. Hough might be discounting something she thought was meaningless, totally unaware of its importance. Cutter intended to glean every last bit of knowledge she had regarding his brother. Even if it was uncomfortable to hear.

Cutter passed the nearest hot table, where pasta was the order of the day. There seemed to be an endless supply—baked ziti, spaghetti, chicken parmigiana— that looked much better than he'd expected it would, considering their remote location, and even a meatless butternut ravioli. The dining room was loud and busy. Most were already seated or making return trips to the soft-serve ice cream machine, so Cutter didn't have to contend with a line. He slid his tray down the rails slowly, looking first, then finally opting for a spinach salad, the chicken parmigiana, and a bowl of rich pasta e fagioli soup to ward off the chill in his bones. He stuck with water to drink, and found an empty table off the end of the salad bar so Bill Young and Jan Hough would have places to sit when they arrived.

He'd no sooner taken his first taste of the bean soup when a familiar sound hit his ears, a sound he almost looked forward to.

The sound of trouble.

CHAPTER 18

*T*ori Whitlock stepped to the side when she passed through the kitchen doors, pitcher in hand, on the way to refill the coffee, moving deftly, like a matador. Richards, the oncoming bull, moved in from the corner of the salad bar.

"Hey, Gene," she said, beelining for the tall stainless steel urn. She tried to sound nonchalant. Friendly, but not encouraging. "I thought you left already."

Richards got his bearings quickly and blocked her path to the urn. He held the fake flower in front of his face, grinning like a schoolboy.

"Not gone yet," he said. "Tomorrow." He shoved the rose forward, pushing it within inches from the tip of her nose. "Thought you could use something to brighten your time up here."

"I can't right now," she said, trying to zig around. "I'm working."

"I can see that," he said. "Everyone in here can see

you're working. Your shift's over at nine, right? We could go for a drive. Look for some northern lights—"

She stepped the other way. "It's cloudy."

He mirrored her movement. It would have been flattering if she'd liked him. Now it only made her feel trapped—and she seriously hated feeling trapped. Mr. Hollifield was nowhere to be seen. *Stinking coward.*

"Come on, Gene," she said, coming off whinier than she would have liked.

"You come on," Richards said, still grinning. "At least take the rose. And promise me you'll think it over. I don't leave until tomorrow morn—"

She stopped trying to dodge and looked him straight in the eye. "I don't want your rose, Richards. Get it? And there's nothing to think over. Now, please. I'm asking you nicely to leave me alone."

The crazy flickered in his eyes again, but only for an instant. His lips quivered. He shook his head. "Let's just . . . We never have a chance to . . . If you would sit down with me and talk for a minute." He took her by the arm—gripping the flesh above her elbow—attempting to guide her toward a nearby empty table. Still no Mr. Hollifield. *Bastard.* The salad bar and milk dispenser hid them from the main dining hall, shielding Richards's actions. He'd planned his ambush perfectly, wanting to catch her away from the herd.

She jerked her arm from his grip, tears welling, eyes blazing. She spoke through clenched teeth. "I said leave me alone."

Richards grabbed her arm again, more forcefully this time, fingers digging deeply enough to make her yelp. She tried to pull away, but he held fast, dragging her toward the table. She cursed under her breath, swinging the coffee pitcher, but missed, sloshing both of them with scalding liquid.

"Shit!" He winced, released his grip for a moment, then grabbed her again, twisting a handful of her uniform scrubs in his fist to get a better hold.

She opened her mouth to scream but was cut short by a flicker of movement to her left, then a whistle. Richards heard it too, and turned to meet it with a feral growl.

It wasn't Mr. Hollifield.

Cutter whistled to get the big guy's attention, causing him to release the young woman's arm. It wasn't completely clear what was going on, or Cutter would have gone ahead and slapped the shit out of the guy.

"Police!" he said. "Everything okay here?"

The big guy turned and wiped a damp hand on the front of a puffy blue down jacket while he looked Cutter up and down.

"I know the cops in Deadhorse," Blue Jacket said. "And you're not one of them. You a trooper?"

"Nope," Cutter said, popping the P. "US Marshals."

Blue Jacket rolled his shoulders, posturing. He had thirty pounds and an inch or two on Cutter. His bluster might have worked had Cutter been one to care about the odds. "Run on," the big guy said. "I got no business with you."

The young woman glanced at Cutter, eyes wild. The tag on her scrub top said her name was TORI.

"Come on," Blue Jacket said to her. "I just want to talk."

Cutter made a little smooching sound, like he was

trying to encourage a stubborn horse to move. He eyed Blue Jacket, but kept his voice low. "How about you talk with me?"

"Do I owe you money or something?" Blue Jacket said, losing patience. "Mind your own business." He put a hand on Tori's shoulder.

"Hey!" Cutter barked. "Knock it off." He met the young woman's gaze. "Tori, do you want to talk to this guy?"

She gave an emphatic shake of her head. "I just want him to leave me alone."

"There you go." Cutter let his right foot drift back a hair, knowing what was about to happen. He spoke calmly but directly. "Listen here." He held open his unzipped parka to reveal his silver belt badge and the Colt Python. "I'm with the US Marshals. Touch her again, and I'll touch you."

Blue Jacket stared straight past him, seething, clenching his fists.

"Guess what?" He was up on the balls of his feet. "I don't give a shit about your big gun. You're not gonna shoot me."

"Tori," Cutter said. "Go to the kitchen. Do it now."

She moved toward the swinging doors, but only a few steps.

"How do you know her name?" Jealousy fanned the flames of Blue Jacket's anger. "Hey . . . Have you two got something goin'?"

Tears turned to rage and the big man snapped. He lunged, swinging wildly, catching Cutter on the point of the shoulder with a massive fist. Undisciplined or not, this guy was incredibly strong. Cutter faded back, robbing the blow of some of its power, but it still spun him. He stepped off line, giving Blue Jacket a left-handed slap to the ear as he went by. Far from a knock-out, the smack certainly got the big guy's attention.

Cutter took the coffee pitcher from Tori's hand and then hooked a thumb over his shoulder toward the doors. "Kitchen!" he said.

She took a few steps, then paused again.

Blue Jacket shook off the slap, wincing, no doubt from a singing eardrum. He bared his teeth.

Cutter gave a slight nod. "What's your plan here?"

"I am gonna beat your ass till you weep."

Blue Jacket tried the bum rush again—since it had worked so well last time—and earned a snootful of coffee pitcher for his trouble. To anyone watching, the blow looked as if Cutter was merely attempting to fend off a larger aggressor. And he was, he just did it cor-rectly, putting his hip into it, hoping to smear this guy's nose across the front of his face during the process. The steel pitcher reverberated with a resounding *pang* when it impacted Blue Jacket's face. A geyser of hot coffee shot into the air, narrowly missing both men as it rained back down on the tile. Blood poured from the big guy's nose. He floundered on the wet floor, roaring like a wild man, coming in for yet another attack.

Cutter stepped off line, keeping his center low and strong. He grabbed a wrist and a handful of blue ski jacket as the guy lumbered past, sweeping a leg and helping him to the tile floor, where he landed with enough enthusiasm to shatter teeth.

Cutter dropped beside him, locking the wrist and maintaining control of his grip on the ski jacket. "You hear me weeping?" he whispered. "This was never going to be a fair fight." He pulled the wrist toward the small of Blue Jacket's back and slapped on a cuff. "Assault is a felony. Assaulting me is a federal felony, and you are under arrest."

"Get the hell off me," Blue Jacket groaned. "I never assaulted anybody."

"Sure you did," Cutter said. "Now give me your other hand."

"You'll have to cuff me in front," Blue Jacket groaned. "I mean, my . . . my shoulders are too wide to get my arms that far—"

One wrist cuffed, Cutter fished a second pair of handcuffs from his pocket and linked them together before he finished the job—behind the back. He rolled Blue Jacket to a seated position. Blood and snot drenched the man's face, hanging in crimson strings from the point of his chin.

Tori stood mouth agape, mightily impressed with that.

Cutter stifled a moan as he pushed himself to his feet. He popped his neck and rotated his shoulder a couple of times to check for damage. Seemed like he hardly ever made it out of one of these without some new niggling pain to help him remember the moment years later.

Tori whispered, "Are you okay?"

"Hell no," moaned Blue Jacket.

Tori ignored him, looking directly at Cutter.

Blue Jacket's head sagged. Tears mixed with the blood and snot, the picture of dejection.

"I'm just fine," Cutter said. "But how are you?"

"I think I'm good," she said, but winced when she rubbed her upper arm.

A pasty-looking guy with a white apron over his

round belly peeked tentatively between the kitchen doors, stepping out when he was sure the coast was clear.

"I'm glad you're all right, Tori."

She scoffed. "Thanks for your help, Mr. Hollifield."

"Aw, come on, kiddo." The man gave a tight smile and winked like they were all in this together. "I would have done something if he'd crossed the line."

Cutter shot a none-too-happy look at Mr. Hollifield. "You and I draw our lines in vastly different places, mister." He turned to Tori again. "I'm sorry I didn't make it over here before he grabbed you."

"Are you kidding me?" she said. "Thank you for stepping in at all." She continued to rub her arm, more gingerly now. "I'm okay, but I'm sure this is gonna bruise."

"We'll get some photos." Cutter dragged Blue Jacket to his feet and recited his Miranda Rights. He didn't plan to question the guy but didn't want to give the lawyers any extra ammo in court.

Officer Jan Hough came up from behind, announcing herself to let Cutter know she was friend, not foe. Hands on her hips, she gave a slow shake of her head, taking in the situation.

"I don't even make it back to my meeting before I get dispatched to a fight." She gave Cutter a half grin. "What's the deal, Marshal? I can't leave you alone for one minute."

Cutter shrugged. "Just trying to eat my pasta e fagioli in peace when this moron decided to get handsy with Ms. Tori there. What's your name, sport?"

"I ain't telling you shit!"

"That works for me." Cutter hooked a thumb toward Hough, who had a strangely perplexed look on her face. "Talk to her then."

"His name's Gene Richards," Tori said. A silk rose lay at her feet. She kicked it away as if it were on fire.

"Gene Richards . . ." Cutter repeated the name slowly. "Where have I heard that name before?"

"I'm afraid you heard it from me," Hough said. "This is the bush pilot I had set up to fly you out of Dead-horse tomorrow morning."

CHAPTER 19

*C*olor photographs of decaying human limbs didn't exactly pair with a medium rare filet mignon, but Lola didn't much care. She was starving, and this case was too important to set aside while she ate.

Brackett sat in the booth across from her, shoving his own food around his plate with the tines of his fork, deep in thought. The sleeves of a blue pinstripe button-down were rolled up to his elbows. His dark hair had that mussed, day-sleeper look. He'd printed the crime scene photos he'd swiped with his phone and assembled them into an impressive case file, which now lay open on the table between their plates.

Club Paris was a tiny restaurant tucked in downtown Anchorage across the street from the Fifth Avenue Mall. A local landmark, the dining room had low, moody lighting and lots of polished wood, what Lola pictured a high-end brothel might have looked like back in the day. More important to Lola, it was a great place to get a steak downtown, quality protein after a workout. It was still early for the dinner rush, and only one other table was filled. There was a bar across the narrow room from Lola and Brackett, but the few patrons sidled up to it were older, and relatively sedate, making it easy to discuss the murder case without raising their voices. No one wanted to be caught shouting about blood and bone during a momentary lull in the ambient noise.

An overly attentive waitress named Erin swooped in to fill Lola's lemon water for the third time in fifteen minutes. Maybe twenty years old, she recoiled when she caught a glimpse of the top photograph in Brackett's file—a severed human foot.

Lola reached across the table and flipped the folder shut in an effort to spare the poor kid an upset stomach.

The waitress's face went pale. "Is that—"

"It has to do with work." Lola patted the table, giving her an everything-is-going-to-be-all-right smile. "Maybe you should just leave the pitcher with me."

Erin nodded, set the water on the edge of the table, and hustled away toward the kitchen.

Brackett toyed with his rib eye. Lola hardly knew the guy, but she'd already decided she was going to eat whatever of the steak he didn't. Leg day in the gym made protein a necessity.

He opened the file again and then gestured loosely at it with his fork. "Sorry I was a little slow to cover them up." He hovered over an image of the severed foot of the Jane Doe with the rainbow pedicure. It lay on a gleaming steel autopsy table with a metal ruler beside it to show scale. Lola wore a size eight runner, and this foot was considerably smaller than hers—maybe a five, judging from the ruler. As a tracker, Cutter had taught her to pay attention to shoe sizes. She pulled the photo across the table toward her to give it a closer look.

"We need one of those big murder boards like you see on the cop shows," she said, leaving the photo on the table so as not to display it to the people at the bar. "It would be easier to study everything at the same time."

Not one to get sick to her stomach, the photo made Lola angry because of the pain and terror it depicted. It was still covered in mud, flecks of grass, and dying sea life. Though it had been subject to the waves and currents of the sea for some time, bits of bone still remained embedded in the granulated, salt-cured meat at the site of amputation.

Brackett jabbed at the air above the folder with his fork, looking young and earnest with his bedhead hair. "This wasn't Henry Farris . . ." His voice trailed off, lips pursed, gravely shaking his head. "These women weren't out jogging. Someone would have reported them missing if they had been. The victims in these photos were already living in the shadows, prostitutes, homeless maybe. I've got to say, though, no homeless woman I ever saw had toes painted like that." He swallowed hard, staring at the photographs, transfixed.

Lola reached across the table and put a hand next to his plate. She had three younger brothers—big, burly, Maori brothers, but still younger, and like men of all sizes and ages, they were in need of nurturing.

"Joe Bill? You okay?"

Brackett shuffled through the file and then slid an

eight-by-ten photograph of what law enforcement had dubbed "The Point Woronzof Torso" out of the stack.

He jabbed again with his finger, only softer, more reverently. "Did I tell you this was my first call?"

"I didn't realize that," Lola said. "I thought one of the feet at Bootleggers Cove—"

Brackett shook his head. "No. You're right. She wasn't the first victim who washed ashore. I'm saying the Point Woronzof Torso was the very first call I was dispatched to after I got cut loose from my field training officer." He took a deep breath. "Hell of a way to start a career."

Lola gave a solemn sigh. "What is it they say? You come on this job to change the world, but the world ends up changing you."

"The detectives are doing a great job . . ." Brackett took a bite of his rib eye, as though he wanted to give his mouth something to do so he wouldn't have to speak.

"But . . ." Lola coaxed.

"Look, I know it's human nature to try and find meaning in things, order and all, but I can't help but think it means something that I got this particular call first thing out of the chute . . . I feel like I'm the one who's supposed to catch this guy." He gave a low groan. "Idiotic, right?"

"Not at all," Lola said honestly. "I feel the same about pretty much every big case I come across. Better to think that way than the opposite, supposing someone else will get the job done."

"True." Brackett touched the photo of the butchered torso. "What turns someone into the kind of person that would do things like this? A father who beat the hell out of his kids. A mother who abandoned the family. Some other childhood trauma . . ."

Lola took a bite of her filet, then another before she answered. She shook her head as she chewed to show that she'd been listening and was about to speak.

"I don't buy the trauma bit for every little wrong turn," she said. "Heaps of people get shit on when they're young and they don't start burning kittens at the stake . . . or doing this to people." She leaned forward, whispering to draw him closer. "I mean, I shouldn't be telling you this, but Cutter's mother ran off when he was a tiny boy. His dad died not long afterward."

"Yeah, well," Brackett said, brows raised. "I'm not sure we can hold up Arliss Cutter as a paragon of sanity."

"True enough," Lola grinned. "But he's no serial killer."

"You have to admit childhood trauma could play a role on some level," Brackett said. "We shouldn't rule it out."

"I'm not suggesting we rule anything out," Lola said. "Still, we talk to heaps of outlaws in the Marshals Service, sometimes for hours during long transports. It's like . . . I don't know, Criminal Psychology 101. Street cops get more day-to-day action, no doubt, but us deputies, we spend so much time hauling outlaws back and forth they start to expect Christmas cards from us. I'm just saying there are a hell of a lot of bad guys out there with mums and dads that loved them when they were little.

"Anyway," she said. "How about Henry Farris? He have some traumatic event befall him?"

Brackett thumbed through the file. "Here it is. Farris graduated high school in Afton, Wyoming, 1990. His mother was a hair stylist and his dad . . . was a butcher. Detectives seem to be very interested in the fact that Dad had a mobile slaughtering truck. I guess some of the farms and ranches around Star Valley used his service quite a bit, and he'd take young Henry along to help with the slaughter. I grew up hunting, but maybe following Dad around watching him off domestic animals could get . . . I don't know. Messy."

Lola stabbed her last bite of the filet and held it up on the end of her fork. "I spent a lot of my younger years on my father's home island of Rarotonga. Strong Cook Island Maori culture there—which means we throw big *kaikai*—feasts, which means we gotta slaughter heaps of chickens and heaps of pigs." She closed her eyes and shook her head slowly. "Nothing much more delicious than a young pig that's been fed a solid diet of fruit and coconuts . . . Anyway, I was strong for my age, so when I was a little girl my dad started making me help out by holding the pigs' legs while he stuck their throats. Let me tell you, Joe Bill Brackett— that was some serious trauma there. Heaps of blood. Trembling flesh. Loud squeals . . . screams, really. Those pigs . . . they don't exactly sit still for the process, so I had to grab on tight, even use my knee to hold them down."

"Sounds rough."

"I was five years old."

"All righty then," Brackett said. "That had to be . . ."

"Traumatic?" Lola popped the last bite of steak in her mouth, chewed it thoughtfully while she eyed Brackett's plate. "It was and it wasn't. I suppose the experience itself could have been traumatic, but *I* wasn't traumatized. I mean, it wasn't something I looked forward to by any means, and I don't go around murdering pigs in my off hours. Would I have my own kids get up to their elbows in blood like that? Damn straight, I would. My dad has a saying, 'You gonna eat the pig, you gonna know how to stick the pig.' His people live life . . . I don't know, closer to the source than we do in most of the US. Unless there's more to the story with Henry Farris, Friday nights at the farm hanging meat with Dad doesn't seem all that nefarious."

"True enough." Brackett waved a hand over the rest of his rib eye. "I'm done. You want any of this?"

She pulled the plate across the table and grinned at him. This guy was a keeper.

He leaned back in his seat. "Would you say Farris is tall?"

"I guess so. What is he? Six feet?"

Brackett drummed his fingers on a copy of the booking sheet. "Six-one."

"Yeah, I suppose I'd call that tall. Why?"

"There are hardly any leads in this case," Brackett said. "Apart from one victim whose sister reported her missing and we were later able to match with DNA, we don't even have IDs on any other bodies to match with missing persons reports—if they've even been reported missing." Brackett leaned forward. "But the girls on the street have their own network. I hear whispers of some unidentified tall white guy hanging around. A girl named Rita Taylor reported another prostitute missing early yesterday morning. A Native woman named

Grace Ayuluk. Taylor mentions this same tall white male."

"She get a vehicle description?"

Brackett shook his head. "She didn't even see him. The desk clerk at the motel thought he saw the Tall Man, but couldn't be sure."

"The Tall Man," Lola said. "That's not creepy at all."

"No kidding," Brackett said. He slouched in the booth. "I don't know, maybe Farris *is* the killer."

Lola chewed on the steak. "What else we got?"

Brackett looked over his shoulder to make sure the waitress wasn't on her way over, and then spread the photos on the table.

Two female torsos, each minus head, arms, and legs; and three feet, also likely female, cut off above the ankle. According to the medical examiner, the dismembering cuts had all been made with the same type of blade, if not the same one—an axe or possibly a machete. The absence of other slashing wounds around the extremities led Lola to lean toward an axe, rather than a lighter machete that, in her mind at least, would have taken repeated blows to get the job done.

"So," Lola said. "Five victims."

"More," Brackett said. "I'm sure of it."

"How about Lacy Geddes?" Lola asked. "The owner of the ID you guys found at Farris's campsite?"

"She has no family in Alaska and no friends who feel close enough that they want to risk interacting with the cops to report her. Downtown patrol officers noticed she wasn't hanging out around the bus stop anymore. That's the only way we knew she was missing."

"I get it," Lola said. "APD is far too busy to stir the pot and open an investigation just because a hooker stops hookin'."

"About the size of it."

"This is a lot of women," Lola said. "I'm guessing your detectives are hitting the streets talking to informants, stitching together whatever they can find as far as possible victim identities. Someone will recognize the girl with rainbow toes."

"That's what Sandy Jackson thinks," Brackett said.

"Jackson," Lola mused. "At Farris's camp? She reminds me of my auntie."

"What?"

"When she's mad, my auntie's go-to phrase is: '*Eia' a koe e maniania mai ka kaikai koe iaku!*'"

"Meaning?"

"Something like, 'Hold your tongue or I'll have you for breakfast!'"

Brackett chuckled, shaking his head. "You have a terrifying family."

"Jackson was giving me that kind of look every time I opened my mouth to talk to you. I think she might be a little jealous."

"Hah!" Brackett blushed. "Let's get back to the bloody murders. I'm not sure how hard homicide is going to work this now that Farris is in custody."

"Maybe he is the killer," Lola said. They both looked at the open folder and shook their heads in unison. "This is a shitload of victims, Joe Bill. Our killer has a voracious appetite. Even if the bodies float around awhile, that's one every couple of weeks—if we're finding a hundred percent—"

"Which we aren't," Brackett said.

He flipped through the files and then slid Lola a report.

"Here's the case I was telling you about. Grace Ayuluk. Stripper and, to hear her friend, Rita, tell it, a reformed prostitute. Case files note that Grace had a custody hearing the next morning where she'd petitioned the court to get her son back from Child Protective Services. Even the CPS case manager says Ms. Ayuluk had turned her life around. They were going to recommend she be granted custody of the kid again."

"She didn't show for court?"

"Nope."

Brackett pursed his lips, like he had a question.

"What?" Lola asked, looking down. "Did I dribble food on my shirt?"

"I just noticed the sticker inside your vest. I was trying to figure out what it was, but I see now it's an orange. 'Freshly squeezed.'"

He blushed when he realized it was from her mammogram.

"Just a checkup," she said. "Though squeezed doesn't come close to describing what they do to my girls."

"I . . ."

"Don't worry," Lola said. "I'm not one to talk too much about titties on the first date."

Brackett looked like he might pass out. She rescued him by returning to the investigation.

"Did the detectives chat with . . . What's the friend's name?"

"Taylor," Brackett said, relaxing by slow degree. "Rita Taylor. Looks like Officer Nafanua took the report."

"Samoan?"

"He is," Brackett said. "He's on mids with me. Good dude. Detectives followed up, but Rita Taylor wasn't at her address of record."

"She needs to be talked to," Lola said.

Brackett shoved the papers in his folder and flipped it closed. "You're damn right she does." He called Erin the waitress over and gave her his credit card. "So let's go do it."

"What time do you have to be at work?"

"I took the night off," he said.

"Last minute?"

He nodded. "Sarge said we have enough coverage. I'm yours for the night."

Lola looked at him, started to make a comment, but stopped.

He gave her one of his earnest grins, obviously thinking the same thing she was. "You know what I mean. Anyway, I have no idea where Rita Taylor lives, but I'm on midnight shift, so I have a pretty good idea where she works."

"It's not even six," Lola said. "A little early for a prostitute to be plying her trade, don't you think?"

Brackett shrugged. "Rita Taylor is . . . how do I say this, very dedicated to—"

"Her craft?"

"I can't speak to that," Brackett said. "But I know she's dedicated to making money. She'll be working somewhere. I'm sure of it."

CHAPTER 20

*C*onstance didn't even try to be quiet when she got home. She and Audrey had seen the two thugs, Koko and Bodie, at school, looking for them. Now Audrey was hiding out with Evelyn.

Constance slammed the door, stomped in from the arctic entry with her shoes on—virtually begging her mother to stop her and demand to know what was going on. *What's the matter with you now? What's your problem, Constance? You're home awfully early? Is something wrong?*

She got nothing, not even a concerned brow raise. Her mom was busy reading that letter she'd taken to carrying around. She barely even looked up from the table.

The twins were making French toast, and the house smelled like vanilla and cooking bacon. Her mom didn't seem to care about that, either.

"I'll be in my room," Constance said, earning an okay-bye-then flick of her mother's hand.

She tried another tack. "When does Uncle Arliss get home?"

Her mother set her letter on the table and looked up. "What?"

"Uncle Arliss," Constance said. "Is he working late tonight?"

Her mom's face flushed crimson. The veins in her forehead began to bulge, a sure sign that she was good and truly pissed. "Not three hours ago you said the most hateful things about him and me. Now you want to know where he is?"

The twins froze. This was news to them.

Constance tried to wave it off. "I . . . I just really need to talk to him."

"So you can lay that same twisted garbage on—"

"No, Mom," Constance said. "I promise. It's not that at all."

"Well, fortunately for all concerned," her mom said, "you're outta luck. Turns out his flight was canceled and he won't be back from the Slope until tomorrow."

"Wait," Constance said. "He's on the Slope?"

"He is. So, there you have it."

"Mom . . . I'm sorry about earlier. I really am."

Her mother just looked at her, vacant, hollow—like nothing Constance had ever seen before. At length, she went back to reading her letter and, without looking up, said, "Well that's good. You're sorry, so I guess everything is all peachy now. . . ."

Constance stood there, dumbfounded. This was all her fault. But moms were supposed to be moms and forgive. She had to think. Imelda Espita was out there somewhere, probably scared to death.

She started to speak, but her mom gave a slow shake of her head.

"Go on to your room," she said, thawing little by little. "The boys just now put the bacon in. It'll be an hour before dinner's ready. We'll get through this. I just need a minute to process."

Constance felt as though an unseen hand gripped her throat. She nodded, unable to speak.

A minute, she thought. *A minute might be too long. . . .*

CHAPTER 21

Joe Bill Brackett was wise enough to know that he had a lot to learn—and learning it from Deputy Lola Teariki was pleasant indeed. She'd been hunting fugitives for half her career.

Still, a year of working midshift in Anchorage felt like a lifetime of experiences, even with a field training officer critiquing his every move. He'd gotten an up-close and personal look at the city's seamy underbelly—stuff he had no idea existed, and he'd grown up here. He'd already developed a handful of informants—a young woman to whom he'd had to deliver a death notice after her husband had been murdered by rival drug dealers; a couple of convenience store clerks, if you could count those; and a forty-one-year-old prostitute named Pauline he'd arrested for assault just a few weeks into the job. She'd not even been mad, telling Brackett on the way to the jail he reminded her of her son. There was a chance she could help him find Rita Taylor, the prostitute who'd reported her friend missing.

Taylor rotated her business among three or four of the seedier downtown motels. Most businesses enforced a three-day gap period between stays—to keep the working girls from setting up a permanent shop in the same room.

Pauline, on the other hand, customarily went to wherever her clients were. She could have been anywhere—but when it came to Brackett, she made herself easy to find. He'd sent her a message before they left Club Paris.

His phone gave an audible chirp as he took his pickup around the block and headed out of town on Sixth Avenue. He fished the phone out of his jacket pocket, aimed it at his face to unlock the screen, and then passed it to Lola since he was driving.

The deputy held up the phone and turned to look at him across the center console. "You and your informant play Words with Friends?"

Brackett gave a sheepish grin. "Her clients can be sorta hinky. The game lets you send messages. It's a good way to communicate without anything showing up on her texts."

Lola gave an approving nod. "Smart."

"Wish I could take credit for it," Brackett said. "Pauline reads a lot of spy books."

"I guess so," Lola said. "I mean, she just played the word *microdot*."

"Dammit!" Brackett smacked the wheel. "I gave her that one . . ." He looked sheepishly at Lola. "I know it's weird."

"Weirdly sweet," she said. "Anywho, according to Pauline, Rita Taylor is working across from Merrill Field tonight. Either room 7 or room 9. Wonder how she knows that . . ."

"She's older," Brackett mused. "Wiser, I guess. Makes it her business to keep track of some of the girls."

"Like a madam?" Lola asked.

"More like a mom, I think," Brackett said.

"Hooker with a heart o' gold," Lola said, sounding unconvinced.

Fifth and Sixth Avenues merged, becoming the Glenn Highway. Brackett hung a U-turn in front of the airport at Reeve, heading back toward town.

"We don't have a warrant," he said.

"Don't need a warrant for a knock-and-talk," Lola said. "We're just following up on her complaint." She chewed on her bottom lip, thinking deeply about something. Finally, she said, "I take it you and Rita Taylor don't play word games on your phones."

"We do not." Brackett chuckled as he turned up Sitka, between a Baptist church and The Castle sex shop. "I arrested her a few months ago for kicking the shit out of another girl in this very parking lot. '*Though she be little she is fierce.*'"

"Look at you," Lola said. "Playing word games *and* quoting Shakespeare."

Located a block off Fifth Avenue, the rundown motel's exterior room doors faced the inside of an atrium. Brackett rolled to a stop in the sex shop parking lot, drawing a side-eye from Lola. He put his pickup in park and heaved a deep groan, steeling himself. There

would be no going back from this with his bosses once
he pulled around the corner.

Lola must have noticed the momentary stutter in his
concentration. "You good?"

"If the homicide detectives find out I'm going around
on my days off sticking my nose into their investigation . . . I'm still on probation for another six months.
They can fire me for about anything they feel like."

"You think Rita will remember you?"

"I arrested her quite a while ago, and she was pretty
drunk," Brackett said. "So maybe not since I'm out of
uniform."

"Then let the US Marshals Service be the ones to
poke our noses into the investigation. I'll do the talking."

"What am I then?"

"Joe Bill, Joe Bill, Joe Bill," Lola said, shaking her
head as if it were all so simple. She gave him a wink
that made his throat go tight. "You're the eye candy."

An elderly Native couple in town from Kotzebue for
medical appointments answered the door to room 7.
Lola smiled and told them she had the wrong room.

As the one making initial contact, Lola stood to the
left of the door outside room #9. Brackett kept to the
right, each of them outside the aptly named "fatal fun-
nel"—the kill zone where they would be silhouette targets when the door opened. They were both in plain
clothes, so Lola let her badge hang from the chain
around her neck. Hands near, but not on their weapons,
Brackett raised his fist to knock—but froze.

He cocked his head, tapping his ear. "You hear that?" he whispered.

Lola leaned closer. A man's voice, oddly familiar, with a strong New Jersey accent. It took her just a moment to suss out who it was—the gravel baritone of Chris Albany, a shock jock on a local drive time radio show.

Brackett's face screwed into a quizzical frown. He mouthed the words, "They're listening to the radio?"

"Nope." Lola shook her head. "They don't let you say the words he's saying on the radio. That's him in the flesh, as it were."

Brackett gave the door a healthy knock, the kind that says whomever it was didn't plan to go away.

Inside the room, Albany's baritone voice fell silent.

Brackett pounded on the door again. He started to announce, but Lola put a finger to her lips.

Nothing but crickets inside, then the creak of a bed when someone got up, followed by the shuffling rattle as an eye peeked through the space between the mini-blinds and the window sill. It was Albany's eye, and it vanished as soon as it spied Lola looking back at it through the glass from less than a foot away.

Hushed voices now.

Lola gave the door another rap. "US Marshals," she said. "I'm not interested in you, Mr. Albany. We're here to follow up with you, Ms. Taylor. You reported a friend of yours missing a couple of days—"

The door flew open, revealing a fragile-looking woman dressed in baggy sweats and a hastily donned T-shirt, hiked up on one side to expose gaunt ribs. She chewed her thumbnail, lips quivering, stricken in anticipation of terrible news. Lola wondered if she didn't always look that way.

"Is she dead?" Taylor asked. Behind her, the bathroom door slammed shut and the vent fan began to whine like a jet engine. Taylor ignored it. She rested her hand flat on top of her head, chest heaving as she began to hyperventilate. "I knew it. She's dead—"

"Hold on." Lola raised a hand and smiled softly. "We haven't found her."

"You haven't?"

"No," Lola said. "But we're trying to. We wanted to ask you a few more questions."

Taylor exhaled slowly. "Oh. Okay. That's a good thing."

Still outside, Brackett gave a nod toward the bathroom door. "What's going on with him, Rita?"

Taylor threw a glance over her shoulder. "He thinks he can sneak out that miniscule window." She shook her head. "Ain't happening. I've tried and I don't even fit."

"May we come in, Ms. Taylor?" Lola asked, motioning for Brackett to keep an eye on the bathroom door.

The wild-eyed woman gave a shake of her head, like she had a sudden epiphany. "Call me Rita. I'm outta my mind worried about Grace. She had a hearing to get her son back, you know. I am telling you, she would never run off. She's gotten clean, doing honest work. That little boy means everything to her." Rita gnawed on her thumbnail again, pacing in front of the minifridge and microwave. "I'm just scared shit-less, you know. You think maybe that serial killer got her."

"Honestly," Lola said. "We're not ruling anything out." She gave Brackett a nod and he pounded on the bathroom door.

"Come on out, Mr. Albany," he said.

They all stood in silence for a beat, then the door yawned open.

"Hands first," Brackett said. "Helps ease our nerves."

Barefoot with a crumpled wool sweater in his fist, Chris Albany only had time to jump into his jeans be-fore attempting to flee.

He was in all ways nondescript. Neither short nor tall, heavy or lean. His lifeless hair was a dirty blond that could have passed for brown in the right light. The kind of man others ignored—but for his resonant voice.

"We got nothing on you, Chris," Lola said, stifling the urge to smack the guy. "You could have just walked out the front door instead of trying to cheese it out the window."

"Wait a sec," he said, working through the scenario in his mind. "You guys are looking for whoever took Grace Ayuluk. I thought you just arrested the guy re-sponsible for all the murders."

Brackett clouded up, looking dark. "That case is still under investigation," he said.

Lola pointed her chin at the door. "And unless you have something to add, you may go. In fact, I insist on it."

Albany pulled the sweater over his head, took the

time to sit on the bed and put on his ankle socks, regaining more and more of his on-air swagger the
longer he was in the room.

"You have no crime to charge me with," he said as
he tied his running shoes.

"Are you asking me or telling me?" Lola said. "I already said you should scoot."

Albany held up both hands. "I'm not trying to argue
with you, Marshal. I'm just pointing out that you have
no evidence of anything going on here other than two
people in a motel room together." He caught Lola looking at his wedding band and slumped. "Which is bad
enough, I know." He raised a hand, shaking his finger.
"Hang on, if there's not a criminal charge, you can't
say anything about me being here, right?" His head
bobbed up and down as he tried to convince himself of
his reasoning. "I mean, isn't there some kind of confi-
dentiality thing, like doctors or priests . . . or you know,
like with your attorney—"

"Ah," Lola scoffed. "You mean the deputy mar-
shal/radio host privilege? Chris, you're such a dumb-
ass. I'd haul ass if I were you. You are getting on my
last nerve—"

"Hang on now," he whined. "What if I helped you
out somehow? Would you be able to keep this off the
books then?"

Brackett glowered. "Helped us out how?"

"You know, if I saw something the night Grace disappeared."

Rita spun, flying at him, pounding on his chest, shrieking. It was primal, something between the keen of a

distraught mother and a wounded animal. "You bastard!" she screamed. "You know something and didn't say? You know where she is?"

She was small, but Lola and Brackett had to help Albany peel her off.

"No!" Albany said, puffed up as if he'd somehow been terribly wronged. "If I knew where Grace was, I'd never keep it a secret. I did see something, but I didn't think anything of it until just now when you were talking to the marshal."

"I'm all ears," Lola said.

"So," Albany said. "If I tell you, then we're good here?"

"Can't promise you that," Lola said. "But I promise you we'll be crossways if you don't spill."

"It's not much," he said. "Not really. But I was visiting . . . another friend of mine a couple of doors down the night Grace disappeared—"

Rita cut him off, throwing her head back in disgust. "Really? You asshole. You slept with Courtney? I hope you catch what she's—"

Lola put a hand on Rita's shoulder. "We should let him finish."

"You're right . . ."

"Anyway," Albany said. "As I was leaving, I saw a guy hanging out by the end of the building. He was parked just around the corner."

"What kind of vehicle?" Brackett asked.

Albany shrugged. "I could only see the hood, but I'm pretty sure it was a SMAV—soccer mom assault vehicle—you know, some kind of minivan."

Brackett looked up from his notebook, tapping his pen on the page. "And the guy you saw?"

"A shadow really," Albany said. "Long coat. Wool hat. I never saw his face and couldn't even give you an age. But I do know one thing. The dude was freaking tall."

"See why we need one of those murder boards?" Lola said when they'd returned to the truck, and were sitting in the sex shop parking lot. Lola half hoped someone saw her there with Brackett.

She reached into her pack and pulled out the Battle-Board Cutter had given her for Christmas. The black multi-cam binder had rooms for files and photos inside its zippered pocket. The front face was covered with a piece of clear Plexiglas under which she'd put a clean white sheet of paper. She used a red grease pencil to write *Grace Ayuluk* in the middle of the board, circled it, and then in connecting circles wrote: *Rita Taylor*, *Chris Albany*, and *Tall Man,* connecting them all to Grace's circle with lines. Beside *Tall Man*, she noted the dark minivan.

"A tall guy in a mom-van," Brackett mused, studying her BattleBoard turned mini-murder board.

"Is this new information?"

"The minivan part," Brackett said. "But this tall guy keeps coming up."

"Enough to go to the detectives," Lola said.

Brackett drummed the wheel with his thumbs, thinking. "There's a lot at play here. We need to—"

Lola's phone chimed.

"Go ahead and take it," Brackett said.

"It's an alarm," she said. "Reminding me I need to get my partner's G-car and stage it for him at the office. You mind running me to his house and then following me back to the federal building. We can make our plan of action in the meantime—I mean, since you're mine for the night and all."

CHAPTER 22

Cutter's white Ford Escape was parked at the far edge of his sister-in-law's driveway. Brackett pulled up behind it and put his truck in park.

Brackett nodded to the little SUV. "You have keys?"

"I do," Lola said. "But I'm going to the door to say hello. Come with me. Cutter has the cutest little twin nephews. One of them looks just as mean as he does."

The porch light turned on automatically at their approach. Brackett, wearing a ballcap against the chill, took it off when they reached the door.

"Well, aren't you the real gentleman," Lola observed.

"My dad's a stickler for headwear etiquette."

Lola heard nothing when she pressed the doorbell, so she knocked. "You and Cutter are going to get along well."

"You think?" Brackett said. "That guy sort of—"

Mim opened the door. Her face was slack, mouth slightly open, like she'd just seen a ghost.

Lola frowned, panicking, thinking she must have heard something about Cutter.

Mim's hand shot to her mouth. She teetered in place, gasping for air.

"No . . ."

The truth dawned on Brackett first.

"Deputy Cutter is fine," he blurted. "We're just here to get his car."

Mim swallowed hard. She lowered a trembling hand. "He's fine?"

"I am *so* sorry." Lola rushed forward and looped an arm around her shoulders. "I didn't mean to scare you. Cutter is right-as. I talked to him only a few minutes ago. He wants me to stage his car for when he gets back tomorrow morning."

Mim heaved a great sigh of relief. "I just saw you and . . . I mean, this is the way they told me about Ethan—two people at the door, looking so somber."

"Well, Arliss is all good," Lola said again. "I promise."

The twins appeared in the background. "Hi, Lola! We made dinner. Bring your boyfriend and come eat some!"

Mim shook off the shock and opened the door wider. "That's a good idea. You guys come in. We've just finished eating, but if you like extra crispy bacon and slightly scorched French toast, we've got leftovers."

"We've already eaten," Lola said.

"Then come in for a minute and talk to me while I

calm down," Mim said. "The boys made Grumpy's Oatmeal Energy Cookies. I'll put on some coffee."

Lola shot a glance at Brackett, who gave her a sure-why-not shrug. He looked particularly pleased that she hadn't corrected the boys when they'd called him her boyfriend.

Mim pushed another oatmeal cookie on Brackett. He seemed like a sweet boy, if a little green. Lola would train him—from the looks of things in a whole lot of ways.

He patted his belly. "I've already had two. These things are addictive."

"Arliss said you guys are trying to find this serial killer."

Lola grimaced. "He knows that?"

Mim nibbled on a cookie and grinned. "Arliss Cutter is an observant man—knows all, sees all . . ."

"Tell me about it," Lola said.

"And he knows you, Lola. I'm certain he wishes he could be out there with you."

Mim shooed the boys out of the kitchen with the promise of a movie. The novelty of Lola's visit fading fast, they vanished at once, all too happy to leave their mother with the dishes.

Mim knew Lola had things to do, but she didn't want to be alone. Not yet. "So you don't think this homeless man is the right guy?"

Brackett shook his head.

Lola shrugged. "We're just following the evidence."

Brackett finally caved and grabbed another oatmeal cookie from the plate.

"Milk?" Mim asked.

Brackett nodded. "That would be great. I'm sure Cutter has talked to you about this, but it doesn't add up."

Mim broke a cookie for herself, leaving half untouched on the plate. "He said as much."

"Evidence washing up along the coastal trail," Brackett mused. "Seems like a lot for a homeless guy."

Mim raised the cookie to her mouth but stopped before taking a bite. She'd grown accustomed to talk of all sorts of horrible things related to Arliss's job. "The news says body parts. Feet mostly."

Lola nodded.

"And we're having a difficult time ID'ing them," Brackett said. "Most of them are probably prostitutes or runaways, but, the weirdest thing, one of the recovered feet had rainbow-painted toes—"

Constance charged in from the hall at that. She must have been listening. "What did you just say?"

"This is Officer Brackett," Mim said. "Lola's—"

Constance threw up her hand. "I heard all that. What did you say about painted toes?"

Mim exchanged glances with Lola, then cocked her head to look quizzically at her daughter.

"Constance?"

"Tell me!" Constance leaned over to look Brackett dead in the eye. She put both hands flat on the table, arms locked, her sullen flap of dark hair hanging straight down. "The news never said anything about painted toes—"

Brackett recoiled. "Listen, I don't—"

"You just said one of them had rainbow toes." Constance began to shake. Her voice caught in her throat. "That means they murdered Imelda! Don't you get it? I helped paint Imelda's toes—and then they chopped . . ." She dry-heaved, putting all her weight on the table to keep from falling. Her wails were loud enough to bring the twins back to the kitchen. Mim sent them straight to their room. The look on her face told them not to argue.

"I . . . I never knew about this . . ." Constance said. "I swear I would have said something. . . ."

Mim stood and put an arm around her daughter, drawing her close. "What are you talking about, sweetheart?"

Constance collapsed in a chair and told them all of it—every horrible detail.

Lola took notes as the girl spoke, patient because she was young, but more than a little annoyed that viable leads had remained buried for so long because of a bunch of stupid schoolgirls. She fought the urge to point out that the faster they caught this guy the sooner girls would stop dying.

She drilled down to fill in as many blanks as possible, while Brackett jumped on the phone with his boss. Koko and Bodie were well-known to APD Vice. Their real names were Solosolo Ipu and Byron Akers. Both had lengthy records for drugs and felony assault. Akers had done two years down in Spring Creek for breaking a trooper's nose during a traffic stop.

"I'm so sorry, Mom," Constance said. "I swear I

never took any acid . . . LSD. Nobody took it when I was there."

"We'll talk about that later," Mim said.

Brackett cupped a hand over his phone. "Constance, I need you to call your friends and tell them APD officers are on their way to Evelyn's house. Tell them to stay put and not to answer the door for anyone except for a police officer in uniform."

"Okay," Constance said, sniffing back tears. "I can't . . . I just can't believe Imelda is dead. . . ."

Audrey picked up on the first ring. Constance put her on speaker and told her the terrible news about Imelda Espita.

Surprisingly, Audrey laughed out loud.

Constance frowned, incredulous. "What's the matter with you?"

"Relax," Audrey said, having no idea there was anyone on the line but Constance listening. "She's not dead, girl."

"I'm telling you right now, she is," Constance said.

"Well," Audrey said. "That's gonna be news to her, because I have my security cameras pulled up and Imelda Espita just broke into my house five minutes ago."

Constance gave Brackett Audrey's address.

"Wait," Audrey said. "Who are you talking to?"

Constance brought her up to speed. "They're sending APD to protect you."

"Protect us?" The other girl fumed. "Evelyn, get your shit. We've got to get out of here." Then to Constance. "Are you kidding me? I can't believe you went to the cops?"

"I'm sorry," Constance said.

"I told you I'm not talking to any cops about this."

"What about Imelda—"

"I said she's fine! I can't believe it. You stupid bitch."

Brackett, still on the line with APD, gave Lola a thumbs-up.

She leaned on the table, looking down at Constance's phone. "Deputy US Marshal Lola Teariki here. The two guys who are after you—Koko and Bodie—they're the real deal, sweetness. Constance spoke with us so we could keep you safe. So unless you're going to thank her, I suggest you shut up with your mean-girl bitching and answer the door."

Brackett gave a quick thumbnail to the swing shift sergeant who then sent patrol units to Audrey Lipton's house. With any luck at all, they would pick up Imelda Espita by the time Lola finished briefing Chief Phillips.

Phillips didn't mind if her deputies worked all hours, so long as she knew they were on the street, just in case the marshal happened to get wind of it and asked her what was going on.

"You're there to provide support to APD," Phillips said.

"Roger that, Chief," Lola said. "Mim's dropping the twins off with a babysitter; then she and I are going to the PD with Constance and the other girls."

"Does Arliss know?"

"No, ma'am," Lola said. "He's my next call."

A baby cooed in the background. Phillips sighed.

"Okay. I'm thinking it's a good thing he's eight hundred miles away. If he thought these two goons were a threat to his family . . ."

"I know," Lola said, dead serious. "There'd be a lot of blood and bone . . ."

"Tell him I'll call in a few minutes," Phillips said. "But make damn sure he knows Mim and the kids are safe. Otherwise, he'll commandeer somebody's dogsled and start home tonight."

"Do my best," Lola said, and ended the call.

CHAPTER 23

C utter pitched his phone on the empty desk across the office from Jan Hough and arched his back, attempting—and failing miserably—to stretch some of the angry kinks out of his spine. Teariki had everything in hand. He knew that. And the chief would see to it that Mim and the kids were taken somewhere secure. But it was killing him that he was so far away. A dozen scenarios played on an endless loop inside his head—all of them bad—when he thought about what could have happened to Constance. Images of severed limbs flashed in his mind, superimposed on his niece's terrified face.

He rubbed his eyes with a thumb and forefinger. The ancient office chair screeched and creaked when he rocked forward and got to his feet.

"You okay?" Hough asked, looking up from her desk phone. She'd been on hold for the last five minutes.

"No," Cutter said. "I'm really not."

To her credit, Hough cradled the receiver and swiveled her chair toward him. "They'll call back," she said. "Anything I can help with?"

Cutter gave her a quick rundown of the events with his niece, mostly so he could make sense of it in his own head.

"So there's some other victim out there with a multicolored pedicure?"

"Looks that way," Cutter said.

"Hell of a coincidence," Hough said, clearly skeptical.

"Yep." Cutter looked Hough in the eye. "Let's you and I talk about coincidences."

She gave a noncommittal shrug. "Shoot."

"Did you find any regarding Ethan's death—unexplained coincidences?"

She drummed her fingers on the desk, then toyed with the corner of a stack of papers. This was the primary reason interrogation rooms were so sterile—to deprive the person being questioned of anything to fiddle with while they contrived a story.

"I want you to know I turned over every stone."

"We have time," Cutter said. "Let's turn them over again. Something in your gut told you Ethan was murdered?"

"Yes," she answered immediately. Absolutely no hesitation.

"And now you believe otherwise?"

"I couldn't find any evidence," Hough said. "And with things as they were, the more people saw me digging, the more it looked like I was trying to cover something up myself."

"The affair?"

Her eyes flashed. "There *was* no affair. But yes. People had all manner of theories. Women are scarce up here. To be blunt, when a girl who . . . fills out her Carhartts like I do becomes friends with a gregarious guy like your brother, people read into it. They project, pissed that they're not the ones who get to be in a relationship. It's primal—and I hate it."

"How'd your husband feel about all this?" It was a personal question, but Cutter was beyond caring.

Hough sighed. "My husband gets all of me he wants," she said. "So he doesn't have to project. The rumors bothered him, though, for sure."

"You're not exactly giving me a denial," Cutter said, watching her reaction.

"Wow," she said. "I thought I already gave you a denial."

"I'm sorry," Cutter said. "I know I'm pulling off scabs, but remember, I'm playing catch-up here, asking questions that have been asked and answered a dozen times. Had someone told me from the beginning that my brother's death could have been a murder, I would have jumped in to investigate with both feet, I guarantee you that. I would have bird-dogged detectives, called in favors, leveraged my position until the Marshals Service Office of Professional Responsibility had me suspended without pay. Whatever it took. Forget turning stones over. I would have obliterated anything that stood in my way."

"Of that"—Hough gave him a hard stare—"I have no doubt."

Cutter banged a fist against the desk. "If all evidence said Ethan's death was an accident, then I'd have let it drop. But here's the deal. The fact that not a single person happened to mention any investigation until today—that any notion of it has been buried for almost two years—I gotta tell you, that makes me curious as hell. I'm not sure you would have told me if you hadn't mistakenly thought I already knew."

"I would have," Hough said. "As soon as I knew I could trust you."

"So, you've said you turned over every stone. But I'm going to ask you one more time. After all that, do you believe my brother was murdered?"

Hough sat with her hands folded in her lap and looked at Cutter through half-closed eyes.

"Yes."

Cutter rubbed a hand over his face, scratching the stubble. This whole thing made him so incredibly tired. Losing Ethan had cut him off at the knees. Now this. Grumpy would have known what to do, Ethan too. Hell, if it had been anyone else, Cutter would have known what to do.

Hough opened her hands like a book, palms out. "I'll answer whatever questions you have. Ask me anything."

And he did, but the exercise amounted to little more than rehashing things they'd already discussed. He could quiz her forever about the known unknowns, while the unknown unknowns remained completely out of his reach. Cutter simply did not know what to ask—and he couldn't shake the feeling that Jan Hough was holding something back.

CHAPTER 24

*A*PD headquarters was located on Fifth Avenue smack in the middle of downtown Anchorage. Lola Teariki, accustomed to tinted windows and the relative anonymity of the Fugitive Task Force offices, felt like a sitting duck in a building that appeared to be made almost entirely out of glass.

Brackett used his proximity card to get them into the underground garage, and then led the way into the building. Mim dropped the twins off at a friend's from church, and she now followed with Constance.

Audrey and Evelyn were already seated in a small meeting room at a wood-veneer conference table. Evelyn gave Constance a smiling nod. Lola caught the flint-hard look in Audrey's eyes and gave a little shiver.

"I bet her mum locks the bedroom door when she sleeps," she muttered to Brackett.

Detective Nakamura breezed in a moment later, looking aloof and more than a little bothered. Lola decided that might just be his way and decided to give him the benefit of the doubt. On the other hand, he did give Brackett an icy stare that rivaled Audrey's. Nakamura plopped a heavy manila folder on the table in front of him and set a handheld Motorola radio on top of it. He kept his feet as he surveyed everyone else in the room, groaning at what he surely felt was a complete waste of his time. Nope, Lola decided. He was just an asshole. They lurked in every department and agency. The Marshals Service had its fair share.

"We're going to interview each of you separately," Nakamura said. He raised his finger like this was a teaching moment. "Remember, none of you are suspects in a crime. You are cooperating witnesses. So . . . cooperate and everyone gets along." He turned to Brackett, but the Motorola on top of his files broke squelch, cutting him off.

"I-17, 24-C-1." Nakamura used the I designator for Investigator.

Lola recognized one of the swing-shift officers who'd responded to Audrey's house.

Nakamura snatched up the radio and turned toward the door. "Go for I-17."

"We've searched the address. Door was clearly forced, but there's no one here."

"You've searched everywhere?"

"Uh . . . affirmative," the swing shift unit said. "We did. No joy."

Nakamura wheeled on Audrey. "Do you have any safe rooms or other hiding spots?"

Audrey went from icy to incredulous. "A safe room? Are you serious? You think my mom's a drug kingpin or something?"

Nakamura held up his hand to shush her and keyed his radio.

"Search again," he said. "And have someone check the grounds."

"10-4," the swing shift officer said.

Constance raised her hand, but Nakamura shushed her too. She caught Audrey's attention and mimicked putting a phone to her ear—and then tapped the imaginary phone's screen.

Brackett saw it and started around the table to Audrey.

"Pull up the archive footage from your door camera," he said. "We'll be able to see when she left."

"Way ahead of you," Audrey said, smirking as she worked the camera app with both thumbs. "A safe room . . . you guys are hilarious . . ." Her jaw dropped and she looked up at Constance. "They got her."

"Who?" Lola's hackles went up. "Who got her?"

Audrey lowered the phone and slumped in her chair, deflated, shaking all over like she might collapse.

"Koko and Bodie," she said, holding up the phone. "They dragged Imelda out of my house by the hair."

Sergeant Hopper drove into the parking lot just as Brackett and Lola were leaving the PD in Brackett's truck.

He rolled down his window and nodded toward his car radio, frowning at Brackett as they stopped door to door.

"You part of this shitstorm?"

"I got here in a roundabout way," Brackett said. "But, yes, sir, I'm part of it."

Lola leaned forward, clicking on the dome light in the truck so Hopper could see her. "Hey, Sarge."

"Marshal." Hopper smoothed his thick mustache and gave his subordinate a somber nod. "You two believe Koko and Bodie are our killers?"

"They're kidnappers," Brackett said. "At the very least. We know they have Imelda Espita." He explained the coincidence of the multicolored painted toes. "Espita has got to be connected to at least one of the victims."

"And since these two shitheels have grabbed her, then they are into it deep."

"Right," Brackett said, glancing at Lola for support and then back at Sergeant Hopper. "Could be they procure the girls for whoever is killing them . . . or maybe they're just a twisted set and they're doing the killing themselves."

"Maybe," Hooper mused, staring straight ahead and tapping to some tune only he could hear on his steering wheel. His head suddenly snapped up. "So . . . I thought you were off tonight?"

"I was," Brackett said. "The Marshals Task Force is helping us locate Ipu and Akers—Koko and Bodie."

"And you are assisting the Marshals Service?"

"Correct," Lola said.

"If it's okay with you," Brackett said.

Hooper gave a low groan. "I get the impression I couldn't keep you out of this if I fired you." He ran a finger over his mustache again and narrowed his eyes. Lola thought they must teach the look in sergeants' school. "And I gotta tell you, son. Firing is not out of the question if you step on . . . yourself out there."

"I won't, Sergeant," Brackett said.

"Kid . . ." Hopper sighed. "You probably already have. Let's just work together to hunt down these turds. We'll find out who's murdering girls around Anchorage and then they can fire you." He put his SUV in gear. "I trust you to take care of him, Teariki."

Lola leaned forward in her seat. "I'm a pretty good Jiminy Cricket."

"We'll see about that," Hooper said. "It should go without saying, but make sure to coordinate everything with Detective Nakamura."

"Roger that," Brackett said.

"You're a good cop, Joe Bill. I sure as hell don't look forward to letting you go. . . ." Hooper studied Brackett a moment, gave one more slow shake of his head—like he was passing a tragic car wreck—and drove into the underground garage.

"You could always apply with the Marshals," Lola said after he'd gone.

"I'm sure the feds are just aching to scoop up an insubordinate ex cop." Brackett rubbed a hand across his face. "I can't think about that right now. Get out your portable murder board and let's figure out where these assholes took Imelda Espita."

CHAPTER 25

Brackett cut down H street past the Skinny Raven running store and then hung a left on Eighth Avenue toward the federal building. It was dark, spitting a mix of snow and rain—just enough that he had to use his wipers, but not enough that the wipers did much good.

Lola took out a grease pencil and her BattleBoard. A quick snapshot with a phone memorialized the work before it was erased and new notes applied.

"Okay," she said. "What do we know about Solo-solo Ipu and Byron Akers?"

"They're muscle for Audrey Lipton's dealer," Brackett said. "Carson Pool. Street name—Deuce. I have his driver's license photo on my phone." He slid it across the center console as he drove.

"I know this guy," Lola said. "We had him in the cellblock a year ago. DEA picked him up. As far as I know the case never went anywhere." She shook her head. "Deuce . . . What a dick."

"No arguments there," Brackett said.

Lola tapped the clear plastic on the BattleBoard with the tip of her grease pencil. "Koko and Bodie are lackeys. Underlings. I don't see a couple of stoogey drug thugs having time to step away and kidnap this many women on their own."

"So if they are involved in the killings, Carson Pool could be the man behind the curtain . . ."

Lola wrote the name *Pool* in the center of the board. Koko and Bodie each got a smaller, attached circle of their own. "We'll look at known associates of all three. But it's a pretty safe bet that the two worker bees grabbed Imelda on Pool's behalf."

"We have UC vehicles positioned around his residence—the house Constance told us about off Dimond. She made it sound like Audrey overheard these guys talking about hunting for Imelda, like she'd run away." He nodded in thought. "But running away from what?"

Lola scoffed in spite of herself. "Oh, I don't know, maybe a sixteen-year-old kid gets a little sick of delivering drugs to bitchy high schoolgirls all day and then coming home to bump uglies with whoever her boss throws her in the pit with for the night."

"Sorry," Brackett said. "I wasn't looking at it like that."

"Or," Lola said. "Maybe Imelda Espita is our serial killer."

"That would be creepy as hell," Brackett said.

"Cutter always tells me to look at things from all angles and then follow the tracks." She tapped the pencil against the BattleBoard and stared out the window at a couple of intrepid runners braving the nasty weather along Centennial Park Strip.

Brackett turned right, heading south again. "Speaking of following tracks," Lola said. "Where are you going anyway?"

"Just driving around while we think," Brackett said. "You get good at meandering when you work midnights."

Lola continued to stare out the window, putting together puzzle pieces in her head.

Back at APD headquarters, Detective Nakamura would be running APSIN checks on everyone involved.

The Alaska Public Safety Information Network, or APSIN, held driver's license, vehicle registration, and records of when anyone came into contact with criminal justice—as a victim, witness, or suspect. APSIN was a good place to start when looking for known associates.

Armed with a lengthy list of anyone who had crossed paths with Pool or his two goons over the past two years, Nakamura would be sending teams to perform knock-and-talks. Brackett wasn't even supposed to be on duty, and the detective left him to scramble to whichever calls he happened to be near, providing backup while other detectives and uniformed officers made contact. The overwhelming police action had the two-pronged effect of alerting everyone connected to Pool that they were wanted men—and tightening the dragnet that was closing in around them. This "blue enema" was used sparingly, but with great effect.

Apart from a good deal of dope being flushed down toilets all across town, all the door knocking and shouts of "Anchorage Police!" yielded little in the way of positive results. It was well after midnight and no one had seen a trace of Bodie, Koko, or their boss.

"This is stuffed," Lola said, yawning, bouncing a fist on her knee. All this sitting was making her pay a price for her earlier leg day in the gym. Her muscles were getting so stiff she wondered if she might fall flat on her face when she next tried to get out of the truck.

"We have to start looking at this another way," she said.

"I'm game for anything." Brackett caught Lola's contagious yawn and wiped away a sleepy tear with the back of his hand. "Tell me what you're thinking?"

"Maybe we should start looking for Imelda."

Brackett laughed out loud. "I thought that's what we were doing."

"I mean instead of looking for the guys who took her," Lola said. She sat up straighter in the seat, feeling like she was onto something. "According to Constance, Imelda's boss had her turning tricks."

"Right," Brackett said.

"Then how about we call your CI, Paulette—"

"Pauline."

"Right. You said she likes to keep track of things. Maybe she knows something about Imelda Espita that we're missing."

"I guess it's worth a try," Brackett said. He dug his phone out of his pocket and passed it to Lola.

"Damn," Lola said when she opened the Words with Friends app and held the screen toward Brackett. "She's winning again."

"Just play something and tell her to call me."

"You have shitty letters," Lola said as she thumb-typed the message.

Pauline called Brackett's cell two minutes later. Lola put her on speaker. He did the talking.

"Don't recognize the name Imelda, sweetie," Pauline said after Brackett explained. "But I do know that piece of trash Carson Pool and the two igmos who work for him. It doesn't surprise me he's running teenagers in his stable. I really do hate that guy."

"When's the last time you saw him?"

"It all melds together, my dear," Pauline said. "I'm thinking it was night before last."

"Hang on," Brackett said. "You hate him and you saw him night before last?"

"Hon," Pauline said. "If I only took jobs from men I don't hate, I'd have an awfully short client list."

"Did he visit you?" Brackett asked.

"I went to him."

Informant/handler relationships were tender things. Lola kept quiet so as not to spook the woman. Excited at this new information, she gave Brackett a hopeful thumbs-up.

"Where'd you go?" Brackett asked.

"Somewhere on the Hillside," she said. "Seemed like we drove forever—way out in the sticks. Stucka-gain Heights or the Glen Alps maybe . . . I'm not sure. To be honest, I was pretty stoned. I remember looking up and seeing a lot of trees, if that helps. . . ."

"Trees?"

"Sorry. I sort of had my hands full in the back seat if you know what I mean."

Lola scanned through her notes for all the known

addresses associated with Carson Pool. She shook her head when she found nothing on the Hillside.

"You remember whose house it was?" Brackett asked. "Maybe one of Pool's friends?"

"It was no one's house," Pauline said, sounding more and more lit the longer they talked. "It was vacant, no clothes, no toothbrushes, not even any shampoo in the shower. But, oh mama, that shower—"

Brackett glanced at Lola. "The house was empty?"

"I mean, it had furniture," Pauline said. "But I didn't get the impression anyone was living there . . . What was I just telling you? Oh, yeah, the shower. It was one of those stone enclosures with a big square showerhead that makes you feel like it's raining . . . I know, my dear, sounds foolish. But believe me, you take what pleasures you can when you're in my line of work—and that shower was fantastic . . ." She gave a deep cough, dry and coarse. Lola imagined her face enveloped in a cloud of thick smoke from a substantial blunt. "Listen, I have to go. I'm calling from the powder room and my date is beginning to miss me."

"Hang on," Brackett said. "Anything else you remember about the house."

"Sorry, sweetie," Pauline said. "I'm afraid you have reached the muddy bottom of my well of knowledge, regarding this at least. I'll call you if I think of anything else."

Brackett double-checked the phone to make sure they weren't still connected and then stuffed it in his jacket pocket.

"She seems nice," Lola said.

"She is," Brackett said. "She'll cut you if you cross her . . . but she'd feel bad about it later."

Lola looked over the APSIN list of Carson Pool's associates again and then glanced up with a wide grin. "Look here," she said, suddenly jumpy with excitement. "Pool got his car repossessed while it was parked in front of a Celina Pool's residence—four years ago, before he was making money hand over fist supplying drugs to high school girls." Lola scanned further. "Looks like Celina is his aunt."

"Please tell me this aunt of his lives on the Hillside."

"Nope," Lola said. "She lives in Peters Creek. But get this, she's a Realtor. Which means she could provide him access to houses she was showing—furnished but vacant houses . . . with interesting showers."

Brackett slapped the steering wheel. "This is good. This is really good."

"Start heading for the Hillside," Lola said. "I'll take a look at her listings."

Celina Pool Realty had a robust website, which was good, since it was searchable, but overwhelming, because she was a very busy Realtor with links to over forty homes. Lola pulled up the map and zeroed in on houses for sale in East Anchorage and worked her way south along the foot of Chugach Mountains in the area known as the Hillside.

Brackett glanced sideways as he drove, adding his two cents. "They'd want someplace that didn't get any attention from nosey neighbors."

"On it," Lola said. "I've got a couple near Stuckagain Heights that are end-of-the-road properties. Isolated enough to fit the bill." She looked up from her notes to get a read on where they were. "Go ahead and cut through Bicentennial Park."

"We do that and we're committed," Brackett said. "No fast way out of the Stuckagain neighborhood. We'll have to backtrack if Pool's safehouse ends up farther south near the Glen Alps."

"True enough," Lola said. "But remember, Pauline said she saw a lot of trees . . . Which could be that long road through Bicentennial Park."

Brackett nodded, digging the phone out his pocket again. "Right. Where Campbell Airstrip turns into Basher Drive. I'll call in and get units headed this way."

"Up to you," Lola said. "But I'd wait a hair. We're operating on little more than a hunch and 'my informant saw trees.'" She shook her phone. "Shit! These photos are taking forever to load."

"Service up here is crappy," he said, trading his cell for the Motorola handheld radio in his cup holder.

The road narrowed and the headlights on Brackett's pickup reflected off more and more snow as they wound their way through the 4,000-acre Bicentennial Park toward the trailheads leading to Chugach State Park and the isolated but expensive Stuckagain Heights neighborhood—presumably so named because early residents found their vehicles so frequently mired in deep hillside mud. There were no streetlights, and the dark forests of birch and spruce felt like they were closing in on the road.

"This is like driving to the Batcave," Brackett mused.

Lola held her phone to the window. More service bars appeared on the screen as they gained elevation, climbing into the Chugach foothills above the city. She pumped her fist when photos began to load again.

"Okay," she said. "Now you can get on your radio."

"What changed?"

"Take the next left, then a right." She gave him an address, then turned the screen, showing him a stone shower with a large rain head. "End of the road with the right water feature. This has to be the house."

CHAPTER 26

Carson Pool's improvised safehouse was surrounded by dark stands of spruce. It wasn't clearly visible from the road, but telltale light from the windows flickered through the foliage.

Brackett and Lola left the truck and crept up the curved drive to get eyes on it. It was a sprawling thing, 3,700 square feet, according to the website. Most of the windows were dark, but lights blazed in the dining room and kitchen adjacent to an attached three-car garage. Lola caught a glimpse of a girl that matched the description of Imelda that Constance had given. The house was supposed to be vacant.

A quick check of the license plate on the Dodge Challenger parked out front revealed it was registered to a Tammy Gregson—who turned out to be Bodie's sister, sealing the deal. They'd ditched the BMW.

The nearest APD unit was Sandra Jackson—over five minutes away. Sergeant Hopper was another couple of minutes behind her. The cavalry was in route, coming in fast but quiet, without lights and sirens so as not to alert anyone of their presence.

Brackett sent Detective Nakamura a link to the property listing so responding units would have a floor plan if it came time to force an entry. There was a lot of back and forth over the encrypted radio about the need for speed versus taking a beat to get a warrant. Someone higher up the food chain than Nakamura was working on a SWAT callout since they were dealing with a possible hostage situation. The fact that it was all related to the Bootleggers Cove serial killer greased the skids. Nakamura would pursue a warrant at the same time other officers converged.

Lola clicked her teeth, rocking slightly in the brush, feeling an overwhelming urge to charge the house. "They could be in there killing her as we speak."

Brackett craned his neck, trying and failing to get a clear look.

"This is stuffed," Lola said. "Five minutes is an eternity if someone's got a gun to your head. The least we can do is move up. If she's not in immediate danger, we just get your people more intel."

Instead of answering, Brackett motioned for her to follow with a flick of his wrist. He stayed in a crouch, keeping to the buck brush along the edge of the circular driveway as he worked his way forward. Less than thirty feet from the back of Bodie's Dodge, they had a direct view into the dining room window.

Neither liked what they saw.

"They're on their feet," Lola whispered. "Koko's talking on his cell . . . Doesn't look happy."

"Can you see if she's hurt?"

"Can't tell." Lola tensed as the trio inside turned and walked out of sight, directly toward the front door. "But I think we're about to get a closer look."

Lola and Brackett moved at the same time, without speaking or making a plan. Each of them had long ago drawn clearly defined lines that they would never allow anyone to cross. Two men dragging a young woman somewhere she clearly did not want to go required action not words.

Lola fanned away from Brackett and drew her Glock.

"US Marshals! On the ground!"

Startled at the sudden noise, the two men froze. Imelda jerked free and ran to the far side of the Dodge. Her wrists were bound in front with gray duct tape. She wore nothing but gym shorts and a T-shirt that was speckled with blood. Even in the dim light from the windows it was easy to see her swollen nose and bruised cheeks. Sobbing and dazed, her head jerked back and forth, as if waiting for another attack.

"On the ground!" Brackett said, fury welling in his voice.

The men raised their hands, tentatively, as if deciding on the next move. Their eyes were still not accustomed to the darkness, and neither could locate exactly where Lola and Brackett stood.

Aimed in, Brackett shot a glance at Lola. He kept his voice to a tense whisper. "Three minutes out. We'll hold them here."

Imelda stumbled, tried to catch herself, but tripped and fell across the hood of the Dodge.

Lola kept her Glock pointed at Koko. "Imelda, stop! We're here to help you."

The poor girl regained her footing, bounced off the

car, and then began to stagger blindly up the driveway, directly toward her captors.

Koko bladed slightly, ready to use her as cover when she got close enough. The smirk on his face said he had his bearings now and wasn't about to be intimidated by some voices in the dark.

"Shit!" Lola spat. She holstered her pistol. "Give me cover. I'll bring her to us."

"Go," Brackett said.

At that same moment headlights arced through the trees. Gravel popped under tires as a car turned up the driveway.

"Must have gone supersonic—" Lola said, half turning, expecting to see a white APD cruiser. Her relief was short-lived when a black Lexus pulled in and crunched to a halt. Caught in the blinding glare of the headlights, Lola didn't see the driver, but Brackett could.

"It's Carson Pool!"

The Lexus lurched forward, tires squealing, directly for Lola.

She shoved Imelda out of the way and jumped, landing flat on her back on the Dodge's stubby trunk. A split second later, the Lexus slammed into the rear tires, spinning the Dodge and throwing Lola to the ground. Dazed, she rolled to her hands and knees, wheezing, unable to draw a full breath. Shots cracked in darkness. Glass shattered. Headlights arced, and the engine revved as the Lexus spun sideways, reversing course to head back toward Anchorage.

Consoling herself that Pool would not get very far, Lola turned to look for Imelda, heard a warning shout, and caught a boot in the ribs.

The kick was devastating, but instead of recoiling, Lola curled around it, pulling Koko's ankle and lower leg into her belly. She was vaguely aware of more yelling. Threats. Footfalls on the pavement.

Imelda screamed.

Every instinct in Lola's body told her she needed air. Holding fast to Koko's leg, she blew out as forcefully as she could. Her ribs were on fire, but her diaphragm relaxed.

Koko kicked with his left foot. The blows took Lola on the hip, sickening, but not enough to get her to let go. Cursing and hopping backward, Koko did his best to rid himself of a hundred and forty pounds of very angry Polynesian woman.

His voice shot up an octave. "Get off me, bitch! . . . Get . . . off . . . That's it, I'm gonna shoot your ass!"

Lola couldn't go for her gun without letting go. Koko's calf muscle brushed her cheek, offering a target. She clamped down with her teeth, growling like a maniac from pain and adrenaline. Koko screamed, jerking upward, becoming light on his feet as he struggled to get away. Lola swiveled her hips, as she'd done a thousand times when wrestling her brothers, rolling into her much larger opponent and using her low center of gravity to send him crashing backward to the unforgiving ground.

Instead of crawling away, she climbed up him as he fell, her left hand jerking the Taser from her belt. Koko flailed, trying to push her away. A massive fist crashed into her ribs. She went with it. His blows started too close to gain any real power—but they were still taking a toll.

Snakelike, she slid up his body, belly to belly until she was directly on top of him. He roared and drew back to hit her again, but she grabbed a handful of hair and twisted. She shoved the Taser against his fat cheek with her left hand and pulled the trigger.

Far from incapacitating Koko as it would have had the twin barbs deployed farther apart, this "drive stun" simply lit him up with tremendous pain as the darts tore into his flesh and fed fifty thousand volts into the apple of his cheek.

He screamed, clawing with both hands at the sudden fire in his face.

Lola rolled away, coming up with her Glock in hand.

"Don't you move!"

Lola stayed aimed in, working to catch her breath.

She was vaguely aware of Brackett a few yards away, a knee in Bodie Akers's back as he applied a set of handcuffs. Blood ran from Brackett's nose. He'd obviously had a fight of his own.

"You good?" she yelled over her shoulder.

"All good," Brackett said.

Imelda knelt in front of the Dodge, sobbing.

Koko screamed. "You shocked me in the face, bitch!"

"Keep your hands where I can see them," Lola said. "And roll over on your belly."

"You coulda put my eye out!"

"You threatened to shoot me," Lola said. "You're lucky I couldn't get to my gun."

* * *

Officer Sandra Jackson and Sergeant Hopper arrived five minutes later. Carson Pool slumped in the back of Jackson's Impala.

Lola flashed her badge at Jackson. "This dickhead been Mirandized?"

Jackson gave a curt nod.

Lola put a hand on the door, then looked at the officer. "May I?"

"You gonna ask him questions or murder him?"

"Still working that out in my head." Lola scoffed. "But I think just questions for the moment."

Jackson flicked a hand at her cruiser. "Be my guest."

Pool leaned away as if he expected to be attacked when Lola flung open the door.

"I wanted to get a look at the guy who tried to run down a federal officer."

"I didn't know you were a federal officer," Pool said. "I just saw a stranger heading across the driveway—"

"So you decided to run down a stranger in the driveway of a house your aunt has listed . . ." Lola shook her head and spit a mouthful of blood on the ground. "Sounds legit."

She slammed the door.

"You know they won't use anything he told you," Officer Jackson said. "Anyway, you're the victim. You really shouldn't be talking to him at all."

Lola spit another mouthful of blood. She fought the urge to clutch her injured ribs, not wanting to give these assholes the satisfaction of seeing her in pain.

"Yeah, right," she said to Jackson. "Pool had no idea

I was a fed, so any part of this where I'm a victim will likely go down as simple assault in state court—and you and I both know the judges up here give a defendant more time for killing a moose out of season than trying to murder a cop."

Detective Nakamura rolled up ten minutes later, following the AFD ambulance into the driveway. Lola insisted the paramedics look at Imelda first. There wasn't much they could do about cracked ribs anyway.

Patrol units poured in and took custody of Koko and Bodie. The senior officers didn't exactly shower Brackett with praise, but Nakamura was impressed enough with his results to start treating him like they were at least part of the same police department.

Sergeant Hopper stood with Imelda at the back of the ambulance while one of the paramedics wrapped her sprained wrist with an Ace bandage. Brackett and Lola followed Nakamura over.

"Miss Espita," the detective said. "I'd like to take you to our office so we can get a statement."

Imelda slumped, sniffing back tears. Her shoulders shook with periodic sobs. "Mr. Pool said . . . this would happen."

Lola shook her head. "Said what would happen?"

"Mr. Pool, he told me if I ran away, he would call Immigration." The girl looked up, imploring Lola for help, or at least understanding. "But I only ran to look for my friend."

"We're not Immigration."

Lola glanced down at Imelda's feet. "I'm friends with one of the girls who gave you that pedicure."

Imelda stared at her blankly, not understanding.

Lola shot a glance at Nakamura, who nodded for her to go ahead.

"The girls who painted your toes," she explained.

Imelda looked up in surprise. "Audrey is your friend?"

"No," Lola said. "Constance is."

"Ah," Imelda said. "I like Constance. They were all very nice to me. They let me take a shower and gave me some bottles of polish to touch up my nails."

Lola gave a broad smile, ignoring the knife-like pain in her side. "You said you left to look for someone?"

"My friend Serafina," Imelda sobbed, still fighting the tears. "One of Mr. Pool's clients hurt her bad. I painted her nails to match mine, hoping to cheer her up."

Brackett and Lola exchanged glances at the news.

"Did Serafina run away?" Lola asked.

"Mr. Pool thinks she did," Imelda said. "That is why he sent Koko after me. He believes I helped her go."

"But you don't think she ran away?" Lola asked.

"She did," Imelda said. "She climbed out the window. I haven't seen her in over a week."

Detective Nakamura could contain himself no longer. He raised his hand to regain control of the conversation. For as abrupt as he could be at the station, his voice and demeanor were remarkably congenial, even honeyed. For the first time since Lola had heard him speak, he wasn't condescending, but brimming with genuine concern. "You said Serafina climbed out the window. Where do you think she went?"

Imelda began to wring her hands and then looked up

at Lola again, wide-eyed. She began to tremble so badly her voice shook. "I am so scared," she said. "He took her. I know it."

Lola held her hand, careful of the bandage. "Who do you think took her?"

Imelda's chest shook with sobs.

"The Tall Man."

CHAPTER 27

*C*utter's phone rang as he walked back from the showers down the carpeted hall to his hotel room. He fished the device from the pocket of his gray sweats, noted it was a 907 number—Alaska. He didn't recognize it but thought it might be Jan Hough. It was late, but she'd said she was going back to the office after she dropped him off.

She'd been at once talkative and cagey, seemingly eager to help get to the bottom of Ethan's death, but speaking in circles by the end of the evening. She was holding something back. Cutter was certain of that. Several times she'd seemed on the verge of some revelation, but then gone back to repeating the same merry-go-round of unsubstantiated rumors.

The call turned out to be Lola, from Officer Brackett's phone.

"My mobile's charging," she said, spilling words over the line in the giddy way of hers when she was excited about something—which was most every hour of the day. "Hope I'm not waking you, boss, but I feel like I need to let you know what's going on."

Cutter smiled in spite of the circumstances. Lola had been known to call him when she reached some personal best in the gym or needed advice about buying a new car. As supervisory deputy, he ran the task force. He was her boss, but she often treated him as a confidant, someone to share in important moments—like an uncle or older brother.

He reached his room and held the phone between his shoulder and his ear while he fished the key out of the pocket of his sweats. Tossing his shaving bag next to the duffel on one of the two twin beds, he stood at the frost-covered window looking out at the ice and snow.

It was after one in the morning. Lola had to be exhausted, but she ticked down the events with a linear clarity that belied her youth and apparent enthusiasm. Better than that, she began her monologue with: "Mim and the kids are safe and secure . . ."

"Smart," he said, after she'd given him a thumbnail of the past four hours. "Checking the aunt's real-estate website. So APD doesn't think Pool's involved with the murders?"

"He tried to murder me," Lola said. "But it doesn't look as though he's connected to the serial killings directly. He gave up the Tall Man in a heartbeat. Stalwart local businessman named Jeffery Grant Tolman, goes by Grant. Owns a bunch of self-storage facilities in Anchorage and Wasilla. Seems he's a regular client of Pool's services. No record of any police contact in APSIN. His DL says he's six-eight, two hundred and ten. Forty-two years old. Not particularly scary looking in the DL photo."

Cutter gave a knowing nod but didn't say anything. He and Lola both knew killers rarely resembled anything like the depraved maniacs that they actually were.

"He looks harmless, like a stick bug." Lola went on. "But Imelda is terrified of him. She overheard his name, but thought Pool was calling him Tall Man. According to her, a date with anybody was better than being set up with the Tall Man. I guess he's a biter."

"Makes sense," Cutter said. "Considering the butchery involved in the killings." He sat on the edge of his tiny bed and groaned, suddenly exhausted and wondering when he'd reach the limit of his ability to learn about the depravity of human beings. "And you think Imelda's friend, this Serafina, is one of Tolman's recent victims?"

"Tracks point that way, boss," Lola said. "Imelda gave her a pedicure and a gold toe ring—consistent with the severed limb found at Bootleggers Cove a couple of weeks ago. It hadn't been in the water long, which matches the timing for when Imelda last saw her. Detectives are getting some hair from her brush at Carson Pool's house to try and get a DNA match."

"Have they got Tolman in custody?"

"Not yet," Lola said. A stripper named Grace Ayuluk went missing a couple of nights ago. APD suspects Tolman has her and may be hiding evidence in one of his storage units—possibly even a body. Their thinking is we can follow him."

"What's this we, Lola? You've got to be running on fumes."

"Everyone is," she said. "Nancy Alvarez is already here. If you don't mind, I'm going to call out the rest of the team."

Alvarez was APD's representative to the Alaska Fugitive Task Force. It made sense that her brass would roll her out for something like this. "That's what we're for," he said, wishing he were there, in the thick of it.

"Nothing short of amazing here, to be honest," Lola said. "Every detective and special unit is saddled up. FBI is boiling out of all the cracks, like fire ants. I honestly forget how many people they have stationed here. It's like the jeans-police there are so many plain clothes coppers."

"The more the merrier for a good rolling surveillance," Cutter said. "Eyes on Tolman?"

"Not as of yet," Lola said, sounding glum. "No cars or lights at his residence of record. Trooper helicopter is standing by at Lake Hood. FBI pilots are about to get the 206 in the air."

"And the chief?"

"Briefing her as we go," Lola said.

"Very well," Cutter said. "Pace yourself."

"That's rich, boss," Lola said. "Coming from you, I mean."

"Just be careful. This could drag on for days."

"Roger that," Lola said. The line fell silent, and for a time, Cutter thought she had ended the call. Then, "Hey, Arliss . . ."

"Yes?"

"You think there could be some chance we could find this Grace Ayuluk alive?"

"Not likely," Cutter said. "But catch this Tall Man and you can make sure she's his last victim."

Cutter's phone buzzed with another incoming call.

"Call me anytime," he said. "No matter when, no matter why."

"Thanks, Cutter," she said, dropping the R so it sounded like Cuttah, in the pleasant Kiwi accent he'd become accustomed to.

He took the new call and was greeted with the harsher, hard R pronunciation of his name.

"Cutter?" Jan Hough said.

"I hope you're calling to tell me you found us a flight out," he said.

"Yeah," Hough said. "About that . . . Alaska Air charter flights are full. The oil companies will want their crews rotating home before this weather blows in. Plus, they're not too keen on having a bunch of felons on board. But don't you worry. I found a guy who just arrived tonight. He's got plenty of room for six passengers."

Cutter corrected her. "Five."

"Think you'd be able to take Richards with you?" she said.

"On the federal charges?"

"We'll still prosecute him for what he did to Tori," Hough said. "But he'll get out on bond by tomorrow morning if all we do is a telephonic hearing up here. He's such a hothead, I don't like the idea of him being around Tori right now. If you guys are planning to charge him, our judge wouldn't be able to cut him loose."

"I'm fine hauling him south," Cutter said. "As long as there's a seat for him on the plane."

He waited for Hough to say something else, something important.

She didn't.

"Okay," she said, "the pilot's name is Dave Larsen. Everyone calls him Mutt. Do me a favor and don't arrest him if you happen to cross paths before tomorrow morning."

Cutter feigned a polite chuckle. His phone buzzed again. A lot of incoming calls for the middle of the night. This one was better, though.

Mim.

"I've got another line," he said.

"Pick you up at 0600 for breakfast," Hough said. "Sleep fast."

Cutter ended the call and connected to Mim.

"Did you find a way out of Deadhorse?" Her voice was tight, distant, like she was trying to pay attention to something else while she spoke.

"Just now," Cutter said. He thought of telling her about the fight in the dining hall, and probably would, but not over the phone. She had too much going on. "We have to drop a prisoner in Fairbanks on the way, but I'm thinking I'll be home by three. Wish I could get back sooner, with everything going on."

"We're fine," she said—almost as prickly as Constance. "Everything is fine. Jill got us set up in a hotel, but now that seems pointless because they caught the bad guys."

"Not all the bad guys," Cutter thought, but there was no reason to suspect this Tolman character was a threat to Mim and the kids. Still, without the whole picture, Cutter felt helpless and uncertain. He picked up the sound of a deep sigh, and Mim softened a notch.

"It's just been a hell of a long day and it feels weird to be in a hotel with armed deputy marshals outside the door instead of my own house."

"I wish I was there."

"Well, that's not in the cards." She sighed again, sounding like she might apologize, but then did not. "The thing is, you would have probably just made it worse. Constance is, I don't know . . . We were having problems before this mess blew up with Audrey."

Mim customarily used him as a sounding board. She wasn't even coming close tonight. The line was silent for so long Cutter pulled the phone away from his ear to make sure they were still connected.

Finally, Mim said, "I've come to realize she and I don't have much in common."

"Does anyone have anything in common with a teenage girl, besides other teenage girls?"

"I suppose," Mim said, still far away. Then suddenly, "Arliss, are you . . . ?"

He counted to ten before prodding. "Am I what?"

"Nothing," Mim said. "We'll talk when you get home. I'm absolutely beat, and this shitty hotel mattress is . . . Never mind."

Cutter wanted to say, hey you called me, but instead settled for, "Yeah, sure. Of course. Get some rest."

She ended the call without another word.

Cutter usually had no problem keeping his imagination in check, but all bets were off when it came to Mim. Something was going on with her. She'd almost told him what it was—but then left him hanging. His third wife had been an expert at that—calling when he was hundreds of miles away on some high-threat trial or judicial protective assignment and spinning him up about something so inane that by the end of the conversation, he wasn't even quite sure what it was that he was supposed to be worried about. She'd done it out of spite, though. Mim had tried to reach out, but for some reason, she'd thought better of it.

Cutter sat on the edge of the bed and stared at the paneled wall. He wasn't really the television-watching type, which was good, because the room didn't provide that sort of nicety. There were two beds, with a footlocker and a small nightstand for each bed. A sign on both the outer door and the wall by the main overhead light switch warned that the hotel might well rent out the empty bed during the night, as well as the floor space, if more guests happened to arrive and there was nowhere else to put them.

Cutter stowed the Glock 27 in his shaving kit and then set the holstered Colt on top of that, inside his open duffel. He slid the duffel under his bed. It would be out of view to anyone who showed up during the night, but within easy reach if the need arose.

He lay on the lumpy mattress with a copy of *A River Runs Through It*, thinking he might read awhile to give his mind a break. No good. It didn't matter how hard he tried, his brain seemed to downshift and gain speed, paying no attention at all to the words on the page. He let the book fall to his chest and closed his eyes. The last few hours had provided exponentially more questions than answers.

A whistleblower at Ethan's engineering firm.

His alleged affairs.

His murder.

Jan Hough and Mim were both holding something back. And now there was a possibility he'd wake up with a stranger in the other bed and another rolled out on the floor.

It was going to be a very long night.

He turned out the lamp and then immediately switched it back on again.

Trying to sleep with so much on his mind was useless.

Sighing to himself, he leaned over the edge of the bed and fished the black notebook out of the vest he'd draped over his duffel beside the Colt Python. He sat up, leaning against the headboard while he thumbed through the pages. The little books were journals of sorts—a map of his thoughts for any given six months, a place to work through ideas. His mind just seemed to perform better when he had a pocketknife or pencil in his hand.

He turned to the first blank page and with the stub of a pencil he kept with every book, drew a circle in the center, and then in block letters, wrote: *ETHAN*.

CHAPTER 28

A team from APD Vice finally crossed paths with Jeffery Grant Tolman when he left one of his storage complexes off Dowling Road in South Anchorage just after four in the morning. He was driving a newer-model gunmetal Toyota Sienna van, not dark, like Chris Albany had thought. The vice officers watched the automatic gate roll shut as he left and then waited in place, calling out over the radio to warn the "take-away" cars stationed at intervals a block away that the subject was heading toward them.

As they suspected he might, Tolman made the block, passing in the front of the storage units again, presumably doing a heat check to see if all was the same as it had been when he pulled away just moments before. Apparently satisfied, he'd sped off for real this time, allowing the takeaway car to fall in behind once he'd made the next turn.

Other detectives stayed near the storage buildings,

search warrant in hand, but held off on their approach in the likely event that Tolman had the place wired with remote cameras. Nakamura had found a judge who was cooperative—or sleepy—enough to grant search warrants for all five of Tolman's known Anchorage properties, including his residence. He was just waiting for the right time to execute.

Unlike plain vanilla storage units, Tolman's more expensive ones were set up like man caves, with indoor plumbing, mini-bars, and sleeping quarters—condo versions of a traditional storage building. Leaseholders had a warm home away from home during the winter to work on classic cars, tinker with custom motorcycles—or fetishize the knickknacks that reminded them of violent murders.

There was always the chance that one of his victims was inside one of the units, but Nakamura and his bosses reasoned that if she was, she was already dead, and it was not worth risking the surveillance with a simultaneous raid.

The rolling vehicle surveillance was exciting and tense—the plum assignment, but the search teams at Tolman's businesses would be pivotal in eventually convicting the bastard.

The FBI made a pitch for command and control early on, insisting that they were much better equipped and trained for massive rolling operations like this one. APD brass held fast, taking all the help they could get, but keeping their deputy chief at the top of tactical command. He'd been an FBI Safe Streets task force officer, a SWAT sergeant, and then lieutenant over the Vice unit before being tapped for the more political position. Even the FBI had to admit he had the chops to run the show. The Bureau ASAC (assistant special agent in charge) and the colonel of the Alaska State Troopers both rode with the deputy chief in the command vehicle to make sure all their kids played nice together.

In the end, the commanders had twenty-seven vehicles to move around the chess board, leap frogging, racing forward, and falling back when necessary.

Lola marveled at the circus-like nature of the event. Simple unmarked cars didn't work for this sort of thing. Ford Expeditions and Chevy Tahoes were police vehicles even if they weren't. A true rolling surveillance required actual undercover vehicles: rattle-can-painted "meth fleet cars," inconspicuous mom-vans, utility trucks, and even a couple of Subarus. Brackett's pickup fit in nicely, blending with the other everyday drivers prowling the Anchorage streets in the early-morning darkness.

Cutter always said there were only three kinds of people on the road after midnight: paperboys, cops, and assholes. Fortunately for this op, Tolman had chosen to move when shift workers were beginning to venture out or returning home, not quite filling the streets, but providing some camouflage to the jeans-police that teemed like flies around the unsuspecting Tall Man.

Brackett and Lola were cooling their heels at the Holiday gas station on Muldoon when Tolman drove by heading toward the Glenn Highway.

"Unit following," Brackett said, giving his location and badge number. "Myself and Marshal 10 have the eye."

"Roger that," the other officer said. "We're getting a

little stale back here. Watch it, though, he's starting to get hinky." The unit, a white jeep that looked suspiciously like a mail truck, turned down a side street about the same time Brackett and Lola pulled out of the convenience store parking lot as if they'd just gotten gas.

Other units would be leap frogging ahead to the highway, in the event that Tolman went outbound on the Glenn or turned back toward town and his residence.

The FBI plane circled overhead, high enough not to be heard, low enough to keep tabs on the Toyota minivan—allowing for a loose tail.

Exhausted and half hypnotized from concentrating on Tolman's vehicle traveling down the dark streets, Lola sat up straight when the van's brake lights suddenly flashed and he whipped into the Holiday gas station a couple of blocks from the highway. Instead of going into the store or even parking, Tolman drove through the lot to the next entrance and watched traffic—including Brackett's truck—go by.

"Marshal 10," Lola piped into her radio, held low in her lap. "Another heat check at the Holiday station, 200 block of Muldoon." It was the first time she'd spoken over the radio in the past three hours and her voice was thick with fatigue.

"We're less than thirty feet from the bastard," she said to Brackett through clenched teeth, ignoring the Toyota as they passed.

Brackett crossed the highway toward the Tikahtnu shopping center, with its multiscreen theater, Texas Roadhouse, Lowe's, and several large anchor stores.

He smacked the wheel when the unit who now had the eye reported Tolman was outbound on the Glenn—apparently heading to Wasilla.

Brackett made a quick U-turn and punched it to keep up.

"It's okay," Lola said. "We don't have to be the ones to capture him. Trackers almost never get who they're tracking. They just provide the direction of travel for other assets to bound ahead and make the arrest."

Brackett grimaced. "Sounds like something Cutter would say to calm you down."

"Every damned day." Lola leaned her head back in a long, shuddering yawn. "You get used to it," she said. "So long as the bad guy is captured. Right?"

"Right. Smart guy, your boss."

Lola pushed up on the armrest with her elbow, working to find a position that didn't make her feel like she was still getting kicked in the ribs, and then nestled deeper into her seat. Brackett said something else, but she drifted off before she could hear what it was.

Lola woke with a jolt when the pickup rolled to a stop. She blinked, smacking her lips much louder than she'd intended as she tried to make sense of her surroundings.

"Morning, sunshine," Brackett said.

She held her arms out straight in a groaning, face-contorting stretch—cut short from the shot of pain across her ribs.

"What time is it?"

"Just after six."

She rubbed the sleep from her eyes. "Are you kidding me?"

Brackett chuckled. "Not a problem. You're a visitor to night shift. I live here. This is my normal."

Lola shifted in the seat again. There was no comfortable position, so in the end, she just gave up and let it hurt.

"Koko did a number on you," Brackett said. "You okay?"

"Right-as," Lola lied, down to half breaths to keep from expanding her rib cage. "Where we at? Tell me they got him."

"We're in the Target parking lot in Wasilla," Brackett said. "And you haven't missed anything. Tolman's been doing heat checks ever since he left Anchorage. He took us all on a merry ride the long way around Eagle River Loop, doubled back to Highland at the Landfill exit, and turned back again to come out here to the Valley."

"You think he knows he's being followed?"

"Beats me," Brackett said. "The bosses ordered us to fall way back and leave it to the FB Eye in the sky as soon as he did that back and forth in Eagle River. We're just now starting to move in closer again. Nakamura has the eye at the moment. Sounds like Tolman just went into the McDonald's a couple of blocks away."

Brackett's radio squawked. Nakamura's voice.

"Suspect is coming out," the detective said. "He's got a big bag of food and two tall coffees."

Lola nodded to a dumpster at the back edge of the lot. "Pull up there and block for me while I pee."

"Seriously?"

"What?" Lola grimaced from the nauseating bolt of pain brought on by her movement. "Guys go behind dumpsters all the time. Now step it up. I need to go, and my ribs are killing me. It's going to take a bit for me to get my pants down."

CHAPTER 29

*R*ollup had been early, leaving the prisoners sullen and quiet. Gene Richards began to sob when he learned he was being transported to Anchorage, away from the influence of a friendlier judge.

The thermometer outside read a balmy twelve below zero, leaving Cutter and everyone else in the van hunched down in their parkas like fluffed birds during a storm. Jan Hough was behind the wheel. Cutter sat behind her, yielding the front passenger seat to Bill Young. Regretting the decision before they'd gone a block, Cutter turned his face sideways, burying his nose in the thick wolverine parka ruff. The faint Windex smell of the tanned fur allowed him a measure of escape from Bill Young's Axe cologne and the prisoners' flatulence. Hough had brought the prisoners to-go boxes of chipped beef on toast—the ubiquitous SOS that could serve as breakfast, dinner, or wallpaper paste in a pinch. The disgusting odor in the back of the van said it was disagreeing with someone in a bad way.

Cutter should have been used to the smell. Human stink. His first three wives had called it some version of that. He'd come home with it on his suits a lot in the early days of his career, when he was a young POD— plain old deputy—working the cellblock in Miami or hooking and hauling vanloads of prisoners for cross-country trips. The odor of confinement was the closest thing Cutter had experienced to life in a third world country—spit baths, hand-rolled cigarettes, and the lingering essence of human excrement. There had been many times he would have burned his clothes if he hadn't been too poor to afford new ones.

Fortunately, the drive from the North Slope Borough offices to the airport was a short one.

Hough got on her phone a quarter mile out, timing it so the hangar staff had the massive door open just wide enough for them to squeeze the van through as they arrived. It began to rumble closed the moment they were inside.

The stadium lights inside the expansive hangar proved blinding after the leaden ice fog of outside. The van's tires squeaked and chirped on the freshly waxed concrete as Hough rolled to a stop at the tail of the only aircraft in the building, a waiting Cessna 208. The high-wing Caravan was a workhorse of the Arctic, as ubiquitous as pickups in Texas. With beefy wheel skis that could land on a regular runway or snow strip, this one was white with a midnight-blue underbelly.

Cutter left Bill Young standing next to the van to

watch the prisoners, and got out to meet the man in the open cargo door. He was busy stowing what looked like a ukulele shrouded in bubble wrap behind a cargo net at the tail of the aircraft.

Hough had identified him as the pilot, Mutt Larsen, when they pulled up.

Squatting in the relatively cramped interior of the Caravan, the man stowed a cardboard box beside the ukulele, continuing to work on the cargo as Cutter approached. Preoccupied, his brow knitted in deep thought about something. The man jumped slightly when Cutter cleared his throat. He duckwalked to the edge of the cargo door, extending his hand.

He had flyaway hair that was sure to be long gone by his fortieth birthday—likely not more than a year or two away—and a sad smile. His grip was firm, and he looked Cutter in the eye. The floor of the plane hit Cutter about shoulder level, making the pilot look down at him.

"Dave Larsen," he said. "Everyone calls me Mutt."

"Thanks for taking the contract last-minute," Cutter said. "Our admin officer should be calling you shortly with particulars, but I can put a deposit on my credit card."

Larsen waved that off. "I'm sure it's fine." He looked at Cutter like he was going to say more but decided not to.

Cutter leaned forward to get a quick look inside the plane. "Have you made a prisoner transport before?"

"Just onesies and twosies for the troopers," Larsen said. "Never hauled anyone for the US Marshals, and I've never had so many outlaws on board at one time."

Cutter gave a solemn nod. "That you know of."

"Touché." He eyed the van. "Anybody I need to be worried about? Hannibal Lecter maybe."

"Nothing like that," Cutter said. "But none of them are in custody for singing too loud in church. It's our policy to keep them in full restraints—handcuffs, belly chain, and leg irons."

Larsen gave an understanding nod. "Good. I'd prefer they didn't get out of their seats."

Cutter gave him something close to a smile. "Me too."

"Is that Gene Richards in there?"

Cutter nodded.

"What's the deal with him?"

"We were scheduled to fly out with him this morning," Cutter said. "Until he decided to fight me last night at supper."

"Yeah, he is kind of a hothead," Larsen said. "He swears I stole a couple of cargo routes from him. Not my biggest fan right now as you can imagine."

"Mine either," Cutter said. "Let us know when and we'll get them on board."

"We're about ready to go," Larsen said. "I'll get Bud to lower the stairs. He's my copilot of sorts."

Larsen whistled, and the airplane rocked as another man made his way back from where he'd been working in the cockpit.

He was a half a head shorter than Larsen with the beginnings of a salt and pepper beard that made him appear older than he probably was.

"Bud Bishop," he said, grinning at Cutter. "Mutt's

your pilot. I'm just a school teacher who happens to fly."

Larsen pointed forward toward the passenger door, and Bud scampered to take care of it.

"Ready when you are," Larsen said. "I'll give you all the safety brief at the same time. I won't mention it to them, but I have a shotgun with the other survival gear under the belly." The odd look returned. If there was something else that needed to be said, Mutt Larsen kept it to himself.

Cutter chalked it up to his imagination. He'd been immersed in conspiracy theories from the moment he stepped off the plane in Deadhorse.

Larsen secured the cargo strapping and hopped down to the hangar floor.

Cutter turned and waved his hand in a circle over his head letting Bill Young know it was time to roll.

Jan Hough, who'd been glued to her phone, came around from the driver's side to help unload.

The prisoners stepped out one by one, hampered in their movements by the restraints. Spivey and Lamp, old pros according to their rap sheets, used their elbows for balance as they negotiated the seats and doorway of the van. Nix and Richards were less balanced. Cutter and Young helped them down, using a plastic crate as an interim step.

Normally, Cutter would not have moved a prisoner in street clothes if he could have helped it. Orange, or even beige, jumpsuits and institutional slippers made it much more difficult to effect an escape. But as with so many things, it was different in Alaska. Each man had

traveled to the Arctic prepared for the weather to dif-
fering degrees. All of them had decent parkas. One
didn't venture this far north without one. All but Nix
had insulated pants or at least long underwear. Everyone but Lamp had decent boots. The gambler made do
with a pair of high-top basketball shoes, reasoning that
he worked inside and never intended to walk outside
except when he was going to or coming from a warm
vehicle. A life-long Alaskan, Bill Young was used to
the far north and dressed in layers of wool and fleece
he could add to or take off. Cutter considered himself a
better-than-average outdoorsman, but he spent a good
deal of time watching old-timers and copying them.
He wore three layers under the bulky Wiggy's parka
with the wolverine fur ruff, wolf and wolverine being
best for keeping breath condensation from freezing
around your face.

Cutter and Young had spent almost half an hour
searching everyone's parkas and other clothing for hidden pocketknives or other tools they might use to
throw a wrench in what Cutter intended to be a mundane transport.

Once the prisoners were unloaded, Cutter lined them
up outside the van. At Hough's suggestion, he'd stopped
by the stock room off the chow hall after breakfast.
Referred to as the Spike Shop, it was like a small con-
veniences store with all manner of sodas and snacks—
free for Slope workers. Cutter gave Hough forty bucks
to ease his conscience and loaded up on bottled water,
Pop-Tarts, and granola bars. He held back on the water,
but gave each prisoner a Pop-Tart. An old salt had reminded him early on that it sucked to be chained up,

and it might make things move a little more smoothly to allow some semblance of control, even if it was only letting the outlaws decide when to eat their own lunch.

Cutter did one last check of the prisoner packets, each with a photo and particulars of the corresponding outlaw taped to the front to aid in booking and, more important, quick identification in the unlikely event of a successful escape.

At Cutter's nod, Young boarded the aircraft first, while he and Hough assisted each prisoner to rattle and shuffle up the stairs one at a time. Young secured their seat belts as they boarded.

Last on, Cutter extended his hand to the North Slope Borough officer. "Thanks for your help, Jan."

Hough heaved a deep sigh, swallowed up in her heavy parka and overalls. She chewed on her bottom lip, keeping a tight grip on Cutter's hand.

"I wrestled with this all night," she said. "I should have been more forthcoming yesterday—but I know how it feels to be accused of something you didn't do."

Cutter pulled his hand away, waiting.

"You should talk to Erica Bell." Hough handed him a yellow Post-It with a phone number. "I spoke with her this morning. She's expecting your call."

"Erica Bell?"

"She worked at the firm with your brother," Hough said. "Same nasty rumors as there were about Ethan and me—though, he'd have hit the lottery with her. She's a hell of a lot prettier than I am. Anyway, sad to pull her back into this, but now you have everything I do."

Cutter stuffed the paper in his vest pocket.

"It's obvious you thought a lot of Ethan," he said. "Knowing him, I imagine the feeling was mutual. Would you mind if I call you periodically and compare notes?"

She gave a wan smile. "Honestly, that would mean the world to me. I loved your brother. Not like people thought—but he was a wonderful friend."

"I agree," Cutter said, turning away to clear the catch in his throat.

Larsen detached the support post under the tail and stowed it in the belly pod before climbing up his own ladder. To his credit, he ignored the glares from Gene Richards. The safety briefing was quick, thorough, and to the point—seat belts, the location of the fire extinguisher, and the survival gear in the belly pod. Bud Bishop checked the door to make certain it was secure, and then helped Cutter and Young with their green David Clark headsets before working his way into the cockpit.

This particular Caravan was equipped with seats for eight passengers and the two pilots. Leaving the front seat on the starboard side vacant, Young had placed three of the prisoners in the remaining seats on that side. He took up a position at the rear on the port side, nearest the cargo door. Richards was directly in front of him, leaving a vacant seat between the prisoners and Cutter, who sat directly behind the pilot.

It was cramped, but workable.

Cutter gave Bud Bishop a thumbs-up, and Larsen called the ground crew on the radio.

The massive hangar doors creaked open along their telescopic rails, and one of the ramp workers pulled the Caravan into the morning gloom with a tug attached to the nose gear.

A gust of cold wind caught them immediately, shaking the plane in its teeth.

Spivey, Lamp, and Nix all looked up, startled at the sudden jolt. Richards gave a scornful chuckle and shook his head. "Buckle up, kiddies. We're in for a bumpy ride with this shit bird at the controls." He nodded at Cutter. "Hope you have your life insurance up to date."

"How about you take a nap," Young said, bumping the back of his seat.

Larsen isolated the intercom while he made preparations for takeoff, leaving Cutter and Young able to communicate over their headsets.

Cutter shifted sideways as they started to move, keeping the prisoners behind him in view.

The takeoff roll was short. Rotation and liftoff came quickly on the cold, dense air.

Up front, Larsen banked the plane to the south. Oddly, Cutter thought, the pilot consulted a folded aeronautical chart on his knee, as if he didn't quite know where he was going.

The Dalton Highway, otherwise known as the Haul Road, ran between Deadhorse and Fairbanks, winding across the snow-swept tundra below like a silver ribbon.

With little to do but sit and stare out the frosted windows, the prisoners began the usual whining, asking for water and bathroom breaks. One led to the other, so the bottled water wouldn't be handed out until they were a little closer to Fairbanks.

Lamp, who sat at the rear of the airplane across

from Bill Young, began to complain about air sickness shortly after takeoff. Young held up a plastic grocery sack to use as puke bag and offered to hang it around the prisoner's ears. Lamp refused, and hung his head. Cutter suggested he nibble on his Pop-Tart to settle his stomach.

Cutter heard nothing but the droning whir of the airplane for a time, then Young's voice came across Cutter's headset. "I just talked to a friend with AST," he said. "Sounds like the troops are closing in on the SOB who's murdering all those girls."

"Hope so," Cutter said, the little boom mic touching his lips.

"Hard to imagine someone that depraved," Young said, obviously getting a little lonely in the back of the plane. "And that's coming from a guy who worked corrections for thirty years. They were hot on his tail when we took off. I heard one of the poor things had a new pedicure . . . I hope they grab the murderous bastard."

Cutter half turned. Young spoke into his mic, but with his ears covered by the headset, he didn't realize the prisoners were listening to every word he said.

"Keep your voice down, Bill," Cutter said. "We have some big ears back there."

"Copy," Young said, suddenly flustered at his gaffe. "I should know better than that."

"No worries," Cutter said. He kept his voice low, nearly eating the little mic on his headset. "Hopefully the arrest will be old news by the time we hit Fairbanks. If not, we may have to keep these guys isolated for a bit."

"Shit!" Young said. "Shit, shit, shit. I am really sorry, Arliss."

"We're good," Cutter said, tamping back a feeling that something was off. Again, he chalked it up to seeing conspiracies in every corner.

Then he looked out the window and noticed the Haul Road—that should have been directly below them—was nowhere to be seen.

CHAPTER 30

*T*he radio squawked—the FBI aircraft. "Rabbit is westbound on the Parks Highway . . . turning left on . . . Knik Goose Bay Road."

Brackett hit the steering wheel again. "KGB Road," he said. "It makes sense. All kinds of country out there for him to hide in."

Nakamura ordered all the ground units to hang back, relying on the Bureau plane to relay information.

An hour later, Tolman was still driving, passing the Goose Bay airstrip, cutting inland toward the prison, and then turning again toward Point MacKenzie.

"This guy is paranoid as hell," Brackett said.

Lola eyed him sideways. "I guess you'd be running heat checks too, if you had girls chained to your basement wall."

The FBI pilot came over the radio again.

"Forty minutes until I'm bingo fuel," he said.

Less than a minute later, the special agent in charge spoke. "Stay on station as long as possible. Nguyen and Welborn will meet you at Goose Bay strip with fuel when needed." The big bosses had returned to APD headquarters, monitoring from the comfort of a warm office—much to the relief of everyone else running the surveillance.

The radio bonked, coming in garbled as someone spoke over top of the FBI SAIC. It turned out to be the pilot.

"Rabbit just turned southeast onto a property off Point MacKenzie Road. Area is heavily wooded beside the road, but it thins out to sparse birch and spruce . . . fifty meters or so in."

The pilot gave the coordinates.

Ever the hunter, Lola couldn't help but grin as Brackett stood on the gas. Units converged from every possible direction. The AST helicopter thundered overhead, seeming to appear out of nowhere as it swooped in from the east.

The FBI pilot spoke again. "Subject's driving behind what looks to be a dwelling. No other vehicles. A couple of outbuildings. Storage sheds. Those units coming up the driveway now, he's spotted you. He's still in his van." The FBI pilot spoke directly to the trooper helicopter. "AST One, if you'd like to make your presence known, that might be helpful."

"Roger that," the chopper pilot said. "Moving above the scene now. Hey, I'm getting a heat signature on the FLIR from one of the small structures behind the barn. Storage . . . No . . . Maybe a shipping container."

The FLIR, or forward-looking infrared, camera easily picked up the image of a human being—running or hiding. It couldn't see through walls, but it did register heat.

The radio was silent for a moment as the FBI plane circled, corkscrewing lower. "We're seeing it too. House and barn appear to be empty. Ground units, suggest you use caution around the shipping container east/southeast—between the back of the barn and the water."

Brackett made the turn into the gravel drive, barreling down the road followed by a parade of at least six other vehicles.

"The bastard's heating that container for some reason," he said. "He brought breakfast and coffee for two. I guess he could have someone in there helping him with a weed grow . . ."

"Or maybe it's Grace Ayuluk," Lola said.

Detective Nakamura, to whom the APD deputy chief had given tactical control, dismounted his vehicle behind Tolman's van. No fewer than twenty handguns and rifles pointed directly at the man's head.

Tolman stuck both hands out his side window, following Nakamura's verbal commands. He opened the door from the outside and then unfolded himself from the van, walking backward until Nakamura told him to stop.

Brackett gasped. "Damn! That is one freaky-tall son of a bitch."

The detective shot him a quick glance. "Your lead got us here, kid. If the two of you want to cuff him, be my guest."

Brackett and Lola holstered their weapons and

moved forward, keenly aware of all the gaping muzzles now pointed in their direction.

Lola stepped to the side while Brackett pulled Tolman's hands behind his back and cuffed him. She rolled her shoulders, the adrenaline that came with every capture chased away much of the pain in her ribs, but it would return. She was certain of that.

Tolman laughed. "I thought I saw someone behind me in Anchorage this morning." He half turned until Brackett gave him a *tsk-tsk* and warned him to face away. "How did you figure out it was me?"

Brackett ignored him, doing a quick pat down for weapons.

Tolman stole another glance over his shoulder, then chuckled again. Genuinely amused. "Frankly," he said. "I am flattered that you believed it would take this many of you." He tipped his head toward the shipping container. "The girl you're looking for is in there. She's terrified if I've done anything right, but still very much alive last time I checked."

"You don't seem very concerned," Lola said.

"I guess I'm really not," Tolman said. The chuckle again, condescending. "Because I still have a card to play."

CHAPTER 31

*C*utter wasn't a pilot, but he made it a habit to glance periodically at the instruments when he flew in small aircraft—which had turned out to be all the time since he'd moved to Alaska. Mutt Larsen had kept the Caravan at a steady 4,500 feet above the ground, cruising the valleys and skimming above patchy clouds. Cutter's ears buzzed, as they often did when equalizing during a scuba dive. He glanced up and saw they were now at 3,000 feet and in a slow descent.

Larsen and Bishop chatted between themselves with animated gestures. Whatever they were talking about seemed awfully important. Their comms were still isolated, so Cutter had no idea what they were saying.

He unsnapped his seat belt and leaned forward, tapping the back of Bishop's seat. The young man jumped as if he'd been bitten, but turned a knob to bring the cockpit back online with the rear intercom.

"What's up, Marshal?"

"You tell me," Cutter said. "We can't be any closer than halfway to Fairbanks, and yet we appear to be going down."

"Just a quick jog to the east," Larsen said. "Had to check on something."

"Due respect, Mutt," Cutter said. "Check on things when we don't have four felons in the back of your airplane."

Larsen nodded as if he understood and agreed, but continued to descend—more rapidly now that Cutter was onto him. Mountains loomed to the east and west. Rivers and streams, lined with trees in an otherwise treeless landscape, braided countless valleys and canyons. Variations of white and silver, everything was still frozen as if locked in perpetual winter.

"No!" Larsen gasped. "No, no, no!" He banked the plane to his left.

Cutter saw immediately what had him worried. On the valley floor directly below them, tucked in among a long copse of scraggly spruce and scrub willow, slumped the charred remains of a two-story building. A remote cabin, or maybe a small lodge, Cutter thought. Like many relatively modern shelters in bush Alaska, this one was built of plywood and traditional lumber instead of logs. A smaller structure beside it had partially burned as well. From Larsen's reaction and the looks of the melted snow around the buildings, the fire had been recent.

Several sets of tracks crisscrossed the snow. There were no people in sight, dead or living, but as Larsen brought the plane around, Cutter could plainly see that many of the tracks were those of a very large bear.

"Does someone you know live here?" Cutter asked.

"Marie Baglioni," Larsen said, scanning so furiously Cutter thought he might forget to fly the airplane. "A friend of mine. She's doing climate and permafrost studies with a couple of interns from UAF. I've been trying to reach her on the radio for two days. Her generator's been acting up, so I didn't really worry at first—"

"I got a brown bear off the right wing," Bishop said. "Holy mackerel!"

"No, no, no," Larsen said again. "It got really warm in early March . . . before it fell off cold again. These long days must have woken him up early."

Cutter didn't say it, but they all knew what Larsen was thinking.

The bear would be hungry.

Larsen brought the plane in just over the treetops, buzzing the bear to try to scare it off. Cutter judged this one to stand a good seven feet tall and weigh close to eight hundred pounds, large for an interior grizzly that lived on berries, ground squirrels, and the occasional caribou calf instead of the steady fish diet of the much bigger coastal brownies.

"That is one huge boar," Young said, confirming Cutter's theory. "Really big for these parts."

Highly interested now that they might get to witness a bear mauling, the prisoners pressed faces against their respective windows, watching the show.

Young spoke again. "He's circling that little—"

"That's the outhouse," Larsen said. "Marie and the others must be hiding in there."

Spivey's laugh buzzed against the window glass. "That's a shitty place to die."

Larsen was too preoccupied to hear. Cutter ignored him.

They buzzed the bear again, low and loud.

Cutter caught a glimpse of a person in a parka when they went by, perched at the top of a gnarled spruce.

"That's Noah Sam," Larsen said, as they flew over and the young Native man gave them a frantic wave. "He's one of Marie's interns."

The tree was twenty feet tall at best and bowed under the weight of the man in the parka. The only reason the bear hadn't dragged Noah Sam down was because it hadn't yet tried. It was still focused on the outhouse.

The second pass made even less of an impact on the animal than the first, hardly even earning an upward glance from the massive face. Instead, the bear stood on its hind legs and began to shove against the side of the tiny building with its forepaws.

Larsen was incredibly low now, and it seemed the bear could have reached up and swiped them out of the sky if it had wanted to.

"This one has seen planes before," Young said.

Larsen adjusted his flaps. "I'm setting us down."

Cutter glanced at the prisoners and then at Young, who nodded, understanding that he would remain at the plane. There was no other choice to make.

"How easy is it to get to your shotgun?" Cutter asked, pressed against his seat as Larsen banked hard toward the snow-covered landing strip that ran in front of the burned buildings.

"Easy," Larsen said. "But I wouldn't mind if you and your Colt came with me."

Cutter watched as a gnarly spruce at the near end of the strip appeared to grow in size, remaining stationary to the nose of the aircraft as they descended. The plane flared, continuing to bleed speed. The stall warning squealed, and the skis settled onto the crusty snow with a loud, clattering hiss.

Larsen was out of his harness the moment the aircraft slid to a stop.

The outhouse was tucked out of sight behind the buildings, a couple hundred feet from the landing strip and the now-stone-quiet airplane.

A light snow began to sift down as if on cue as soon as they landed.

"I'll take care of the plane," Bud Bishop said, not keen about getting out with the bear running loose.

"Keep your seats," Cutter said to the prisoners.

"What if we have to pee?" Spivey smirked.

Cutter set his teeth. "Bill," he said. "If they move, deal with them."

"Happy to," Young said.

Mutt Larsen slipped and fell on the ice as soon as he left the plane, scrambling toward the belly pod before he'd even regained his footing. He ripped open the door and dragged out the survival pack, strewing shotgun shells and other gear onto the snow.

"Shit!"

"Slow down," Cutter cautioned. "You can't help your friend if you shoot your foot off . . . or mine for that matter."

Larsen gave a noncommittal nod, but he took a deep breath. A good sign. Rummaging through the bag, he came up with a red twelve-gauge slug and dropped it into the open breech of a simple over and under survival gun. The lower barrel was chambered for shotgun shells, the smaller, upper barrel for .22 caliber rimfire.

He snapped the gun closed and flicked a gloved hand toward the trees, starting off at a trot.

Cutter wore thin wool glove liners, but let the heavy beaver mittens dangle beside his parka.

"You're bringing more rounds?" he asked. "Right?"

Larsen reached in his coat pocket and came out with a handful of shotgun shells—all bird shot from the look of them. Not optimum, but exponentially better than the tiny .22 when it came to bear defense.

Cutter left the .357 in its holster and followed, unwilling to get in front of a panicked man wielding a shotgun.

Repeated landings and takeoffs had packed the airstrip, making for slick, but relatively unencumbered travel. Larsen sank to his knees when he stepped off the edge, wallowing, holding the shotgun up with both hands to keep it out of the snow.

Cutter stopped in his tracks, listening.

"Does your friend have a dog?"

Frenzied barks came from the far side of the burned structure, muffled, like they were coming from inside a barrel or the bottom of a well.

"A big Tamaskan," Larsen said. "Looks just like a wolf, so don't shoot him."

Cutter nodded and they started moving again.

The going was more than difficult, and the men post-holed to midcalf even when they found a trail of relatively packed snow. Unaccustomed to the repetitive movement of lifting their knees to their waist each time they took a step, both were sweating despite the near-zero temperatures and panting heavily by the time they rounded the burned timbers that had once been the back of the main dwelling.

A hoarse "woof" greeted them from the trees.

A male voice, high in the spruce, shouted a warning. Noah Sam.

"Bear! Forty feet to your right!"

Cutter turned, drawing the Colt, and faded out a few steps so he was beside Larsen and would have a clear shot.

"Hey, bear!" Cutter said, firmly, but not threateningly. He'd learned even as a boy in the Florida swamps, you didn't threaten something as big and potentially aggressive as a bear—black or brown. You left it alone, asked it to leave you alone—or you killed it. That seemed to go double with these interior grizzlies.

Another "woof" came from the shadows.

"Marie!" Larsen shouted, shotgun at his shoulder, pointed at the trees. They moved forward until they could see the outhouse, a sturdy structure of weathered gray plywood, almost hidden behind a large willow. "Marie! It's me. Where are you?"

Branches crashed and snapped, causing both men to swing left, until they realized it was Noah, shimmying down the spruce.

A female voice cried out, "Mutt!"

The muffled barking grew louder and more frenzied.

Then the bear appeared, silently, suddenly just there amid the underbrush thirty feet away. It rose effortlessly onto its back legs and canted a massive head from side to side, staring at the men with dark pig-eyes. Interior grizzly or not, this one was huge, the top of its ears above the ridgeline of the outhouse—at almost eight feet tall.

Larsen fired at the same instant the bear dropped to all fours. The shot shook the snow, but it went high, passing harmlessly over the bear's head.

"Reload!" Cutter said, his eyes fixed on the bear over the sights of his Colt Python at low ready.

The big boar tilted its head again, as if considering which one of the men to eat first—and then simply turned and ambled back into the brush.

Larsen ejected the spent shell and dropped in a round of bird shot, snapping the gun closed with an overaggressive thunk. "Marie—"

The outhouse door creaked open slowly. A female voice tried vainly to shush the dog. "Fig! Be quiet!" Then more tentatively asked, "Mutt?" A fur hat with dangling earflaps obscured much of the roundish face that peeked through.

A second head poked out, disheveled red curls spilling from beneath a wool beanie pulled low. Piper, the other UAF intern.

The two women and a large dog that did indeed look like a wolf all but exploded out of the tiny outhouse once the door came open. It was difficult tell much about them in the bulky red Canada Goose parkas favored by Arctic and Antarctic explorers alike.

Noah tromped through the snow, wearing an identical red parka, sinking to his knees, huffing and puffing from effort and fear, looking over his shoulder with every step.

The Native youth sniffed the air. "The word my grandmother used for grizzly literally means 'smells like dung.' It's still out there."

Larsen found the packed trail and ran to the women while Cutter watched the spot where the bear had disappeared. Noah was right. The bear was close.

CHAPTER 32

"*I*'m going to ask you this one time," Captain Osborne said, standing at the open door to Detective Nakamura's back seat.

Hands cuffed behind his back, Grant Tolman adjusted his posture to take the pressure off his wrists and gave a wan smile.

He smirked. "Just where do you think we are, Captain? Iran? North Korea? What? You're going to ask me once and then start pulling out my toenails?"

Lola shrugged in spite of herself, thinking that sounded like a good idea.

"You know very well," Tolman continued, "that you will ask me the same question over and over ad nauseum, even if I give you the same exact answer each time."

The captain closed his eyes, grinding his teeth. "Listen, Ichabod, is that shipping container rigged with anything that will hurt us? Explosives? Booby traps?"

Tolman blinked up at him, forehead against the seat in front of him. "No," he said. "That isn't the card I have left to play."

"You're sure?"

"And there you go," Tolman said. "Just like I thought. That's the same question twice."

Nakamura put a hand on the captain's shoulder and pretended to have an important question, leading him away before he did anything to jeopardize the case.

Tolman craned his head and looked at the shipping container out the opposite passenger window before turning back to Lola and Brackett. "I could pinky swear if that would carry more weight. But I promise you, we didn't rig anything to explode. What's the fun in that?"

Voices in front of the metal container rose, indicating something was happening. Officer Pagan nodded to Brackett. "Knock yourself out, kid. It's one more report that I don't have to write if I stay here with the prisoner."

Brackett and Lola hoofed it quickly across the clearing, past a stump and an overturned wheelbarrow that would surely get more scrutiny later.

Nakamura cut the padlock with a pair of bolt cutters and swung the latch. The door opened with an eerie groan, revealing a terrified woman cowering on a mattress in the back corner. She wasn't chained, which Lola found odd. In fact, she was well stocked, with juice boxes, a six-pack of bottled water, and as many empties. Trash from various fast-food joints littered the metal floor. A plastic bucket in the opposite corner served as her toilet.

Two small LED bulbs on the ceiling cast a pool of

eerie blue light in the center of the container but made the edges of the boxy interior feel that much darker.

Detective Nakamura led the way in, turning off his flashlight so it didn't shine in the girl's face.

"Anchorage Police," he whispered. Even then she pressed against the wall, visibly flinching at each word. "I'm Lee Nakamura. Are you Grace?"

Her chest began to heave. She nodded. Blinking back tears. Breaking down. Nakamura shot a glance at Lola, the nearest female with a badge.

"If you don't mind . . ."

Lola stepped forward. Wincing, she crouched down to bring herself eye to eye with the terrified woman. She reached out with an open hand. "My name is Lola," she said softly. "US Marshals. Grace, we got him. You're free."

Wrapped in a blanket in the back of an ambulance, Grace Ayuluk proved to be remarkably resilient, despite her ordeal. A female paramedic started an IV and got fluids going.

Ayuluk demanded to know about her little boy first, refusing to answer any more questions until she found out who had him and that he was safe. As soon as the captain assured her she would be seeing him soon, she provided a brutally clear picture of Grant Tolman and what he'd done to her.

She told them how she'd been taken outside the hotel, and then got teary when she rehearsed how she'd woken up in what she thought would turn out to be her own grave.

Tolman had assaulted her, many times, but Nakamura encouraged her to wait until she got to the hospital and had a full examination to go over the details with a female investigator.

She choked back a quiet sob. "Did you find the pit?"

Nakamura perked up at that. "Pit?"

"Grant . . . that piece of shit . . . chained me up and took me back there once." Her eyes remained distant, unfocused. "He said I should look at it so I could understand what was happening to me."

Lola and the others were silent, letting Ayuluk speak at her own pace.

She took a deep, shuddering breath and then looked up, steadier now. "There's a pit behind the container, I don't know, fifty feet maybe, behind a dirt berm in the trees. They . . ." She clenched her eyes shut.

Nakamura was on the radio, sending part of the search team to check out the trees behind the shipping container. One of the officers came back almost at once, hollow.

"Send a supervisor behind the container," the officers said. "We have a shallow depression with partially burned remains."

"Remains?" Detective Nakamura said, stepping away.

Grace Ayuluk heard him and glanced up at Lola. "Heads and hands," she said. "Grant told me they planned to cut mine off too, so no one could identify my body if it was found."

Brackett gasped in spite of himself. "Shit."

Ayuluk shuddered again. "He thought it was fun to torment me, telling me twisted stories like that. I got the impression they were trying to find another girl. He said there were always two, one to watch while they . . . did things to the other."

"Shit . . ." Brackett gasped again under his breath.

Lola took over at Nakamura's silent nod. "I hate to ask this, but did you ever see any other captives? Other women like you?"

Ayuluk shook her head, still flinchy. "No. I guess the girl before me pissed them off so they killed her early or something. Maybe she tried to escape or . . . or maybe she just died. They never told me so, but whatever happened, I could tell it screwed up their plans." Her frail shoulders trembled. "Eventually . . . they would have gotten someone to watch them do all those things to me . . . That asshole, Grant, would sit in there and eat his sandwich and tell me all about it, calm as ice, like he was talking about the weather. I know there were cameras in there. He knew things. You know? Things I did while he was gone and he'd locked me in, like trying to unscrew a bolt near the door. I think they put it there to give me something to work on. Give me false hopes . . ."

Nakamura spoke again. More softly this time. "Who else besides Grant Tolman?"

"Tolman?" Ayuluk mused, blinking her eyes like she might drift off. "That's his name? I guess it makes sense . . . Tolman . . . Tall Man . . . I never saw the other guy. Only Grant. But he was always talking about someone else. Whoever his partner is, he's the one coming back soon with a new girl. . . ."

"Did Tolman ever mention a name?" Lola asked.

"No—" Ayuluk grabbed her jaw. "My tooth is broken . . ." She rolled her arm, wincing from the act of moving it so quickly. "And I think that asshole popped out my shoulder last time he . . ." Her voice trailed off.

The paramedic shot Nakamura a stern look.

"Okay," the detective said. "Let's get you to a hospital. We'll talk later today, after you've rested—"

"And seen my son," Ayuluk said.

Tolman was smiling when they got back to the car. Lola fought the urge to stomp on his balls . . . or worse.

Nakamura flung open the door. "Who's your partner?"

Tolman chuckled. "And there we go," he said. "My ace in the hole. I'm sure the little woman has told you what I did with her."

"To her," Lola said, in spite of herself.

"True enough." Tolman gave a little shrug, looking Lola up and down in an effort to intimidate her.

She felt her temperature rising, but a nudge from Brackett caused her to wave it off.

"I'll be quite happy to confess to everything Grace told you—kidnapping, even the assault . . ." He smiled, remembering the moments. "Assaults. In any case, I'll give you all of that and the name of my partner in these misadventures, so long as I am not charged with the murders. He killed them. All of them. I had no hand in that. Get a lawyer here and I'll make it official."

One of the crime scene techs came trotting up, iPhone in hand. "You need to see this." He held the phone out to Nakamura, then whispered something in his ear.

The detective studied the image, enlarging it to look more closely at something. He was smiling when he turned back to Tolman.

"Any deal with you just seems wrong to me." He crinkled his nose as if it tasted bad. "It'd be great if you confess, but I'm thinking we'll go ahead and charge you and your partner for every murder. It shouldn't take the lab too long to match our list of missing women with the remains you kept in your pit behind the container."

Captain Osborne strode up as Nakamura slammed the door on a bewildered Tolman.

"Get this piece of shit to the station for a taped interview," Osborne said. "I just got off the phone with the Mat-Su Borough tax office. This parcel of land comes back to Edward Nix."

Lola's mouth went dry. "Did you say Nix?"

"That's right." Nakamura held the crime scene tech's phone so she could see it. "The placard on the side of the container has been scraped, but the name is still readable. NIX TRUCKING."

Lola snatched the cell from her pocket and punched in the number for Cutter's satellite phone. It failed to connect. That made sense. He used it for making calls, not receiving them, and usually kept it powered off in his pack. Lola thought over her options, then called Jan Hough in Deadhorse.

Mutt Larsen and his airplane were out of radio range for the moment, but she gave Lola his sat phone number. Hopefully, the pilot would have his on.

CHAPTER 33

Nix knew Chance Spivey just well enough to trust him to be Chance Spivey—which meant he was certain to wreak havoc whenever and wherever the opportunity presented itself. If there was something to break, he'd break it. It was his nature. Not as big or smart as Gene Richards, Spivey's lack of any semblance of an emotional governor made him twice as imposing and exponentially more dangerous. Years of getting thrown off bucking horses made pain a relative thing, forging him into a hard man to put down in a fight.

Nix was counting on it.

Bill Young had moved to the front of the plane and was half turned, busy chatting with Bishop. He'd left his parka at the rear of the aircraft on the back of his seat. His fleece vest hiked up over his belt, exposing his sidearm—a revolver, simple and straightforward to use.

"I've been to prison," Nix lied, leaning forward to whisper to Spivey. "And I don't feel like going back."

Spivey gave a slight nod, fuming, staring at Young's gun. "That guy was a hack last time I was in Goose Creek."

"Richards's a pilot," Nix whispered. "We'll toss these two and he can fly us out of here while the marshal is gone."

Richards rolled his eyes. "I'm not flying you shit-birds anywhere."

"Fly yourself out then," Nix said. "We'll just come along for the ride." He leaned in closer to Spivey, lowering his voice even more. "You and me can take the guard. Richards will get on board with everything once he sees we mean business."

The big cowboy gave a slow, cave-man nod. "Okay . . ."

"Follow my lead," Nix whispered. "I'll call him to check on my cuffs. He won't do shit to loosen them, but when he turns to go back up, you grab his gun. I'll join in and we'll take care of business. Then we're off the ground in no time."

This earned another sullen nod from Spivey.

Nix raised his voice, calling out, "Hey, Marshal."

Young looked back, annoyed, but stayed where he was, in the middle of some story.

"Come on," Nix pleaded. "These cuffs are tightening up on me. I think my hand's about to fall off."

"Pipe down and keep still," Young said. "I'll check on them when the others come back."

"I'm serious," Nix said. "It'll be your ass when they have to amputate my—"

The satellite phone in the cockpit began to ring.

The little bearded dude answered it, then listened for a few seconds before his mouth fell open. He turned and shot a terrified look at Nix.

"Go now!" Nix whispered.

Spivey humped up. "Now?"

The guard followed the kid's gaze at the prisoners, they froze, like lions caught midstalk. Then he made the mistake of turning again to the cockpit to get more information about the phone call.

Spivey lunged the instant his back turned.

The interior of the Cessna Caravan was small and even hampered as he was by the leg irons, Spivey had his hands around the gun in a flash. Nix followed, shuffling forward, nearly tripping himself from stomping on his own chain.

Richards growled behind him, but Lamp dove in front, tying him up in a tangle of leg irons and handcuffs, preventing him from rendering aid to the embattled guard.

All in now, Spivey held fast to the gun. He gave Young a brutal headbutt to the temple, staggering him backward so he fell into the forwardmost seat.

Nix slid the crook of his arm over Young's head, and down around his windpipe as best he could with his wrists affixed to the chain around his waist. He threw his body sideways, jerking Young away from Spivey.

Young roared when he saw what had happened. He redoubled his efforts to get free, lifting Nix off the ground as he staggered forward toward the cockpit.

"Help me!" he gurgled to the bearded kid.

Spivey pressed the revolver against the guard's ribs and pulled the trigger.

The gunshot was deafening inside the closed cabin.

Young staggered, bellowed again, but there was no life in it.

Bud Bishop scrambled out of the cockpit and jumped between the seats into the fray. Spivey fired wildly, striking the kid with two rounds. A third shattered the glass instrument panel, bringing a plume of black smoke from the engine compartment.

"You idiot," Richards screamed from the rear of the aircraft. "You hit a fuel line! It's spraying on hot metal."

Flames began to lick the cowling. Smoke poured from the engine quickly to obscure the prop. In seconds, it began to fill the cabin.

More familiar with the plane than the others, Richards was able to work the cargo door latch quickly despite the cuffs and belly chain. He shoved it open with his shoulder and jumped without looking back.

Lamp followed him out, grunting when his knees slammed into the ice.

Frigid air flooded the plane, giving momentary relief from the cloying smoke. The fire grew quickly, fed by vaporized Jet A spewing out of ruptured lines and fanned by the wind. Nix wasn't sure how much fuel was on the plane, but he knew it was a lot. There was a tank up front near the nose gear, and the wings were full of it.

Hacking and coughing, Nix rummaged frantically through the dead guard's vest pockets. For this to work, he'd need a handcuff key. He found a small pocketknife and shoved it in his boot, then located the single speed loader for the Smith & Wesson. Spivey had shot four times, and they were going to need a lot more than two rounds to take care of the marshal when he got back.

Tears streaming down his face, Nix was unable to see anything but Spivey's shadow in the clouds of noxious yellow-black smoke. He shoved Bill Young's body aside. "The key." He fell into a momentary coughing fit. "We . . . need . . . that key!"

Heat from the fire was already melting the instrument panel.

Spivey bumped him with his shoulder, moving toward the cargo door—and fresh air. "I got it already! Now move!"

The handcuff key was on a six-inch bar of milled aluminum. Meant for close quarters self-defense, this Kubotan made it easy for a deputy or guard to keep track of, but was cumbersome enough to slow Spivey down when he tried to manipulate the key while in handcuffs himself. He was able to get one cuff off shortly after he hit the ice. This freed him of the belly chain but left the other bracelet dangling from his right wrist. Richards had already made it off the packed airstrip to deeper snow, trying, no doubt, to gain enough distance he could warn the marshal.

"Stop him!" Nix shouted.

Lamp, who floundered just behind Richards, reached for him, caught the leg of his pants, and then sank to his knees.

Eyes fixed on Richards as he moved, Nix ran head-long into Spivey, making him drop the key.

"I'll get it," Nix said. "You have to stop him!"

Richards was up again, easily disengaging himself from the much smaller Lamp.

Marshal Cutter had insisted they roll their boot tops down that morning when he'd applied the leg irons, leaving them unlaced and floppy, which further encumbered their flight.

Under other circumstances, Nix would have laughed at the awkward ballet of the men's skipping lope after one another through the snow, trying to keep from tripping themselves with the short stride of the leg irons.

Steel bracelets bit their ankles at every step. Short chains made progress jerky at best and threatened to upend them if they attempted to go too fast.

But Spivey had an advantage. He'd spent the better part of three years in prison, gaming with other inmates, tying pieces of string between their institutional deck shoes and practicing the short-stride runs necessitated by leg irons.

Looking almost graceful, he caught up to a wheezing Gene Richards less than fifty yards off the nose of the airplane, which was now fully engulfed. From Nix's point of view, it was a beautiful sight, watching Spivey hop forward to stomp on the other man's leg chain, slamming him face-first into the snow.

Nix and Lamp reached them moments later, pulling up short to give Spivey room to do what they all knew he was going to do. Richards lay on his back, half buried where he'd fallen through the crust—a snow coffin. He looked skyward, panting thick clouds of white vapor with each breath. A cutting breeze blew flecks of snow on his lashes.

Fear flashed in his eyes. Nix smiled and gave Spivey a nod.

Richards tried to raise his arms, but the chain kept them low, at his belly, unable to fight or even protect himself.

"I got no love for Cutter," he said, gazing up, panting harder now. Pleading. Begging. "Hell, he's why I'm in here. But he's a fed. You get the needle for that."

Snow began to fall harder. Nix shot a glance over his shoulder. Still no sign of the marshal.

"Do it and let's get out of here."

Richards let his head fall back in the snow, apparently resigned to his fate. "Where you gonna go? You're miles from anywhere."

Spivey kept the revolver aimed at Richards's face. "I'll tell you where I'm not gonna go," he said. "I'm not going back to the joint. I'd rather take my chances out there."

"That's because you've never spent time 'out there' not in weather this cold." Richards's face relaxed. He smiled softly, closing his eyes. "Feel that? That's the cold seeping into your bones. Killing me isn't going to warm you—"

"Worth a try, though," Spivey said, and pulled the trigger.

CHAPTER 34

*C*utter crouched instinctively at the staccato cracks bouncing off the trees. He waved the others behind him. Snow dampened the shots, but he'd been down-range enough to know exactly what the sound was.

Where he grew up in Florida, one shot might mean a snake. Three could be a signal. Four was the sound of serious trouble.

Larsen gave him a worried glance. "You think the bear made it all the way to the plane? Maybe they're trying to scare him off?"

"I hope that's all it is," Cutter said, already moving. "But do me a favor and keep an eye on the trees, just in case it's something else and the bear is still watching us."

The group moved as one, none of them wanting to be too far from the guns.

A mushroom cloud of black smoke rose above the

trees before they'd gone ten steps. Cutter froze, listened for more gunfire, any sound that might give him a clue.

"My plane!" Larsen gasped. He took a step, like he was going to run ahead, but Cutter grabbed the sleeve of his parka.

"Listen to me," he said. "Someone over there has a gun, and it may not be my guard. Let's go, but let's go smart."

Even retracing their original tracks made for an agonizingly slow process, post-holing, high-kneeing for every step forward.

The Cessna Caravan was fully engulfed by the time Cutter rounded the charred ruins of the cabin. Oily black smoke boiled and rolled off tongues of fire. Intense heat had turned the snow and ice directly around the aircraft into a sizzling, steaming lake.

Black and orange flames against the otherwise white background were hypnotic. The crack of another gunshot on the frigid air jerked Cutter's attention to the right. Half a football field away off what had once been the nose of the airplane, two prisoners huddled together around something on the snow and ice, stark in their dark parkas against the white backdrop.

Cutter drew his Colt and scanned the trees beyond the prisoners, moving instinctively in front of Larsen and the others while he motioned them back toward cover. There were only two prisoners—and there should have been four.

Black boot toes sticking up from the snow told him Richards was down. The spray of pink snow where the man's head should have been gave him a pretty good idea of what happened. Lamp stood hunched over, shivering, still in chains as far as Cutter could tell from that distance. Nix worked feverishly on his restraints with a key—that had to be Bill's. One hand was free and he was working on the other. A line of tracks, gray in the flat light and quickly covering with snow, led directly to the trees another thirty yards beyond.

Spivey must have gotten Bill's Smith & Wesson.

Five shots, so one in the gun. Spivey might have gotten Bill's speed loader, but it would hardly matter if he got close enough to snipe Cutter from the tree line. One round was all it would take.

Piper, the female intern, stood closest to Cutter. She jumped when he began to bark orders.

"Edward Nix!" he shouted over the breeze and muffling snow. "Stop messing with your chains and come to me. Do it now!"

Lamp took a step to comply, but Nix said something to stop him.

Snow fell in large, popcorn flakes, serenely beautiful, belying the severity of the moment.

Larsen moved obliquely to Cutter, fanning, creating space. He looked around, dumbfounded.

"Where's Bud?"

"It was Richards did it!" Nix shouted. "He killed your guard and started the plane on fire. We stopped him for you."

"Awfully good of you," Cutter said, deadpan. "Come to me. Do it now!"

Nix stood still for a long moment, staring him down across the white expanse. If he was nervous, he didn't show it. At length he shouted, "You wouldn't sink low enough to shoot an unarmed prisoner—but even if you did, I don't think you could hit us from there with your pistol. Besides, you gotta be worried about Spivey taking potshots at you, otherwise you'd have come to me."

Even from fifty yards away and in the shadows of his parka hood, Nix's shit-eating grin was clearly visible.

Cutter turned to Larsen and nodded at his rifle/shotgun combo. "You have a .22 in the chamber of that thing?"

Larsen nodded, "I do."

"Mind if I borrow it a sec?"

Larsen passed the gun to him, holding out his hand as if he expected to be traded the Colt Python for bear watch.

Cutter took the long gun but holstered the revolver. He didn't know any of these people well enough to hand over his side arm.

It was difficult to say for sure, but Cutter thought he made out a flash of momentary panic on Nix's face. He aimed at the gray pile of chains a foot to Nix's left, barely visible in the tromped snow next to Richards's upturned boots.

The round kicked up a puff of snow an inch from Nix's foot.

Larsen grimaced sheepishly. "She pulls a little to the left."

Cutter broke open the chamber and dropped in another cartridge.

"Holy shit!" Nix said, raising the hand he'd gotten free of his cuffs. "Okay. Okay." He slogged forward in the snow, slamming into Lamp with his shoulder in frustration. "We're coming to you. I'd worry a hell of a lot more about Spivey, though."

"Bring those loose chains with you!" Cutter barked. He kept the long gun aimed in.

Cutter had seen death before—too much of it, involving people he knew well. Gene Richards was a prisoner, Bud Bishop a stranger, and before this trip, Cutter only knew Bill Young in passing from his time as a contract guard. But he was responsible for all three of them. It would have been easy to give up hope, but Cutter had learned long ago to triage his emotions, to deal with the things he could control—and fight his way through the rest as targets presented.

When their father died, Grumpy had put his grandsons in his boat and taken them out to the middle of Gasparilla Sound. He'd somberly told the boys that grieving the death of a loved one was a natural and even healthy thing to do. With tears in his eyes and a fishing rod in his hand, he'd not shied away from the fact that though Ethan and Arliss had lost their dad, he'd lost his only son. Grumpy quietly pointed out that they all had a choice—to curl up in a ball and cry, or mourn on the move.

Almost always, Arliss chose the latter.

Mutt Larsen's once-beautiful Cessna Caravan was a hissing hulk of twisted black metal and plastic by the time Cutter got Nix back into full restraints. Rainbow slicks of oil shimmered on the filthy lake of melted snow that surrounded the wreckage—and obliterated any tracks that might have told Cutter what had transpired immediately after the prisoners got off the airplane.

The Cessna was a turboprop, meaning it burned jet fuel instead of gasoline. Essentially clean kerosene, Jet A was not as volatile as gasoline, but it burned with a wicked frenzy when vaporized. A fuel line clipped by a bullet would spray just enough fuel to provide the right conditions. Once the blaze was going, the wing tanks ruptured, creating a fireball almost a hundred feet in diameter.

The charred bodies were visible too, what was left of them. Burning metal and jet fuel left them hardly recognizable. The wreckage pulsed and glowed like some alien object hurled down from space, much too hot to approach. Cutter choked back his anger and focused on the task at hand—capturing Chance Spivey.

Cutter led Nix and Lamp behind cover of the burned building and secured their cuffs. Nix swore he'd dropped the handcuff key in the snow, but Cutter found it stashed under the man's tongue. "Shooting at an unarmed prisoner," Nix sneered. "You're gonna have some 'splainin' to do when we get to court."

Cutter ignored the banter and dragged the two outlaws through the snow toward the outhouse to a stout fir tree six inches in diameter. "Sit yourselves down on either side of the trunk," he said.

Nix turned to face away from the wind, made more bitter by the circumstances. "That's a big hell no, marshal. I'm not going to—"

Cutter helped him to the ground with a boot behind the knee. "I don't have time to argue," he snapped.

Lamp knelt on his own and nestled into the snow.

Cutter used the chains Spivey had shucked to secure the two men to the tree.

Nix yowled as if he'd already been shot. "We'll freeze to death if we can't get up and move around."

Cutter glowered down at the outlaw, his neck burning despite the frigid weather. "Desperate times," he said. "Brought on by yourself. Let's not forget, you *were* trying to get out of your cuffs. And I'm reasonably sure you killed my friends and started the fire."

"Look here now," Nix said. "I admit we ran, but I already told you, Gene Richards killed your friends. He shot your guard with his own gun. That's what started the fire. I swear to it. Tell him, Lamp!"

Lamp nodded like the lap dog he was. He shivered, as much from nerves as the cold, but he said nothing.

Nix leaned his head against the spruce tree, moaning up at the falling snow. "You can't leave us like this."

Cutter kicked him in the boot sole. "Hush! Your racket's going to call in the bear."

"I'll come with you," Noah Sam, the young Native man said. His parka hood was thrown back, exposing high cheeks and a strong jaw. Thick black hair hung well past his ears.

Cutter started to protest, but Noah said, "I know the area. You need me, Marshal." He smiled, leaning in as if to reveal a secret. "But don't worry. I'm awful stealthy."

Piper, the other intern, and Professor Baglioni huddled together, keeping their distance from the two prisoners like they had the plague. Both looked down their noses in disapproval. Larsen clutched the shotgun, red-eyed, still trying to process the fact that his friend, Bud Bishop, had died in the aircraft fire. He shot a glance at Cutter.

"You're not . . ." he stammered. "I mean . . . you're really going after him? Spivey?"

Nix spoke again, quieter now, apparently regaining his nerve. "I'd be careful if I were you. That big cowboy son of a bitch is a hell of a hunter."

Cutter ignored him.

"I'm serious," Nix buzzed like a bothersome mosquito. He spoke to Cutter but studied the women to see how they reacted. "You go after him, he'll gut you for sure."

Cutter glanced at the tree line, then down at his Colt as he opened the cylinder. He made sure it was loaded with six before snapping it shut and returning it to the holster under the heavy parka. He looked Noah up and down and groaned at the situation. Desperate times, indeed. But the kid was right. Cutter did need his help.

Noah leaned closer, whispering. "You think he'll really try and gut us?"

Cutter gave a little shrug, almost lost in the heavy parka. "I wouldn't worry about that. He doesn't have a knife. More likely he'll try to shoot us in the face."

"You are a disturbingly honest man," Noah said. "My grandma would have liked you."

"We have to move fast," Cutter said. "While this asshole is still trying to figure everything out. I don't want to give him a chance to plan an ambush. Right now, he's on the run, flushed with adrenaline. Everything he does is a clumsy reaction, taking advantage of the situation. He's making things up as he goes along."

"What are we gonna do?" Noah asked.

Cutter gave him a little wink. "Not sure," he said. "I'm making things up as I go along."

CHAPTER 35

*C*utter whispered a few last-minute instructions to Mutt Larsen, out of earshot of the prisoners, and then nodded at Noah, ready to move. Spivey had been gone no longer than fifteen minutes, but that was plenty long enough to be dangerous. The outlaw would have zero doubt Cutter would come after him, just as Cutter had known that Spivey was going be a problem from the first time he'd seen the man. He had that self-important look in his eye that said he was the only star of the little movie playing in his head, and everyone around him were just extras whose sole purpose was to see to his needs, bugs to be squashed for his enjoyment.

Sociopath or not, Spivey was smart—and he was out there in the trees somewhere, waiting.

On Cutter's signal, Mutt Larsen, Piper, and Baglioni began to pound against the north end of the charred cabin wall with sticks, calling out "Hey, bear!" and generally causing as much noise as possible. The noise wasn't likely to have much effect at keeping the big boar away, but Cutter needed Spivey's attention somewhere besides him and Noah. If he thought the bear was coming back, he'd want to watch that.

The bear's tracks ambled into the trees northwest of the burned cabin. Spivey's had fled almost due west. Eleven and nine o'clock, respectively. Cutter moved out at four o'clock, southeast, kicking his way as quickly as possible across the no-man's-land of knee-deep snow, all the while feeling that tense, tight-in-the-jaw sensation he got when the prospect of getting shot was all too imminent. Noah followed, moving with the easy stride of a youth who'd grown up in snow country. There was no way to be sure which way Spivey had gone once he'd made it inside the tree line, but Cutter assumed he was smart enough not to run toward the bear—the snow was deep enough that the bear's low belly plowed a deep trench almost three feet wide. The trail would have been impossible to miss.

If Cutter figured the angles correctly, the shell of the burned cabin would provide cover for at least part of his and Noah's journey across the open snowfield. He guessed that Spivey would seek cover inside the tree line, staying back enough to remain out of sight, while watching for Cutter's next move. It was a gamble. The outlaw might already be working his way around to the south, just waiting there with the Smith & Wesson out and ready to shoot. All Cutter could do was make an educated guess. His grandfather had often pointed out that guesses didn't make for optimum strategy.

Movement, on the other hand, was.

So Cutter moved, hoping he hadn't spent so much time seeing to the other two prisoners that Spivey had had time to set up a proper ambush.

Cutter kept a weather eye to his right as he high-kneed it through the thick snow, breaking through the crust a foot into the powder and falling hard enough to jar his teeth. It was exhausting work, using muscles he didn't normally use, threatening to wind him quickly like a fight gone out of control. Breathing heavily and starting to sweat, he scanned for any sign of Spivey as they neared the bunch willow and berry bush that preceded the edge of the spruce forest. Shape, color, movement—anything that looked out of place.

Both he and Noah threw back their heavy parka hoods once they were inside the tree line. Cutter peeled off his wool beanie, feeling the heat from exertion leave out the top of his head. The chill brought on by sweating could bring hypothermia all too quickly. It was imperative that he regulate his body temperature. The old saying, "If your feet are cold, put on a hat," worked in the converse as well. He counted to ten, letting the heat bleed off, feeling the pinch of the bitter cold on his forehead and ears before he replaced the wool beanie. He left the hood off so the thick wolverine fur rough lay across his shoulders, allowing him to listen for snapping twigs or crunching snow that might indicate Spivey.

The trees were gnarled things, unlike the towering cedar or Sitka spruce forests of southeast Alaska or the ponderosa pines of the Rocky Mountains. Long, brutal winters and fierce winds left these stunted and sparse with trunk bases several inches wider than the tops. Cabins, if someone happened to be bold enough to build one of logs made from these trees, had often been made by placing the logs vertically, like a fence, every other log turned upside down to ensure a uniform wall, rather than the traditional horizontal stack.

The trees themselves were far enough apart they gave little cover, but they slumped with new snow, making them appear denser than they actually were. This, combined with thick if low underbrush, would provide enough shadow for Spivey to set up a decent ambush.

Cutter pictured the terrain from when they'd flown in. His focus had been primarily on the grizzly, but he recalled a large river at the mouth of a valley where they now were and a slight draw or frozen stream running out of the mountains, generally east-west just a few dozen yards south of where Spivey had hit tree line. There was a large, flat spot in the open snow that Cutter took for a frozen pond.

Noah Sam confirmed that there was indeed a creek running through the trees on the far side of the clearing nearer to the burned airplane.

"How deep is the creek?" Cutter asked.

"Not too deep to cross," Noah said. "But it's frozen solid, so it wouldn't matter. No overflow or anything like that so far as I know."

Well inside the relative protection of the forest now, Cutter crouched behind a thick tangle of alder that offered some concealment, if not actual cover. "How deep are the banks?" he asked. "Flying in, it looked like a ditch if I'm remembering it right."

The Athabaskan youth gave a contemplative nod, seeing where Cutter was going with this. "Walls maybe four or five feet deep," he grinned. "It'll be full of snow. A bitch to try and push across. He'll sink up to his neck."

"What's to the north of us?" Cutter said. "The way the bear went?"

"The trees are way sparser, thinning out completely as you move up the valley," Noah said. "Mountains on the west side. But that bear's not goin' anywhere if that's what you're thinking."

"Agreed," Cutter said. "He's smelled food. The long days got him up early, but this spring cold snap makes it hard for him to find something to eat. He's not going to give up on a sure thing. Bears are smart enough not to leave meat to go find other meat."

"That puts Spivey smack between the bear and the creek," Noah said, keeping his voice low. "That other guy said Spivey's a hunter. That worry you?"

"There's hunting, and then there's hunting," Cutter said. "I'd imagine he's got some woods sense, but he's not prepared. He's got my friend's revolver, but he's got no knife or gloves or hat. Temps are in the single digits, if not colder. He'll want to keep his fingers tucked into the parka sleeve until he's ready to shoot."

"Good to have the gun with the bear around," Noah said. "But for making it out here, you'd need a knife."

"Yep," Cutter said, still surveying the blue shadows through the trees. The kid was right. Once the gun was empty it would have no practical use in this environment. A knife could be used to make shelter, a rudimentary weapon, butcher meat . . . Still, Cutter was glad he had both. He didn't relish the idea of fending off a hungry bear with his brother's knife.

Cutter sat for a moment, working out his route. At first glance the forest seemed lifeless, frozen in time, but the longer he looked the more he found. A squirrel skittering from bough to bough, sending down cascades of sifting snow. An ermine slithered along the top of a piece of slanted deadfall, like a furry serpent, white but for the black tip of its tail that looked as if it had been dipped in ink. It was hunting, listening to hushed squeaks of mice and voles that spent their winters in the slightly more temperate zone between earth and snow. Wolf tracks crisscrossed the forest floor— too many of them to be Professor Baglioni's dog. Snowshoe hares had nibbled at almost every willow shrub.

But there was no sign of the bear or Chance Spivey.

Noah shivered, doing his own scanning. He saw the ermine at the same time Cutter did. "Spivey's not going to survive very long out here," he said.

"No," Cutter said. "He's not. He'll need shelter and food." Cutter rolled his shoulders, shuffling from foot to foot to keep his blood flowing. "If we don't find him by nightfall, he'll creep up and start picking us off."

"The bear should keep him from moving around the north side," Noah said. "I know a wide spot in the creek bed. We'll have to swing out to the west, so it's a bit out of our way, but we won't have to wade through chest-deep snow."

*   *   *

They made good time to the creek, snow-laden trees dampening the sound of their movement. But Spivey's noise was dampened too. Cutter nearly walked out in the open before he had eyes on his target.

Cutter held up his left hand, fist clenched, signaling Noah to stop. Post-holing and high-kneeing through even relatively shallow snow had both of them out of breath. Spivey was less than twenty yards away at the edge of the tree line, peering out toward the burned cabin. He rocked back and forth. Cutter had made the prisoners roll down their boots in order to get the leg irons over their ankles. Floppy boots also made it harder to run away. Spivey, apparently feeling like he was well hidden, was bent over, finally in the process dumping snow out of his boots and snugging up the laces. His parka hood was back so he could hear, but absent a functional hat he was losing a lot of heat.

Cutter waved Noah behind him. A trickle of snow hissed down from the boughs above at the movement. Cutter braced himself for confrontation, but Spivey was too busy hunched over his boots to hear.

A scant twenty yards should have been an easy shot—the Marshals Service qual course went out to twenty-five—but Cutter was sapped and cold. Closer would have been better, but that would only make it easier for Spivey to return fire.

Cutter could almost hear Grumpy's words in his ear: *"If you can't get closer, get steadier."*

He leaned against a tree, more for support than cover, and rested the front sight of the Python in the center of Spivey's back. Clouds of vapor enveloped his face from slow, deliberate breaths.

"Don't move!" he barked, sending more snow skittering down from the branches to his left and right.

Spivey stood up and turned to face Cutter, hands out to his sides, open, pink from the cold.

"Where's Bill Young's revolver?" Cutter yelled.

Spivey chuckled. "What revolver? I'm unarmed. Just trying to get away. You can't blame me for that. I mean, this is some shit you got us into." Eyes locked on Cutter, he took a step forward, then another, closing the gap between them.

"Far enough," Cutter said, still aimed in.

Spivey smirked, a dozen yards away now. "You wouldn't shoot an unarmed prisoner just 'cause I'm trying to get away, would you? You got me on what, a gambling charge and a couple of old warrants. How about you just let me go. I'll still be wanted next week, and you can capture me then. One less person to worry about out in the wild."

Cutter shrugged. "I could let you go . . . but the parka belongs to the North Slope PD. You'll have to leave it with me."

Spivey took another step. "I'd freeze to death with no coat."

"Mister, you won't have time to freeze to death if you don't stop moving."

"I don't think you're—"

The snowball launched from Noah Sam's hand skittered through the boughs directly above Chance Spivey's head, sending a huge avalanche of snow cascading down around the outlaw's shoulders, filling his parka hood and covering his eyes.

"Get on your face!" Cutter yelled, expecting Spivey to reach for the revolver.

Looking like a great powdered sugar cookie, he held out his arms and slowly dropped to his knees.

"Smart move," Cutter said. "Giving up."

"I ain't giving up," Spivey said. "I'm just puttin' off the inevitable."

CHAPTER 36

Noah had to link two pairs of handcuffs to get Spivey's arms behind his back. Spivey merely shrugged when the kid found the Smith & Wesson tucked into his waistband under the parka. It was the way of things. Deputies expected prisoners to lie—and prisoners rarely let them down. Cutter looked on with the Colt, out of reach, but close enough the outlaw realized any further attempt to escape or fight would earn him a bullet and not another snowball. The return trip to the burned cabin took only a few minutes following the trail Spivey had already broken through the snow. Cutter watched the prisoner, while Noah kept an eye out for the bear.

Cutter had been gone for less than a half an hour. The others were huddled in the cold exactly where he left them when he returned. He got the idea that they had hardly spoken a word to one another.

Putting the restraints back on Spivey was fraught

with danger. The belly chain and cuffs were fairly straightforward, but just complicated enough Cutter needed to do it himself instead of relying on Noah or Larsen. Cutter left Spivey cuffed behind the back. Instructing the outlaw to lean his head against the standing wall of the cabin and kick up one ankle at a time, he was to ratchet on the leg irons. Once his legs were restrained again, Cutter handed off his Colt to Noah and then unlocked the handcuffs, feeding a set through the chain that went around the prisoner's waist. Spivey seethed, rolling broad shoulders and glaring down at Cutter in a display of dominance. He made no secret of the fact that he would relish the idea of pulling Cutter's head off. He'd be a handful in a fight. That was certain. So Cutter had to be smart and make sure he never presented the opportunity. Nix and Lamp were unchained from the spruce tree, but he left them in full restraints.

Together again, the three outlaws stood glumly, backs to the charred wall of the main cabin, hunched down in their parkas against the cold, staring at their feet.

"One of you killed Bud!" Larsen said through clenched teeth, breaking the momentary silence. He sniffed back angry tears. Cutter considered asking him to put down the shotgun, but decided against it.

The big cowboy shrugged, teeth chattering. His chains jingled like sleighbells. "I told you," he said. "Richards's the one who shot your guard. One of the bullets must have gone on through and killed the kid—"

Larsen leaned in, getting much too close. "Bud Bishop wasn't a kid!"

Cutter guided the distraught man away. "We'll get

this sorted out." He eyed Spivey. "I promise you that. But at the moment, we need to decide our next move." He turned to Professor Baglioni. Her parka hood was thrown back, and a layer of fresh snow covered the top of what Cutter guessed to be a sea otter hat. "I'm assuming that the whole reason for this visit is because your radio is inoperable."

"Correct," Baglioni said. She leaned close to Larsen but peered at the prisoners as she spoke. "It's been broken for some time. Piper and I tried to repair it, but . . ."

"And you don't have a satellite phone?"

She shook her head. "No, it was inside with my gear when the fire started." A flash of something Cutter thought might be pain flashed across the professor's face. She made a fist, invisible in her mittens had he not been looking for it. Whatever it was passed, so he didn't mention it.

"You can see why I needed to look in on them," Larsen said.

Cutter checked his cell phone. As he suspected, no service.

"Nearest cell tower serves Anaktuvuk Pass," Noah Sam said. "Out this valley and then twenty plus miles west of us."

Cutter turned the phone completely off and tucked it into his inside pocket close to his skin to save power. It was still fully charged, but temperatures hovered just a few degrees above zero and would likely drop hard at night. If left out, the battery would be toast in no time.

"Okay," he said. "Maybe someone saw the smoke from the burning jet fuel. That fire mushroomed up like a small bomb."

Baglioni nodded at the burned cabin, giving an exhausted sigh. Her parka hood was back exposing her chipmunk cheeks and intense eyes. "This place burned for hours—and that fire was even larger. Two barrels of heating oil and fuel for the generator went up in a plume of fire and black smoke. Absent a random passing airplane . . . Well, let me put it this way. That was three days ago, and you're the first people we've seen."

"This valley doesn't really go anywhere," Larsen said. "It's not on a normal flyway."

"All right then," Cutter said. "When we don't arrive on schedule, won't someone backtrack your flight path?"

The pilot stared at his boots. "They will," he said. "But we're almost thirty miles from where I'm supposed to be. I only planned to do a flyover to make sure there wasn't some emergency and then come back once I'd dropped you in Fairbanks."

Cutter eyed him, knowing the answer, but asking the question anyway. "But you notified someone of this change in route?"

"I did not," Larsen said. "I'm sorry to admit it, but nobody knows we're here."

Lamp shuffled forward, impeded by his ice-caked chains. "So it's your fault we're stuck—"

Cutter flat-handed the outlaw in the chest, nearly lifting him off the ground. "*He* didn't burn the plane."

Lamp sputtered, coughing, trying to catch his breath. "Well, I sure as hell didn't." He'd likely breathed in a lungful of toxic smoke, but Cutter couldn't bring himself to care.

"Oh," Cutter said. "I doubt you've got the balls to

do something like that. But you know who did it, and that means you're a liability to them."

"Not going to work, Marshal," Nix said.

Cutter forced a smile. "We'll see."

Nix gave an emphatic shake of his head. "We all saw the same thing. Even you know Richards had a temper. I mean, hell, wasn't he in custody for going apeshit on you in the dining hall. Should come as no surprise that he grabbed your friend's gun and shot him while he was talking to Bud. The rest of us chased him off the plane. That's the end of it."

"We're a long way from the end of anything," Cutter said. "But we will . . . What do they say? Circle back to that later. For now, I need to concentrate on more immediate concerns." He turned to Baglioni again. "You say the cabin burned three days ago. What have you been using for shelter at night?"

"Noah's quarters." She pointed a mittened hand at a ten-by-ten wooden structure between the charred remnants of the main building and the outhouse. The heat from the main fire had been intense enough to ignite the smaller cabin, which looked to be little more than a shed. The near side had burned almost completely away by the time they'd been able to put it out, and it was now patched with a blue tarp and scrap lumber. The rear wall was lower by several feet, making for a slanted roof that allowed snow to slide off and form a massive ramp against the back wall that reached all the way to the roofline.

"Fortunately, he had a few blankets and such stashed away." She shot an accusing look at Piper, who raised her hands.

"Okay," the young woman said. "Let's just get this out there. Noah and I are an item, and Professor Baglioni's not happy about it."

"No one cares, my dear," Baglioni said, though it was obvious that she cared a great deal. "Anyway, the cabin is quite small, but the north wall blocks the wind. . . ." Her gaze fell suddenly on the prisoners. "Wait just a minute." She wheeled to face Cutter. "You're not putting them in there with us. There's no way we would all fit."

Cutter stomped his feet against the cold, trying to get some feeling back. "Ma'am," he said. "We're going to have to. I need to safeguard all of us. Including the men in my custody. This is a real mess, I don't mind telling you, so we have to make some hard decisions." He turned to the pilot. "Mr. Larsen, I need to take a look at Noah's cabin and make a plan for how to house all of us safely. Think you can watch the prisoners for a minute?"

Larsen adjusted his grip on the shotgun and gave the shackled men a hard stare. "That I can."

"Thank you," Cutter said. He turned to focus on Spivey as he spoke. "Every one of us standing here is in danger if we do not work together. And if any one of you move off that wall, Mr. Larsen is going to take that as a sign that you have chosen not to work together and he will shoot you in the chest with number nine bird shot. Now, I once saw a man shot at this range with number nine bird shot. You could put a fist through the hole in his ribs."

Nix started to protest, but Cutter shushed him. "That's how it is." He glanced at Larsen. "Understood?"

Larsen gave a curt nod and took a long breath through his nose, settling himself. "Got it."

Cutter started for the shed and then stopped, turning to face the group. He raised a finger toward the prisoners but looked at Larsen as he made his point. "Right now, they're thinking, 'What if we all move at once. . . .' If they do that, take your pick. But don't talk. Don't give them a second warning. Just shoot one of them—and then beat the others to death with the shotgun."

CHAPTER 37

*L*ola tried three times to reconnect after the satellite call went dead. She'd heard something right before. A muffled sound, like the guy on the other end caught his breath. He'd said Cutter couldn't come to the phone. That pissed her off something royal. How the hell could he not come to the phone? Bush planes didn't even have a john, for crying out loud. Cutter was probably so close he could just reach out and take the damned thing. Instead of arguing, she'd driven home her point with information, all but screaming into the phone.

"I need you to tell Deputy Cutter that Edward Nix is a serial killer! Would you do that for me, mate?"

In retrospect, the guy on the other end could have been startled in response to her tirade, which would have explained the quick intake of breath. But then the connection had dropped, leaving her with three fast pulses and a dead line.

Lola's brain could do all sorts of mental gymnastics in two minutes, imagining every terrible possibility for the dropped call. Terrible things seemed all the more possible when she stood yards from the cadaverously creepy Tall Man and his blood-rusted wheelbarrow.

Phone to her ear and hugging her ribs as she turned back and forth, she called Chief Phillips. To his credit, Joe Bill Brackett stood by to offer emotional support.

"I stuffed it all up, boss," Lola said, chin quivering. "What if the person I was talking to on the sat phone *was* Edward Nix?"

"Calm down, Lola," Phillips said—not her usual no-nonsense voice, but soft, like she was soothing her baby. "If Nix answered the phone, then Cutter already had a problem. You didn't cause it. Let's look at what we *can* do, not what we should have done. Call that North Slope Borough officer back. Get her to have any other aircraft in the area relay a message for Cutter's pilot to contact us ASAP. I'll contact the Fairbanks Trooper post and ask them to do the same thing for planes headed north. That's a wild route between Dead-horse and Fairbanks. With any luck they'll come back into radio range any minute."

"Right," Lola said. "It's just that . . . Cutter is always careful, but he has no idea what kind of prisoner he's got on board."

"Oh, I talk a big game, my dear," the chief said. "But I'm as worried as you are. Come on back to the courthouse. Your Tall Man is in custody, so your work there is done."

Lola snapped her fingers to get Brackett's attention. He turned dutifully from where he was talking to a couple of senior officers. She mouthed, "Can you give me a ride to the federal building?"

He nodded, puppy-like. "Of course."

Lola gave him a thumbs-up and turned her attention back to the chief.

"You think maybe we can get a GPS read on the satellite signal?"

"I'm not hopeful," Phillips said. "Since it's not an active call. Any historical records probably won't tell us much beyond the fact that he's somewhere in Alaska."

"But—"

"I'll try." Phillips gave a tight chuckle. "Hell, Lola, I'd get NASA to re-task satellites if I thought headquarters would back me. You and I have a sense that something may have happened, but the Troopers are sure to tell me that all we have now is a dropped phone call. The plane isn't even overdue yet. We have—"

"I know," Lola said, pacing again, free hand to her forehead. "We have to trust Cutter to be Cutter. But this is bad, Chief. I can feel it."

"Me too," Phillips said. "So, get your ass back here. We'll make ourselves a plan. Together."

CHAPTER 38

*T*he professor's rangy dog sat on its haunches and frowned at Nix, looking a hell of a lot like a wolf. Nix had never thought about dogs frowning, but this one was, even with his eyes. It looked to be superprotective, which was definitely going to make things interesting.

Nix ranked his adversaries and put the snarling dog just a fraction behind Cutter on the danger scale. Shortly after the plane burned and Cutter had caught up to them, Nix had come to the conclusion that he'd just take care of whichever threat presented the opportunity first.

Until then, he'd smile sweetly, play nice, and pretend he was just as upset about being stuck here as everyone else. There was no way the marshal could stay awake and aware for long. If Nix was anything, he was a student of human nature. Cutter had had the weight of the world on his shoulders from the moment he met them at the holding cells that morning. He'd been running on fumes even then, preoccupied about something, probably girl troubles, if Nix had to guess. The bags under his eyes said he'd not slept well the night before. Now, cold, fatigue, and a near-constant flood of adrenaline would be Nix's allies in wearing the marshal down.

It might take a while. This lawman was a hard case. But when he fell, he would fall hard. Nix just had to be patient. He had to remember not to stare at the professor. The younger one, Piper was her name, was prettier, riper, all of that. Professor Baglioni was a little on the heavy side for his tastes, but she was also scared shitless—which was far more appetizing.

This was better than anything Nix had ever dreamed up—and he'd dreamed up some pretty twisted shit. Stranded in the middle of nowhere, for who knew how long. Best of all, it looked as though they would all be crammed in on top of one another. Everyone was scared and cold, but bitchy Marie Baglioni was lashing out, pissed at the world. Terrified. Nix could taste her fear. It would get worse at night. The shelter was miniscule. He licked his lips just thinking about it.

He would save the younger one for later, after she'd ripened some. She'd lose her shit as time went by—as things started to unfold. His plan wasn't concrete yet. Too early for that. Whatever it was, it would prove soul-crushing for these bitches—which made it a very sweet plan indeed.

One thing at a time. He'd get to the tender young redhead in due course. For now, he'd focus on Baglioni's magnificent chest heaving with the anger she used to cloak her fear.

Beside him, Nolan Lamp broke into another coughing fit, knocking Nix from his reverie. The little weasel was always choking on cold air like it was a piece of gristle stuck in his throat. He shot Nix a side-eye, one of those pleading looks that said he was about to drown and just might drag everybody else down with him.

Nix tore his gaze off the delicious angst in Baglioni's flushed face and stared down past the frost-covered front of his parka so he could think.

Lamp was a problem that needed to be dealt with before Nix could enjoy himself. If he worked it right, maybe dealing with the little pussy would stir things up a little. Tolman was always pointing out how he was so good at "adding to the anxiety."

Things were going to be more difficult than Nix had originally thought. Difficult, but still doable. The marshal had taken Young's revolver, which was good. That meant he had it with him, so there was another weapon in play. Even a well-trained lawman had to let his guard down sometime. He'd slip up. Of course, Young's revolver had only two rounds left. Nix hadn't wanted to risk getting caught with the dead guard's speed loader and extra ammunition, so he'd let that drop into the snow when no one was looking. He took a chance and kept the pocketknife, which was still stuck down the top of his boot.

Lamp choked on his own breath again. It was a wonder that the asshole had lived to adulthood. Nix opened and closed his hands, flexing them against the cuffs and belly chain, then stomped his feet to get the circulation going.

"Marshal," he said. "I'm really not trying to be a bother—"

Cutter looked up from his conversation with the kid. Noah something.

"Good."

Nix chuckled. "Seriously, though. We're gonna freeze to death just standing here. We can't move around like you free citizens. I'm sure you have a plan to get us rescued, but won't you get in trouble if your three prisoners are the only ones who lose toes to frostbite?"

"Desperate times," Cutter said. He sighed, nodding slowly before turning to the professor. "Let's take a look at the provisions."

"I'll get the bags," Noah said, and then stomped off through the snow to the shed.

Professor Baglioni harrumphed, her face twisted like a hissing cat. "We couldn't salvage much. Noah loves his Earl Grey, so we have plenty of that, but only two small duffels of food, mostly Spam and Pilot Bread. At best we have enough for only nine or ten days, and that's when there were just three of us. I'm not sharing what little food we do have with criminals, murderers— the very people responsible for stranding us."

Oh yeah, Nix thought, this bitch deserved everything he had planned for her.

Spivey hawked up a mouthful of phlegm and spat it contemptuously onto the snow, where it froze into something too disgusting for even Nix to look at.

"Maybe they should have let that bear eat your fat ass," Spivey said. "Then you wouldn't have lorded your food over us."

"That'll do," the marshal said, measured, quiet.

Piper kicked at the snow with her boot, embarrassed at her teacher's selfishness.

Larsen tried to put an arm around Baglioni's shoulder, but she shrugged him off. He gave the rest of the group a she-doesn't-mean-that smile.

Baglioni proved otherwise. "I'm completely serious," she said. "Who knows how long we'll be here?"

"There's always the dog," Spivey said. "That damn thing's bony, but it's got some meat on its bones." He looked around the group. "What? Anyone with half a brain is thinking the same thing."

The big Tamaskan stood up and ran a long tongue over his lips again, sensing that the conversation had turned to him.

"This is exactly what I mean!" Baglioni said. "You want me to share my food with that?"

Instead of getting rattled, the marshal gave the professor a polite shrug—like she was actually the one in charge. "It's your food. But if they don't eat, I don't eat—"

A sharp cry from Noah at the shed cut him off.

Baglioni leaned into Larsen, trembling, but Nix didn't take the time to savor it. He was just as jumpy as everyone else.

"Watch them," Cutter said to Larsen, flicking a hand toward the prisoners. He'd not taken a step before Noah walked around the corner of the cabin. Only thirty feet away, the kid looked small standing at the edge of the fire-carved snow drift piled high as the roof. He held aloft the tattered remains of two duffel bags.

Piper took off her wool hat to run a glove through red curls. An exhausted groan escaped her lips.

"The bear."

CHAPTER 39

*T*he wind seemed to shift at the mention of the grizzly, pelting exposed faces with snow. Temperatures had risen a few degrees with the coming storm—which essentially meant they would all freeze to death a few seconds more slowly than before. Fatigue and the constant flutter of near panic made the cold all the more debilitating.

The bear was still out there, lurking somewhere, probably flopped down in the snow watching them, sniffing the air with its black nose. As big as it was, the animal was still on the skinny side, depleting all its stored fat over the long winter sleep. It had woken up early, ahead of the green shoots of new growth and freshly dropped caribou calves that normally would have filled the emptiness in its belly. This bear wasn't going anywhere. Food was difficult to come by in these mountains, and now that it had found a source, there would be no giving it up just because a couple of humans with noisemakers had dropped out of the sky.

Piper stayed tight on Noah's heels. She was brave to be out in the bush working in the first place, but the idea of a hungry grizzly had her seriously rattled.

Cutter understood.

"There are a lot of us," he said. "That should help keep it away."

"That's bullshit and you know it," Spivey said. "Those big boars are eating machines."

Cutter looked the prisoner in the eye. "Okay, now."

"He's not wrong," Baglioni said, shaking her head, sounding like the Eeyore she was. "They're magnificent animals, and I admire them, but they are far from the cuddly teddy bears of children's cartoons."

"I've seen 'em eat their own cubs alive," Spivey said. "Just to bring a sow back into heat—"

Cutter bowed his head against the wind and gave the man a little shove between shoulder blades, pushing him toward what was left of Noah's cabin. "That's enough color commentary, Marlin Perkins."

Cutter moved the prisoners into Noah's cabin, seating them on the plywood floor with their backs to the north wall, knees to their chests. This would have been the back of the building before the fire. Now the structure was a three-sided shed. The south-facing door remained closed while the slanted void where the west wall had burned away provided easy entry and exit.

It was sparsely furnished—a folding camp chair, a set of bunk beds along the east wall, and the charred remains of a squat three-drawer dresser like one might find in a hotel. Noah had already told them he didn't have any guns. Cutter did a quick search for anything the prisoners might use as a weapon. He found no knives or clubs but moved a five-foot piece of straight wood Noah had apparently been whittling into a walking stick or some kind of spear. Spivey appeared to be keenly interested as Cutter moved it to the far corner of the room next to a pile of assorted gear and clothing, some of it Piper's from the looks of it.

Noah stepped to the burned opening next, pausing to lean around the charred wall and grab a piece of peeled willow that hung on a nail just inside. He used the wood to brush the snow off his parka before stepping inside to escape the weather.

"My grandma used to keep a grooved piece of caribou antler by her door," he said. "She always made us scrape off before we came inside so our clothes didn't get wet with melt water—"

Spivey scoffed. "None of us give a shit about your grandma unless she's bringing us something to eat—"

Cutter kicked the outlaw hard in the boot, jingling his leg irons.

"That's enough!"

Spivey drew his legs up and slumped against his knees while the others filed in one by one, using Noah's willow snow scraper. Marie Baglioni leaned away from the prisoners, keeping the big Tamaskan as a shield. She called him Fig. She dragged a foam mattress off the bed and found a spot on a pile of blankets in the northeast corner as far away from Chance Spivey as possible.

Noah's tiny cabin would have been tight for four people. Eight left them toe to toe and shoulder to shoulder. It would get even more cramped when any of them tried to lie down and sleep, but at least they were out of the wind. Barely.

Cutter kept his feet, rocking to keep warm while he worked through his options. He wasn't yet sure what to do with the prisoners during the night.

He'd let the oversize beaver fur mittens dangle around his parka, unwilling to trade the dexterity he might need to use his gun for warmth. The thin wool glove liners weren't doing the job. He put his right hand under his armpit to warm it and pointed at the open west wall with his other before finding a spot for it under the opposite arm, deep inside his parka. "I'm surprised the bear didn't try to come through here last night."

"It hadn't shown up here yet," Piper said. She'd moved closer to Noah, her parka still zipped high and tight so it covered even her chin.

"She's right," Noah said. "It didn't show up until this morning. Most of our food supply was in the cabin. Even if the bear was a long ways off, the smell of burnt sugar and bacon would have drifted for days after the cabin went up. My grandma used to say that a sugar burn was the quickest way to catch a—"

"Learning more than I ever wanted to know about old Grammie," Spivey muttered.

Cutter shot him a look but instead of saying anything began to dig the snacks he'd gotten from the Deadhorse Spike Shop that morning out of his pocket. He'd already given a Pop-Tart to each prisoner but had five granola bars and three packs of mixed nuts. He pitched them all to Baglioni.

Spivey and Nix both sat up straighter.

Lamp coughed again, leaning away from the two men like he no longer wanted to be associated with a single word they said.

Spivey scowled. "Professor Bag-a-donuts gets all the food?"

"I was kinda wondering about that too," Nix said. "The professor already made it clear that we're not welcome here."

"The things you 'kinda wonder about,'" Cutter said, "are way the hell down my list." He nodded to Baglioni and the food piled in her lap. "We don't have much, but we'll kick this in with the rest."

The bear had torn into almost everything in the duffel bags, ruining most of what it didn't eat on the spot. They were left two unopened boxes of Earl Grey tea—Noah Sam's personal stash, a half-full squeeze bottle of strawberry jam, and a can of Spam with only two tooth punctures in it."

"We'll need to eat this tonight," Baglioni said, holding up the Spam.

"Think it'll be okay?" Piper said, studying the tooth punctures, turning it over in her fleece mittens.

"I'd watch that," Noah said. "Getting food scent on your clothes."

Piper held up the can. "It's frozen solid. Spam-cicle."

Cutter shivered, despite his heavy coat. This was an occasion when a little extra body fat might have been welcome. "It should be fine to eat."

"Yeah," Spivey said. "The smell of grease won't draw the old griz in or anything . . ."

Cutter resolved to find something to gag the man with if he didn't shut up. Low morale had gotten people killed in situations less dire than this one. Spivey was savvy enough to see the flash in Cutter's eyes and gave a tight-lipped smile, an unspoken signal that he was going to be good. For now.

Cutter looked at the sparse pile of food. "Twelve ounces of meat and some granola bars aren't going to get us very far in this cold. Any game animals around?"

"Besides the bear?" Larsen said.

"Oh, we won't waste the bear," Cutter said, "if it comes to that."

Noah turned up his nose, drawing a look from Piper.

"What?" she said. "Your people eat brown bear."

"My people eat a lot of shit I don't particularly care for," he said. "I mean, I can eat moose nose, but I prefer a spicy Italian from Subway. Anyway, brown bear can be a bit . . . wormy." He wagged his head. "That little thing called trichinosis."

"So I hear," Cutter said. "We'd cook the hell out of it. Though, to be honest, I'd rather eat something else."

"We see caribou once in a while," Noah said. "But it's a great year for snowshoe hares. They're on a seven-year cycle with lynx . . ."

Cutter smiled in spite of the situation. Brackett had told him and Lola the same thing only a day before—though it seemed like forever ago.

"I'll set some snares on their trails before we turn in for the night," Noah added. "We'll catch one or two for sure, but the bear might get to 'em before we do."

Cutter cupped his hands together and blew in them for warmth. "I assume you don't have much in the way of sleeping bags or blankets."

Professor Baglioni held up her index finger. "One sleeping bag," she said. "Plus four blankets, the two mattresses from the bunk beds, a six-foot piece of old carpet, and this chewed-up caribou hide that looks and smells as though the bear urinated on it just to spite us."

"Okay," Cutter said, blowing in his hands again, his breath forming a cloud in the still air. "Shelter, food, water . . ."

Noah used his chin to point at the meager pile of gear in the corner. "Babe," he said. "Wanna show them my Svea?"

Piper reached behind her and dragged a one-burner backpacker's stove out of the meager gear. "One Svea camp stove coming up," she said.

Not a whole lot larger than a can of soup, the simple brass stove came with an aluminum lid that looked like it would double as a small cook pot. "And about a half a gallon of white gas. It's not the greatest stove for a group this size. We used to eat our meals over in the main building. Lucky for us, Noah is addicted to Earl Grey, so he kept an old saucepan in here. Since the fire, we've been using it to melt snow for water. His Nalgene bottle is the only one to survive the fire."

"We're lucky to have it," Cutter said. "What else?"

Along with the shotgun shells, Mutt Larsen had a pocketknife, a half a roll of wintergreen breath mints—which he deposited in the food pile—a pair of reading glasses, and a fantasy adventure novel called *The Doomfarers of Coramonde*—which Cutter thought was an appropriate title for their present circumstance.

Cutter reached in the pocket opposite where he'd kept the granola—the same pocket that held Young's revolver—and pulled out a single bottle of Aquafina. "Forgot about this."

"I have two elastic bands for my hair," Baglioni

said, chin quivering. "So as you can see, we are pretty much—"

"Hang on now," Cutter said. "Anybody have matches?"

"I have a lighter," Piper said.

Noah tapped his pants pocket. "Me too. And a knife. And my survival bracelet. I'll unravel the 550 cord in the bracelet to make some snares."

"Oh," Piper said. "And I've got a pocketknife too."

"How about a flashlight?" Cutter asked.

They shook their heads.

"I had some candles." He sighed. "But they were on the dresser by the wall and melted into a big wax puddle during the fire." He brightened. "We could use the lighter in a pinch if we needed to and make a spruce torch."

Piper reached into the corner where she'd gotten the stove and pulled out a kinked coil of quarter-inch sisal rope of unknown quality or strength and a steel Estwing construction hatchet with a hammer head opposite the blade.

"We had some extra clothes," Noah said, but besides a few cotton T-shirts, the three of us divvied most everything up to stay warm."

Cutter dug his everyday carry out of his pockets. The dog leaned in to sniff him as he spread the items out on the caribou hide at Larsen's feet.

A pocketknife, a small flashlight, a ferrocerium rod or fire steel, and a Zippo lighter he'd refilled with lighter fluid two days earlier. Ethan's MAK fixed blade was on his belt, but he left that there, out of sight along with the small Glock in the holster over his right kidney. There was no reason to lay all his cards on the table with the prisoners looking over his shoulder. They were, no doubt, already plotting an escape as if it was their duty.

"How much ammo do you have for the shotgun?" he asked Larsen.

"Four bird shot," the pilot said. "And ten rounds of .22 long rifle under the butt plate."

"That .22 will come in handy if we don't catch something in the snares right away," Noah said.

"Well, there you go," Cutter said, forcing a smile. "We have shelter, food, water, a way to make fire, and the means to protect ourselves."

"What are we going to do about the bear?" Baglioni whispered, leaning back from Larsen so she could look him in the eye. The pilot shrugged and passed the question off to Cutter.

"We still have six hours or more of daylight," Cutter said. "That gives us enough time to drag up enough wood to keep the fire going all night."

"There was a decent stack of split spruce on the far side of the main cabin," Baglioni said. "Not all of it burned."

"That's a start," Cutter said. "That plus whatever else we can find should help warm our shelter and hopefully keep the bear away."

"Hopefully?" Lamp said, breaking into a coughing fit again.

"Let's go," Cutter said. "Gathering firewood will help warm you twice."

Nix clamored to his feet and stretched his cuffs as far out in front of him as the belly chain would allow.

"What?" Cutter asked.

"You don't expect us to be much help trussed up like this?"

"Oh, every little bit helps," Cutter said, nodding to the door. "You prisoners will get the easy stuff that's already split."

"And if we don't?" Spivey said.

"You can sleep by whatever fire you help build," Cutter said, before turning to the others. "We could use all hands and eyes. Piper, do you know how to use a shotgun?"

The redhead laughed. "My parents were teachers in Minto when I was growing up," she said. "Big duck hunting area. Shotguns were pretty much mandatory in our house."

"Good enough," Cutter said. "If you don't mind pulling bear guard while the rest of us take care of the wood. Pieces of the old cabin, dead trees, anything that burns." He put a hand on Spivey's shoulder as they walked into the blowing snow. "And don't worry. I'll search you all really well when we're done, just in case a nail or screw or anything sharp happens to end up in your coat pockets. Wouldn't want you to hurt yourselves."

CHAPTER 40

*T*o Lola's surprise, Joe Brackett asked if he could accompany her inside the federal building.

She swiped her proximity card to get his truck into the garage via the Seventh Avenue entrance. The building security at the guard shack on the other side would have pitched a fit if they'd gone in that way because he didn't have a vehicle decal. They were only doing their job, but Lola didn't have time to argue exigency.

They found a vacant parking spot outside the Marshals Service sallyport. Lola entered her code in the scramble pad about the same time the court security officer in the control room saw her on the camera. The prisoner elevator was waiting for them when they got in, and the CSO buzzed each door from then on as they approached.

Two deputies came out of the squad room to the right of the secure hallway when they heard Lola and Brackett exit the heavy steel door. They were worried about Cutter too. Lola could do little but raise her hands and shrug—and that hurt like hell. The chief's office was to the left as they came out the door, a few steps up the main hallway. She was the bridge between operational personnel (who referred to themselves as gun-toters) and admin.

Jill Phillips rolled away from her desk and stood when Lola and Brackett walked in, two parts Southern manners and one part nervous energy.

"Cutter's plane is now officially overdue," the chief said after she'd shaken Brackett's hand. "Everybody under the sun has been trying to contact the pilot via radio, but they're getting nothing. They should have been in range for well over an hour. And by now they should be on the ground."

"Bad weather between there and Fairbanks?" Lola asked. She'd already checked every website she could think of but hoped Phillips had in-person information. "Maybe they had to set down because of fog or something."

Phillips fell back in her chair, rocking while she spoke. "That heavy weather we talked about is moving in," she said. "But they should have beaten it. It sounds like it was relatively good for that part of the north when they departed Deadhorse, but the Brooks Range is getting dumped on as we speak."

Officer Brackett raised a tentative hand.

Chief Phillips shook her head, more curt than she surely intended to be. "Just talk if you have something to say."

"What kind of plane are they on?"

"Same as ours," Phillips said. She glanced at Brackett, explaining. "We have a Cessna Caravan as well, but our only pilot is in advanced deputy training in Glynco. Otherwise I'd have it in the air now."

"That sucks," Brackett said. "And Cutter's is supposed to be flying toward Fairbanks?"

Phillips nodded. "That's right. Why?"

"I'm thinking any plane that small would fly the Haul Road through the Brooks Range to get between Deadhorse and Fairbanks. Especially if the weather was supposed to be sketchy."

Lola turned to him. "So you know the area?"

"My dad and I have hunted the Brooks Range for years. We've flown out of Bettles, around Galbraith Lake, the Sag River, all over. There are a couple of pump stations along the Haul Road if the pilot got into trouble. For that matter, this is Alaska, pilots land right on the road more often than people realize."

"That's what the trooper lieutenant in Fairbanks told me," Phillips said. "Though he did admit he transferred in from Bethel two weeks ago, so he's sorely lacking in local knowledge."

"I hate to even say the words," Lola whispered. "But should we consider the off chance that Arliss and Bill were overpowered and Nix took control of the airplane?"

"Nothing is off the table," Phillips said. "Do we trust the pilot?"

Lola grimaced, shaking her head. "I suppose he could be involved, but according to North Slope PD, it was a last-minute deal. Cutter arrested the guy who was supposed to fly them."

"That's right," Phillips said, tapping the tip of a pencil on her desk blotter. "I signed the 157 to approve the charter contract as soon as I got in this morning. How

about Nix then? Does he have any friends along the
Haul Road?" The pencil lead snapped. Instead of sharp-
ening it again, she threw the whole thing in the trash
can beside her desk. "I mean, he's a truck driver. He's
got to have contacts up and down that road."

Brackett held up his phone. "I understand Tolman is
singing his heart out. I'll call and see if he's giving up
anything on his partner."

"Do it," the chief said. She got a new pencil from a
ceramic Marshals Service mug on her desk, considered
the freshly sharpened point for a moment, and then
began tapping it on her blotter.

"Should we tell Mim?" Lola whispered after Brackett had stepped into the hall.

Phillips dropped the pencil and rubbed her face with
both hands. Lola had never known Jill Phillips to be
anything but a paragon of strength—a stone, chiseled
from the same granite quarry as Arliss Cutter. Seeing
her worried made Lola feel as if the ground beneath
her feet was unsteady, opening up to swallow her
whole.

"We'll have to tell her eventually," Phillips said. "If
only to make sure he hasn't checked in with her."
Phillips's chair squealed as she leaned way back. Her
spine gave an audible pop. "Cutter didn't say anything
else when you spoke to him last? Nothing to lead you
to believe he was in any kind of duress?"

"Not a thing." Lola began to tear up. "Chief, what if
the plane just crashed without any help from Nix?"

"We'll keep looking until we find it," Phillips said.

Brackett came back in the office, phone in hand.
"Sergeant Hopper said Tolman is doing his best to

make a deal. According to him, Edward Nix rents a storage unit at one of Tolman's facilities. A box of Nix's photos spilled as he was moving it out of his truck and revealed what Tolman described as 'intersecting interests.'"

Lola pretended to spit. "What kismet that these two shit sticks found each other."

"No kidding," Brackett said. "Anyway, I'm not sure it holds water, but according to Tolman, Nix would sometimes bring back girls he picked up in Fairbanks or even hitchhikers along the road. They like to have two at any given time. Overlapping." His voice dropped to a reverent whisper. "You sure you want to hear the rest of this?"

Phillips gave a somber nod.

Lola said, "Yeah, nah . . . but yeah."

Brackett sighed. "Okay. Nix apparently forces one girl to watch him . . . torture and murder the other. Most of the time the victim is still alive in the beginning. Nix feeds off the fear of the girl he kills but mostly off the one who watches. The one who is left alive knows she'll be next—after he comes back with a new prisoner. He calls the freshest girl a 'companion,' and he always gives the two of them a few days to get to know one another, to talk, and hatch futile escape plots. He and Tolman watch them on CCTV, then Nix shows up and does his work while the newest companion has to watch the veteran. Tolman says the last one, the girl with the painted toes, had a heart attack or stroke and just died on them before they could make her watch anything. Nix was pissed because she robbed him of his fun. He planned to get a new girl on the way back from his trip north. Detectives have a warrant for his storage unit and are headed that way now."

Phillips and Lola were both grimacing by the time Brackett finished, looking like they'd eaten something bitter.

"Twisted," Lola said. "This sick bastard had it figured out. He gets to terrorize the girl he kills, the girl who watches, and the entire city of Anchorage every time we find some piece of remains."

"Okay." Phillips snatched up her desk phone and hit speed dial. She waited a moment for the other party to answer. "Hey, sweetheart," she said. "It's me . . . Yes . . . Well, you know that thing I told you might happen someday? It's happened . . . Right . . . Thanks . . . Me too." She hung up and turned her chair to dig through one of the drawers in her cabinet. She found what she was looking for and swiveled, stuffing a red paper booklet into a daypack under her desk.

"What is that?" Lola asked, fearing the answer. She'd heard of the "Red Book" that walked district management through the necessary steps after the death of a deputy.

"It is what it is." Phillips pushed away from her desk with an exhausted groan and stood, grabbing her coat. "Thank you, Joe Bill," she said. "Lola, you're with me."

"Roger that," Lola said. "Where to?"

"First, Nix's storage unit," Phillips said. "Then, Fairbanks. I just let my husband know he's home with the baby for the duration. I'll be damned if I'm going to let the Troopers run a search for one of my deputies when my Kentucky ass isn't on the scene."

Brackett raised his hand again, then dropped it quickly when Phillips gave him one of her looks.

"What is it?"

"Ma'am," he said. "I've hunted the Brooks Range since I was ten years old. I know I'm APD, but Alaska peace officers have jurisdiction all over state. I'd really like to come along and help if I may."

"What about your brass?" Phillips asked. Then, seemingly thinking better of it, she waved the question away. "Never mind. I'll talk to your chief and make my case. If he'll let you go, we'll pick up the cost of your travel. We need all the help we can get."

"We should swing by and tell Mim," Lola said. "She might take it better if we're on our way to do something."

"We should," Phillips agreed. "But we're in a hurry. I don't see a scenario where she takes this well, but she might panic more if we make a big deal of it." Phillips stopped at the door to the secure hallway and whistled to the two deputies in the squad room.

"Hey, Chief," the taller deputy said. His name was Don MacKay. "What's up?"

"Teariki and I are leaving on the next available flight for Fairbanks. I need you and Cindy to head toward Mim Cutter's."

"Sure thing," MacKay said. "Don't we have her at the Marriott?"

"She returned home early this morning," Phillips said. "Don't make contact. Just park down the street. I'll call her on the phone and then get back with you. I might have you hang around to make sure she and the kids are okay."

"Roger that," MacKay said. "We'll go grab our gear and start that way."

"Get us some flights," Phillips said to Lola as they walked down the secure hallway on the way to the cellblock elevator. Security officers in the control room saw them and each door unlocked with a metallic whine as they approached.

"That was a good idea," Lola said. "Having Don and Cindy stand by with Mim."

"I'd like to believe I would have thought of it anyway," Phillips said. "But it's page one of that damned Red Book."

CHAPTER 41

*T*hey worked for four hours straight, stacking a rough pile of wood that was almost as large as the shed. Even the prisoners dug in and helped, grumbling the entire time, but working hard. No one, including Cutter, relished the idea of venturing out in the dark to get more fuel. With few blankets and temperatures plunging well below zero, they had to keep a fire going or risk freezing to death.

Cutter and Noah rigged a makeshift wall of wood pallets, a dozen empty jerry cans, and four 55-gallon plastic barrels that were normally used for water storage, forming wings off either side of the shed's opening. This made for a half-decent windbreak and a bunker-like barrier that Cutter figured would hold off a determined bear for a grand total of a half a second. Hopefully the collapse of the rickety fortification would make some noise if the bear did decide to breach the walls.

Every one of them, including Fig, was caked in a layer of snow and ice by the time they were done. The wind had died down, and the thermometer on Noah Sam's zipper pull said the temperature was holding steady at a balmy five above zero. Snow fell in huge popcorn clumps, some almost two inches across. Cutter estimated they'd gotten at least six inches since they'd started dragging up the wood.

Leaving Larsen with the shotgun again to guard the prisoners—outside the shelter where he could keep an eye on them—Cutter went with Noah to set the snares. Cutter's job was to watch for the bear.

He'd heard countless stories since moving to Alaska about brown bears exploding out of the brush. Sourdoughs seemed to delight in terrifying newcomers, recounting with morbidly vivid descriptions of faces torn away, heads knocked off with the single blow of a paw, or giant bears absorbing round after round of high-caliber ammunition only to keep up their attack. One man apparently had his back broken by a bear that then proceeded to sit down to feast on the poor paralyzed guy's tender kidneys during the last few moments of his agonizing life. Little in the world frightened Arliss Cutter, and most bears left people alone, but he would have been foolish not to respect half a ton of tooth and claw that considered him food.

The snares were simple loops of parachute cord with sliding knots that Noah hung over forked twigs so any unsuspecting snowshoe hair would have to pass through them as it moved down the well-used trail. Noah said he'd rather have used thin picture-hanging wire like his grandmother taught him, but having none, he made do with the parachute cord. Neither Noah nor

Cutter expected much movement tonight. Any self-respecting hare would be hunkered down in some warm pocket or den during a storm like this. Still, hunting was a game of odds, and the odds of catching anything were zero if they didn't set any snares.

Piper and Marie Baglioni had a fire started and two large pieces of corrugated tin propped up behind to reflect heat into the shelter by the time Cutter and Noah returned.

Three feet wide and approximately six feet long, the fire was built on a bed of the cut stove wood and another long piece of roofing tin they placed in a trench dug out in the snow with the hatchet. They hadn't quite reached bare ground, but they built the fire big and hot enough it would still be burning as the last few inches of ice underneath melted away.

Cutter got the snow dusted off the prisoners, then, as he'd promised, searched each one for anything sharp they might have picked up while hauling wood. He handed off his Colt and Young's Smith & Wesson to Noah for safekeeping, since he was danger-close to the prisoners, and had Larsen stand by with the shotgun during the search.

Finding no contraband, he took the revolvers back from Noah and situated the prisoners along their spot on the north wall. Then, for the first time since they'd landed over six hours before, he sat down to rest, using the thick beaver mittens as a cushion.

Mim would know by now that his plane was overdue. She'd been distant when they'd spoken last, but she expected his call and it bothered him that she'd be distraught. Lola had to be beside herself. For all her youthful bluster and bravado, she was still a kid at heart. A naïve, inexperienced kid, especially when it came to personal loss.

Cutter shook his head to clear it. No point in fretting over things he couldn't control.

Noah flopped down on a mattress between Piper and Baglioni. "With your permission, Professor, I say we break into the Spam and granola bars."

"I agree," Piper said. "We all need something to warm us up after that."

"Situations like this," Cutter said, "it'll be better if we make it into a soup. I know Spam soup doesn't sound that palatable, but it's better for us in the cold."

Baglioni rolled her eyes. "You have lots of experience in this sort of situation? Stranded in the cold with no rescue on the horizon."

"Rescue will happen," Cutter said. "And yes. I spent a fair number of cold nights in Afghanistan."

He didn't like talking about that time in his life, but it seemed important to establish his bona fides if he wanted these people to listen to him.

"Wait," Lamp said. "I thought Afghanistan was a desert. It gets cold there?"

Baglioni blurted out a derisive laugh. "You belong in jail."

Mutt Larsen piped up. "So, soup or—"

"Let's just eat it," Baglioni said. "We have the tea. That will warm us enough."

Cutter raised a hand in surrender. "Fine with me. Forcing everyone to eat Spam soup is not a hill I want to die on."

Noah used the little metal tab to peel back the lid and then pushed the Spam can out to Cutter. "You want to do the honors, Marshal?"

"How about we have Piper do it," Cutter said. "She looks honest."

Noah scoffed. "Ha! You've never played cards with her."

Piper used her pocketknife to cut eight relatively equal pieces of the semi-frozen potted meat while it was still in the can. She pushed the can to Baglioni. "You go first, Marie."

The professor grabbed a piece farthest away from the punctures made by the bear's teeth and wolfed it down in three quick bites, cupping her free hand under her chin. Larsen and Noah went next.

Cutter pushed the can back to Piper, who held up her hand. "I cut it," she said. "I go last."

Cutter fished out three pieces and handed one each to the prisoners, not worrying over niceties like washing his hands or using a fork—since he didn't have one anyway.

Spivey held his piece in both his hands and studied it in the light of the fire. "Looks like frozen tongue."

"I'm sure someone else will take it if you won't," Cutter said.

Spivey hunched forward, lifting his hands as high as they would go in the chains, and then meeting them halfway by craning his neck.

Cutter had never minded Spam, if it was all he had, but he didn't go out and look for it. Still, hunger was the best spice on earth, and these few bites had to be some of the most delicious food he'd ever tasted.

"I'll fire up the stove," Noah said, fiddling with the little brass Svea. "We'll get us some water going for tea. Too bad we don't have any sugar."

"We can drink it the Russian way," Cutter said. "Sweetening it with strawberry jam."

"Sounds like a way to ruin good Earl Grey." Noah grinned. "But I'm kind of a purist. Guess the extra calories from the jam will help keep us warm tonight." He stepped outside, into the shadows at the edge of the fire, and dug down to get snow from deep within a drift as tall as his head.

"We'll have the granola bars for breakfast," Larsen said.

Noah came back in with a metal cookpot full of snow. "And more tea."

Lamp coughed, Spivey glared, and Edward Nix watched Arliss Cutter's every move.

The tarnished brass stove whirred like a tiny jet engine against the bottom of the blackened stewpot. It heated the water, but more important, the glow of the little stove added a measure of much-needed cheer to the cabin. The fire outside cast primitive dancing shadows, but the constant circle of blue flame from a fifty-year-old stove represented something civilized.

Twenty minutes and four tea bags later, the citrusy smell of bergamot helped push back the pinched odor of scorched snow from the fire outside. The Earl Grey was ready.

Noah and Piper cuddled together under a blanket, passing one of two ceramic mugs back and forth between warming sips and fortifying smiles. Larsen appeared to expect the same from Marie Baglioni, but though she leaned against him for warmth, she cupped the only other mug in both hands and blew across the top, drinking periodically and gazing out at the flames. Piper was aware enough to see what was going on and nudged Noah until he poured some tea into his Nalgene bottle and offered it to Larsen. Pursed lips led Cutter to believe the strawberry jam wasn't sweet enough to hide the bitterness of the pilot's guilt over getting them stranded.

The bear had ruined or eaten most of the food, but Cutter was able to cobble together enough mangled cans to get three serviceable drinking implements for the prisoners.

He used the Spam can himself, covering the holes made by the bear's teeth with his fingers. Earl Grey, strawberry jam, and a sheen of floating Spam grease might just have become his new favorite beverage.

Fig, the big Tamaskan, got a decent dinner from food that the bear had ruined. He stood to stretch, went to the edge of the cabin to peer at something beyond the fire, and then turned to curl up beside Cutter.

Baglioni's face fell into a pout, like she might chastise the dog for abandoning her.

The dog hadn't even gotten settled before he raised his head, ears perked, tracking something outside in the darkness. He stood, turning to peer intently past the fire.

"He hears something," Baglioni whispered.

A low growl rumbled in the dog's chest.

"Figaro!" Baglioni said. "Leave it!"

The professor threw off her blanket and sprang forward, grabbing a handful of collar at the same moment the Tamaskan leapt toward the fire. The dog squirmed and whined, never taking his eyes off the darkness and falling snow.

Cutter downed the rest of his Earl Grey and dropped the Spam can. A long day of cold and fatigue combined with the bulky parka to hamper his movement as he pushed himself to his feet. He caught Nix watching him and wondered if the greatest danger was outside the cabin or in it.

A riot of snarling yelps cut through the night beyond the burned cabin, sending the already chargey Tamaskan into a frenzy.

"Coyotes?" Piper said.

Noah shook his head. "There are a few up this far. But I'm thinkin' that's wolves."

A grating roar, long and low like a far-off waterfall, joined the chorus of yelping squeals.

"Yeah," Noah said. "The bear is running wolves off his food."

"Food?" Piper asked, realizing what he meant the moment the word left her lips. Her hand flew to her mouth, covering a gasp.

"The body."

"Holy Mother," Baglioni whispered. She dragged a squirming Fig to her blanket next, using the opportunity to reclaim him from Cutter. "We should have done something."

Larsen bounced the back of his head on the wall. "Like what, Marie? The ground is too frozen to dig— and we don't have a shovel. We could have hoisted him up a tree, I guess, but we can't afford to use the only rope we have. What should we have done, brought him in with us?"

Lamp coughed, hacked up something, swallowed it, then said, "No thank you."

Baglioni turned up her lip. "You don't get a vote."

"Apparently you don't either," Spivey chuckled.

The pandemonium outside fell quiet. Silence did little to appease the dog, and Baglioni had to loop the end of the sisal rope through his collar.

"You think it's gone?" Piper asked.

Cutter shook his head. "No."

Noah pulled his girlfriend closer. "It's awful, but look at it this way. That bear's gonna be busy for a good while now. And not as desperately hungry as it was before."

"That's just fantastic," Baglioni said. "We are saved because the bear's out there eating someone else."

"Richards is past feeling," Larsen said.

The gruesome drama at least out in the open, if not over, Cutter settled again into his corner. His hands were finally thawing out enough to whittle. He took out his pocketknife and began to work on a fist-size piece of alder he'd found in the woodpile.

"Bud was a school teacher, you know," Larsen said out of the blue. He continued to bang his head on the wall, but softer now, punctuating his words. His speech was slightly slurred as if someone had spiked his Earl Grey. "Elementary. Wanted to make it his career, but I talked him out of it."

Spivey half lifted his tea can as far as the belly chain would allow, jingling the links.

"Well, that sucks."

"My experience," Cutter said. "We can't talk anyone out of doing something they really want to do. It's their decision."

Larsen shook his head, sniffing. "He was a hell of a teacher too. Taught up in Nuiqsut. The teachers there sometimes called it 'No Exit' because it can be hard to get a transfer out. Tough place, but Bud Bishop loved it, and the kids loved him. He'd still be alive if I woulda kept my mouth shut . . ."

Cutter waited a beat, and then attempted to steer the subject away from Mutt Larsen's confession.

"We need to set up a rotation for fire duty. Once this snow stops, search and rescue personnel will be more likely to see us if we keep the fire going."

He could almost hear Baglioni's neck crack she turned so abruptly. "Either you are deluding yourself, Marshal, or you're just not listening. I've already explained it to you. Our entire main building burned to the ground and not a single soul noticed the flames."

Cutter glanced up from his carving, careful to gesture with the wood. This woman seemed the type to freak if he so much as held a pen blade in her general direction. "Ah," he said. "But when your house burned, no one was looking for you."

Larsen groaned, then leaned forward and used the tip of his finger to draw a line in the tawny hair of the caribou hide. "It's a little less than four hundred miles between Deadhorse and Fairbanks." He jammed at the hide a few inches down the line. "My last contact on the radio was here, about seventy miles south of Deadhorse. I would have normally checked in somewhere around here, a hundred miles or so north of Fairbanks. So . . . you're right. They will mount a search and rescue, probably as soon as we're overdue. They'll assume we went down somewhere along this two-hundred-mile stretch in the middle of our reported flight path through the Brooks Range." Larsen ran both hands over his hair, hard, like he had a headache or wanted to clear away bad thoughts—probably both. "The Troopers take SAR seriously. I wouldn't be surprised if they've got ground teams driving the Haul Road already, even in the weather."

Noah gave an enthusiastic nod. "Those Alaska Search and Rescue types live for this kind of shit."

"They do," Larsen said. "But there's a problem. We are here." He touched a spot on the caribou hide a few inches over from his line. "Thirty miles west of the route they expected us to be on." He studied his crude map for a moment and then rubbed the marks away, covering his palm with countless brittle caribou hairs. "They'll probably search a corridor, let's say ten miles on either side of the road. In order to find us, they'd have to expand their search thirty miles west, and if they do that, they'd expand it the same amount to the east. That's a hell of a lot of ground. . . ."

Cutter worked his blade around a stubborn knot of alder and pondered the gravity of their situation while he did the math.

"Twelve thousand square miles," he said.

CHAPTER 42

Mim nearly broke her leg scrambling across the kitchen to get to the counter where she'd left her phone. Arliss should have called a long time ago. She'd been short with him when they'd spoken that morning, but that wouldn't have stopped him. She could have cussed him out and he still would have called as soon as he landed to check in and see if she was okay.

Her heart sank when Lola greeted her on the other end of the line.

"I was afraid we'd scare you if we dropped by," Lola said. "But I did want to let you know that Arliss's plane is a little bit overdue."

"Overdue?"

"Yeah," Lola said. "Maybe a weather detour or the pilot might have had some engine problems and had to land somewhere to take care of them."

Mim found her way to the couch and sat down, knees together, elbows on her thighs. "I don't understand. Don't y'all always take a satellite phone on these prisoner trips?"

"We do," Lola said. "But you know technology. Those sat phones can be finicky, especially if there's much cloud cover, like now."

Mim couldn't help but think Lola was working very hard to convince herself that Arliss was okay.

"What can I do?"

"Not a thing," Lola said. "Just have him call whenever he checks in."

"And you'll do the same?"

"Of course—"

Mim heard a voice she recognized in the background.

"Are you with the chief?"

Silence on the line, then, "Yes . . ."

Mim felt as if she'd been gut-punched. "It's late. This must be really bad if the chief's still out."

Jill Phillips came on the line next, speaking the forced sort of chipper that parents used to tell their kids the dead dog was running free on a make-believe farm somewhere.

"Hey, Mim. We would have stopped by in person, but Lola told me about the misunderstanding yesterday. Didn't want to make a bigger deal than this is."

"Stopped by in person to tell me what?"

"That's the thing," the chief said. "There's not much to tell. We're implementing a search and rescue out of an abundance of caution. I fully expect Arliss to call in anytime wondering what all the fuss is about."

"There's got to be something I can do!"

"There's really not," Phillips said. "Lola's right. Just tell him to call us whenever he checks in."

"Who's heading up the search?"

"Alaska State Troopers out of the Fairbanks post. I talked to the lieutenant a few minutes ago. They get this kind of scenario all the time. We're on our way to the airport now."

"Wait," Mim said. "*You're* going to Fairbanks."

"Don't read anything into that," Phillips said. "I'm just being overcautious."

Mim ground her teeth so hard her jaw began to ache.

"Do you think the plane crashed?"

"Don't even go there," Phillips said. "There's no evidence to suggest that it has."

"But you haven't heard any news at all?"

"That's true," Phillips said.

"Then there's no evidence that it hasn't."

CHAPTER 43

*J*oe Brackett met Lola and Jill Phillips at the airport with little time to spare. Clearing security while armed was a double-edged sword. They got to bypass the metal detectors and X-ray machines, but then they had to wait for the right TSA person and then Airport Police to meet them and check their credentials. As federal officers, Teariki and Phillips simply showed their creds, provided their unique code, and signed the TSA logbook. Brackett had to show his credentials as well as a signed letter from his chief and a trip-specific code.

They'd made it to the gate with just enough time to present their armed boarding passes before the door shut.

Lola couldn't help but notice how traveling with the chief deputy US marshal for the district greased the skids. There was no wait to get the electronic travel authorization forms signed, no explaining why they needed a rental instead of a taxi. If Jill Phillips wanted to rent a car, she rented it and filled out the paperwork later.

Chiefs, Phillips explained, could not break the law, but policy was another story.

It was dark and snowing hard by the time they retrieved their bags of winter gear and made their way out to the Fairbanks Airport rental car lot. Brackett crammed himself in the back seat with their canvas duffels and stacked parkas.

Lola drove, turning right out of the parking lot onto Airport Way. Huge flakes of snow zipped toward them from the darkness, starkly white in the headlights. Lola had always thought driving through falling snow at night looked like a starship going into hyperdrive. Thick stands of white birch lined the road on either side. The city glowed a sullen orange gray ahead of them.

She crossed under the Parks Highway. Left would have taken them the four hundred miles back to Anchorage. To the right, the highway looped around Fairbanks proper, toward Fort Wainwright army base, Costco, Barnes & Noble, and all the other stores that made the far-flung city of ninety-some thousand seem just a little less like the frontier outpost that it actually was.

Lola shivered. If she'd been on her own, she would have settled for a little Subaru sedan, but with the snow coming down in buckets, she was glad the chief had opted for at least a Jeep Cherokee—the biggest vehicle they had—to slog through the mush.

Lola groused to herself, fingers cramping as she gripped the steering wheel. "Did I ever mention that I'm from a nice warm island in the middle of the South Pacific?"

Phillips stared out the passenger window. Sometimes she was so broody she could have been Cutter's sister.

Lola could see Brackett in the rearview mirror, doing the same, deep in thought.

A rattle-can pickup with a lighted pizza delivery sign clinging to the roof shot by them, blinding her with a flash of blowing snow as it fishtailed around the corner onto University Drive. Blizzard conditions notwithstanding, the Fred Meyer grocery store parking lot was packed with vehicles, each nosed in against an upright post.

"Remind me never to move to a place where you have to plug in your car to go buy milk," Lola muttered, feeling the fire in her cracked ribs as she struggled to stay in her lane.

Fortunately, the slog to the AST D Detachment was just a little farther up Airport Way on Peger Road. She turned into the lot, busy for this time of night, crunching through the hashmarks of countless tire tracks in at least eight inches of new snow.

Phillips phoned ahead, and a sergeant named Miller met them at the back door, showing them to the ad hoc emergency operations center set up in a conference room off dispatch.

The aroma of strong coffee and carpet cleaner hung heavy in the air.

The smell of a command post, Lola thought.

To Lola, the trooper post felt like the home of an eccentric relative who hated to throw anything away. She doubted the place had changed much since the eighties. Stacks of files sat on a long table beside the dispatch center next to potted ivies and Ficus trees that administrative personnel had brought in from home. Though it was clean, it had a dusty, almost shabby feel in comparison to the glitzy offices of the US Marshals in Anchorage.

Whether intentionally or not, the message was clear: troopers were too busy working in the field to care about snazzy digs.

As was par for offices in Alaska, the walls were decorated with dead animals, many of these seized from illegal hunting or trapping operations. Phillips, not as avid a hunter as some, called them "skin and bones clubs." There were stuffed grouse, a musk ox skull, and the top jaw of a walrus with Alaska Native art scrimshawed down both massive tusks, each over two feet in length. An *oosik*, or walrus penis bone the size of a toy baseball bat, was mounted on a wooden plaque below the tusks. Much of the wall opposite a white board was covered by a rug made from a large brown bear, mouth open to expose wicked yellow teeth. Beside the white board was a wall map covering the area that stretched from the Yukon River north to the Arctic Ocean—approximately the top third of Alaska.

At least two dozen men and women were stationed around the room, poring over nautical charts, working the phones, or fine-tuning pieces of winter gear. Some wore blue Alaska State Trooper uniforms, others were dressed in civilian clothes with their radios in chest rigs that identified them as Civil Air Patrol, or WSAR— Wilderness Search and Rescue—who handled Interior Alaska, an area of responsibility larger than any state in the Union but for Texas. It was at once heartening to see so many involved in the search and rescue operation, but upsetting to see them milling around at the post.

After cursory introductions, Phillips got straight to the point.

"Where are we at with the search?"

Lee Terry, Lieutenant of D Detachment, pointed to the wall map. He'd just come inside and the impression of his Stetson's hat band was imprinted on the stubble of his crew cut. "Last radio contact would have put them about here," he said. "Not quite to Pump Station Number Three. We have an AStar chopper and a Piper Super Cub in Coldfoot, but the weather's a no go for flying. We do have teams on the ground going north and south out of Coldfoot and Pump Station Number Four."

"Is there a trooper at Pump Station Number Four?"

"No," Terry said. "Oil companies keep a small crew there. It's where they put in the Pigs . . . the little missile looking things they send down the inside of the pipeline to clean out sludge. Anyway, a couple of them volunteer to help on SAR events like this. A Bureau of Land Management ranger is there at the moment, so he's out on his snow machine as well."

"Seems like I heard the pipeline folks have drones?" Phillips asked.

Lola looked up in surprise. "Drones?"

"I told you nothing was off the table."

"The university uses them some," the lieutenant said. "They're small, though. Nothing that could go out in anything remotely close to this storm."

Phillips stepped closer to the map, pulling a pair of reading glasses from her fleece vest to study the details. "But we'll get planes up at first light?"

"As soon as the weather allows it," the lieutenant said. "I don't know if this helps, but if these were my people out there, we'd be doing this the exact same way we are right now. Mutt Larsen is a good pilot from all accounts. I don't know him, but I understand he's capable enough. Lots of experience in the bush."

"That's good to hear," Phillips said. "Deputy Cutter knows his way around the woods as well."

Lola gave an emphatic nod. "Hell yeah. And Bill Young, the contract guard who's with him, he's hunted in Alaska for years to hear him tell it."

"Outstanding," Terry said. "Then so long as the aircraft is intact, they're probably sheltered up somewhere with the prisoners waiting for first light. My suggestion is for you three to get some sleep. The search will ramp up tomorrow. We have several aircraft so we might be able to use you as spotters."

"The weather forecast holding?" Brackett asked.

"Same." Lieutenant Terry took a sip of his coffee. "We're hoping this snow will taper off sometime tomorrow, but when it does, temps are expected to plummet for a couple of days." He patted the Brooks Range on the map with an open hand. "It's going to feel an awful lot like winter in this part of the world."

"It feels like winter in your parking lot right now," Lola said.

The lieutenant held up his coffee mug and gave a sad shake of his head. "No, ma'am. Sure, we're getting dumped on, but this is just a wet spring. My dad calls this 'nuisance cold.' Excuse my language, but we're about to get what he called 'break-shit cold.'"

CHAPTER 44

*T*he eight hefty pieces of split spruce, each as big as Cutter's leg, began to pop like a string of fire crackers moments after Cutter stacked them on the coals. Sparks zipped upward, disappearing in the blackness. Driving snow hissed when it met the flames. According to Noah's thermometer, the reflected heat from the fire had warmed the interior of the open cabin nineteen degrees. Comfortable enough as long as one kept moving.

Guard duty was a problem. Cutter could get by on less sleep than most, but he was still human. Eventually, his body would sag and he'd simply nod off without realizing it. The prisoners had been dozing off and on throughout the evening, unincumbered by worry over anyone else's welfare but their own. They were watching him, Cutter could feel it, biding their time until he closed his eyes.

Mutt Larsen wallowed so deeply in guilt over Bud

Bishop that he was likely to be more hinderance than help during a confrontation. Something was going on with Marie Baglioni. She was injured or getting sick and spent an inordinate amount of time either holding her stomach or demanding Larsen accompany her to the outhouse. Even at her best Cutter doubted she'd do more than spit and fuss. Spivey and Nix responded to action, not words.

It was clear Cutter would have to depend on the interns for help. They were young, both in their first year of graduate school, but Cutter had been younger than that when he joined the army.

Cutter glanced at the prisoners out of habit, making certain they hadn't somehow slipped their shackles. The tiny cabin was so small that when stretched out, everyone's feet were virtually touching. The tight confines were less than ideal for security, but Cutter hoped they might help with the warmth.

They needed every degree of heat they could get.

Larsen and Baglioni shared two of the four blankets. Piper gave Cutter one of the other two. Cutter thanked her and used it to cover the prisoners' feet. He'd sleep on top of the old caribou hide and make do with his Wiggy's parka, which was exponentially better than anything the prisoners had.

"Legs only," he warned. "Keep your handcuffs visible at all times."

Spivey was on the end, nearest the fire, followed by Nix in the middle, with Lamp closest to the corner and the bunks. Cutter used the restraints he'd taken from Richards's body to secure the men together, running the five-foot belly chain between the knees of all three, above the leg irons, allowing them limited movement while they slept, but making it difficult for any one of them to stand up on his own. The extra leg iron looped around the timber leg of the bunks, before being secured to Lamp's end of the chain.

Cutter talked Noah out of an old T-shirt—cotton, so it did them little good in the cold anyway. He'd torn it into strips five inches wide and a couple of feet long.

Nix watched the procedure intently, but in silence.

Spivey jerked insolently at the chains. As usual, he was the one who groused.

"You expect us to sleep like this?"

"Yep." Cutter held up the strips of cloth. "And blindfolded."

Spivey blustered, gathering himself up like he might try and stand. "And if we refuse?"

Cutter sighed, letting his hands fall. "Honestly," he said, deadpan. "That would only make my job easier. I told you before, we're playing by a different set of rules at the moment."

"There ain't no rules," Spivey said.

"Oh, son," Cutter said. "You better hope there are rules."

Nix yanked on the leg chain to get Spivey's attention. "It's not worth it, Chance. Just let him have his way." Then as Cutter tied the strip of cloth around his eyes: "I guess you learned this in Afghanistan too?"

"Among other things," Cutter said.

Cutter asked Noah to take the first two-hour prisoner watch, bringing a derisive sneer from Professor Baglioni.

"I'd think you'd want to lead by example."

"You would, would you?" Cutter said without further explanation. He settled in on his caribou hide mattress, facing the prisoners. His legs hung off the end at midcalf and they'd likely act as an alarm clock as they chilled enough to wake him from whatever sleep he might get.

"I don't mind pulling first watch," Noah said. "I'm too jazzed to conk out now anyway. Smarter he takes the next shift when everyone else is passed out."

"Whatever," Baglioni said.

Larsen stared into the flames, looking lost.

Piper leaned her head on Noah's shoulder. Firelight danced on her oval face.

"So, no one is coming?"

"We'll have to see," Noah said. "I'm sure they'll be up looking as soon as this snow stops. Won't they, Mutt?"

Larsen tore his gaze away from the fire, blinking. "What?"

"They'll start searching for real tomorrow," Noah said. "Right?"

"Yes," the pilot said, hollow and distant. "I'm sure they'll have aircraft from both Deadhorse and Fairbanks."

"Yippee!" Baglioni scoffed. "A handful of planes to search an area the size of Vermont. I am absolutely giddy with hope."

Fig stood from his spot beside the professor. The rope still connected the wolf-like dog to the bunk bed, but he'd learned that he could move freely around the cabin. He yawned, turned to look at Baglioni, and apparently sick of her attitude, sauntered over to flop down beside Cutter.

The cabin fell quiet but for snoring prisoners, the snap of the spruce fire, and the distant growl of scavengers fighting over what was left of Gene Richards's frozen remains.

Nix waited an hour for the marshal to fall asleep, listening for the change in his breathing.

He wished he still had Bill Young's pocketknife, but he'd had to dump that earlier, after the wood haul before Cutter searched them. He'd let it fall outside the door, a step from the corner of the shed, beside their trail. It was covered with new snow now, but he knew where it was. With any luck, retrieving it later would be a simple matter of stumbling and snatching it up.

Lamp was still sawing logs beside him. On the other side, Spivey slept restlessly, but at least he slept. He was the biggest of the three and, outwardly at least, the meanest. Every few minutes, when he got sore from sleeping in one position and decided to roll over, all three of them had to move with him. Nix didn't mind the constant movement. This cold was paralyzing, made worse by the cramped circumstances and the unforgiving floor. Nix had always hated camping, but at least you got an air mattress and sleeping bag for that. Sandwiched between two stinking federal prisoners, he got a third of a blanket that didn't even reach his crotch. He treated the girls he kept prisoner on KGB Road better than this—until the end at least. The thought of the shipping container made him smile on the inside—until he remembered the look on Bud Bishop's face. Tolman must have gotten himself caught. That's the only way to explain it.

The fire burned less fiercely now, with fewer pops and snaps from the spruce resin. It still put out a fair amount of heat, but the flames were small, emitting much less light.

Perfect for what Nix had in mind.

He rolled a hair to the side, careful not to disturb Spivey and earn himself a kick. Lamp knew better. The belly chain kept Nix's handcuffs secured too close to his waist to be any use adjusting the blindfold, but he'd been able to rub his head against the floor enough to allow a tiny sliver of vision. He craned his neck to get a lay of the situation.

Noah sat beside his redheaded girlfriend, awake, but dazed. He spent much more time letting himself be lulled by the fire than watching three sleeping prisoners.

Nix moved slowly, timing his efforts to match Lamp's labored snores. Straining against the handcuffs, he wrapped his fingers around a chunk of Spam he'd saved back from the meager dinner. It was large, roughly a third of his portion. Saving it back left him hungry, but it was about to go to a much more noble cause.

Spivey and Nix had to lay on their left sides. Lamp, facing the bunks, had a slightly longer bit of chain and was able to lie almost flat on his back.

Nix gave Spivey three quiet tugs on the leg irons, the signal that it was time to take care of the weak link. Spivey got the message and tucked his long legs, giving Nix as much slack as possible in the chain that held them together.

Nix lifted his head, peeking out from under the strip of T-shirt, listening, waiting.

Lamp gave him the opportunity he needed moments

later. His snores paused, and he opened his mouth wide, sputtering and gasping like a beached fish.

Nix moved at once, rolling onto his knees so his waist chain and cuffs were directly in line with Lamp's face. Shielding his movements with his body, he jammed the chunk of Spam into Lamp's gaping mouth. Hands held together by the cuffs, he used both index fingers to stuff the meat down the back of his throat.

"He's choking! Someone help!" Though he sounded the alarm, Nix continued to push the piece of meat deeper into the other man's windpipe.

Lamp flailed, but chained as he was, could do little but bite down on Nix's fingers.

Nix roared. "I am trying to help you, asshole!"

He'd known this would happen. One of the girls had bitten him years before and he'd learned then that the greatest danger came when one tried to jerk away. Much better to keep pressing.

Cutter was up in an instant, yanking away the blanket to see what was going on. He was armed, and obviously didn't want to wade into the thick of things too quickly.

"Get away from him! Now!"

"I'm trying to, Marshal." Nix screamed in genuine pain. This son of bitch has sharp teeth. "He won't let go!"

Nix kept pushing, working his fingers and the potted meat deeper each time Lamp convulsed. He wished the fire were brighter so he could have the pleasure of watching the poor bastard's eyes as he reached the end.

Larsen was on his feet now, holding the shotgun, blinking stupidly and unsure of what to do.

A powerful hand closed around Nix's shoulder as

Cutter dragged him backward, dumping him on top of Spivey.

The marshal pitched Noah his small flashlight, and the kid shined it on Lamp's crimson face.

"He's choking!"

Nix lay on his side now, still facing the action, which he watched with stifled glee through the tiny gap below his blindfold. The dying man sputtered and groaned, arching his back so only his heels and the back of his head touched the floor.

"I told you," Nix shouted, adding to the confusion. "I heard him—"

Cutter kicked his feet. "Quiet!" Then, to Larsen: "Cover these two with the shotgun."

Lamp's body went slack.

Noah put a hand alongside his neck, feeling for a pulse. He looked up and shook his head, his face glowing orange in the firelight.

What was that all about?" Cutter asked, standing over Nix and aiming the small Streamlight directly into his eyes.

"I told you," Nix said. "I heard him choking."

"And you suddenly turned into a good Samaritan?"

"You say so," Nix said. "I just reacted."

Noah pried open Lamp's mouth and looked inside, remarkably calm considering his youth and the circumstances. "Can you point your flashlight over here?"

Cutter gave Nix a hard stare and then turned to Noah.

"What have you got?"

"I can't be sure," Noah said, pointing down Lamp's gullet. "But I think that's a piece of Spam."

"See!" Nix said. "What'd I tell you? He choked."

"I'm not buying it," Cutter said. "It's been too long for him to be choking on a piece of Spam he ate hours ago."

"And yet," Nix said. "There he is with Spam in his windpipe. He must have saved some back."

Spivey raised his head, attempting to see Lamp but hampered by the T-shirt. "Damn," he said, looking like he might spit in disgust. "I wish that asshole would have died before he ate his share of the food."

CHAPTER 45

*M*im sat on the edge of her bed, dressed in her sleeping shorts and one of Ethan's old Tampa Bay Buccaneers T-shirts, and took the letter out of the envelope—again.

This was far too big a decision to make on her own. She wished she would have talked to Arliss about it. She'd been so short with him last time they talked. Constance's idiotic notions weren't his fault. . . .

And now he was missing.

No. He couldn't be. People like Arliss Cutter didn't die.

Then again, neither did people like Ethan.

Mim couldn't even remember the last words she'd said to her husband. Something mundane, she was sure of that. They never fought. Ethan wouldn't have it. If she accused him of being wrong about something, he would just smile and say something like, "Okay, what can I do to make amends?"

Arliss was just like him, at least in that regard.

She should have told him about the letter, gotten his advice. He certainly deserved to know. Instead, she'd used their last conversation to complain about the bed in her hotel, the hotel he'd set up to keep her safe.

He'd come back. She knew he would. He had to. She'd tell him then.

She fell on the bed, holding the well-worn paper above her while she read it for the hundredth time.

The letterhead was from Ethan's old firm, which she'd found odd at first. They never sent her anything directly, insisting before Ethan was even buried that any and all communications be conducted through their respective attorneys.

This letter had been sent directly to her home address. It was short and to the point—obviously having been written by lawyers.

Miriam Cutter,
We are pleased to inform you that the investiga-
tion regarding the circumstances surrounding
your late husband's death has been concluded.
Though the company admits no responsibility as
to the cause or manner of Ethan Cutter's death,
we see no further reason to delay the life insur-
ance settlement. Payment will be disbursed im-
mediately.
Yours very truly,
Signed—
(Blah, blah, blah . . . a bunch of corporate ass-
holes who stomped the shit out of you for two years
after your husband was blown to pieces . . .)

Still on her back, Mim let the paper flutter down to her chest. The few tears she had left streamed down her cheeks wetting her ears. This was enough money to pay off everything—and put Alaska in the rearview mirror.

CHAPTER 46

"*W*ho oversees your research?" Cutter asked, seated against the wall, carving. The chunk of alder was taking the shape of an arctic grayling, complete with prominent dorsal fin.

A silent snow continued to sift down outside in the blue light. It was still cold, and miserable, like the low clouds had decided to skip spring altogether and stick around until summer. Cutter had taken the prisoners out to pee—keeping a weather eye for the bear. Everyone was happy to be back inside the relative warmth and safety of the little three-sided cabin.

"I'm a tenured PhD and department head," Baglioni said. "I oversee my own research." She touched her stomach as she spoke, wincing.

"You okay?" Cutter asked.

"I'm fine," she snapped. She moved her hand away, though it was obvious from her face that she was still in pain.

Larsen put an arm around her and let her lean on him. "She's just cold and hungry," he said. "Like all of us, I guess."

Noah and Larsen had gone out to check the snares at first light and brought back a single snowshoe hare. One bunny wasn't much for seven people, but it was now boiling in the stewpot on the little Svea stove that whirred between Noah's feet. He'd dug down to get the much denser "water snow," like his grandmother had taught him.

They'd not seen the bear, but there were fresh tracks beyond the outhouse.

"The reason I asked about your research," Cutter said, "is that there must be someone at the university who feeds your statistics into the computer, that sort of thing. People who know that you're out here."

"Of course people know I'm here." Baglioni winced again, speaking through clenched teeth. "What kind of question is that? I'm not one of your fugitives on the run."

Cutter bit his tongue. She was scared and obviously hurting. "What I'm saying is that anyone who knows Mutt will eventually think he's come to check on you and then they would naturally come looking for him here. Right?"

Larsen gave one of the long, groaning sighs Cutter was beginning to get used to. "I'm not sure that's in the cards."

"So, your relationship is a secret?"

"It is," Larsen said. "Technically, I'm still married."

Baglioni jerked away, fuming. "Technically and otherwise. You still live with her. I'd imagine you bring her flowers and take her to The Turtle Club for prime rib every other weekend—"

"Marie . . ."

"Just leave it," she said, sounding like she was talking to her dog. "I'm not in the mood to hear about—"

Spivey gave a low chuckle. "I don't know your wife, mister, but I'm having a hell of a hard time seeing how you could leave her for this moon-faced piece of—"

"That's enough," Cutter said, though he couldn't help but wonder the same thing. He blew wood shavings off his carving and peered up at the graduate students. "Won't someone at the university eventually check your welfare."

"Eventually is the key word," Piper said. "We call in over the sat phone every two weeks, but we called . . ." She looked at Noah.

"The day before the fire," he said.

Cutter carved for a bit, thinking. "So, we're looking at almost another week and a half before anyone expects to hear from you."

"About the size of it," Piper said. "We've been completely off social media since we've been working here. Most of our friends probably think we've ceased to exist. It's easy to be forgotten if you're not part of the daily noise."

"What are you going to do, Marshal?" Nix asked. "The tea and jam are going to run out, and I can't see us surviving long on rabbit water."

"I'm not sure yet." Cutter pointed his knife. "But I am fairly certain you killed Lamp in his sleep."

"Come on now." Nix recoiled, incredulous. "I tried to save him. Everyone saw it."

"We need to move," Larsen said.

Cutter shook his head. "Better to sit tight when people are looking for us."

"Usually," Larsen said, becoming animated. "But hear me out. Anaktuvuk Pass is maybe twenty miles to the west. They have a cell tower. If we could get within range of that—"

Baglioni threw up her hands. "Have you gone completely insane?" She rolled her neck around in a slow circle and then slumped forward, shaking her head. "I swear, Mutt, talking to you is like talking to a small child. We have no snowshoes. No camping gear. We'd make, what, two miles a day? And then what. Sleep in the snow? We'd freeze to death the first night."

"No, no," Piper said. "Mutt's got a good point. We'd only have to make it to the river. The wind off the glacier blows down that valley practically nonstop. In places where the snow isn't broomed away, it gets packed into hard drifts that would be a lot easier to walk on."

"She's right," Noah said, backing his girlfriend's play. "Much of the area outside this valley is low tundra and rock. I mean, this pocket of trees is why they built this camp here in the first place. The river valley is the same. It's mostly willow, but there are a few good-size spruce trees along the bank. Those should give us firewood and some semblance of shelter from the weather." Noah shrugged. "Still, Marie's not wrong, either. The river is almost two miles away. It'll be a bitch to get there. My grandma used to talk about tying spruce bows onto her boots like snowshoes. We probably have enough rope."

Spivey threw his head back, eyes closed. "Good old grammie gonna get you killed, son."

"Noah and I can go," Larsen said.

Baglioni snapped around, her face pulled in a horrified grimace. "You're not leaving me here with them."

"You're forgetting about the bear," Cutter said, whittling again. "I still don't like it."

"I'm not sure what makes you think you're in charge," Baglioni said. "But you're not."

"Be that as it may," Cutter said. "Separating is a bad idea."

"Or," Baglioni said, "we chain your criminals to a tree and let nature take its course—the bear or the weather. It's obvious that they had something to do with burning the airplane. Why do we all need to risk our lives by allowing them to eat our food, use our blanket, and make plans to murder us while we sleep at night. Who knows when one of them will try to shove a piece of Spam down our throats?"

"She makes a good point," Cutter said. "Larsen's trying to eat all the blame for this predicament, but the bulk of it is on you two—"

The professor let out a keening cry, like an injured bird, and fell sideways into Larsen.

"I'm going to be sick . . ."

Larsen and Noah half helped half dragged her outside. Piper took the shotgun and pulled bear watch.

Baglioni hadn't made it far before she began to heave. She had nothing left in her stomach to vomit.

"She doesn't sound so good, Marshal," Nix said.

Baglioni walked back on her own, apparently feeling better. "Just a spell," she said. "I must be coming down with a bug."

Cutter returned the knife and nascent wood carving to his pocket and stood. He arched his back, hearing the cracks and pops that seemed more and more prevalent with each passing year.

"It's not getting any warmer," he said, "and we're going to need more wood to make it through today and tonight. You prisoners come with me." He gave a nod to Larsen. "If you and Noah want to come help, that would be most welcome. I know I'm not in charge, but I suggest Piper stays back and keeps Professor Baglioni company."

"Happy not to go out there," Piper said, snuggling down in her parka, arms folded tight across her body.

Baglioni's lips pinched into a disdainful sneer, but sweat beaded on her forehead—worrisome, considering how cold it was.

"I already told you," she said. "I am perfectly fine."

Larsen looked at Cutter and gave a furtive shake of his head. Marie Baglioni wasn't fine at all.

CHAPTER 47

L ola sat slumped over a long command-post table, head on her arms like a kid in study hall who'd stayed up all night playing video games. Jet-black hair escaped its usually tight bun to frizz like a bottle brush. Each shallow breath sent a jarring bolt of pain up her side, a vivid reminder of her hammered ribs.

"Maybe we're looking at this the wrong way," she said without sitting up.

"How do you mean?" Brackett asked, unbelievably chipper since neither of them had had more than a few hours of sleep in the past two days.

Chief Phillips had gone up in one of three Trooper search planes, but they were RTB—returning to base. The weather, the pilots said, had turned "bum."

"This is going to take forever." Lola pushed back from the table and walked gingerly to the wall map. As bad as standing hurt, it felt better than sitting down. "Look at this. We're searching twenty miles on either

side of this two-hundred-mile stretch of Dalton Highway. That's an area almost the size of some eastern
states, with mountains that are what, ten thousand feet
high?"

"Seven thousand and change," Brackett said.

"The point is, where there are mountains, we're also
gonna have valleys." Her shoulders slumped in despair. "Unless search planes fly right over top of Cutter, he might never be found."

"He would know to stomp out an SOS or put up
some other signal."

"He absolutely would." Lola sniffed, furious with
herself for getting tearful. "But it's been snowing all
night and all day. Everything, including their airplane
and any survival gear, is going to be little more than
white lumps on an endless landscape of the same."

"Okay," Brackett said. "What do we do?" He put a
tentative hand on her shoulder.

It felt astoundingly good, so she let him keep it there
while they stood side by side, looking at the map.

"Cutter says virtually everything leaves tracks."

"Right . . . but . . ."

"You're thinking, 'She's crazy. Airplanes don't leave
tracks.' And you'd be right. But I'm talking about the
pilot. And Bud Bishop. And Edward Nix. Let's look at
the possibilities. If Nix overpowered Cutter and the pilots, there are two options: he seized some unforeseen
opportunity, or he had a preexisting plan. If he had a
plan, he'll have someone coming to pick him up, wherever he is."

"So we should check with the local flight service
and see if anyone had a remote pickup."

"Check with any and everyone who has an airplane.

There's a possibility that this is a hijacking and not a plane crash. We should be looking on the ground, as well as flying over it."

"And you think the pilot could be involved?"

Lola rolled her shoulder, gingerly stretching her injured ribs, stifling a groan. "Your guess is as good as mine. It doesn't sound like it."

"Or maybe it has nothing to do with this Nix guy," Brackett said.

"That's another scenario," Lola said. "The Troopers have gotten a look at most all of Haul Road by now, and the plane didn't go down there. Maybe Larsen had to skirt some weather or had engine problems. Just maybe he has a little hidey-hole somewhere he flew into."

"And if that's the case," Brackett said, "Someone will know about it."

Most everyone involved in the search effort was in the field. The entire Fairbanks AST post felt hollow, like an abandoned building. Only two uniformed Alaska State Troopers were left in the conference room, one a sergeant, the other a relief pilot named Ricks, waiting to give one of the incoming crews a break when they got a break in the weather.

Lola turned and addressed them at the same time. "Does the pilot have a family?"

The sergeant looked up from his laptop. "Mutt Larsen? Yeah, I talked with his wife, Ruby, last night. She's understandably worried. Didn't say much except he was supposed to come straight home after Deadhorse."

"She lives here in Fairbanks?" Brackett asked.

"Out Chena Pump Road," the sergeant said. "I'd

imagine she's gone out to her mother's now, though, up by Fox. Ruby did tell me she's had no contact with Mutt since he left for the airport to fly north day before yesterday."

Lola drummed her fingers against the wall map, pondering. "Her husband flies to the end of the world, spends the night, and then leaves the next morning with a surprise load of federal prisoners barely ahead of an approaching blizzard—and they don't talk?"

The sergeant and the trooper pilot exchanged glances.

"What is it?" Lola asked. "I have three brothers and heaps of male cousins. I can tell the look of a bro conspiracy a hundred miles away."

"No conspiracy," the sergeant said. "I just don't want to start a rumor that leads us up the wrong tree and wastes resources."

"Yeah, nah . . . I'm not buying it. What's the rumor?"

The sergeant nodded at Ricks, who dropped his pencil on the aeronautical chart and leaned back in his squeaky chair. "Word around the hangar," he said, "is that Mutt might have a little something going on the side."

"An affair?" Lola mused. "With whom?"

Ricks gave an honest shrug. "That's what we're all trying to figure out. The mechanic thinks it's someone who works on the Slope, but my fuel guy thinks it's a school teacher over by Salcha."

Lola went back to the table and flipped through the notes in her BattleBoard. "Larsen's copilot is a teacher. Maybe this mystery woman is connected to him."

"Bud did teach up on the Slope," the sergeant said. "Before he started flying more."

"How about his family?" Lola asked. "Bud Bishop, I mean."

"From somewhere in Alabama, I think," Ricks said. "The school district administrators go to job fairs in the lower forty-eight every year to try and convince a bunch of graduating teachers they need to come north to the future . . . or something like that. Bishop's got no family in Alaska that I know of."

"It sounds like your pilots are pretty close," Lola said.

"I guess," Ricks said. "Big state, small skies. There's a shitload of weekend pilots in Alaska. You know, folks with a plane they keep like the flying family Suburban to get them out to the cabin or whatever. But those of us who fly for a living depend on one another."

"Why do they call him Mutt?" Lola asked, changing tacks. "It's not his real name, is it?"

Ricks smiled. "Larsen found this village dog up in Wainwright, on the coast by Utqiagvik. Typical inbred mutt, crooked nose, flop ears, and sawed-off legs, like a cross between a German shepherd, a corgi, and some bent-nosed Roman emperor. Damned thing had been getting into everybody's trash, knocking over honey buckets, everything a dog can do to get itself in trouble. No one would claim it, so the village council put out an execution order. Fortunately, Wainwright falls under North Slope Borough PD jurisdiction so we didn't have to deal with it. Anyway, I guess Larsen was flying a 206 for another air service back then. He heard of the execution order, found the stinkin' mutt, and smuggled her out of the village. His boss nearly fired him because the plane smelled like shit from the honey buckets it had been knocking over."

"What happened to the dog?"

"Probably up in Fox with Larsen's wife and mother-in-law right now."

Lola leaned over the table, resting on both hands, and forced herself to take a deep breath. She looked sideways at Brackett. "If Mutt Larsen is having an affair, we need to find out who it's with. And that means we need to go talk to the wife."

"Who, Ruby?" the sergeant said. "She didn't seem to know anything about it when we talked."

"You guys," Lola said. "I hate to break it to you guys, but if all you flyboys suspect Mutt is having an affair, his wife suspects it too. She might not even admit it to herself. But she knows. The wife always knows."

CHAPTER 48

Nolan Lamp had turned on his side and drawn his knees up toward his waist at his moment of death. No one had bothered to straighten them out. Rigor kept them bent when Noah and Larsen moved the body outside the next morning, propping him with his back to the south wall of the cabin. They'd hoped to keep the corpse close enough to discourage ravens and the bear, but away from the direct heat of the fire. It froze in no time, before the rigor had a chance to pass, knees up, head back, mouth agape as though howling at the moon.

Nix trudged back and forth through the snow on firewood duty and found his eyes lingering on the delicious twist of terror frozen on the dead man's face.

The marshal refused to remove Nix's or Spivey's restraints, but tromping around in leg irons and a belly chain was better than sitting on his ass in the cabin. It gave Nix a break from being chained directly to Spivey.

The rodeo cowboy was beginning to give him looks and make snide comments, like he was the one who should be making the decisions.

"I know your secrets," he'd whispered earlier, wagging his fool head like he held winning lotto numbers or something. Evidently, getting bucked on his head countless times didn't kill all his brain cells because he'd been able to guess Nix's connection to the missing girls. Maybe from listening to Bill Young's discussion about authorities closing in on the Anchorage killer, and then putting two and two together when Nix had reacted so intensely to the incoming satellite phone call. Perhaps Bud Bishop had blurted out something incriminating. If he had, Nix hadn't heard it. His ears were too full of the sound of his own heartbeat, his mind too busy finding an immediate way out.

Spivey hadn't said anything else, but the threat was implied. The only reason to say something like that out loud was to exert dominance—control. Something with which Nix was intimately familiar.

He stopped for a moment, catching his breath in the bitter cold air while he watched the big man kick his way through the snow with a large piece of deadfall, dragging it toward the woodpile. Chance Spivey was a problem that would have to be dealt with—eventually. For now, Nix needed his thuggish strength, and more important, he needed the man's savvy. Nix had been to jail a few times, but he had no idea how to shim handcuffs or move deftly in leg irons. Spivey had spent time in prison, learning from masters.

The marshal wanted them to stay close while they worked. It made it easier to keep an eye on both of them at the same time. But it also allowed them to communicate more freely than they could while inside the cabin with so many prying ears right on top of them.

"You gonna do it when we get back?" Spivey muttered, turning to face Nix as he dropped his wood at the pile. Someone else would have to stack it because the belly chain made it impossible to raise their hands.

"After dark," Nix whispered. Larsen and the kid were busy with a large deadfall of their own for the moment, and something in the trees had grabbed the marshal's attention. "It won't take much more to get the staple out. Then we're in business—if you think the staple will work."

"It'll work," Spivey said.

The marshal glanced their way again, so they fell silent until he looked back at the tree line.

"You can't just use the Spam key?"

The metal ring had broken off when Noah had opened the can, and Nix had covered it with his foot. Everyone had been so focused on the food, they hadn't seen Nix pull it up to his waist and eventually hide it in a crack in the baseboard by his head. It took some contortion and misdirection, but he was able to retrieve it during the night and use the flat tip to pry on a loose staple in the plywood floor. It was maddeningly slow, working without getting caught, but time was not exactly in short supply. The colder and more exhausted everyone became, the easier his job became.

Spivey shook his head. "The older-type key might have, but that pull tab is all wrong. The lumber staple will work. But then what?"

Nix double-checked on the marshal before speaking.

"We watch and wait. He's getting tired."

"Yeah, well, so am I," Spivey groused. A drip of moisture from the cold hung on the end his nose. "I'm ready to end this shit now."

"Patience," Nix whispered. They started to walk again, going for more wood. He inadvertently stomped on the chain of his own leg irons, jerking him to his knees. As fascinating as all this was, maybe the time had come. He gave Spivey a wink.

"Tonight—"

The marshal's shrill whistle cut him off.

The lawman cut across the trails, tromping through deeper snow to reach them, quickly. Even the short trip of a few yards left him panting from fatigue and effort. He didn't tell them to stop talking, but that was implied by his scathing look. Instead of speaking at all, he took a willow twig out of his pocket and began to chew on it while he looked them up and down, waiting, it seemed, for one of them to break the chilly silence.

Spivey cracked first.

"Can I help you with somethin'?"

The marshal chewed on the willow twig a bit longer and then took it out of his mouth—with his left hand, Nix noticed, keeping his gun hand free.

"You boys are scaring me again," he said. "Making me fear for my safety."

Spivey harrumphed. "Yeah, well, whoop-de-do and good for us, I guess."

"I don't know what you're scared of, Marshal," Nix said, shivering. "We're all freezing our asses off out here, working hard for you."

The marshal lifted the twig as though to put it back

in his mouth, but peered over top of it instead, giving a slow nod. "Is that right?"

"Can't help it if you're scared," Spivey said.

"I'm not bullshittin' you," the marshal said. "I'm tired and I'm cold, and you boys chatting each other up like you were, I start feeling outnumbered. So . . . I need both of you to stay in line, stacked as it were so I can take both of you out with one shot. If one of you steps out of line, I'll consider that person is moving for me—and shoot you both."

"Wait, what?" Spivey said. "You can't talk to us that way."

"That so?" The marshal's tone grew darker. "I could tell from the very start of this by the soot on your boot tracks that you two went forward in the plane during the fire. Gene Richards's tracks had no soot . . . Meaning one or both of you two murdered Young and Bishop and started the fire—"

"Tracks?" Spivey hawked up a mouthful of phlegm and spat it into the snow. It crackled when it froze. "You don't have shit if you're banking your theory on a couple of sooty boot prints."

"Is that right?" The marshal looked at Spivey but jabbed his willow twig toward Nix. "This smarmy son of a bitch shoved a piece of Spam down another man's windpipe. The way I see it, you boys aren't operating under any rules at all—so why should I? If I feel threatened or get the slightest notion like you're threatening one of the others—I'll kill you both without a word." He chewed on the twig again, letting it sink in. "That's just how it's going to be."

"Good for you, Marshal," Nix said, clapping his gloves together as best he could, considering the handcuffs. "This is the most I've heard you speak since we've gotten to know you. Warms me to see a little fire in your belly."

The marshal stood mute as stone for a full minute, his already hard-barked face chapped and bitten from the cold. For a time, Nix thought he might shoot them both where they stood.

CHAPTER 49

*T*he Alaska Pipeline hove into view through blowing snow a few miles north of Fairbanks. The "four-foot-fat" pipeline snaked along the Elliot Highway and then turned north with the Dalton Highway, or Haul Road, eventually crossing the mighty Yukon, and continuing some four hundred miles north over the Arctic Circle, Oh Shit Corner, Coldfoot, the Brooks Range, and eventually, Deadhorse. It was one of the most desolate isolated strips of road in North America, with hundreds of miles between services—and Arliss Cutter was out there on it. Somewhere.

Brackett drove, suggesting Lola rest and take some of the pressure off her ribs—which she'd decided had to at least be cracked, if not shattered into a million pieces. Leaning back didn't help, so she sat up and looked out the window, brooding at the falling snow.

"We should just keep driving," she said. The defrost fan was on full blast, but her breath covered the side window with fingers of ice as she spoke. "My friend is somewhere out there in this, and we're just camped out in a warm car."

"I'm with you on that," Brackett said, smart enough to know argument was futile. "Let's talk to Mrs. Larsen and then make a plan."

"I know it won't do Cutter any good if we get ourselves frozen, but . . ."

Again, Brackett read the mood well enough to know Lola wasn't asking for him to "fix" the situation. She simply wanted to air her frustration.

Brackett slowed, glancing at the GPS on his phone, and then made a quick left.

"So this is Fox," Lola said, looking out the window at trees and snow.

"There's a bit more, farther north on the highway. The Troopers' notes show that Opal Runyon, Mrs. Larsen's mother, lives out here off Goldstream Road. It's still a pretty wild place. A step or two off the road will take you from civilization to the wilderness in a heartbeat."

"You've been here then," Lola said, relaxing a notch. One of Cutter's many rules: *Don't go anywhere for the first time.* Study maps, do in-depth recon online, send scouts, or, best of all, go with someone who'd gone before.

"My grandparents had a homestead in the Goldstream Valley," Brackett said. "My dad grew up not far from where we are right now. Like I said. Wild place. My grandpa used to tell me stories about the winter of '74 to '75 when wolves killed and ate something like a hundred and sixty dogs."

"Killer wolves . . ." Lola stared out the window

through the snow at the ghost-gray trees. "This just keeps getting better and better."

Brackett slowed the Jeep to a crawl, getting his bearings again.

"Right there." Lola used her hat to point at a narrow driveway, invisible but for a snow lump that was probably a mailbox and the tall whip reflector poles on either side.

Ruby Larsen met them at the door. Blond hair pulled back in a ponytail, she wore a thick Nordic sweater of gray wool and matching flannel pajama pants. Taller than Lola, she was sturdily built. Her sweater was pushed up to her elbows, revealing strong farmgirl forearms that reminded Lola of photos of her own grandmother.

Mrs. Runyon was an older version of her daughter, though slightly stooped from years and the hard work of carving out a home at the edge of the wilderness.

Ruby invited them into the living room while her mother brought coffee and bread she'd just taken out of the oven.

"No word yet?" Mrs. Runyon asked as she set the mugs down on a table cluttered with a collection of snow globes and hand-knitted doilies. A grandfather clock in the corner ticked so loudly that Lola began to imagine it vibrated the walls.

Brackett thanked her for the coffee and shook his head. "None yet," he said.

"I knew your father," Mrs. Runyon said, smacking her lips after a drink of her coffee. This was a woman used to running the show. "He used to help muck our kennels."

"Thought I recognized the name," Brackett said.

Larsen's wife didn't say much, seemingly happy to let her mother do the talking.

A short-legged dog wandered in from the kitchen and came to sniff Lola's plate on the coffee table.

"Go lay down, Abby," Mrs. Runyon said, then turned to her guests. "Sorry about that. She's shy on manners sometimes. David rescued her in one of the villages— from certain death, to hear him tell it."

"That's kind of what we wanted to talk to you about," Lola said, looking at Ruby. "We think your husband might have had to land in some spot off the beaten path. Is there anyone you could think of, a friend along the Haul Road, where he might seek shelter in an emergency?"

Ruby shook her head, a little too quickly.

Lola tried again. "I don't have to tell you, but the weather is pretty bad in the Brooks Range right now. From all accounts, your husband is an excellent pilot and would have done his best to skirt the bad stuff or land and wait it out."

Mrs. Runyon took another sip of coffee, coaxing. "Doesn't he usually just follow the Haul Road, sweetie?"

"I think so," Ruby said. "That's not something we talk much about."

"We're under the same assumption," Lola said. "Crews up and down the Dalton Highway are out looking on the ground and, weather permitting, in the air. We're just hoping you might know of any other acquaintances your husband might have between here and Deadhorse, somewhere he might wait out bad weather . . . someone he may have called . . ."

Lola asked the same question five times, coming

just short of asking if she knew about any affair. No matter how many times she asked it, Ruby only shook her head and stared down at her coffee.

Mrs. Runyon, on the other hand, could hardly stay still. Finally, she'd had enough and set her cup on the table with enough force to slosh some over the side. She used her sleeve to wipe it up before it reached one of the white doilies and then sat back in her chair with a resigned sigh.

"If she's not going to tell you, I will."

"Mom!" Ruby Larsen shook her head, her pale complexion flushing bright pink.

"We're not just talking about your husband out there, sweetie," Runyon said. "There are other lives at stake."

Ruby's eyes welled with tears. "Okay," she whispered. "David has a friend, a professor at UAF. He thinks it's a secret . . ."

Ruby Larsen told them everything she knew, which wasn't much, but for a name and place of employment. She didn't even know what the other woman looked like, though a simple Internet search would have revealed that in no time.

Mrs. Runyon left her distraught daughter in the house and followed Lola and Brackett out to the car. They were in their parkas, but the older woman wore only a wool cardigan against the bitter cold.

"I'm sorry about that," she said. "Mutt's not a bad man. He's always reading novels and studying this or that. Damned intelligent in a lot of ways, pitifully stupid in others."

Lola had to push back her hood to hear, and the wind blew a thick strand of hair across her face. She tucked it back and turned. "Could this woman and Mutt have a place together somewhere remote, a cabin on a lake or something, maybe between here and Deadhorse?"

"I'm sorry," Mrs. Runyon said. "No idea. I never met the lady and never want to. You'll have to talk to her. As you can imagine, Mutt was never very forthcoming about this." The older woman pulled the sweater tighter across her chest, finally noticing the cold. "A professor at the university . . ." She shook her head. "Not right, but it does make sense. My daughter isn't dumb, not by any stretch, but she's not a big reader, nor was she someone who Mutt could talk with about math or science or whatever the hell else he was interested in at the moment. A lot of stuff goes into making a marriage—but it doesn't seem to take much to break one . . . I don't pretend to know all the details, but I suspect Mutt just plain got tired of my Ruby and figured he needed somebody smart to talk to . . ." She shook her head. "Anyway, I hope you find your friends."

She made no mention of her son-in-law.

"I don't care if Mutt Larsen did save a cute little village dog," Lola said when she'd eased herself into her seat and shut the door. "We need to find him so that Ruby can have the opportunity to kick his ass."

Lola called the chief, putting her on speaker so Brackett could hear.

"How about the search on your end?" she asked after she gave a quick rundown about Larsen's side chick.

"Weather has turned shitty," Phillips said. "Everyone seems to be cooling their heels here at the Trooper post. We're talking whiteout conditions. Apparently two snow machines ran off the road near one of the pump stations."

"Injuries?"

"Just pride," Phillips said, sounding as exhausted as Lola felt. "I ordered fourteen pizzas for the SAR guys. There's plenty if you want some."

Brackett shook his head.

"We're not hungry," Lola said.

"Me either," Phillips said. "But you need to eat to stay warm."

"Roger that, Chief," Lola said. "We'll pick something up. We're heading to UAF now to talk to this Marie Baglioni. The university website says she works in the Department of Atmospheric Sciences. I'll let you know what we find out."

Lola ended the call and stared out the windshield, hypnotized by the thump of the wipers that barely kept ahead of the heavy snow. It was one of the rare moments in her life when she was happy her companion didn't want to talk. This Baglioni chick had better know something, or they were back to square one—and Cutter was screwed.

CHAPTER 50

Noah killed a porcupine while he and Larsen were out checking the snares. Rather than stay in the woods and risk drawing unwanted attention from the bear, he dragged the carcass back to the cabin, quills and all.

Not exactly simple, skinning was a theoretically straightforward process of flipping the beast over and starting at the quill-less belly to avoid getting stuck.

In Cutter's experience, food prejudices started to fade after a couple of days of hunger. After three, people who insisted their eggs be cooked hardboiled would drink one warm and raw straight out of the shell.

The hapless porcupine was at least something other than snowshoe hare, and everyone sat with rapt anticipation while Noah skinned and gutted it.

"My grandmother always kept track of where the *dekehone* were. She taught us we should never kill one unless we didn't have anything else to eat." He spread the skin quill side down on the snow and used it as a makeshift bag in which to store the offal. "It's too easy," he said as he worked. "I didn't even have to use one of the .22 shells. Just a stick."

Even Spivey kept his mouth shut and let the boy tell stories of his grandmother. It was worth the price of fresh meat.

Larsen boiled the front legs and ribs, cracking the bones to make soup, but they splurged and roasted the rest of the animal between two green willows in front of the fire. It took the better part of two hours, but the smell of sizzling meat gave them a much-needed boost in spirit—even if it was likely to entice the bear.

Cutter gave each prisoner a piece, careful to remove anything sharp. He'd seen deadly weapons made from flimsier stuff than porcupine bones.

Smoke and hunger were two of the best spices on earth and the meat was delicious, if a little on the sprucy side.

Marie Baglioni refused any of the roast, which was good because it went fast with six of them eating an animal that turned out to be made more of quill than meat.

She sat in the corner, sipping porcupine broth. For a time she appeared to feel better, until a sudden cramp doubled her over in pain. She handed off the mug to Piper and hissed at Larsen, who helped her stumble quickly outside. They returned a short time later, only to turn the moment she set foot back in the cabin for another trip toward the outhouse.

She was pale and panting with exhaustion by the time she was finally able to lie down.

"Anyone else feel sick?" Cutter asked.

"I'm sick of this," Piper said. "But no."

"Marie," Cutter said. "The broth made it worse?"

She nodded through a shuddering breath, not even wanting to speak.

"Gall bladder," Spivey pointed out, as though it should have been obvious to everyone. "My old lady had an obstructed bile duct. Professor Baglady is a prime candidate—fat, forty, and fertile—"

Larsen lunged, getting a glancing blow on Spivey's face to defend his girlfriend's honor before Cutter pulled him off.

Spivey looked up at Larsen and snarled. "That, little man, was a bad mistake."

"Enough!" Cutter said.

"I was pointing out the obvious," Spivey said. "And you let him hit me while I'm chained—"

"I said that is enough!" Cutter said again. He looked at Larsen. "He's goading you, trying to make you get close. Don't."

"You should listen to Wyatt Earp," Spivey said. "'Cause I'll kill you if you ever do that again."

"Watch them for me," Cutter said to Noah.

The young man nodded, gnawing the last shreds of meat off a bone from the porcupine haunch as he traded spots so he could keep an eye on the prisoners while Cutter checked on Baglioni.

"He could be right about the gall bladder," Cutter said. "Have you had spells before?"

Baglioni gave a shuddering nod. "Nothing recent," she said. "Until a few days ago. About the time of the fire. I'm careful with my diet, and they've always sub-sided on their own."

Larsen looked up, terrified. "Appendicitis maybe?"

"That's possible," Cutter said. He put his wrist to her forehead. As he expected, she was burning up.

"Marie," he said. "I'm going to press lightly on your stomach."

She nodded, but said nothing.

Cutter double-checked on his prisoners and got a thumbs-up from Noah. Spivey looked on with interest, but Nix seemed transfixed, the corners of his mouth perking into a slight smile that matched the gleam in his eyes.

"How does this feel?" Cutter asked, working his way across Baglioni's gut, low, along the waistline of her pants.

She groaned, but didn't recoil like he thought she might. "Hurts whether you touch it or not."

"Okay," Cutter said. "This could be serious. I need to try something, but I have to be honest. It might hurt."

Her eyes flickered open. "What is it?"

"It's called Murphy's sign, a test to see if this is your gall bladder."

"You have medical tra—" She caught herself. "Let me guess. Afghanistan? They teach you guys something besides killing people . . ."

"A fair amount," Cutter said, softly, hoping to put her at ease—but a bedside manner wasn't exactly one of his strong suits. "I saw a couple of guys with gall bladder issues when we were a ways off from what you might call decent care. Field medicine is a necessary skill."

Cutter knelt directly beside her, his hand hovering

over her belly. "I'm going to push under your ribs for just a second."

She gave a quick nod, eyes clenched. "Okay."

Larsen and Piper held Baglioni's hands while Cutter pressed his palm firmly under her bottom right rib and asked her to inhale.

She tried to comply, but the pain was so great she arched off the foam mattress, unable to draw a breath.

Cutter removed his hand immediately.

"Sheeeeit!" Baglioni said, once she could breathe again. Tears pressed from her lashes. "Are you trying to kill me?"

"I'm afraid it is your gall bladder," Cutter said. "If the bile duct is blocked bad enough, you could become septic."

Baglioni licked dry lips. "That's not good."

"No, ma'am," Cutter said. "It is not. Normally, I would say it was better to stay put, but this makes me rethink my position. I agree with Noah. Sending someone to try and reach the cell tower is risky, but Marie's condition may warrant the risk."

"It's doable," Noah said. "I was thinking it through last night. Depending on how clear the river is, I might be able to make it in two days, a day and a half if I'm really, really lucky."

"I don't know," Cutter said. "Luck's in short supply out there."

"I'll go with him," Piper chimed in. "Safer with two."

"You're forgetting about the bear," Baglioni said.

"She's right," Piper said. "Even if we take one of the revolvers, that's one big-ass bear. And we'll be sitting ducks camped out without shelter. And we have to walk right past where it has the rest of Richards's body cached . . . if there's any of him left."

Cutter and Larsen exchanged glances.

"Then we'll give the bear something else to cache," Larsen said. "Somewhere in the opposite direction from where you'll have to walk."

"Something else to cache?" Piper caught on even as she formed the words.

No one said it out loud, but they all knew Larsen meant moving Lamp's body away from the cabin. Procuring food in the wild was a matter of economy. The less energy a predator had to expend to get a meal, the better. The grizzly would be much less likely to follow Noah and Piper if it already had Nolan Lamp to eat.

CHAPTER 51

Nix retrieved the metal ring from the can of Spam and began working to pry out the flat metal staple while the others were focused on Marie Baglioni. He'd passed it to Spivey at about the same time the marshal jammed his hand into the woman's ribs, bringing on one of the most tragically beautiful whimpers of pain Nix had ever heard.

Spivey hid the staple in a crack in the floor beside him, within easy reach, but immediately began to bend the ring back and forth in the middle, eventually breaking it into two even pieces. It would have been visible had there been sufficient light, but in the dancing shadows from the fire, the staple looked like it belonged there.

The two outlaws were able to talk in fits and starts while they returned from helping move Lamp's body. That was a surreal maneuver, Nix thought. In his wildest dreams, he'd never imagine that a deputy US marshal would force him to help dispose of the body of a man he'd killed.

"We should wait," he whispered to Spivey as they walked. He timed his words to coincide with Noah or Larsen speaking. The marshal hardly ever talked, but he listened when the others did, and sometimes he even answered.

Spivey kept walking without acknowledging.

"We have to wait," Nix said again. "Fewer eyes on us after they leave."

Spivey said nothing until they were back at the cabin and the marshal had run the chain from the bed-post to their ankles. With Lamp's chains no longer in use, he could be more creative, and ran a line through their belly chains as well, which he also affixed to the bed. It was supremely uncomfortable, but the marshal didn't appear to care. For that matter, neither did Chance Spivey, who rolled over on his side and closed his eyes.

Frustrated at the new restraints, Nix shook his cuffs, rattling the chains against the plywood floor. "How do you expect us to sleep like this?"

The marshal nodded to Spivey. "He's not having any trouble with it."

Spivey opened one eye. "Maybe I hit the ground so hard coming off so many bucking horses that I'm fine sleeping here as long as I can lay down nice and easy."

"Or maybe you're just brain damaged," Nix said.

"Maybe so," Spivey said, yawning. "But I sleep like a baby, wherever I lay my head—no matter what I've done during the day. . . ."

CHAPTER 52

*D*eteriorating weather had pushed searchers in from the field, many of them packed into the Trooper command post, which at this point smelled like stale coffee, pizza, and wet dog from all the gear sodden with snowmelt.

The entire post had taken on the air of a law enforcement reunion, with friends from far-flung outposts seeing one another for the first time in months—or since the last major search. Wildlife Troopers, Bureau of Land Management Rangers, US Forest Service Resource Officers, all familiar with the Brooks Range, had shown up to assist, along with troopers from other posts.

Lola recognized Sergeant Don Yates at once. He had been the sergeant in Ketchikan, overseeing the post on Prince of Wales Island until they'd gotten their own sergeant. Lola and Trooper Sam Benjamin had tried the long-distance romance for a time, after she and Cutter had worked a case on Prince of Wales. Long enough for her to learn that Yates had once lost his temper and done a hat dance on top of Trooper Benjamin's Stetson, stomping it flat. Those blue Stetson campaign hats were sacred things among troopers, and a petty anger-management issue like that would have been enough to get him demoted, had Benjamin reported him. Yates knew it and left Benjamin alone, more or less. He must have burned enough bridges in Southeast that the Troopers did what most agencies did with their bad apples—shuffled him around to be someone else's problem for a while. He was now a sergeant in Palmer, close enough to AST headquarters in Anchorage that the top brass could keep an eye on their problem child but far enough away that they didn't have to look at him every day.

For some reason, probably to get him out of their hair for a time, decision makers had sent him to help out with the search operation in Fairbanks.

Jill Phillips must have known him too. She came in from taking a phone call in the lieutenant's office and saw him. "Well, hell." She groaned. "Gaining that guy is like losing three good men."

Lola resolved not to talk to him unless absolutely forced to do so. Instead, she directed her inquiries to Lieutenant Terry, who stood perusing the wall map with a US Fish and Wildlife pilot who wore a desert tan flight suit.

"So Baglioni's camp is there," Lola said, nodding at the map.

The lieutenant tapped a spot in a narrow valley with the clicker end of his ink pen. "Yes, ma'am," he said. "Right here. UAF Climate Research Center station.

But it's thirty miles off Larsen's flight path. That's a long way to fly when you're in a jam."

"True enough," Lola said. "But no one has been able to make contact with Baglioni or anyone else at the station. Either via radio or satellite phone."

"Maybe Larsen wasn't the one in trouble," Brackett offered. "Maybe Baglioni called him for help."

"And then what?" Sergeant Yates said, crossing the room with a slice of pizza in hand and insinuating himself into the conversation.

Lola did her best to ignore him. "I'm assuming you'll get aircraft up at first light," she said. "I'd like to go along if that's all right."

The lieutenant clicked his pen against the map again, measuring his response.

"That's my partner out there, sir," she said. "I didn't come here to be *tangata matakitaki*—a bloody tourist."

"You misunderstand my hesitation, Deputy Teariki," Lt. Terry said. "I'm happy to put you on board one of our aircraft, as soon as one is able to go."

Sergeant Yates saw his opportunity to make points with his boss.

"I agree, Lieutenant," Yates said, gesturing at the map with his pizza. "Larsen's aircraft has been overdue and out of commo now for, what, two days and nights by tomorrow morning. Given the extreme cold and all this snow . . . We need to weigh the risk of more human life for a search and rescue operation against what is starting to look a hell of a lot like a body recovery—"

Lola flew at him, intent on gouging his eyes out. "Body recovery my ass!"

Phillips grabbed her by the back of the fleece jacket

and dragged her away before she connected—assisted by Joe Brackett.

Sergeant Yates looked to his boss as though he expected him to do something, but Lt. Terry merely turned back to the wall map as if nothing had happened.

The chief nodded toward the door, and Brackett helped escort Lola out into the hall.

Lola stood seething, arms folded, eyes full of angry tears. "I wonder what he'd say if it was his friend out there."

"I doubt he has any," Brackett said.

"The weather *is* bad," Phillips said. "We have to realize that. Lieutenant Terry is a good hand. We have to trust him to do his job."

Lola closed her eyes and took a deep breath. "I'm sorry, Chief. Won't happen again."

"It might," Phillips said. "If he says something like that around me. Frankly, it's lucky for me that I had to worry about your career, or I'd have kicked him in the nuts."

Brackett grimaced. "Always the nuts with you ladies."

"Sends a message," Phillips said.

A female trooper in a blue BDU work uniform came out of the command post carrying a plastic water bottle. "Hey, Joe Bill," she said, gathering him into a big hug. "I thought that was you. Geeze, what has it been, two years?"

Brackett introduced her as Julia Montez, a former classmate at UAA. She'd been hired by the Alaska State Troopers a year before he went with Anchorage PD.

Trooper Montez glanced over her shoulder toward the command post door. "Nobody likes him, you know. Not even his bosses."

"Why do they put up with him?" Lola mused.

"We have plenty of our own," Phillips said.

Lola nodded. "I guess."

"In our case," Montez said, "I think they keep Yates on board to make sure none of us can get too happy. I mean, this is a great job, so you have to have someone like Yates in the mix to keep us down to earth. I think the bosses like us to be lean and hungry . . . and a little bit pissed."

"That sucks," Brackett said.

Montez gave a shrug. "Troopers gonna troop. Anyhow, Yates gets in trouble for being an asshole all the time, but he serves a purpose to the bosses—hatchet man who everyone hates already, that kind of thing."

"We've got a couple of those," Brackett said.

"I suggest we get some sleep," Phillips said. "All we can do is wait for the weather to clear up enough to fly."

"And hope Sergeant Yates spontaneously combusts," Lola said, still fuming.

Montez held up her water bottle as if to toast. "I'd be okay with that."

Phillips gave a tired chuckle and led Lola a few steps away, out of earshot of the others. She put a hand on her shoulder and looked her directly in the eye. "My advice," she said. "Sleep. Nothing else."

"What?"

"You know *what*," Phillips said, giving a nod to Brackett. "I was single when I joined the Marshals Service. I've been down this road before, or one very much like it. It's easy to fall into some cute guy's arms for solace when we're upset."

Lola stifled a laugh, wincing. "No worries on that front, Chief. My ribs are way too sore to fall anywhere for comfort tonight."

"Good," Phillips said. "I don't need you comforted. Like the lady said, you're better off to me and Cutter if you're lean and hungry—and a little bit pissed."

CHAPTER 53

*T*he fire began to die down just before eleven, leaving a noticeable drop in the temperature inside the cabin. Noah got up to stoke it. Cutter helped him, taking the opportunity to get his blood flowing and warm up a little between fitful catnaps on the ratty caribou skin—which provided little padding from the plywood floor.

Noah stood at the edge of the cabin opening when they were finished, orange light reflecting off exhausted faces as the flames began to build again. He gazed out at the trees for a moment, thinking, before glancing sideways at Cutter.

"You doing okay, Marshal?"

The simple question hit Cutter like a brick. This kid was impressive. Surely cold and numb himself, he was about to embark on a journey that might well freeze him to death, and he still had the empathy to worry about someone else.

"Better than I deserve to be," Cutter said, giving an honest smile despite his half-frozen face. He opened and closed his hands, desperate for warmth from the fire.

Noah nodded at that and then turned to look into the darkness again.

"*Duhtseedle,*" he said. "*Snow in trees.*" Hands open and stretched toward the fire, he gestured to the tree line with his chin. "Hunting is good when there's lots of *duhtseedle.*"

Cutter chuckled. "It helped us catch Spivey," he said. "Thanks to your aim with the snowball."

"Makes it easier to sneak up on moose too." Noah took a deep breath, blowing vapor. "Snow seems like it's slowing up some. It's going to get really cold when these clouds clear off.

Spivey spoke from behind them. "Colder?" He was just a few scant feet away, listening to everything that was said. Cutter hated that, but it couldn't be helped.

Everyone except Larsen had generally learned to ignore Spivey's mouth.

"I think I should go right now," Noah said. "Get on the trail before the cold really sets in."

"Well, shit," Spivey said. "I'm cold as hell already."

"You sure you want to go before first light?" Cutter asked. He would have felt the same way but wanted to give the young man a venue in which to talk out his plan, look at all sides.

"I've hiked up and down this valley dozens of times," Noah said, his face all but glowing in the center of the traditional fur parka ruff he'd added to his Canada Goose parka. "My grandma says I got a compass in my nose."

Spivey scoffed. "Again with grandma . . ."

Nix chuckled softly, but said nothing.

Noah kept going. "No way I'll get lost, Marshal. The snow reflects what light there is coming through the clouds. Once we're away from the fire and our eyes adjust, we won't even need a flashlight until we get to the river and have to look for overflow. By then, it will be close to daytime. We might even make it before nightfall tomorrow. But we would have to get going now."

Piper and Fig came to stand beside him.

"You're right," Piper said, her voice hushed, at once excited but unsure. "We should go now."

Baglioni lifted her head, grimaced, and fell against Larsen's lap. "What about the bear?" she said, breathy, concentrating hard to stave off the pain.

Noah shrugged. "I heard him when I went out and got that last rabbit right before dark. He's . . . where he's supposed to be."

Spivey chuckled. "Crunchin' on Lamp's bones—"

Cutter gave the man's boot a stiff kick. "Shut it, Chance."

"Marie's fever is getting worse," Piper whispered. "She can hardly keep still anymore. Bear or no bear, she needs help now."

Cutter rubbed a hand across his face and groaned. "I get why you want to go," he said. "But you won't do anyone any good if you die on the way."

"We'll be fine," Noah said. "So long as we don't freeze to death, fall off a cliff, get eaten by a bear, or fall through the river ice . . ." He put a hand on Cutter's shoulder. "Seriously, wouldn't you want to get going yourself if you didn't have the prisoners?"

"I would," Cutter said.

"Okay then," Noah said, sounding much older than he actually was. "We'll take the Svea and some tea, and leave you the pot. You guys keep the rabbit. We'll take that piece of the porcupine that's left. There are beaver lodges along the riverbank. Not very sporting, but we can dig into one if the trip takes a little longer and we have to get meat."

Cutter fished the cell phone out of his pocket. "Keep it off and in your pocket until you think you might have a signal. If you do make contact, give your location first."

"Got it." Noah stuffed the phone inside his parka near the heat of his body.

Noah lashed a set of feathery spruce boughs to Piper's feet while she sat on the edge of the cabin floor. She shivered, as much from anticipation as the cold. Temperatures hovered just above zero, turning the snow into a fine powder. The clouds seemed higher, like they might not stick around.

Cutter pushed his mittens and the Smith & Wesson revolver to Noah, who'd tied spruce boughs to his own boots. "I need these back after you're done saving us," Cutter said. "The mittens were made for me by a friend, and Bill Young's wife may want his gun."

"I'll take care of them," Noah said. He lifted a foot, adjusted the knots on the makeshift bindings, and then nodded in satisfaction.

"Nice knowing you, kid," Spivey said. Both prisoners sat up now, watching, shaking their heads in disbelief.

Cutter couldn't really blame them. A painful cold

seeped into his bones every time he stepped more than a few feet away from the fire.

Piper stood in front of the flames, careful not to ignite her spruce snowshoes, while Noah used a willow walking stick to climb up makeshift steps he'd tromped in the now-elbow-high wall of deep snow at the edge of the firelight, beyond the reach of the heat. The dog bounded back and forth, sensing that someone was going to go for a while and intent on going along.

Noah sank to midcalf, took an unsteady step, sank again, high-kneeing it each time he moved forward like a soldier on parade. He threw back his hood and exhaled a cloud of vapor.

"It's tough going," he said, panting already. "But doable. The snow's probably four feet deep in places, but these snowshoes float me in the first foot."

Spivey, who was closest to the cabin opening, leaned out to watch. "Is it true that you guys have a hundred words for snow?"

"Don't know about a hundred," Noah said, still testing the depth. "But we have a lot. English is the same. Powder, frost . . . slush . . . drifts . . ." He stopped, leaning on his willow stick to catch his breath. "My grandma woulda had a word for this too—heart-attack snow."

CHAPTER 54

J oe Bill Brackett clicked off the television in his hotel room, the glow of the bedside clock and the red LED on the smoke detector on the ceiling providing the only light. Brackett rarely watched TV at home but thought he might find something to take his mind off the fruitless search . . . and off of Lola. That was hopeless. He was sucking fumes, so tired his skin hurt, like he'd been rubbed all over with sandpaper. He desperately needed to sleep, but his brain just wouldn't cooperate.

He'd never met anyone like Lola Teariki. He could have sat and watched her all night.

Her room was just across the hall, a scant eight feet, door to door. He fantasized about marching over there and knocking, wondering what she'd say . . . what she'd do.

He banged his head against the pillow, flipping it over to the cool side.

What the hell, Joe Bill?

His eyes flicked open when his phone pinged on the nightstand beside the bed.

A smile spread over his face when he saw an invitation to play Words with Friends from a player named LolaMoana—and Teariki's grinning pic in the avatar circle.

Ironically—or perhaps part of Teariki's plan—the banner above her opening word—*fond*—said: IT'S YOUR MOVE.

He tapped the Chat bubble—the twenty-first-century equivalent of walking across the hall and knocking on her door.

You okay?

Can't sleep. Wish my ribs didn't hurt so bad.

He typed quickly.

I do too.

So you know, I'm a fast healer, she wrote back, just as quickly.

I'll keep that in mind.

Good night Joe Bill Brackett. Thank you.

Get some rest.

Brackett pitched the phone back on his nightstand, imagining Lola Teariki's thick black hair. . . .

He flipped the pillow over again and stared up at the ceiling. This little Words with Friends convo wasn't going to make it any easier to sleep—but now he didn't care.

They felt the wolves before they saw them. Piper trudged a little closer, crowding in with every step. Noah didn't say anything. He was scared too. He counted at least a half-dozen sets of yellow eyes ghosting through the forest each time he turned with his headlamp. The wolves found it easier going inside the tree line.

They'd been at it for three hours now with barely even a pause for rest—slowing now and then, just enough to keep from sweating. The snow came down heavier now, driven by an angry, unforgiving wind that burned skin if they turned their hoods wrong.

Noah wrapped Fig's rope leash tighter around the wrist of Cutter's thick beaver fur mittens, bracing himself. A low growl rumbled in the dog's chest, but it trudged straight ahead, knowing instinctively it was smarter to ignore this threat. Fig was a large dog, a fit eighty pounds of muscle, but he was no match for a big male gray that might tip the scales near one-eighty. An uninformed person might look at the Tamaskan as a wolf—but the wolves looked at him as an easy meal.

Wolves had never been something to worry about when Noah was growing up. He'd always been excited when he heard one on the wind or caught a glimpse of one. His uncles cussed the things for killing too many caribou and moose. They learned to fear people and kept their distance. Noah had read that they went after people over across the Bering Sea in Siberia, but wolf attacks on humans in Alaska were almost unheard of—unless you ran. Or, he supposed, if the wolves were especially hungry.

A mournful howl carried through the inky darkness ahead, lingering as if it had frozen there. Another wolf answered from well to the rear, long and wobbly and low.

Piper veered closer as they trudged along, stepping on Noah's makeshift spruce-bough snowshoes with hers and nearly upending him. She wasn't usually the panicky type, but this was even scaring the shit out of Noah.

Piper leaned sideways, whispering above the squeaky Styrofoam crunch of crusty snow as they trudged. "You think they're—"

Noah raised a hand, straining to make sense of the noises in the trees to his left. He passed the dog's leash to Piper and eased the revolver out of his parka pocket.

Another howl came from up the trail—yip, yip, yowl—wolf Morse code.

A short yip in the trees preceded the swish of running feet.

Then the wolves were gone.

Piper stopped, turning slowly, shuffling her feet carefully in the ungainly snowshoes to check behind them. Vapor whooshed out the tunnel of her parka hood, curling like smoke in the beam of her headlamp.

"What was that all about?"

"I have a guess," Noah said. "But I don't know for sure."

A quarter mile down the trail his guess was proven correct. A line of moose tracks, a cow and yearling calf from the looks of them, crossed the trail into the thicker forest. Snow had been kicked up on the tail end of each hoofprint.

Fig pulled harder at the rope, much more interested in chasing moose than a hundred and eighty pounds of fang and claw.

"Moving fast." Noah pointed his light into one of the deep holes to get a clear look at the actual footprint at the bottom. "This one is young. Easy pickings for the wolves."

"Lucky for us," Piper said, making a little yelp of her own as she bent to look at the track.

"You okay?" Noah asked.

"Honestly?" She winced, straightening up to look him in the eye, angling her headlamp down so she didn't blind him. "I feel like shit, Noah. My hips aren't built for the duck waddle we have to do in these snowshoes. I wanted to help, to come with you so you wouldn't be alone, but I'm only slowing you down."

Noah glanced upward, thinking. No gently falling snow-globe here, this snow bit and slashed as if it were angry. As temperatures dropped the snow usually tapered off, but these mountains didn't appear to know about that little weather rule. Air and ground melded together into a flat white wall, their headlamps reflecting back at them, making it almost impossible to pick out a trail.

Noah's shoulders slumped inside the thick parka, distraught at the idea of letting Professor Baglioni down. He'd promised Cutter he could do this.

"This is going to get worse before it gets better," he said. "We'll both die if we don't stop for a bit and get warm."

"Warm?"

"Well," he said. "Warmer."

Deep snow made travel agonizingly slow, but digging a shelter was a cinch—if you had a shovel, which they did not.

Judging from the moose tracks, the snow on the flat was at least three feet deep, but the wind had piled it well over Noah's head against any rock or hill tall enough to catch it. He found a likely spot and stomped around until it was firm enough that he could take off the unwieldy spruce boughs, and then used the beaver fur mittens to burrow out a rough, T-shaped opening, through which he excavated enough snow to give a place out of the wind. When he judged he had a bench large enough for the two of them to crowd in together, he filled in the outer edges of the T, leaving only a hole at the bottom large enough for them to crawl up into.

More burrow than cave, the inside resembled a boxy mushroom, climbing up through the "stem" and stretching out on the ledges under the domed mushroom cap. He'd dug dozens of such snow caves as a boy using shovels, Frisbees, and even a large plastic spatula from his mother's kitchen. This one was rough, taking less than an hour to excavate, but he was prouder of it than anything he'd ever built.

Crawling on all fours, he used a stick to punch a vent hole in the roof and then stuck the same stick in the snow wall. The headlamp hung there, illuminating the dome-shaped interior.

Fig came in next flopping down beside Noah. Piper poked her head up like a groundhog, cheeks cold nipped, lashes covered with frost. "Sounds like the wind stopped."

"It's still blowing," Noah said. "We just can't hear anything in here." It was already getting warm enough he had to unzip his parka to keep from sweating.

"You think the wolves are still out there?"

"Oh, yeah," Noah said. "But they're too busy with moose at the moment."

He leaned against the wall so Piper could stretch out and rest her head on his thigh.

Tears pressed through clenched lashes. Her face drew back in pain.

"I'm so sorry. You'd still be going strong if I hadn't started whining."

"Nah," he lied. "It's good we hunkered down for a minute. We'll get the stove going and melt water for tea."

Piper's eyes flicked open. "I'm going back. My hips are shot. You'll move so much faster without me."

"This snow is pretty intense," Noah said. "Mercury is falling so it's gonna stop, but there won't be much of a backtrail for you to follow."

"I'm not worried about finding my way," she said. "You're not the only one with a compass in your nose."

Noah got the little Svea stove hissing at once. The aluminum lid made a convenient, if small, boiling pot. The tiny blue ring of flame not only raised the temperature to the high teens but lifted their spirits as well. The smell of bergamot and black tea soon filled the chilly air.

"I don't like it," Noah said, passing the steaming cup to Piper. "But if you have to go back, you need to take the gun."

Fig suddenly lifted his head, eyes locked on the entrance. A low whine revved into a growl. Piper gave him a scratch behind the ears and he calmed down.

"I'll be fine," she said, as if trying to convince herself. "You have got to make it to the cell tower and call for help. Marie . . . all of us are counting on it."

Noah closed his eyes. Piper drank the last of the tea and leaned against him, still wincing from pain each time she moved her legs. He patted her on the shoulder, happy for the warmth and closeness.

"I'm gonna close my eyes for a minute," he said. "But you're taking the gun. That's all there is to it."

Noah woke with Fig licking his face. He called for Piper, but she was gone. The revolver lay on top of the beaver mitten that she'd been using for a pillow.

She couldn't have gone far. He zipped up his parka and crawled out of the cave, hoping to catch her. It was still dark, still snowing, but it had slowed some.

But no Piper.

A wolf howled again, jerking Fig's attention toward the forest.

Noah gave him a pat and began tying the spruce boughs on his boots.

"I sure wish she'd taken the gun, Fig," he said. "I can't shake the feeling that there's a lot more to be scared of back there than there is out here."

CHAPTER 55

*S*now sifted steadily down through the glow of the parking lot lights when Lola, Brackett, and the chief arrived at AST D detachment headquarters at a quarter after eight in the morning. Lola thought it might be letting up some, or maybe the flakes were just smaller. Probably just wishful thinking. They'd been up for a while, but Phillips had to make some phone calls from the hotel. Lola and Brackett had sat in the lobby studying topographical maps of Mutt Larsen's flight path relative to the University of Alaska Fairbanks remote climate research station.

"You think this is tapering off?" Lola asked, stomping her feet at the employee entrance while the chief entered the security code.

Brackett stared skyward, catching flakes on his lashes. "Maybe so," he said.

"You think?" Phillips said, ever the realist.

The thermometer in front of the bank on the way over showed the temperature at twelve degrees—cold enough to make Lola's face hurt. She was disappointed to see the parking lot was almost as full as it had been last night. If people were here, then they weren't out there, looking.

Julia Montez met them inside. Today she wore her blue AST patrol uniform instead of the coveralls from the day before.

"Doesn't look like you're dressed to go search," Lola said.

"I want to be," Trooper Montez said. "Believe me. But unfortunately, the wheels of Alaska crime continue to turn, even during a search and rescue op. I'm oversight trooper for Minto, and one of my village public safety officer's needs help with a domestic violence issue out there."

"Understood," Lola said. "Is Yates going with you?"

The young woman scrunched her nose. "Lord, I hope not."

"Too bad." Lola shrugged off her coat, shaking off the snow on the rubber mat inside the doorway. "Because I have resolved to pull the head off his neck if he gets in my way."

"Do what you think is best." Montez grinned, then settled a thick beaver fur hat on her head and picked up a heavy nylon duffel. She paused at the door. "I almost forgot to tell you. There is some good news. Earl Battles just passed by Farewell coming up from Bethel."

"Earl Battles?" Lola said. "Yupik man with a great sense of humor who flies for C Detachment?"

Phillips gave a slow nod, exchanging glances with Lola. "I understand he once landed on a moving ice floe to save a hypothermic snow-machiner."

"That's just one of the stories," Montez said. "He's the real deal when it comes to bush pilots. Hell, people write songs about him . . ."

"Still," Phillips said. "How is he able to fly in this when no one else will?"

"He's coming up between McGrath and Farewell," Montez said. "Bethel is fairly direct from here. He doesn't even have to cross the Alaska Range. The L.T. says his ETA is around eleven am—if he's able to make it."

Lola put a hand on top of her head and looked at the ceiling. "Eleven? Cutter's out there in this shit and we're all just sitting on our asses warm and safe."

"Look," Montez said. "Nobody can fly north in this weather, but if it gets anything close to flyable—Battles will be first in the air. The guy's got balls—and he'll need 'em to fly in this." She bumped the door open with her hip, facing the gray wall of bitter cold and falling snow.

CHAPTER 56

*C*utter woke with a start. He'd only taken a short catnap, but Larsen was nodding off. He could hardly blame the man. They were all hammered from cold and fatigue and fear. Fortunately, the prisoners were sapped as well, and neither appeared to have noticed the momentary lapse in guard duty.

Cutter rolled his shoulders and bent his legs, slowly getting the circulation going again. The cold attacked his knees the worst, leaving them stiff and aching even after they were relatively warm. The fire had died down again, allowing the deathly chill of the white silence outside to creep into the three-walled cabin—and cranking up the ache in his knees.

Any other time, Cutter might have been upset that the prisoners had been unguarded, even for a minute, but exhaustion and hunger and cold were fast replacing adrenaline with ambivalence. A dangerous notion, but he still had enough wherewithal to fight it—for now.

He half rolled, got to his knees, and then used the wall to help push himself to his feet. Everything was so much more difficult in the bulky parka. He'd not taken off his boots since they'd gotten stuck in this godforsaken place, and trench foot was going to be a real problem if he didn't do something about that. For now, it seemed insane to worry about dry feet when he had two killers chained mere inches away.

Tonight.

He'd take off his boots tonight—if he remembered.

Any attempt at food, even weak broth, sent Marie Baglioni crawling from the shelter with painful vomiting and diarrhea. She'd long since given up making it to the outhouse and frequently made it no farther than around the corner—half frozen each time Larsen helped her stumble back inside. Her face had taken on a yellow pallor, and she'd not eaten anything since trying weak rabbit broth at breakfast, leaving Cutter to wonder which would kill her first, sepsis or dehydration.

Cutter had just gotten to his feet when she called out, startling the prisoners awake.

"Noah!" she said, shivering uncontrollably. "I'm s-s-so c-cold. S-s-stoke the f-f-fire."

Larsen reminded her that her two interns had gone for help.

"How long ago?" She cast around the cabin, dumbfounded. "I was only j-just talking to him."

Cutter checked his watch. "Sixteen hours ago. With any luck, he's been on the river—"

Spivey yawned, stretching as far as the chains allowed him to. "That's a joke," he scoffed. "Those kids are bear shit by now and you know it."

Baglioni stared at him for a time as though trying to

figure out who he was, and pulled the blanket tight to her chin and began to snore.

Spivey rolled over on his side and gave Nix a somber nod, raising a bushy brow. He'd done it. He'd defeated the cuffs, at least one side. That was really all it took to get out of the belly chain.

The marshal had finally conked out long enough to make some progress, and Larsen was too preoccupied with his sick girlfriend to pay attention to what the prisoners were doing with their hands. Spivey knew how to pick cuffs. He just needed the privacy to do it. Larsen was pulling guard duty, but he was too tired and worried to notice when he'd pulled the blanket up a little higher so it covered his belly chain. He'd slid the single, toothed bar past the mechanism, alongside the double bars, making them look as though they were still securely locked unless directly inspected.

Early on the marshal had physically checked each cuff every time they ventured outside. Now it was hit and miss. The lawman was so tired he stumbled around like he was drunk, which would make Nix's plan all the easier. Spivey had to play his part, as did Larsen. Nix knew they would. They couldn't help it, and neither could the marshal.

Nix had to work to suppress the smile that started deep in his belly. When he thought about it, he couldn't help what he was going to do, either.

"I gotta piss," Spivey said.

Cutter stared at him for a long moment, like he

might shoot him where he sat, then said, "Both of you on your feet."

"I'm good, Marshal." Nix sucked his head deeper into his parka. "It's too damned cold to go out when I don't have to."

"You have to," Cutter said. "We all go at once. Now, on your feet."

"Anybody ever tell you you're a hardass?" Nix said.

"Nope," Cutter said. "I suspect I am universally loved and admired by all."

"She's sleeping," Larsen said. "And I need to take a leak too. I'll come with you and help watch them."

Nix shot Spivey a quizzical look, but Cutter wrote it off to irritation at having to go out in the snow.

Cutter checked the location of his revolver—the holster had a tendency to move an inch or two on his belt when he was sleeping. He'd have to raise the tail of the parka to reach it, but that couldn't be helped. Leaving his parka unzipped for any length of time would render him too cold to be able shoot straight anyway. He pulled his hood up over his head, folding back the ruff enough so it didn't impede his peripheral vision, and then gestured outside. "Quick piss break, then we'll add some more wood to the fire."

"Keep our eyes open for the bear," Larsen said. He tapped his coat pocket, rattling the plastic shells for his shotgun.

Cutter directed Spivey to lead the way. Nix followed. The outlaws hopped down from the cabin floor to the ground, careful of their chains, shuffling around the edge of the fire, avoiding the motes of melted snow and floating ashes.

Spivey made it just a few steps beyond the fire before he stopped in his tracks. "Holy sheeit!" He looked over his shoulder, grimacing as if he were in pain. "It's not enough that I'm trussed up like a goose and freezing my ass off? Now I gotta worry about stepping in that fat bitch's puke."

Larsen prodded him with the shotgun barrel, earning a chiding look from Cutter.

"Don't let him get to you."

Larsen backed off quickly. "Yeah, right . . . Sorry."

Spivey and Nix hobbled along their previous trail through the four inches of new-fallen snow since they'd last brought in wood for the fire. Cutter ordered them to stop in the relatively packed area beside the charred remnants of the main cabin, so he and Larsen could keep an eye on them while still keeping Marie in sight inside the shelter.

The cold burned Cutter's lungs, bringing on a spasmodic cough. His eyelids sagged with fatigue allowing his lashes to freeze together at the corners, forcing him to blink constantly.

Deep snow swallowed up surrounding sounds, making Cutter keenly aware of his own breathing and the jingle of the prisoner's chains. A raven *kerlucked* in the trees to his right, sending a skitter of snow cascading down through the branches.

Spivey groaned, half turning, as men do when they're about to relieve themselves. Nix shuffled sideways a couple of steps, getting some privacy of his own.

Belly chains rattled as the men fumbled with parka and zipper fly.

Spivey whispered something Cutter couldn't make out. Whatever he said, it caused Larsen to perk up.

Then Spivey spoke louder, over his shoulder, while

he continued to urinate in the snow. "She's gonna die, brother. Just do us all a favor and shoot her fat ass now while—"

Larsen sprang forward, something between a whimper and a scream escaping his throat. Cutter was less than ten feet away, but Larsen was a hair closer and reached the prisoner first, shotgun raised to shoot Spivey in the face.

Spivey turned as if he expected the attack, deftly for a man wearing leg irons in heavy, uneven snow. The two men struggled, locked together with the shotgun between them. Too late, Cutter realized Spivey was free of his handcuffs. The outlaw deflected the shotgun barrel, twisting it straight down. Larsen hung on, screaming in earnest now.

Cutter barked, "Drop it!" lifting his parka and drawing the Colt. He took a half step sideways to keep from hitting Larsen. From this distance, he didn't need to aim—

Something hit him hard in his side, bowling him over and knocking the revolver out of his hand.

Nix!

Cutter rolled for the gun, digging in the snow where he'd seen it disappear. He caught a glimpse of Nix in his peripheral vision. He was still in handcuffs and struggling to get to his feet in the deep snowdrift where he'd ended up after plowing past Cutter.

The shotgun roared, shaking the still air—and parting the chain between Spivey's leg irons, freeing him of his last restraints.

Cutter's fingers closed around the butt of the Colt Python at the same moment Spivey delivered a staggering headbutt to Larsen's nose and gained control of the empty shotgun. Spivey brought the gun up quickly, slamming the stock directly into the side of Larsen's temple, dropping him where he stood. An accomplished fighter, Spivey knew not to waste motion. He kept spinning in the direction of his attack, now bent on braining Cutter.

Cutter was close now, less than three feet away, digging his revolver out of the snow. He faded backward as the empty shotgun whirred by like a baseball bat, connecting with his arm instead of his head.

The Colt flew from his hand, disappearing again in the powder.

"Anytime, Nix!" Spivey screamed, swinging the shotgun a second time, this one whistling past Cutter's jaw.

Cutter sidestepped, attempting to gain distance—and time to draw the Glock. Snow, the heavy parka, and the car-wreck dynamics of Spivey's attack made it impossible.

Spivey was on him in a flash, roaring, swinging, chopping with the empty shotgun as if it were an axe. Cutter was no small man, but Spivey had him in reach and weight. The outlaw was everywhere at once, and it was all Cutter could do to duck or parry the blows. He worried that Nix would find the revolver in the snow, but there was no time to deal with it now.

Spivey attacked with such force and ferocity that he began to tire almost at once. Cutter ducked a powerful swing and then rushed in, bent low so he caught the larger man in the solar plexus with the point of his shoulder. Any other time the maneuver might have earned Cutter a knee to the face, but Spivey was too focused on braining him.

The shotgun fell away, disappearing in a deep drift. Both men went to the ground. Cutter clawed at his back, trying for his Glock. Spivey rolled him with a sickening blow to the temple. A geyser of sparks and colors exploded behind Cutter's eyes. He forgot about the Glock and spun, half blinded from the blow, kicking at whatever was there. The heel of his boot caught Spivey in the groin, doubling him over and giving Cutter a split second to crawl away, hand over hand, plowing a foot of snow as he went. He scrambled to his feet, intent again on drawing the Glock.

Spivey grabbed him from behind, looping a powerful arm around his neck and drawing him tight. The parka slowed down the choke, but it also hampered Cutter's ability to free himself. He turned his head sideways, keeping his airway open for the moment, at the same time squatting to lower his center and raining blows backward against the other man's unprotected thighs and groin. Winter clothing rendered the strikes all but useless.

Spivey cocked his wrist inward slightly, allowing his grip to focus against Cutter's carotid artery, despite the thick parka. This guy had choked people out before. Cutter stomped, attempting to drive his heel into the top of Spivey's foot. Nothing. The heavy winter boots protected him.

Then Spivey yowled, loosening his grip a hair.

Cutter stomped again, feeling the leg iron tick against his foot as it slid down the other man's boot. Though Spivey had shot the chain between the two leg irons, the steel shackles in effect extra-large handcuffs—still bit into the tender flesh of his ankles and Achilles tendon where Cutter had him roll down his boots. Cutter exploited the weakness, gaining more room to maneuver each time he raked down the side of Spivey's leg.

Enraged, Cutter ducked out of the choke and spun, driving Spivey's chin upward with a devastating palm strike that slammed his teeth together with a crack that sounded like gunfire. Cutter pressed his attack, slamming a fist directly into the other man's exposed throat again and again as he staggered backward.

Spivey teetered, croaking for air before collapsing into the snow.

Cutter turned quickly, pushing the parka hood back so he could see. Nix was on his feet again, sugar-cookied in snow, within arm's reach. Too close, but his hands were still secured to the belly chain, his face passive.

A faraway noise, like a keening bird, pulled Cutter's concentration off the prisoner. Larsen lay motionless in the snow and the cry had come from the wrong direction; it had to be Marie Baglioni. Cutter's head was on fire, his vision blurred, but he could just make out a small figure floundering through the deep drifts toward them, a hundred yards away.

It was Piper—and she was alone.

And then Nix hit him like a runaway truck, knocking him off his feet and shoving him face-first into the deep snow.

Cutter clawed blindly, swimming, unable to push himself up or lift his head. Nix sat on his shoulders, using the resistance of the heavy snow on either side to keep him down. Sharp crystals seared Cutters face as it was shoved deeper and deeper into the cold blue darkness. He flailed wildly, but there was nothing to grab but more snow. He arched his back, attempting to buck Nix off, but it was useless. The snow trench penned him on either side while Nix held him in place, bearing down, grinding his face into the snow until his mouth and nose were packed full of ice—and he could no longer breathe.

CHAPTER 57

*E*arl Battles didn't get to the command post until almost two p.m. He'd arrived in Fairbanks well before noon, which made Lola want to scream, until she learned that he hadn't been killing time or stopped off for a burger. He'd been on standby at the airport, ready to launch during a supposed weather window that never materialized. Lt. Terry had briefed him on the information about Marie Baglioni's UAF research camp and knew where to focus his search.

The lieutenant motioned Chief Phillips into his office just before Battles arrived, giving Lola a chance to make a beeline directly for the pilot as he walked into the SAR command post. A younger Native man who looked like he might not even be out of high school came with him, carrying a black computer case like Battles was the president and he had the nuclear "football."

Lola guessed Battles was probably in his early

fifties, about five-seven—several inches shorter than his protégé. He carried a seal-skin winter hat and beaver mittens that were like Cutter's—larger than oven mitts. The sleeves of his fleece jacket were pushed up to his elbows, a ball cap pushed back at an angle on his head as if he'd forgotten it was there.

"Marshals, right?" he said, extending his hand when he spotted Lola. "I flew you to Stone Cross." His tone became more somber and he gave a nod to the wall map across the room. "That's your partner out there?"

"It is," Lola said. "Arliss Cutter."

Battles introduced his nephew, Cyril Chiklak. Already an accomplished private pilot at twenty-one years old, the young man was gaining hours and valuable experience working with his uncle, who was arguably the most well-known bush pilot in Western Alaska.

The location of the UAF climate research camp was marked with a red triangle on the wall map. Battles hovered over the area with an open hand, moving it back and forth.

"It's this valley where the climate station is located that's the problem." He traced lines on the map with the tip of his finger. "It opens up here, toward the river, but it's a dead end . . . here—what the old cowboy movies used to call a box canyon. I have no way of knowing what conditions will be until I turn into it. If they suck, I'm flying blind and we risk augering into the side of a mountain. I thought I had a window a bit ago to take a probing flight, see what we might be able to see, but it didn't happen."

Brackett studied the map, though Lola was certain

he had it memorized as much time as they'd spent looking at the damned thing. "How about flying north and then circling west to come in from Anaktuvuk Pass?"

Battles tipped his ballcap back a bit farther with his knuckle and looked at Cyril. "You want to take this one?"

"We looked at that route," the Yupik youth said. "Weather Station in Anaktuvuk reports visibility is still below minimums. If we ran into trouble, we wouldn't be able to see where to land—let alone find anyone on the ground. But it's a good idea if the ceiling lifts at all."

"Not to mention my plane turns into a two-million-dollar lawn dart if it ices up," Battles said. "We have a TKS system that bleeds deicer on the leading edge of the wings and a slinger for the prop—but it's for use in the event of trouble. I'm not supposed to head into icing conditions on purpose. Let me ask you. How sure are you Mutt Larsen went to visit this Marie . . . ?"

"Baglioni," Lola said. "Not a hundred percent, but sure enough I'll walk there to check it out if I have to. Larsen's airplane has gone dark, and no one has been able to reach Professor Baglioni via radio or satellite phone for days."

Joe Brackett folded his arms, still looking at the map. "Both of them out of commo is pretty convincing."

"I see your point." Battles rubbed his chin and then gave a sad shake of his head. "Look. I've got weather watchers up and down the Haul Road—not to mention Wiseman, Anaktuvuk, everywhere I know somebody with a phone. They'll call me the moment they even think we might have a weather window. I have to take care of a few things here with Lt. Terry, but as soon as that's done, we're heading back to the airport to be in a . . . What do they call it in the military? Alert Five status. You have my word. We'll be airborne in minutes as soon as it's safe."

A commotion in the hall pulled Lola out of the conversation. Jill Phillips's Kentucky accent stood out over the other voices.

"Cutter's phone just pinged off the tower by Anaktuvuk," the chief said. She looked directly at Lola. "It was only once. He appears to have gone dark again, but I have Scotty Keen monitoring it from Anchorage."

Lola wheeled on Battles at the wall map. "How close is the tower to the climate research station?"

Sergeant Yates strode across the room. Battles looked as though he might tell him to get lost, but the guy was a sergeant, so he yielded the map. "Caribou Shit Pass," Yates said, pointing to Anaktuvuk. "The UAF research station is fifteen or twenty miles east, up this narrow slot. Anaktuvuk's cell tower sits well above the village, but still, there are too many mountains to get a signal from that far away." He shrugged. "Looks like your friend didn't make it to the UAF station. As far as we know, that signal is from a phone on its last leg in the wreckage of Larsen's plane."

His cavalier attitude was all it took to get Earl Battles into gear. "If you ever want me to fly in and get your ass, Sergeant Yates," the pilot said, "I'd suggest you move it out of my way." He scratched his chin again while he peered at the map. "Cyril," he said without turning around. "Get that chart for this area and all the latest weather—Notices to Airmen, NOAA, Windy.com, gossip from moose hunters, I don't care, so long as it's the most recent."

Moments later, Battles stood at the conference table beside Cyril Chiklak poring over various routes on the chart. He weighed the recent news about Cutter's cell signal against the extreme cold, icing conditions, and near-total lack of visibility.

Always a teacher, he lined out the facts, but then asked his young protégé for an opinion.

By now, everyone in the command post—almost two dozen people—had gathered around the table, waiting to hear the decision. Many of them had been on the receiving end of Earl Battles's expertise—plucked off the ice or picked up from remote locations that were socked in by weather for days and days and days . . . They trusted him. Some joked (but seriously) that he should run for senator.

Chiklak scrunched his face, thinking for a time without saying a word. He was quiet long enough Lola thought she might have to poke him with a stick.

Finally, he said, "The Caravan is a two-million-dollar airplane that belongs to the people of Alaska, not us. We're not supposed to fly in icy or instrument conditions . . ." He tapped the printed pages of weather info on the table. "And as of now, we have both in the area where we need to go."

"Okay," Battles said. "So, you're pilots in command for a minute. What do we decide?"

Chiklak took a deep breath and blew it out slowly,

clearly avoiding Lola's gaze. "A single ping from a cell phone tower gives us some information, but nothing definitive. We have to weigh the probability of finding anyone alive and the severity of the conditions against the risk to our own safety, the value of the state aircraft, its use in future rescues. Like they teach us in flight school—there are old pilots and bold pilots, but no old-bold pilots."

"So that's an assessment," Battles said, "not a decision. Call it. Go or no go?"

Chiklak stared down at the table and shook his head, nose scrunched, the unspoken "no" in Yupik culture.

"No go," he whispered.

To Lola's utter dismay, Battles nodded his approval. She wanted to scream.

Sergeant Yates gave one of his well-what're-you-gonna-do shrugs and turned to go refill his coffee mug.

Lola tensed, shaking with pent-up frustration, on the verge of a tirade. Phillips touched her arm and gave an almost imperceptible nod toward Battles.

This wasn't over.

"You absolutely made exactly the correct call, Cyril," the senior pilot said. "Considering the weather info we have, you're right. One ping on a cell tower doesn't give us proof enough to take the risk . . ." Battles rested a hand on his nephew's shoulder and gave a resigned sigh. "But guess what. We're goin' anyway. There are people out there waitin' for us in this mess. I don't want to make them wait any longer than we have to."

"Now, hang on," Yates said.

"Shut it," Lieutenant Terry said. "I'm not a pilot. Are you?"

"No, sir," Yates said. "I am not, but—"

"Then let's let leave it to the subject matter experts."

Battles nodded to the lieutenant and then glanced at Lola. "The weather may make it impossible to land, but if we get a positive location, the Air Force PJs should be able to get in for a pickup. Sometimes a fly-over is enough to keep people going when they're in a jam. Just knowing they're found makes a person hang on. Gives 'em hope."

"We're coming too," Phillips said. "That is, if you don't mind, Earl."

"Okay by me," Battles said.

Lt. Terry folded his arms across his chest and shook his head. "I'm sorry, Jill," he said. "Not enough room. We're looking at a six-passenger pickup with the prisoners, and that's not counting Professor Baglioni and her interns if they've run into trouble. I need to send one of my troopers who's trained in emergency medicine. I maybe have space for one of you and that's pushing it."

Lola groaned, leaning against Joe Brackett for support. She didn't care who saw. There was no way the chief was going to give up the only spot on the rescue plane.

But Phillips stepped back and gave Lola a little wink. "Get your stuff together, my dear. Let me know the moment you have any news."

"I'd hug you, boss," Lola said. "But my ribs are killing me."

Yates laughed out loud and raised his coffee mug. "I got no idea why you're all so giddy. You're volunteering for a one-way flight."

Phillips gave Lola a tight smile. "Just go. What's that Grumpyism Cutter is always saying? 'Sometimes, to lead from the front, you have to stay the hell out of the way.'" Her face fell solemn when she looked to Sergeant Yates. "Staying the hell out of my way is something you'd do well to consider."

CHAPTER 58

*C*utter woke flat on his back feeling like he was frozen to the floor. The spruce fire cracked and snapped, going strong again, but seemed to do little to warm the cabin. He had no idea how long he'd been unconscious, but it was still light outside. It took nearly a full minute for his vision to clear.

Memories of the fight with Nix rushed back, flooding him with adrenaline. He jerked, tried to sit up, but realized he couldn't lift his wrists. A rattling jingle told him his legs were shackled as well. He opened swollen eyes wider to find his feet were chained to the bunks, Nix's old spot.

Nix stood above him, warming his hands on a steaming mug of tea. He sneered down at Cutter, prodding him with the toe of his boot.

"Well, doesn't someone look like warmed-over dog shit. . . ."

Cutter felt like it too. Everything about him was a raw nerve, tenderized meat. He'd swallowed a considerable amount of snow when Nix was grinding his face into the sharp crystals—surely breathed it in too, judging from his hacking cough and the sullen weight on his chest. His lips were hamburger, swollen, weeping fresh blood. He had no mirror, but felt certain that frostbite covered his face.

He felt like a hot nail was being driven through the top of his head, and he could hardly see out of his left eye. A concussion, frozen lungs, a face ground to pulp—and that wasn't the worst of his problems.

Nix had unzipped his parka revealing the butt of the Colt Python in the waistband of his jeans.

"Can I sit up?" Cutter asked, his voice a hoarse croak. He needed to buy time, to take stock of the situation. Nix hadn't killed him—a surprising but welcome revelation.

"Knock yourself out. . . ." Nix gave a derisive chuckle. "I forgot. Guess I already did that."

Cutter used his elbows and the wall to wallow himself into a seated position. Nix had pulled the belly chain tight around his parka—tighter than Cutter usually did it and he had a reputation for chaining snugly. His back to the wall, he was surprised to feel the bulge of the Glock still in the holster over his right kidney. He'd never allowed the prisoners to see the pistol, and Nix apparently hadn't noticed him trying to reach it during the earlier fight with Spivey.

Cutter's excitement faded quickly. He was right on top of the gun, literally sitting on it—but the cuffs and belly chain kept him from reaching even his side, let alone behind his back and beneath the folds of the thick parka. The Glock might as well have been in a lockbox across the room.

Baglioni lay in her corner, whimpering, out of her head. Piper sat beside her, wracked with sobs. Her hands were cuffed in front, but absent the belly chain. Cutter saw why. Nix had wrapped the chain around and around her neck and locked it in place with one of the extra pair of handcuffs that hung like an amulet in front. The chain necklace didn't attach her to anything and served no purpose but to intimidate, to brand, to demonstrate to Piper that she was Nix's slave.

Across the cabin in the spot Cutter had once occupied, Mutt Larsen leaned against the wall. His head lolled, half conscious from a beating that looked even worse than Cutter felt.

Spivey was nowhere to be seen.

Cutter coughed, driving the white-hot nail deeper into his skull. He cringed, closing one eye at the pain. "Where's your partner?"

"Chance?" Nix stifled a smirk. "If I was to guess, I'd say he's outside choking to death in the snow. You did a number on his windpipe. I'll tell you what, the moment I met you I said to myself, 'Now there's a man just achin' to throat-punch everybody he meets.'" Nix took a sip of tea. "Anyway, last I checked, Spivey was still out there. Mercury is dropping like a rock, so I'd imagine he's already died of hypothermia if he didn't suffocate on his own vomit first. For all I know, the grizzly's dragged him off already."

Nix squatted low on his haunches, cocking his head from side to side, examining Cutter close up. Cutter could smell the bergamot on his breath. "I've gotta say, you are one lucky bastard. Chance Spivey was a brawler. In a fair fight I think he would have pulverized you . . . all things being equal."

Cutter spit a mouthful of blood on the floor. He swallowed, working up the energy to speak. "All things being equal, I would have beat that guy to death with a two-by-four if I had to fight him."

"You've still got a sense of humor," Nix said. "Even after all this. . . ." His face fell dark. "That's good. You're going to need it."

Nix stood, nodding to the trembling girl. "Lucky for us, Piper decided she just couldn't keep up with her boyfriend—"

"Is Noah okay?" Cutter asked, sitting up straighter, wincing. The interruption drew a frown from Nix.

Piper patted the back of Baglioni's hand in an effort to comfort her. She nodded. "He was just going so fast . . . We thought it would be better if I came back and waited here. He could get to the tower quicker without me slowing him down. I'm sure he's made it to the river hours ago. I . . . I wish I would have stayed with him now."

"Tell him about the wolves," Nix said, prodding.

"They followed me," Piper said. "I counted five, but they never got close or anything."

"Oh," Nix said, relishing the story. "They were hunting you, my dear. If you had run, they would have ripped you apart. Have you ever seen what a wolf can do to an animal's belly? They often eat the guts while their prey is still very much alive—"

"But they didn't," Cutter said.

"No," Piper said. "They started to fall back when I was still a half mile away from here. Must have smelled the smoke because they were gone by the time I hit the clearing."

"They smelled the bear," Nix said. "Funny how the beast that wants to eat you saved you from the others that also want to eat you. . . ."

Across the cabin, Larsen stirred. "I am so sorry," he said. "Sorry . . . for everything . . ." Blood and spittle hung from his gaping mouth. "None of this would have happened if—"

"How did you slip your cuffs?" Cutter asked, looking at Nix. This was no time to wallow in guilt.

Nix gave an isn't-it-obvious shrug. "I unlocked mine with the keys from your pocket. Spivey's the one with skills. He shimmed his with the pull ring off the Spam can or a staple from the floor. To be honest with you, I'm not sure which."

Nix turned in a slow circle, surveying the room. He nodded slowly to himself as if reaching an important decision.

"So, I need us all awake . . ." He reached down and pinched Baglioni hard on the back of her upper arm, bringing a pitifully hoarse yowl.

She rubbed her arm, cowering. "What's the matter with you?"

"I want you alert, Marie, for the next little bit at least." Nix set his mug on the top bunk and rubbed his hands together like a housefly. He drew Cutter's Colt Python, gesturing back and forth with it on a loose wrist as he spoke. "None of this is any fun at all without an audience. I mean, if I blow someone's brains out in the forest and there's no one there to witness it, did it even happen?"

His grip tightened on the gun as he turned and shot Mutt Larsen in the face.

Cutter clenched his jaw. Piper screamed. Baglioni's eyes rolled back in her head.

Nix leaned in close to the carnage and gore that had only seconds before been Larsen's skull.

"Well . . . this really happened . . ." He licked his lips, smiling when he turned to study Piper's stricken face. "And you were all here to enjoy it with me."

CHAPTER 59

L ola sat in the forwardmost seat on the right side of the airplane so she could keep an eye on Earl Battles in the left seat of the cockpit. Troy Meeks, the tall, snake-hipped trooper with wilderness medical training, sat across the aisle from her. Both wore every stitch of their winter gear but for hats and mittens, which they carried in their laps. If for some reason they did have to suddenly put down (that's what Earl called a crash landing—putting down) they would have to leave the aircraft with whatever they had on their backs. Just jump out whichever door was closest. No time to put on your parka. No time to grab a bag. There would be time, Earl said, if he was unconscious, to consider dragging him and Cyril along with them.

Lola had been nervous during the preflight and engine runup before takeoff, but Battles's confidence and easy nature helped her relax. Trooper Meeks leaned back in his seat and closed his eyes, completely at ease. He'd evidently flown with Battles before, many times. The two had traded hairy, blood-curdling stories before takeoff. By the time they rolled down the runway, Lola had decided that she wouldn't panic unless Meeks started to look like he was scared.

Battles was running wheel skis on the caravan, with regular tires penetrating the wide aluminum skis, allowing him to land and take off on a conventional runway or snow-covered strip.

Lola relaxed by degree as the plane leapt off the Fairbanks strip on the cold, dense air.

The whirring drone of the aircraft rendered communication impossible without headsets. Unlike many pilots Lola had flown with, Earl Battles left his intercom open, so his passengers could listen in on his radio traffic with the tower and passing aircraft—which were few and far between in the low clouds and spitting snow.

Battles probed the mountains from the south, flying in and out of low fog banks. He was supposedly always able to see the ground. Lola had her doubts. The air outside of the plane seemed palpable, thick as pea soup, but she said nothing. She was heading toward Cutter and that was all that mattered. A southern route proved impossible. Every pass and valley they tried was curtained off with a white wall. In the end, Battles cut his losses and flew the Haul Road, necessitating backtracking to the east for a good twenty minutes and then cutting west again on the north side of the Brooks Range—like Joe Bill had suggested earlier. The trip was a little longer, but Battles reasoned it would be faster than repeated unsuccessful attempts to pick his way through the Endicott Mountains to Anaktuvuk Pass, where Cutter's cell had pinged.

The Cessna Caravan cruised at a little over two hundred miles an hour, and the moment Battles had a view unobstructed by clouds, he wrung every ounce of horsepower possible out of the engine.

Lola unzipped her parka and settled into her seat, propping herself against her hat and gloves to protect her aching ribs—and drifted off.

She awoke with her stomach being pressed toward the floor of the airplane. When she looked out the window, snow-clad hills looked directly up at her. Battles was in the middle of turning back to the south.

Lola smacked her lips and shot a quick glance at Meeks to see if he'd caught her drooling while she slept. He leaned slightly forward, ignoring her to scan the frozen landscape below.

"This is the Anaktuvuk River?" he asked, pushing the tiny boom mic on his headset against his lips.

Cyril answered, loud and clear over the intercom. Pilots always had better headsets. "Yep, weather's moving through, so the ceiling isn't quite as low on this side of the Endicotts."

"This place hasn't even heard of spring this year," Lola said, looking at the snow-shrouded valley and mountains below. It was difficult not to imagine it was an outpost on some far-flung ice planet.

"They get snow here in June," Battles said.

Cyril pointed with his chin. "Anaktuvuk village is ahead there. That jagged pyramid off the right wing is Soakpak Mountain. The UAF research station is up the little valley on the backside of that toothy one to our left, Mount Stuver."

"They all look toothy," Lola said, her voice crackling until she moved her mic closer. Everything around her was white—the ground, the mountains, the sky itself. "How do you even tell which way is up?" she heard herself ask.

Battles spoke this time. "We got our ways. But to be honest, that's what makes us so careful. Flat light plays heck on depth perception. Pretty easy to fly straight into the ground and not even realize it."

"That would suck," Lola said, fogging the window with her breath as she looked out. "You think that's what happened to Cutter's pilot?"

"Let's go see." Battles banked left again, over the tumble of small, snow-shrouded houses in the middle of a desolate plain a thousand feet below. "That's Anaktuvuk—The Place of Caribou Droppings. Nunamiut—mountain Eskimos—settled here decades ago so they could have a school. Before that, they were more nomadic, like all Arctic people had to be to survive. The Nunamiut followed the caribou herds as they drifted out of the mountains to the tundra. They traded with coastal Iñupiat for whale meat and seal oil. Hard life back then. My great auntie is Iñupiat. She used to tell me—"

"Got him," Cyril said, his head whipping to his right. "Two o'clock off the nose, quarter mile . . . about to pass abeam the wing."

Lola scanned the endless white expanse of the valley below, seeing small pockets of spruce trees, windswept gray rocks . . . and there he was. A lone figure walked aimlessly over the snow. Then, what she had thought at first was a rock, turned out to be a dog, bounding and plowing through the powder. Hearing the plane, the man began to jump up and down, waving his arms frantically over his head.

"Is that your partner?" Battles asked.

Lola pressed her face against the window as Battles put the plane into a steep bank. "No," she said. "He's too young. I think it's the UAF intern. Noah Sam. What's he got on his feet?"

"Spruce boughs," Cyril said. "We used to make snow-shoes out of 'em when we were kids. Look at that. He's stomped out SOS in the snow."

"That bothers me," Trooper Meeks said. "Larsen would have had a couple of pairs of snowshoes in his plane. If this guy is reduced to using trees, it can't be good."

Battles leaned sideways, looking over his shoulder at Lola. "Mind opening that duffel strapped in the seat behind you and pulling out the bright orange stuff sack?"

"Sure." Lola unbuckled her safety belt and did as she was asked. She held it up. "What now?"

"There's a sleeping bag, bivy sack, a flashlight, and some Snickers bars in there, along with a satellite phone and instructions on how to use it."

"Water?" Lola asked.

Earl chuckled. "I learned a fifteen-hundred-dollar lesson dropping a water bottle in the same bag as a sat phone. Once was enough for me. Water and a couple of MREs are in the yellow bag."

Cyril pointed out the left side of the airplane. "Over there?"

"Looks good," Battles said. "We'll make two passes." Then he explained to Lola and Meeks. "We want a spot with snow, but not too many drifts for him to have to dig through . . . if we can help it." He reached back. "Would you pass me the orange bag, please."

"I have the airplane," Cyril said, both hands on the yoke.

"Hang on," Lola said. "You're going to just open your window and drop it out?"

"Sort of," Battles said. "But first, Cyril's going to take us to five hundred feet and slow to just under seventy knots . . ." He shot a serious glance at his nephew. "Keeping in mind that this bird stalls at sixty-one . . . *Then* I'm going to open my door and throw it out."

Dropping the bags turned out to be a simple procedure with Battles triple-checking his seat harness and then pushing open his door against the buffeting wind. The sudden rush of freezing air made Lola doubly glad she didn't have to do it. She pressed her nose to the window and watched the brightly colored bag plummet into the snow, landing less than a hundred feet from Noah.

He had the phone powered up and the antenna extended by the time Battles brought the Caravan around over top of him again to drop the yellow bag. Lola used her sat phone to call him. He answered immediately, breathless.

"You guys came . . . You really came." His voice quavered, close to tears. "I have never been so happy to see an airplane!"

Lola told him about the food and water in the second bag. "We can't land here," she said. "But we're going to send someone for you. Are you injured or sick?" It took everything she had not to ask about Cutter from the start.

She didn't have to.

"I'm fine," Noah said. "I appreciate the food. I have a stove and another sleeping bag, so I'll be fine for a little longer. Deputy Cutter and the others are up the valley at the UAF research camp. . . . Do you know where that is?"

Lola pumped her fist. "Yes."

"Excellent," Noah said, a shiver apparent in his voice.

"We're seeing some bear activity in the snow," Lola said. "We'll get you help as quick as we can."

"I'm good," Noah said. "I have a handgun. . . . My girlfriend might be between me and the camp. Would you keep an eye open for her, please?"

"Of course," Lola said, hearing the worry in the young man's voice.

"Professor Baglioni . . ." he continued as if rehearsed. "She's very sick. You need to go there fast. I'll fill you in about the rest of it while you're on the way. . . ."

And he did, every painful detail of it. Lola told Noah to keep his phone powered on and then hung up so she could contact Chief Phillips and get help rolling to his coordinates. That done, she brought the others in the Caravan up to speed on the details.

"They fed the bodies to a bear to keep it busy?" Trooper Meeks said when she'd finished. His face looked like he'd accidently downed half a carton of curdled milk.

"Honestly," Lola said, "that sounds like something Cutter would think of." She gave the Glock on her belt a comforting tap, wishing she'd brought a bigger gun.

Battles must have read her mind. "There's a Remington 870 in the belly pod," he said. "Loaded with slugs."

"That's good," Lola said, thinking how different things were in the bush than they were in urban America. She'd long ago decided that wild places were *real* life. City living was a sham, a glitzy imitation. Out here you did what you had to do to survive. You killed what you needed to eat, and hopefully killed anything that wanted to eat you before it got the chance. It didn't get more real than that.

Battles's voice crackled over the intercom.

"Seven minutes out."

CHAPTER 60

*N*ix left Larsen's body where it was, a constant reminder of what would eventually happen to all of them. Cutter was no stranger to carnage, but this was different. Terroristic. Carnage not as the result of a weapon but weaponized itself.

"I don't understand," Cutter said. "What's your endgame? You can't think you'll be able to wait here until spring and then just walk out."

"I might fool you," Nix said. He stood at the open edge of the cabin, staring beyond the fire at the silent white landscape. "The truth is, all my life I have only ever worried about the big details and let the little things take care of themselves. It's served me pretty well."

Piper pounded her cuffed hands against her lap. "Noah is bringing help. They'll put you in prison—"

"Oh, hon," Nix said. "You'll all be dead, then it's my word against a bunch of corpses. As far as they will know, Chance Spivey killed everyone here and then I killed him."

"I wouldn't be so sure about that," Cutter said.

"They need evidence." Nix turned and hunkered down again. There was something more sinister about him in the daylight, as if every shred of evil was exposed. He spun the empty stewpot on the cabin floor absentmindedly as he spoke. "Let me ask you this, Marshal Cutter. Were you one of the ones in Anchorage chasing your tail trying to find the . . . what did they call me? The Bootleggers Cove Killer." He snorted. "Doesn't exactly roll off the tongue. I'd hoped for something more suitable for history, like 'The Alaska Axe' or—"

Cutter scoffed. "You're not making history, asshole. A couple of feet wash ashore. So what? Hardly anyone noticed but law enforcement."

The smile bled from Nix's face. "That's a lie and you know it. I have half the state scared shitless. Your brothers and sisters in blue already have my associate in custody. I'm sure my picture is all over the Internet by now. Oh, I'll get my own Wikipedia page and maybe a couple of books. I'll probably go down for a kidnapping and a killing or two—but not yours." He peered across the cabin at Piper and then Baglioni. "Or yours, or yours. Spivey killed everyone but me . . . Scout's honor . . .

"And speaking of that, I guess I should get started. As our dear Piper pointed out, Noah may bring help in a few hours—and I'd like to relish this time we have left."

Cutter jerked at his restraints, croaking now, barely audible. "You worthless piece of shit!"

Nix laughed. "Nice try," he said. "I know you want to make me angry so I kill you first. But guess what? You don't have to work so hard. That's exactly what I plan to do. Oh, I'd thought about keeping you alive to watch, but if Spivey shimmed his cuffs, then you probably could too. And I can't risk that." His face began to twitch with every word. "No, I'll shoot you . . . in the knee, I think . . . Let you flop around awhile, and then finish you off—maybe in the eye, so you can see it coming. And then . . . then I'll spend some time with my moon-faced beauty before she dies on me. Our sweet little Piper will have a front-row seat to it all. Then she and I . . . well, I have amazing plans for her."

Cutter had arrested many bad men, but few that were truly evil—and fewer still as twisted as Edward Nix. He'd thought the man insane before, but now it was as if Nix had shed the last thin shell of humanity to reveal the monster beneath.

Piper cowered in the corner, trembling so violently that the chains that were looped around her neck jingled like sleigh bells.

Nix threw the stewpot at her, shrieking. "Shut up! I can't hear myself think!"

The pot hit Baglioni in the face, which appeared to enrage Piper more than if it had hit her. It clanged to the floor and landed in the corner beside the Estwing hatchet, the blade of which had been hidden under *The Doomfarers of Coramonde*, Mutt Larsen's paperback novel. The hatchet was just close enough for Piper to reach.

Nix was too spun up to notice.

He knelt beside Cutter, gun in hand, careful to stay clear of his kicking.

"You sure you weren't involved in hunting me?"

"I was not," Cutter said. "US Marshals don't investigate weak-minded little pricks . . . until they've already been convicted. But I wish I had been."

Piper picked up the hatchet and crept forward, holding it up in both hands. Her chains still shook and jingled, but Nix thought nothing of it. She was weak. A captive bird. Not someone to fear.

Nix leaned closer, holding the Colt loosely, swinging it back and forth again, leading the music as he'd done before shooting Larsen.

Cutter spit in his face. "Get on with it then!"

Nix's lips pulled back in a malignant grin, exposing yellowed teeth. "I'm sure you have questions," he said. "Cops are always so curious . . . I'll bet you're just dying to find out why—" The grin faded and his grip tightened on the gun. "Have a preference for which knee?"

Cutter spit again, keeping Nix's attention focused on him.

Piper brought the hatchet down hard, slicing into Nix's leg an inch above the top of his boot. The blade was heavy and sharp. The Achilles tendon parted with a satisfying snap. The little hatchet cut completely through the much smaller fibula, but buried in the backside of the shin bone. She grunted, sprayed with blood, heaving with all her might to pull the blade free.

Nix threw back his head and howled. The gun slipped from his hand at the same moment Cutter gathered up and put a boot to his injured leg, kicking then raking as hard as he could.

Cutter rolled to try to reach the Colt with his feet, but the chain caught him short—inches away. He yelled at Piper. "Hit him again!"

Nix, preoccupied with stopping the geyser of blood, made a halfhearted attempt to grab the revolver.

Piper struck again as Nix clutched his wound, thrashing. The blade hit the side of his leg, cracking the shinbone and taking three fingers with it.

Shrieking, Nix grabbed her by the hair with his good hand and threw her across the room. She slammed against the wall, stunned—the Colt Python at her feet. She kicked the gun to Baglioni, who rolled on top of it.

Nix grabbed the hatchet, red-eyed and screaming. Blood and spittle flew with each curse.

Cutter thought Baglioni would be angry enough to shoot, but instead, she slid the gun across the floor as if it were on fire.

Nix was so caught up in his blood lust that he missed it completely.

Cutter rolled onto his side, catching the gun at his belly, fumbling in the handcuffs and tight chains to get it turned around into a shooting grip.

Nix knelt in a lake of his own blood, looming over Piper. He brandished the stubs of his butchered fingers in her face, holding the hatchet in the other. "You biii-itch—"

Cutter gave a shrill whistle.

Nix turned, but Cutter didn't have a good shot without jeopardizing Piper if the bullet went through and through. Cutter took what he had, sending a round into Nix's pelvis—chipping away at the foundation, Grumpy called it. Nix listed sideways, far enough away from

Piper for Cutter to put two shots in his chest and another in his head.

Overwhelmed, Cutter felt himself begin to fade immediately after the last shot. The Colt slipped from his hands and he collapsed against the cold plywood floor. He was just so damned sleepy.

Outside, the fire was dying again, embers hissing against the melted snow. Another faraway sound he couldn't quite make out grew louder and louder. . . .

CHAPTER 61

*C*yril Chiklak saw the smoke before the others. Trooper Meeks gave a low whistle at the fire-damaged buildings.

"Is that . . . ?"

"The burned-out plane," Battles said. "Afraid so. Easy to miss with all this snow."

A young woman, presumably Piper, ran from the tiny cabin next to the fire and waved frantically with both hands at the Caravan.

Lola pressed her face to the window as they flew by. There was no sign of Cutter.

Earl Battles made his downwind run over the airstrip low and slow, studying every drift and divot in the snow. Instead of landing straightaway, he touched down softly, applying only partial weight to the skis as he slid down the runway. Nearing the end, he increased power, taking off to come around and do it again, settling in with a little more weight on each run, packing tracks in the snow. He repeated the maneuver six times, explaining that he if did not, he could very well sink the plane up to her wings.

He let the Caravan settle gently on the seventh pass, skiing to a stop adjacent to the smoky fire.

Lola had the back door open in an instant, throwing out the folding steps. She sank up to her hips as soon as she stepped off the newly packed strip, but wallowed and plowed her way forward, forgetting completely about her ribs. Trooper Meeks was tight on her heels, dragging his medical kit through the snow.

"Cutter?" she said when Piper floundered out to meet her, sobbing uncontrollably. Lola blanched at the smears of blood and soot on the girl's face.

Piper nodded, speaking through ragged breaths. "I'm not sure . . ."

Lola nearly threw up when she saw the blood and carnage inside the half-burned cabin.

Cyril did.

CHAPTER 62

Twenty-two hours later

*C*utter's eyes fluttered. He was warm—finally—
but everything about him was so very heavy, much too
heavy to move. It dawned on him that he might be
dead. If he was, then he was in Hell because his feet
were on fire. Hushed voices drifted into his conscious-
ness, needling him. He wanted to sit up but couldn't
quite figure out how to do it. A sudden rush of calm
washed over him. He relaxed. Maybe Hell wasn't so
bad. . . .

He woke again with a start sometime later, out of a
dream where he'd run through a field of goat-head
stickers and Ethan was pulling them out of his feet—
chiding him for going barefoot and threatening to get
out the Merthiolate. . . .

"Arliss . . ."

Cutter opened his eyes, blinking at the bright light. How did Mim get here? He needed to stoke the fire. . . .

She put a beautiful hand on his forehead. So warm . . .

"Are your feet bothering you again?"

He managed to muster his right eye into service and turned his head sideways on the pillow, toward the sound. What an amazing invention, the pillow.

"Hi," he whispered, smacking chapped lips.

Mim stood beside his bed, backlit by the window. She took his hand. "I'll get the nurse," she said. "Maybe she can give you something more for the pain."

He gripped her hand when she turned to go, weakly, but enough to send the message that he wanted her to stay.

His voice came breathy and coarse, like he'd swallowed a bucket of gravel. "Could . . . could I get some water?"

"They brought you a pitcher of crushed ice."

"Ice?" Cutter would have laughed, but it made his head hurt. "No, just water."

He nodded off before she could fill the plastic cup.

"You gave us a scare, Mr. Cutter." A tall Asian woman said when he woke up the next time. "Tell me about your pain level."

Cutter mulled that over as the cobwebs receded to the corners of his brain. He felt better, which was to say, he felt like crap, but a hell of a lot better than he had the last time he was conscious.

He let his head loll to the side, looking at the woman. He tried to raise an eyebrow but gave up. "Doctor . . . ?"

"Dr. Watanabe," she said. "Your partner is outside. She's already told me all about her Japanese ancestry."

Cutter attempted a half smile. "She's never met a stranger."

"Your pain," Dr. Watanabe prodded.

"I'm good," Cutter said. "Just need some rest."

"Your pain?" she said again.

"Well," Cutter said. "My left elbow feels pretty good."

"Okay . . ."

"Other than that, I'd say I'm about a twelve on a scale of one to ten. Worst thing is my feet. They feel like I'm standing in a bed of red ants."

"Trench foot," Dr. Watanabe said. "You must have worn your boots for several days. . . ."

The doctor listened to his breathing, clucked a bit at whatever she heard, and then shined a small light in each eye, clucking at that too. She finished her exam and promised she'd be back to check on him in a few hours. She stopped and turned when she reached the door. "Your friends are in the hall. You feel up to me sending them in?"

Cutter managed a nod.

A moment later, Lola burst in, followed by a much more sedate Chief Phillips and, oddly enough, the Brackett kid.

"You're APD," Cutter said. "I don't remember coming back to Anchorage."

"You didn't, boss." Tears streamed down Lola's face. "I just can't get rid of this guy."

Chief Phillips smiled her omniscient smile, as always, looking as if she could read minds. "Officer Brackett insisted on coming to Fairbanks to help in our search. Evidently, he's familiar with the area."

"Thank you for that," Cutter said.

Lola stood at Cutter's bedside, hand resting gingerly on his shoulder. "I thought we'd lost you, boss. I couldn't . . . I mean I can't imagine." She sniffed, then wiped her face with her sleeve. "Can you move your arms?"

Cutter gave her a quizzical look. "Gingerly," he said. "Why?"

"Because I know you don't like people to touch your face and I don't want you to stop me." She leaned in and kissed him on the forehead, dripping tears.

Crying was contagious and Jill Phillips joined in. Arliss found himself tearing up and managed to raise a hand.

"Okay now," he whispered. "I'm alive—" His throat convulsed and he found it impossible to speak. He swallowed, waited a beat, then managed to say, "Thanks to all of you." He gave a groggy laugh. "I leave town for one little minute and the whole world turns to crap." A sudden thought occurred to him. "Noah made it?"

"He did," Phillips said. "Air Force PJs picked up him along with his dog. Your phone pinging the tower confirmed what Lola and Brackett had already figured out. They learned of Mutt Larsen's affair. One lead led to another and they eventually found out about the professor's research station."

"How is Baglioni?" Cutter asked.

"She's doing better," Lola said. "Recovering from emergency gall bladder surgery a few rooms down the hall as a matter of fact. Piper and Noah are with her now."

"The others?"

"Weather has cleared enough that the Troopers got the helicopter in to pick up the bodies."

"I screwed this one up bad, Chief."

Phillips scoffed. "To hear Professor Baglioni and her two interns tell it, they'd all be dead were it not for you."

The memories washed in, coming back stronger like waves on a rising tide. "Bill Young's family?"

"Everything's taken care of," Phillips said. "You get some rest."

"The dogs are going to be fine," Lola said out of the blue. "In case you were wondering."

"Dogs?"

"The French bulldog puppies," Lola said.

"Our friend in the US Attorney's office is having a fit," Phillips said. "It seems as though someone leaked a story to the media and now *Good Morning America* reports that the government considered sending three hundred malnourished puppies back to Russia and the puppy mills from whence they came."

"It wasn't me!" Lola said.

Phillips gave a wan smile, a sparkle in her eye. "Oh, I'm absolutely sure it wasn't you." She clasped her hands together at her waist. "We should let Arliss get some rest."

"Can I borrow a phone?" Cutter said. "I need to call Mim."

Lola grinned, nodding at the chair by the window across the room. "I don't think Mim's left your side since we brought you in."

"I'll be back to check on you in a few hours," Lola said.

"Thank you," Cutter said, "for not giving up."

Lola shot him a double-finger-gun thumbs-up. "You're my partner, boss. It's what we do."

She held Brackett's hand when they went out the door, politicking the chief to send her to a training course on wilderness medicine.

Mim pulled her chair next to the bed after they'd gone.

"I thought I only dreamed you," Cutter said.

"Nope," Mim said. "I'm here in the flesh. Constance and the boys say hello."

"Constance too?"

"I know, right?" Mim laughed, easy, not forced. "No, she's still Constance, but she's coming around. The boys made Oatmeal Energy Cookies. I brought you a couple."

"That sounds terrific," Cutter said. "But maybe just some water for now." He fumbled for the controller for the bed.

Mim finished pouring his water, then helped raise the bed to a semi-sitting position. Cutter took a sip, but his throat was too sore to enjoy it.

"So," she said. "You're letting yourself get beat up an awful lot lately."

He tried to shrug, stifled a grimace, and settled for a nod.

"Dr. Watanabe says you'll heal," Mim said, stroking

the back of his hand. "Severe dehydration, frostbite on your face, trench foot—not to mention a concussion."

He gave her hand a squeeze. "Like she said, I'll heal. I'm feeling a lot better than I was five minutes ago."

Another squeeze.

For the first time, he saw a long, official-looking envelope on the table beside the bed.

"I have some mail?"

Mim snatched up the envelope, maybe a little too quickly. "No," she said. "This is mine." She changed the subject. "Your clothes should probably be burned, the parka too, but I got the stuff out of your pockets. Her face grew somber. "Can I ask you something?"

"Of course," he said. "And then I'll ask you something too."

"Ask me what?"

Cutter couldn't help but smile. "You started this. You go first."

"No," Mim said. "I decided I want you to go."

"What's in the envelope?"

"What?"

"Looks like it was postmarked just a few days ago, but the flap is about to fall off you've taken the contents out and put it back in so many times. Must be important correspondence—"

Mim gave an exasperated sigh. "Okay," she said. "I've decided I *will* go first with my question." She took his notebook from her pocket and held it up. "This was in your parka. I apologize for prying, but you were unconscious for so long. I thought maybe I could find out what happened to you by looking in here."

"That's no problem." He gave a hoarse cough. "I might not say everything out loud, but that doesn't mean I want to keep secrets."

"I've seen how you do your investigations," she said. "How your mind works."

"Okay . . ."

She opened the notebook and turned it toward him. "You have Ethan's name written here in the middle. It's circled, with lines running to different names and places. That's what you do when you're working through some burning question. So, why is Ethan the center of . . . whatever this is? And why now?"

He told her everything he knew, which wasn't much. There were hardly any details and virtually no concrete evidence, but even the suspicion that her husband had been murdered was enough to make Mim collapse into the chair with the notebook in her lap.

"You think his firm had something to do with it?"

"I have no idea," Cutter said. "Did they ever mention to you that his death might not have been accidental?"

"Not a word, the bastards . . ."

Cutter closed his eyes. "When we were growing up, Grumpy always told us we better have a damn good reason for hiding the truth."

Mim held up the envelope. "Okay. The truth is, they released Ethan's life insurance settlement. The money has already cleared and is in my account."

"That's great," Cutter said. It didn't dawn on him what that meant until the words left his mouth. "I guess you're going home—back to Florida?"

"Someday," she said. "I mean, it definitely crossed my mind. But not until we figure out who killed Ethan."

"Or *if* he was killed."

"Right," Mim said. "But this . . ." She looked at the notebook. "This Officer Janice Hough thinks he was murdered."

"She does," Cutter said.

"How about you? What do you think?"

"I have nothing to go on but the fact that it was covered up," Cutter said. "That and a gut feeling."

"I know some doctors that are saying our gut is like a second brain."

"Makes sense."

Mim dug Cutter's knife from the pocket of her fleece vest along with the chunk of wood that he'd been working on while he was stranded. "We need to think this through," she said, "and you think better when you're carving."

She spread a copy of the *Fairbanks Daily News-Miner* across his lap to catch the shavings.

Cutter had to will his fingers to simply open the little whittling knife, gritting his teeth as the muscles in his hands and arms slowly began to loosen up. "So, you are going to stay in Alaska?"

She sat down by the bed again and tapped the notebook against her leg. "At least until we figure this out. Then we'll have to see. Frankly, I don't think the boys could live without you."

He worked the knife slowly, carefully. His hands behaved like stones at first, but it felt good to move them. He looked up and gave what he hoped was a teasing smile. "Just the boys?"

Mim shook her head, tight-lipped, blinking away tears. She started to say something, then seemed to think better of it. She nodded at the carving, not quite changing the subject, but giving her brain a beat to catch up with this new revelation.

"Whatcha making?"

Cutter ran a bandaged thumb over the smooth wood and thought about his brother.

"Some kind of fish, I expect."

A tear rolled down his cheek and popped against the newspaper on his lap.

"Arliss, what if . . . ?" Mim whispered. "I mean . . . what if someone did kill him?"

The monitor at Cutter's bedside noted a sudden uptick in his pulse. He took a deep breath, bringing his heart rate back down, and then dried his cheek with the back of the same hand that held the pocketknife before locking eyes with her.

"Then someone's gotta pay."

ACKNOWLEDGMENTS

Much of the research for COLD SNAP occurred over the years, without my realizing I was doing research for this or any book in particular. I did, however realize that I had a great many friends who I constantly pestered to help sate my curiosity about their particular areas of expertise.

Pilot friends Sonny Caudill, Earl Samuelson, Richard Cobb, and Joe Huston, have flown me countless miles over the ruggedly beautiful terrain of Alaska as well as walking me through all manner of hypotheticals for this and other stories.

Over the course of several books, aircraft mechanic and dear friend, Steve Szymanski, has often discussed at length what it would take to bring down this or that aircraft.

James Hoelscher, Perry Barr, Nathan Joseph, Lila Peterson, and Brian Kroschell, among others, have shown me around bush Alaska in all kinds of weather, fed me, and sat by the fire to answer my endless questions about living far away from the road system.

Besides their friendship, Rob and Michelle Heun of High Lake Lodge have given me a place to write that is beyond beautiful.

My friends and family with the United States Marshals Service, and coworkers from Anchorage Police Department and the Alaska State Troopers have helped me for years with research merely being their impressive selves.

My dear friend, man-tracking expert and jujitsu master Ty Cunningham, is always quick to talk through fight scenes and man-tracking minutia.

Robin Rue of Writers House literary agency and Gary Goldstein (along with all the folks at Kensington Publishing) are top-notch professionals, some of the very best in the business. I'm fortunate to have them in my corner.

Many thanks to Ben and Cate and Dan and their spouses for letting me bounce all manner of ideas off them.

And to my bride, Victoria for . . . well, for everything.

RECIPE

Grumpy Cutter's Oatmeal Energy Cookies

5 sticks (2½ cups) softened butter
1½ cups firmly packed brown sugar
1 cup granulated sugar
2 eggs
2 teaspoons Mexican vanilla
3 cups all-purpose flour
2 teaspoons baking soda
1 teaspoon cinnamon
1 teaspoon salt
½ teaspoon nutmeg
1 cup chopped dates
1½ cups chopped pecans
6 cups uncooked rolled oats

Beat softened butter and sugars until creamed. Add vanilla and eggs and blend well. Note: other kinds of vanilla may be substituted but the flavor may not be quite as intense.

Combine flour, baking soda, cinnamon, nutmeg, and salt and mix into dough.

Fold in dates and nuts. Fold in dry oats. Note: if using a brand of oats that contains a lot of oat flour, cut back a quarter cup on the all purpose flour or your cookies will be cake-like.

Grease cookie sheet or line with parchment paper

Drop rounds of dough roughly the size of ping pong or golf balls onto sheet, then press down once with fork to flatten slightly (should still be fairly thick with rounded edges)

Bake at 375° for 10 to 11 minutes, depending on your oven.

Cookies will flatten considerably as they cook. If they flatten too much, add a touch more flour.

Remove from oven when edges are brown but the top of the cookie still looks a little moist and not quite done.

It's easiest to use two pans so the first pan out of the oven can rest and cool for a few minutes so they can be more easily moved to a wire rack. They will be delicate at first but should be easier to handle without breaking when cooled.

Keep Reading for a Special Excerpt . . .

BREAKNECK

An Arliss Cutter Novel

by

Marc Cameron

A train ride into the Alaskan wilderness turns into a harrowing fight for survival for Deputy US Marshal Arliss Cutter and a mother and daughter marked for death.

Off the northeast coast of Russia, the captain and crew of a small crabbing vessel are brutally murdered by members of the Russian Mafia. After the *Bratva* thugs stuff the dead bodies into crab pots and throw them overboard, they scuttle the vessel off the coast of Alaska and slip ashore.

In Washington DC, Supreme Court Justice Charlotte Morehouse prepares for a trip to Alaska, unaware that a killer is waiting to take his revenge—by livestreaming her death to the world.

In Anchorage, Alaska, Deputy US Marshals Arliss Cutter and Lola Teariki are assigned to security detail at a judicial conference in Fairbanks. Lola is tasked with guarding Justice Morehouse's teenaged daughter while Cutter provides counter-surveillance. It's a simple, routine assignment—until the mother and daughter decide to explore the Alaskan wilderness on the famous Glacier Discovery train. Hiding among the tourists, eccentric locals, and other passengers are the terrorists, who launch a surprise attack when the train reaches a remote area. While they seize control of the engine, Cutter manages to escape with Justice Townsend by jumping off the moving train—and into the unforgiving wilderness.

The chase is on. Wih no supplies and no connection to the outside world, Cutter and the judge must cross a treacherous terrain and commandeer a raft through an icy river canyon to stay alive. Two of the terrorists are close behind. The others are on the train with the judge's daughter—and they plan to execute her on camera. With so many lives at stake, Cutter knows there are only two options left: catch the train and kill them all . . . or all will be killed.

Look for **BREAKNECK,** *on sale in May 2023!*

"O, from this time forth,
my thoughts be bloody, or be nothing worth!"
—Shakespeare, *Hamlet*

PROLOGUE

Alaska

Gladys Ayuluk's husband, Pete, was the one who decided they should all go upriver to catch ducks—and she would never forgive him for it.

It was June, *Kaugun* in Gladys's native Yup'ik, when fish would soon be so plentiful you could hit them with a stick. The ice had gone off the main Yukon just the week before with much destruction and shrieking.

Gladys made almost as much noise when she spied the new hickey on her fifteen-year-old son's neck. That damned downriver girl, Agnus Polty, was the culprit. Gladys called her *Utngucegnaq—one who looks like a wart*.

Pete assured her Emmett was just going through a phase. Boys would be boys. When Gladys pointed out that those same boys were already cozying up to their twelve-year-old Winnie, Pete started getting the boat ready for duck camp.

Emmett took care of the shotguns and the .270 Winchester rifle—Gladys's camp gun. There were bound to be bears about. Winnie helped pack their basic supplies—flour, oil, salt, sugar, coffee, and a gallon baggie full of smoked salmon strips—the last of the previous year's harvest. Two dark blue boxes of Sailor Boy Pilot Bread went on top of everything. More of a hard cracker than bread, each piece was the diameter of a hockey puck—and good with everything from peanut butter to seal oil. It was a staple in bush Alaska.

All chubby cheeks and smiles, baby Martha enjoyed the ride up and down the riverbank swaddled in soft cotton in the back of Gladys's summer kuspuk.

Moose camp, berry camp, fish camp, or duck camp, the Ayuluks were pros, and they had the boat loaded in no time. Gladys's worries began to melt away from the first growl of the propellor biting the turbid brown waters of the mighty Yukon. The river was wide here, swollen by spring floods to almost a mile across. Sandbars had popped up in new places since last summer and rafts of ice floated by like killer torpedoes.

The mouth of the main Andreafsky was less than two miles upriver, just around the corner. St. Mary's, a couple of miles north of that. A series of crescent sloughs and side channels, the East Fork of the Andreafsky snaked between the main river and the Chuilnak, meandering south and east before turning northward through the low Nulato Hills. It was called *Qukaqlik* in Yup'ik—*The Middle One*.

Pete pulled the tiller toward him, avoiding a sandbar as he cut up the channel. A grayling leaped on the sun-dazzled surface, biting at some unseen insect or bit of fluff. The sight of it filled Gladys with hope for a good supper.

The normally clear waters churned and frothed, swollen and cloudy with silt. Jagged rafts of old ice grew more plentiful as the little boat motored up upstream. Pete wove his way carefully, keeping well clear of the bergy bits. His dad had died falling through rotten ice and he harbored a healthy respect for it.

Two hours after the Ayuluks departed Pitka's Point, their little boat nosed around the protected bend they all knew so well. Gladys marveled at how much of the bank had simply vanished. Thick cottonwoods that she'd known for decades were gone, sheared away during breakup and taken downriver. What had once been a gentle slope had been gouged into a steep muddy cliff, five feet high.

Emmett gave his sister a stiff elbow and called dibs on any fossilized mammoth teeth or ivory they might find in the newly exposed earth. Gladys clapped her hands, elated when she saw the plywood shelter was still intact. Pete reversed the prop for a short burst and then lifted the motor out of the water. Momentum carried them in.

Skunk cabbage and purple sedge sprouted on the wet bank amid patches of ice and snow. Twenty feet upriver, an otter zipped down a mud chute and slipped beneath the surface with a squeak.

Emmett and Winnie crowded into the bow, their bulky life jackets fighting for the best spot. Winnie grabbed the bow line, the sleeves of her purple hoodie pushed up on her little forearms, ready for work, and scrambled over the side the minute they scraped gravel. She sloshed up the bank to take a loop around a cottonwood that had survived the ice dams. Emmett gripped the bow with both hands and threw his weight backward, tugging the boat closer to the bank so his mother wouldn't get her feet wet.

The grunt of winging ducks drew everyone's attention upward. If there was a more beautiful duck than the strikingly black and white eider, Gladys had never seen it. Pete stood at the sight, teetering the aluminum hull against the gravel. Never much of a talker, he turned his head to follow the birds.

Gladys smiled, happy her husband was such a good hunter. "You boys catch us dinner," she said. "Me and Winnie will unload the boat."

Pete raised both eyebrows. In other parts of the world the expression might convey amusement or surprise, but to Gladys's people, who might have to sit silently for hours waiting to catch their food, it was a quiet way to say "good idea."

Baby in the back of her kuspuk, Gladys trudged up the hill to the little cabin. It was a shack, really, with a blue tarp roof, weathered plywood walls, and one long window Pete had salvaged from the rear of an old Ford pickup truck. The door was unlocked—a thief would just break it down, and someone caught in a blizzard might need shelter.

"Tea pot's been moved," Gladys said as soon as she stepped inside.

Winnie crowded around her mother and surveyed the sixteen-by-sixteen interior. There was plenty of light thanks to Pete's pickup-cab window.

"Did they take stuff?"

Gladys scrunched her nose. *No.*

The furnishings were sparse—four metal folding chairs, a set of bunk beds built from two-by-fours, a similar crib, and a double bed with a rusted metal frame. A plywood shelf ran along the wall beneath the window. Spattered grease stains marked the spot where Gladys would put her two-burner camp stove. The Coleman lantern was still hanging from a wire on the center two-by-four rafter—right where they'd left it.

Gladys took the lid off a blue metal bear barrel in the corner and peeked inside.

"They mighta took some tea . . ." she said, the hushed clucks of a mother hen. "Probably hunters who needed to warm up. That's okay . . ."

A half hour later the beds were laid out, a fire snapped in the wood stove, and the baby snored softly in her crib.

Winnie reached into her daypack for a paperback copy of *The Hunger Games* she'd gotten from the Trooper book-boat.

Gladys held out a five-gallon bucket.

"Fill this up. Then you can read."

Winnie went out the door, book in one hand, bucket in the other.

It took fifteen minutes before Gladys started to worry. She opened the door and called out, cupping her hand so as not to wake the baby. No answer but wind and water.

She was probably lost in her book.

Gladys called again.

Nothing.

Exasperated, she scooped up the startled baby and stomped down the hill, .270 rifle in hand.

The river that only minutes before had brought her

so much joy now took on a sinister gulping sound—as if it were hungry.

Heart in her throat, Gladys searched up and down the bank, bending willows, parting grass, looking for any sign or track.

Then a cake of dirty ice the size of a car door slammed into the mud exactly where Winnie would have been getting water. Seconds later, a huge log came around the bend. It caught the same eddy and gouged a furrow in the bank before spinning back into the current.

All the blood drained from Gladys's face. If Winnie had been reading and shown the river her back . . .

Beyond panicked, Gladys set the baby on a patch of grass and fired three shots into the air. She worked the bolt quickly, screaming all the while for her missing child. The baby flinched at the gunfire and began to wail along with her mother.

It seemed like forever before Pete and Emmett crashed through the willows. Emmett carried not only his shotgun, but a yellow five-gallon bucket.

"I found this floating downriver," he said. "Mom? What's—"

"Winnie's missing . . ." Gladys pointed at the churning brown water. Her knees buckled and she had to grab her husband to keep her feet.

Emmett scuffed at the bank with his boot. He looked up at his father.

"Here's one of her tracks."

Gladys clutched the baby to her chest.

"Look at this, Dad," the boy said. "She's facing away from the water, leaving. We shoulda passed her when we came up."

Pete wheeled. "Come on. She might be hung up in a sweeper, or some willows." He stopped abruptly, turning back to Gladys, his bronze face twisted with worry of a man who'd lost his father to the river. "How long's she been gone?"

Gladys told him.

"Come, come." Pete flicked his hand at Emmett.

"Hold on, Dad," the boy said. "This track . . . it's different."

Pete glanced at the mud. "Probably when we were unloading the boat. Now come!"

"I don't think so," Emmett said. "Different heel—"

Pete cuffed his son on the shoulder. "I told you let's go! Dirt's too tore up to see anything for sure." He crashed into the thick brush with Emmett on his heels, both shouting Winnie's name.

Gladys waded knee-deep into the water beside their skiff, screaming for her little girl until her voice cracked.

In her haste, she missed the fresh boot track in the mud.

Fifteen hundred miles to the east, a man with feral eyes and a hatchet face held court from a tufted leather booth in the back of *Ogon' i Led*—Fire and Ice—his back-alley nightclub off Primorskaya Street in the Russian city of Petropavlovsk. A hint of rotting seaweed from nearby Avacha Bay muddled with the pungent body odor and eye-watering perfumes of the three women crammed into the booth with the man. Low, moaning music throbbed in time with pulsing lights, illuminating three cages and, more important, the nubile dancers inside them. Two dozen men sat at low tables around the stage, all entranced, swaying, drinking the hatchet-face man's booze and throwing wads of cash at his women.

When Maxim Volkov was a boy, his friends had called him "*Toporok*," meaning "Little Axe"—and not only for the severe angles of face. He was a fighter, prone to fits of rage. The tail of a black dolphin tattoo the size of his thumb peeked above the rat's nest of gunmetal chest hair spilling from the open collar of his silk shirt. The ink was a memento of another time when the air smelled not like the sea, but of misery and urine and fear. In Penal Colony #6, he'd earned another name.

Kostolom.

Bone Breaker.

Volkov's lieutenant, a handsome silver-haired man with a pencil-thin mustache, stood at the end of the booth with a phone pressed to his ear. He pulled the device away and gave a slow shake of his head.

"No answer, boss," he said. The music made lip-reading a necessity.

Five years Volkov's junior at forty-six, Ilia Lipin had earned tattoos in the Black Dolphin prison as well. All had been applied with a jury-rigged electric razor motor, plastic from a melted toothbrush, and a straightened staple from a fat book in the prison library. Ink was made of bootblack and piss, preferably from the person getting the tat. Volkov had decided early in their acquaintance that Lipin's handsome face and prematurely silver hair made him perfect for politics or the cinema. Even in prison, he'd advised the man to keep his tattoos concealable under his clothes, mindful of a time when they might wish to blend with the world.

"No answer?" Volkov muttered, as if the notion was inconceivable.

Lipin shook his head, his mouth pinched in a frown, demonstrating to his boss that he, too, was disappointed at the current situation.

The tendons in Volkov's neck thrummed as if carrying high voltage. People, he could bend to his will. Phone lines, satellites, undersea cables—those did not care that he was a feared leader of the Bratva, called the Russian Mafia by the West.

One of Volkov's many mistresses, a raven-haired waif named Kira, cuddled up beside him. Even she was not sure how old she was, but Volkov put her at around sixteen, if he happened to think about her age at all.

He gave a nod to Lipin to try the call again and then turned his attention to the pudgy naval officer standing before his table. The man kept his head up, shoulders back, but rubbed his sweating hands at his waist like a housefly—at once nervous and defiant.

"It is Bukin, correct?"

"Yes," the man said. "Gennady Arkadyevich Bukin."

Volkov toyed with an empty vodka glass, turning it back and forth as if grinding something against the table. "Captain of the third rank," he noted. "Stationed across the bay at Rybachiy Naval Base aboard special mission submarine BS 64 Podmoskovye—"

"This . . . this is sensitive information," the captain stammered. "How did you come by—"

Volkov cut him off. "You owe me money, Gennady."

"And I will pay," the captain said. "I only need—"

"You have money to spend at my competitor down the street."

"That was an error in judgment," the man said. "It will not—"

Volkov pushed the glass away and sat back in the soft leather between his women. "I am curious," he said. "The Russian navy is very strong . . ."

The captain squirmed. When no question came his way, he said, "Yes?"

"Stronger than me, do you suppose?"

"The navy is . . . is larger . . ."

Volkov nodded, considering this. "I am not large," he said. "Does that mean I am not strong?"

Bukin flinched like he'd been slapped when Volkov snatched up a mother of pearl spoon and slathered a blini with caviar from a large bowl in the center of his table. The mafia boss eyed the younger man while he chewed.

Then, out of nowhere, Volkov grabbed young Kira by her face and squeezed, hard, grinding her hollow cheeks against her teeth. The girl hung there in his grip, sobbing quietly, obediently. She was startled, but not at all surprised. Bloody saliva trickled from her pursed lips. Volkov held her for a time, his nose inches from hers, face canted to one side as if puzzled.

He pushed her away just as suddenly as he'd grabbed her. She collapsed into the booth beside him, rubbing her face, obviously too terrified to run or make a sound.

"And there you have it, Captain Gennady Arkadyevich Bukin." Volkov used a linen napkin to wipe the girl's tears and spittle off his fingers before popping another bite of caviar into his mouth. "That—" He nodded sideways to the quivering girl. "That was for *nothing*. Can you imagine what I would do to her if she had done *something* . . ."

The captain trembled more than the girl now. Volkov studied him for a moment and then glanced at Lipin.

"Still no answer?"

The bratva lieutenant shook his head.

Ignoring the navy man, Volkov snatched the phone away and pressed the button to redial, cursing the fast busy signal.

"I told the boy to expect my call," he said, drawing a nod from the stoic Lipin. Finally, on Volkov's third attempt, a male voice crackled over the line, an American speaking barely passable Russian.

"Sashenka!" he said, using the informal diminutive for Alexander. He wished the boy's Russian was better, but that would be remedied soon enough. For now, Volkov spoke English, getting straight to the point. "It is your father."

"Papa!" the boy said. "I was hoping you would call. Do you have any newspaper clippings about grandfath—"

"I need you."

"I'm on a fishing boat," the boy said. "We should be in Kodiak—"

"Not Kodiak!" Volkov snapped. "I thought your boat berths in Homer. I expected you would come to Anchorage from there."

"Wait!" Alex said, suddenly more animated. "You're in Anchorage?"

"Soon," Volkov said. "And I want my son there to

meet me. We have much to discuss. When do you arrive in Homer?"

"I don't know," the boy said. "Four days, maybe five or six. We only left Dutch Harbor yesterday."

"No, no, no," Volkov said. "Why five or six days? It should not take you this long even all the way from Dutch Harbor."

"I already told you," Alex said, sounding flippant—far too much like his mother. "The skipper wants to stop in Kodiak for a few days."

Volkov rubbed a hand across his jaw and barked an order to Lipin, who took another phone from his pocket.

"Very well," Volkov said to his son. "I will make you a reservation to fly from Kodiak to Anchorage—"

Lipin looked up from his phone and shook his head. "Flights full for the next five days," he said.

"I'm not surprised," Alex said, hearing Lipin's end of the conversation. "Weather's been bad in the Gulf for a week. Kodiak flights get canceled all the time for fog. Backs everything up like crazy. Don't worry. I'll be in Homer in a week, tops."

"Nyet!" Volkov snapped. The girl beside him jerked, fearing he might grab her face again. "A week does me no good. No good at all. Tell your captain he must sail directly to Homer."

"You don't really *tell* this skipper anything," the boy said. "He's kind of a—"

"Talk less." Volkov cut him off. "Listen more."

"Okay. . ."

Volkov closed his eyes, forcing himself to calm. "You are my son, Sasha," he said. "Inform the captain you have family emergency. You must stress to him that you have no choice."

Alex chuckled. He not only had his mother's laugh, which was galling enough, but her glib nature as well. "What's so important? It's just a couple of extra days."

Had any of Volkov's men spoken to him this way he would have cut off their balls with a carpet knife, one by one so they would have time to think on their behavior.

The bratva boss took a deep breath and then said, "I must see to someone personally. I want you by my side."

The boy was uncharacteristically silent for a time. "Okay . . . when you say 'see to someone' you usually mean . . ."

"Correct."

"And you want me to help you?"

"No!" Volkov said, harsher than he intended to be. "And yes. Explanations will come. For now, convince your captain."

"I'll try," the boy said. "Can I ask you something?"

"Of course."

"I need proof about grandfather. The crew doesn't believe—"

"Focus, Alexander!" Volkov chided. "Call Uncle Lev when you have a time of arrival in Homer. He will work out transport to Anchorage. Then we will discuss your grandfather."

Volkov ended the call and slipped the phone in his pocket.

He glanced at the Navy man. "You are still here."

"I thought . . . you wanted me to stay—"

"I did," Volkov said. "We could spend an endless amount of time on this . . ."

"I—"

"Do you want to know what I think?"

The captain ran a trembling tongue across his lips. It was clear that he did not want to know at all, but he gave a tentative squeak. "Yes . . ."

"I think that you believe your military rank gives you a certain latitude. You believe because you work aboard a secret nuclear submarine your debts should—"

"N–no," Bukin stammered. "I promise—"

At a nod from their boss, Lipin and young man named Gavrill grabbed the captain by both arms. Gavrill was Alexander's age, dark and handsome, with a superman curl on his forehead. He drove a boot into the side of the navy man's knee, causing him to double over in pain.

The crowd drew back, heavy with anticipation and dread. They knew what was coming. Volkov's men pushed a terrified Bukin to his knees, and then forced him facedown so his head was on the step of the booth while his body trailed downward at an angle to the carpeted floor.

Gennady Arkadyevich Bukin, Captain of the third rank in the Russian Navy, painted the floor with tears, begging forgiveness for his debt. Music throbbed. Dancers writhed in their cages. Kira, the sweating waif on whom Maxim Volkov had recently demonstrated his cruelty, passed her employer a heavy wooden walking stick. He shooed her out of his way and rose from the booth to place the thick mahogany against the base of the wailing navy man's skull.

The wooden stick was nothing ornate. Bland, in fact, like a table leg. But it held great sentimental value to Maxim Volkov, its frequent use providing his Bone Breaker nickname.

Gennady Bukin gurgled and pled, his hand flopping against the carpet like a pallid fish.

The girls in the cages stopped dancing. The bartender climbed up on a stool to get a better view. Lipin had the house lights raised and Volkov waited a beat so everyone's eyes could adjust. Sometimes men needed to be killed in private, but an audience was exponentially more powerful at driving home his point.

"I have no time to discuss." He put his full weight on the stick. "I must see to someone in America."

Depending on the case before the United States Supreme Court, half the country loved Associate Justice Charlotte Morehouse. The other half wanted to see her hanged from a gibbet. Those halves swapped sides on a frighteningly regular basis.

She'd learned long ago—and was still trying to teach her teenage daughter—not to fret over what people thought. Do the right thing because it was right, not because one screamed the loudest.

At forty-five, Morehouse was the youngest and, according to *Rolling Stone* magazine, the "most handsome" justice on the court. Five feet ten inches tall, the days she wasn't on the court's basketball court, she spent an hour in the gym reading on the treadmill or stair climber. Shoulder length hair fell somewhere between dun and silver. Her late husband had called it gruella. She considered her hair the most interesting thing about her. He'd always said it was on his list, but he'd had a few other ideas.

John Morehouse had passed away a month before the president appointed her to the court—just over a year ago. She missed him terribly but saw his eyes every day when she looked at their fifteen-year-old daughter.

Morehouse pushed away from the desk and stood at the same moment her clerk—a fellow Duke alum—breezed in with stack of folders, each containing briefs for pending cases.

"Good morning, Libby." Morehouse strode to her chambers window and looked out toward the Library of Congress.

"Good morning, Madam Justice." The clerk set the briefs on the corner of her desk. Libby Weems wore a dark A-line skirt and smart silk blouse—like a thousand other young lawyers working inside the Beltway. Her brow was knitted, clearly concerned. "Apparently, one of your hosts, a US District Judge Markham, would like to show you around Alaska after your speech at the Fairbanks conference. He's taken the liberty of planning a couple of extra excursions."

"Excursions?"

"He calls them 'wilderness excursions.'"

"Sounds—"

"Terrifying?"

"I was going to say exciting." Morehouse paced to the other side of her chambers—much more commodious than the ones she'd had as a district court judge. She'd always been a walker, especially when deep in thought. By now, Weems and the rest of her staff estimated the carpet *might* last two years if they were lucky.

Weems nodded, lips pursed as if she'd sucked on a lemon.

"What?" Morehouse said. "You mean you don't love a good adventure? Feast your young eyes on this." She moved to her desk and brought up the image of a blue and yellow Alaska Railroad locomotive winding its way along a section of track between the sea and endless snowcapped mountains. "Ramona is super stoked."

"Wait." Weems pulled up short. "Your daughter's going?"

"We notified the Marshals Service this morning." Still standing, Morehouse scrolled the photos. "You can't tell me that a rail journey through this supremely wild place wouldn't be amazing."

"Honestly, ma'am," the law clerk said. "My idea of wild adventure is a foreign film with subtitles. What if something were to happen? You're going to be . . . I don't know, a million miles from the nearest big hospital."

"Pffft," Morehouse chided. "Alaska has hospitals."

Weems leaned in, as if confiding a secret. "Did you know that there are twice as many people inside the Beltway as there are in the entire state of Alaska? I checked."

"So, you're saying you'd like to come?"

Weems blanched. "No. I mean, of course I'd go if you—"

"Relax, Libby," Morehouse said. "I won't drag you along."

"You should watch a couple of episodes of *Alaska*

State Troopers," the clerk said, slightly breathless. "Volcanoes, earthquakes, plane crashes, not to mention ten-foot grizzly bears and ginormous moose that all want to stomp you to death. And . . ."

Her voice trailed off.

"Spill it," Morehouse said. "What else?"

"With all due respect, ma'am," Weems said. "You have a way of . . ." She paused, chewing on her lip, holding back the words.

Morehouse narrowed her gaze, chiding. "Libby . . ."

"The Marshals say you can be a bit too . . . spontaneous," Weems said. "Like you're not worried about your own safety."

"I'm not," Morehouse scoffed. "That's their job."

Visit our website at
KensingtonBooks.com
to sign up for our newsletters, read
more from your favorite authors, see
books by series, view reading group
guides, and more!

Become a Part of Our
Between the Chapters Book Club
Community and Join the Conversation

Betweenthechapters.net